REINVENTING EMILY BROWN

JODI GIBSON

ALSO BY JODI GIBSON

The Five Year Plan

The Memories We Hide

Sign up to my mailing list to keep updated on my latest books on my
website www.jfgibson.com.au

PRAISE FOR JODI GIBSON
THE FIVE YEAR PLAN

'The Five Year Plan is a lovely, happy read, just right to escape lockdown with. But be warned. Don't read if you're hungry!'

SANDIE DOCKER, AUTHOR OF THE REDGUM RIVER RETREAT

'...Beautiful, funny, realistic cast of characters that have stayed with me...The perfect escape.'

MICHELLE BARRACOLOUGH, HOST OF THE WRITER'S BOOK CLUB

'A wonderful read!'

CLAUDINE TINELLIS, HOST OF THE TALKING AUSSIE BOOKS PODCAST

'A sweet heart-warming book with relatable real characters, a storyline that keeps you interested all the way through, and, my favourite, fun descriptions of food and scenery.'

TRAVELS BOOKS AND MOVIES, INSTAGRAM

ABOUT THE AUTHOR

Jodi Gibson is an Australian author of contemporary women's fiction. Her debut novel *The Memories We Hide* was published in 2019, and *The Five Year Plan* was published by Brio Books in September 2021 and was shortlisted in the 2021 Booktopia's Favourite Australian Books awards.

Jodi is also a passionate advocate for aspiring authors and offers her knowledge and experience in writing and publishing through mentoring as well as through her *Ask The Author* podcast.

Jodi lives in country Victoria, Australia with her family including her writing companions a rambunctious Border Collie, a hungry Golden Retriever, and a demanding Ragdoll cat. When Jodi isn't writing, she loves spending time baking, rewatching 80s and 90s rom-coms, and is a self-confessed trivia addict.

Reinventing Emily Brown is Jodi's third novel.

Cover design: Stuart Bache

ISBN eBook 978-0-6485512-5-6

ISBN print 978-0-6485512-6-3

Published in Australia by

Verb Publishing PO Box 627 Wangaratta 3676

❀ Created with Vellum

DEDICATED TO

All the mums out there who feel suffocated by the guilt and pressure society places on the modern woman. This is permission to step away from those expectations and rediscover your own sense of self. (And have some fun while you do!)

CHAPTER ONE

Present Day

IF YOU GOOGLE THE PHRASE, 'things you should have achieved by the age of 40', you get two distinct search results.

The first one illustrates the financial milestones you should have achieved, such as having bought a house, having savings of at least six months living expenses, having a detailed financial plan for retirement, having money put away for your children's future, and having your career on track.

The second one talks about the wild adventures and life experiences you should've had. Things like showering in a waterfall, spending New Year's Eve in New York City, floating in the Dead Sea, and having made peace with your younger self.

Well, I'm turning thirty-eight this year, and I should be well on the way to achieving those things but I can tell you I can tick none of those boxes. Zero. Zilch. Nada. Especially the last one.

My name is Emily Brown, and I've successfully failed in almost every aspect of my life to date. Marriage? Yep. Career? Big fail there.

Motherhood? My fifteen-year-old daughter hates me, so yeah. Friendship? Travel? Experiences? Fail. Fail. Fail.

I didn't think I'd be one of those women affected by turning a certain age. After all, it's just a number. But as I creep closer to the four-decade mark, and as more information comes into my stratosphere, the clearer it becomes that—according to Google at least—I haven't achieved what I should have by this age.

Instead of 'it all', I'm sitting in my childhood bedroom, being swallowed by a mountain of throw cushions, and being stared at by a life-size Justin Timberlake cut-out. I've just left my husband. I'm broke, homeless (not technically, but still), and, as I mentioned, my daughter Hayley hates me for dragging her to the sleepy hollow of my parent's house in Curlew Bay, two hours from Melbourne and the life she loves.

So, how did I get here?

CHAPTER TWO

Two Days Earlier

'YOU KNOW it would be a help if you could push the trolley for me,' I huffed to Hayley dragging behind me, thumbing at her phone as if her life depended on it.

'Huh?' She didn't look up.

'Here! Push.'

She expelled a grunt and rolled her eyes as if I'd asked her to push a semi-trailer up a steep hill with her bare hands.

'Don't worry about it.' I forged forward. You have to pick your battles with fifteen year olds. And this one wasn't worth the effort.

Was there anywhere worse than the supermarket? Everyone navigating wonky-wheeled trolleys down the aisles, yelling into mobile phones, invading each other's personal space, grumbling, and rolling their eyes, wishing they were elsewhere. And let's not talk about what happened in the toilet roll aisle. Every time I was here, I berated past Emily for not making the time to organise online shopping or, at the very least, click and collect. One day I'd get around to it.

I wrangled the trolley around the end of the one isle and into the next, proceeding to almost slam it into a display of shampoo on sale as the wonky front wheel rattled and set off in its own direction. A man with a shopping basket scowled at me as if I'd done it intentionally. Hayley dragged behind, none-the-wiser. Passing by the canned fruit, I mentally calculated what I'd already got in my trolley and how much was left on the budget. Maths never used to be my strong suit, but since Anthony had been out of work, I'd become quite good at it. I could usually calculate to the nearest dollar or two at the check-out. You could often see me fist pumping when I scored an item on special. Yep, that was what my life had become. Getting excited about fifty cents off a box of cornflakes.

'I need a can of chickpeas,' Hayley declared in the canned vegetable aisle.

I dodged a toddler sucking on a piece of apple, his other hand grasping the side of his mother's trolley. 'Chickpeas?'

'Yes. Chickpeas.' She picked up a three-dollar can of certified organic, no added salt chickpeas and threw it in the trolley. I discretely replaced them with the ninety-nine-cent store brand one.

Organic chickpeas? Seriously? Ever since Hayley turned vegetarian—and I used that term very loosely, more like vegetarian-when-it-suits—she had requested the most bizarre and bloody expensive additions to the weekly shopping. Whatever happened to taking a Vegemite sandwich to school and being satisfied with meat and three veg for dinner? Choice. That was what happened. Kids these days had too many choices and too many options, and we parents obliged. It was our fault. It was that mother guilt thing. Fear of being judged by other parents, our children pitied—or worse still, bullied—for store-brand chickpeas. We all carried it. An invisible weight that made us question every decision, waking us up at precisely three am every morning to question whether we should've just bought the damn organic chickpeas. Would it ever go away? Or would I still be worrying about Hayley when she was thirty? Surely my mother wasn't lying awake in bed worrying about me at three am. She'd more likely be tutting and wondering why I couldn't be more like my perfect sister, Lucy.

After removing a liquid eyeliner from the trolley that Hayley had also tried to sneak in, I handed the trolley to Hayley as we arrived at the check-out. While I began loading things onto the conveyer belt, Hayley of course, returned to her phone, her thumbs frantically dancing across the screen, no doubt catching up on every minuscule thing that had happened in the past ten seconds she'd missed. The check-out girl scanned and bagged the items into my tattered cloth bags at a sloth-like pace while I loaded the bags into the trolley like a game of Tetris. One, I might add, I was very skilled at.

'One hundred and forty-two dollars and ninety cents.' The girl behind the register avoided eye contact; her voice was monotone. Personality plus, not.

Okay, so a little more than I thought, but still under budget. I tapped my credit card, keyed in my pin, and waited, only to be greeted with a long beep from the uncooperative EFTPOS machine. I tried again, same result.

'Sorry.' I fumbled with my card as the bored check-out girl stared at me with vacant eyes. This time I swiped the card. Maybe the machine was broken. I selected savings instead of credit. The machine whined again.

The girl chewed her gum without missing a beat. 'It's declined.' Nothing like stating the obvious.

The lady behind me tapped her long, manicured nails on the trolley handle and my cheeks heated. Involuntary blushing, a bonus of being a strawberry blonde with fair skin.

Even Hayley had looked up from her phone, her eyes questioning.

'Here, let me try another card. Sorry, I don't know what's going on.' I shuffled through my wallet, feeling the dampness in my armpits and pulled out another card. But the stupid machine beeped again.

This time it was as if the beep was on loudspeaker. People in the adjacent check-outs threw curious glances my way. Even the apple-wielding toddler, now clinging to his mum's skirt, was staring at me.

'Do you have, like, cash?' the teen said, flatly.

Why did every second word have to be like? When did that even start? Oh God. I was starting to sound like my mother. I scrambled through my handbag, knowing there was nothing more than a few gold coins covered in strands of hair and fluff at the bottom. Who carried cash these days? Weren't we moving towards a cashless society?

'Mum?' Hayley's big brown eyes widened, and I felt sick to my stomach.

It was one thing to be mortified but to have Hayley with me ... My heart hammered in my chest, and I thew another cautionary glance at the lady in the queue. She raised a perfectly plucked eyebrow. No random acts of kindness I'd heard about on the news from her. The teen behind the counter rolled her eyes, no doubt wondering why it was her dumb luck to land me on her shift.

I looked to the trolley laden with bags of ninety-nine-cent spaghetti, over-ripe bananas, home-brand cornflakes, and canned chickpeas. Then, before I questioned my decision, or even realised I'd made a decision, I grabbed Hayley's arm, ignoring the sheer panic and embarrassment in her eyes. 'Come on!' I whispered and dragged her towards the door. The mid-winter air slapped me in the face as the doors whooshed open, and still holding Hayley's elbow, I hurried us towards the car.

'Oh my God, Mum!' Hayley shrieked, covering her head like she was being hounded by the paparazzi. It wouldn't surprise me if they were around to capture this epic life failure. Another one to add to the growing list.

We piled into the car; I slammed it into reverse and exited the car park like I was Daniel Ricardo before coming to a screeching halt at the traffic lights, my cheeks still burning hot, blood rushing like a wave through my entire body.

'Mum! What the hell?' Hayley turned to me, eyes wide, nostrils flared. 'I can't believe you! I've never been so embarrassed in my whole entire life.' She dramatically sunk into her seat.

Neither have I. It even topped that time in my first year of uni when I emailed my best friend a photo of me in my new bikini, only to realise I'd emailed it to my entire legal ethics class!

'I'm sorry.' I could barely get the words out, still catching my breath.

'What's wrong with your card?' Hayley's question hung in the air like a foul odour. 'Are we broke?'

A heaviness pressed against my chest and I rubbed my clenched fist over the spot to try and relieve it. The only thing running through my head right now was: What the actual ...? Of course we weren't broke. Although, I had no idea what was going on.

'Of course not, hon.' I took her hand, squeezing it, relieved she didn't pull it away. 'It's just ... just a misunderstanding. I panicked, that's all. I'll sort it out with the bank.' Hayley pulled her hand away and rolled her eyes before directing her attention back to her phone. I took a shaky breath and shifted the car into gear.

As we drove home, my brain was scrambling for answers to the one question that kept barging to the forefront of my mind: What had Anthony done now?

CHAPTER THREE

When we arrived home, Hayley bolted upstairs to her bedroom, no doubt to hide from her excruciating mortification courtesy of her mother. I wasn't proud of running and leaving the cashier with a trolley full of bagged, unpaid groceries. But what choice did I have? It wasn't like I was going to return the groceries to the shelves. 'Sorry, I'll just pop these back, shall I?' I'm hoping to God nobody I knew, or Hayley knew, had seen us.

My head was still spinning as I walked into the kitchen. It took all my resolve not to call Anthony and scream at him, but that wouldn't fix things. I needed to log onto our bank and see what was going on with my own eyes. Arm myself with the facts before I go shooting him down. Maybe it was a simple mistake? A bank error. Lord knows they've been known for those in recent years. Or maybe we'd been hacked. The thought sent razor-sharp pricks across my skin.

I picked up the laptop from the study nook and threw my bag on the end of the breakfast bar littered with breakfast dishes, toast crumbs, and dried milk stains. The tea towel was on the floor (because where else would it be?), and two shoes (not even a pair) were kicked under the table. Just another day. I pushed the urge to clean it up aside and logged into our bank account, holding my breath as the screen loaded. Our account balances appeared, and I inhaled sharply. I needed wine.

For the next couple of minutes, in between sips of wine, I glowered at the zero balances staring back at me. Where was it all? Anthony was the one who handled the money. Made sure the loans were paid, the direct debits were up to date, and the credit cards paid off each month. Or at least the interest. After all, he was the one with time on his hands. I clicked through to the account transaction history and waited for the page to load and then I saw them. All of the debits. The Camden, The Glasshouse, The Railway, The Inkerman. All local hotels. The amounts were sometimes miniscule. Five dollars fifty here, eight dollars there, and some were bigger amounts between forty and one hundred dollars. Then there were cash withdrawals from ATMs a few hundred at a time. My hand was beginning to cramp as I scrolled the list. Occasionally a credit would appear in the right hand column where my pay had gone in, but it was nothing compared to the number of withdrawals. My stomach dropped like I was skydiving from fifteen thousand feet. I knew Anthony had been drinking a lot. Okay, too much. But, it was understandable. Well, at least for the first few months after he'd lost his job. But, it was worse than I thought. And, there was more to it. He couldn't be drinking *that* much. A thought snagged and I opened up a new browser tab and looked up all of the hotels. Yes, they all had gaming or TAB facilities. Oh God, Anthony. No.

How could I not have known? Not realised?

I took another slug of wine and tried to remember the last time I looked at the balances or transactions for that matter. I couldn't. Guilt wedged its way into my thoughts. Guilt for letting things slip. Not noticing. But, what the hell? How could he do this to us! I slammed the laptop shut and gathered bowls and plates from the dishwasher, the clanking of crockery echoing in my ears as I put them away. I slammed the dishwasher shut, slammed the fridge door shut. I yanked open the oven to slam it shut, along with a few cupboard doors for good measure.

I picked up the cleaning cloth and began wiping down the bench. Then I stopped, hung my head, and heaved in a breath. Why the hell was I cleaning up this mess? The kitchen had been clean when I left this morning. This was Hayley's and Anthony's mess. My eyes flicked to the living room, where the throw cushions lay scattered on the floor, and a coffee cup and an empty bag of potato chips cluttered the coffee table. A basket of unfolded washing sat on the couch. The kitchen clock ticked loudly, and the drum of music from Hayley's bedroom seeped through the walls. My shoulders crept towards my ears and a heavy weight twisted in my gut. Anger, frustration, helplessness all building from its depths, moving up into my head until it threatened to explode. But I couldn't let it. I didn't have time. I was the one supposed to hold all this shit together. Every. Single. Day.

I stretched my neck to release the tension. God, I could do with a massage. A five-day relaxation retreat. Not like that was ever going to happen. I poured another glass of wine as the front door banged shut, and Anthony's heavy footsteps lumbered up the hall.

'Hey.' He shrugged off his puffer jacket and threw it on the kitchen stool, then raised his eyebrows at my over-size glass of wine. 'Big day?'

I bit the inside of my lip. Was I the only one who could see the irony in this situation? Anthony was the one who usually came home smelling like a brewery after wiling away his days away, apparently at the local pub or TAB under the guise of 'job seeking' I now knew.

'You could say that.'

'What's for tea?'

Ignoring him, I cut straight to the chase. I never was one for a poker face or waiting for the right moment.

'Do you want to hear about my day?'

Anthony grabbed a beer from the fridge and flicked off the top. I watched it roll onto the kitchen counter. It circled round and round until it came to a stop. Anthony leant against the end of the bench. 'Ah, yeah. Sure.'

I leaned on the counter, grateful for the distance between us. 'Well, my day was going well until I tried to pay for the groceries at the register.'

Anthony's mouth dropped slightly, and recognition dawned on his face. 'Em. I can explain.'

'Really. Well, first, why don't you ask Hayley how she felt when I grabbed her and ran from the supermarket, leaving a full trolley behind at the register because it declined every single account?'

Anthony slow blinked and stood up straight. 'I forgot to transfer the money, that's all. Simple mistake.'

'You forgot to transfer the money? From where?' I flung the laptop open, spinning it around on the counter for him to see. 'All our accounts are overdrawn!' I stabbed at the screen with my pointer finger. 'Thanks to all these withdrawals.'

Anthony's face paled, his eyes unable to settle on the screen.

'The pub? Multiple pubs? What the hell, Anthony?'

'Em, look. Don't stress, it's fine. I—'

'It's fine? Really? If this is your idea of fine, I'd hate to see what *not* fine looks like.'

'I can explain. It was, it's not as bad as it looks.' He ran his hand over his forehead. 'We can transfer some over from the other bank.'

'The other bank? As in our daughter's university savings?' Surely, he was joking.

'Just a bit. Just 'til we get on top of things.'

'Get on top of things? You're supposed to be handling this, Anthony. You're supposed to be on top of things. But instead, our savings are zilch, our credit card's overdrawn, and our mortgage is behind four payments! All because of you!' I spun the laptop back around. 'And what's this one?' I pointed to the screen.

Anthony stepped around the counter and bent down to look. 'Oh, yeah. I had to buy a new suit for that interview I had yesterday.'

'From Peter Jackson! What was wrong with your old one?'

'Come on, Em; I need to look the part if I'm going to get a job, you know that.'

I scoffed. 'Meanwhile, I go to work every day in a ten-year-old suit and scuffed shoes.' The sarcasm in my voice was thick.

Anthony stood up to face me. 'I have a good feeling about this one, Em. I think this could be the one.'

I shook my head and turned away, threw the rest of my wine down the sink, rinsed the glass under the tap, and set it on the dish rack. I couldn't bear to look at him right now.

Rationally, I knew it wasn't his fault he'd lost his job. It had been the start of the pandemic, and the law firm where he worked underwent a restructure. They closed the entire property law division to focus on family law, wills, and estates. Anthony had worked in property law his entire career, and there wasn't a role for him in the new structure unless he was willing to retrain. In hindsight, that's what he should've done, but he decided to chance something new, thinking with his experience and reputation, he was sure to find a new role. That was three years ago. In the meantime, we'd been living on my wage, trying to cover a mortgage and fund Hayley's private school education. Oh, and little things like eating and keeping the electricity connected.

'They were impressed with my experience,' Anthony continued. 'I'd need to touch up on the new legislations and reform changes, but they seemed positive.'

I dried my hands on the tea towel, threw it on the bench and crossed my arms.

'We'll just borrow a bit of money; it'll be fine.'

'Fine? God, Anthony. Things haven't been fine for such a long time.' I tried to keep my voice low, knowing Hayley was upstairs.

'I'll sort it. I promise. And I'll call the bank,' he continued. 'I'm sure some of those charges are double ups.'

Hayley's quick feet thumped down the stairs like a herd of elephants. I turned and opened the freezer under the guise of looking for dinner options but really just hoping the blast of chilled air would temper my burning face. I couldn't let Hayley see us like this. See me like this. I sucked in deep breaths of cool air.

'Hi, Dad.' Hayley bounded into the kitchen. Seemed her mood had improved; I only wished I had her ability to forget. But somehow, Anthony had that effect on Hayley. One guess who the fun parent was?

'Hey, chicken. How's things?'

I closed the freezer, turned around, and forced a small smile, but Hayley shot me daggers—okay, so she hadn't forgotten. She returned her gaze to Anthony. 'Can I have some money to buy a new dress? It's for the formal.'

'You have a dress for the formal.' I'd bought it for her at the start of the year when we were filling in a Saturday afternoon window shopping. Phrases like 'I love it, Mum' and 'It will be perfect for the formal' and 'pleeease' had been thrown about.

'I know.' Hayley threw herself dramatically on the kitchen chair as if this was the biggest disaster since the dawning of time. 'But it's not the right colour anymore.'

'Not the right colour?'

'Well, Coco already has a navy dress, and Savannah does too. I don't want to be in navy as well,' she replied as if I was daft and I didn't realise that would be social suicide. 'And they have an amazing dress online at Pretty Things that would be so perfect.' She pulled out her phone and tapped away at it madly. 'Here, see!' She practically swooned at her father in an expression worthy of an Oscar-winning performance for Most Enthusiastic Rendition of 'How to get your parents to buy you a dress when you don't need one'.

'How much is it?' Anthony squinted at the screen.

I glanced over and my eyes popped open. 'Two hundred and twenty dollars!' That would've covered the groceries today.

'It's on special. Half price!' Hayley ignored me and spoke directly to Anthony, which irked me even more.

'There's no way.' I shook my head, turning back to the fridge and gathering the limp lettuce and a few other shrivelled salad items.

'Hang on.' Anthony drew Hayley in for a hug. 'Maybe—'

'Anthony!' Surely, he wasn't serious! We'd just argued that we were broke, and he was now agreeing to buy Hayley a dress she didn't need. 'She already has a perfectly good dress, brand new, unworn, bought specifically for this occasion, that she loves—or once loved.' I slammed the chopping board down and began hacking at the lettuce.

Hayley frowned at me, her pout childlike, then switched her attention back to Anthony. 'Please, Dad. I can resell it on Depop. And I can sell the other one too. It'll work out cheaper.'

Don't you love the way kids' brains work? As if they're actually doing their parents a favour. If I wasn't so mad, I'd laugh.

'We'll see.' Anthony was all full of smiles, and Hayley cuddled up to him before spinning to me.

'Oh, and Mum, Coco's coming for dinner. We have an English presentation tomorrow, and we want to practice it. Can she stay the night too? Her mum said it was okay. Maybe we could get takeout?'

The frustration that I'd been shoving down like an unruly shirt that wouldn't stay tucked in violently whooshed through me, and before I knew it, my hands were in the air, tiny pieces of lettuce flying every which way.

'You know what?' I said through gritted teeth. 'You deal with this, Anthony. The dress. Dinner. Everything. I can't do this.' I grabbed my bag off the counter and stormed to the front door.

'Mum! Where are you going? What about Coco?'

'Em?'

I resisted the almost unbearable urge to turn back and fix things. Like I always did. But instead, I pulled the door closed and pressed the button on my keyring. The lights on the car flickered; I hopped in, slammed the door, and reversed down the driveway, my hands shaking on the wheel.

CHAPTER FOUR

The local pub was noisy for a Wednesday night as I entered through the bar door. A waft of stale beer and sweat greeted me from the throng of men in team jerseys, a local hockey club by the look of the logo, their rambunctious voices competing to be heard. I veered towards the lounge area which was, thankfully, more subdued, with soft chatter and the hum of an eighties classic coming from a jukebox in the corner. At the other end of the lounge area was a long table with a silver 'Happy 80th' balloon hanging from the back of a man's chair. His cheeks were rosy red, his glasses perched halfway down his nose, and now and then, he touched his ear, perhaps adjusting his hearing aid. Apart from myself, sitting in the club chair, there was only one other couple eating a counter meal.

I took a sip of my lemon squash that I'd paid with the loose change in the bottom of my handbag. Twirling the straw, my mother's voice swirled in my head. *It's the last straw that breaks the camel's back.* It was exactly how she'd explain this situation. With one of her annoying clichéd sayings.

Considering the wine I had at home, I probably shouldn't have driven here, but it's not like I'd been thinking straight. I'd acted on impulse. Something very out of character for me. At least for the last twenty years. The last impulsive decision I'd made led me to the city. The memory suddenly overwhelmed me with shame, and I drew my thoughts back to the present. I'd never walked out of the house in anger before. I'd never walked out of the house without a plan or somewhere to be, something to do, and having organised things at home first. Because that was my job. Now, here I was on a Wednesday night in a pub, alone, upset, and angry. Absolutely not where I expected to find myself, late thirties, approaching the big four-oh. In fact, if you'd told me when I was twenty, that me, Emily Brown, lawyer-to-be, would be sitting here feeling helpless, ashamed, and confused, I would've laughed so hard the vodka and lime I would've been drinking would've spurted out my nose.

Back then, I was in my third year of a law degree, dating Anthony —five years older than me and already a hot-shot lawyer on the rise— and dreaming of seeing my-Gucci-suited-self parading my Manolo Blahniks around a mahogany courtroom.

'And that, your honour, is why my client is not guilty.' Bam! Or mic drop. That's what they say these days, isn't it?

I cringed at my innocence. Or naivety. Or perhaps just plain stupidity. I'd had it all planned back then. Or so I'd thought. After leaving Curlew Bay in circumstances different from what I'd planned, I had something to prove. I was hell-bent on doing something totally different. Hell-bent on making something of myself in the city. But somewhere between that naïve determination and dreams of success, I'd gone off track. Way off track. Maybe I should've returned home when I'd had the chance. Before it was too late to undo everything I'd done. Maybe I should've gone around Australia for a gap year with Simon selling my artwork for cash along the way. Like we originally planned.

Simon. Every now and then, he'd cross my mind along with the shame and regret remembering how much I'd hurt him. How I'd lied. I pushed the thoughts away. I couldn't go there. The past was the past. Twenty years ago. So much had happened since then. So much. And things always happen for a reason. Or so Mum always said.

My phone vibrated on the wooden table. Anthony. Again.

Where are you? Are you okay?

I ignored the message and switched my phone off. There you go, Anthony. Your turn to worry.

Worry. I picked at the coaster on the table. Worry was a constant state for me. Worrying about Hayley. Worrying about money. Worrying about work. Worrying about my marriage. A fresh swell of tears pricked at my eyes, and I took another drink of fizzy squash to hold them back. A roar erupted from the bar, and the couple eating looked up from their meals before resuming their conversation.

I rummaged in my bag and dug out a pen and a crumpled docket. I needed to get these thoughts out of my head before I did something stupid like walk away from everything. People did that, you know. I once listened to a podcast about a mother who got so overwhelmed with life, that one day, she kissed her husband goodbye as he left for work, ushered her kids on the school bus, packed her bag and disappeared for a year. She left her husband a note, telling him she needed space because the thoughts she was having were worse than just leaving her family. It was pretty chilling stuff. Walking away from your family. Your kids. People shamed her for it. Her husband took her back when she returned, but it wasn't long before the marriage disintegrated, he gained custody of the kids, and she was alone. But remarkably, she didn't regret her actions. Said it was a catalyst moment in her life, and now, ten years on, she was happy. She had a good relationship with her kids and was proud that she put herself first for the family's sake.

That was some brave stuff there. There was no way I could do that. Nor did I want to. But, at this moment, I didn't want to go back either. The thought snagged in my chest, and it took everything to hold back the emotion lodged there. Instead, I picked up the pen, smoothed out the crinkled docket, and began to write:

I can't go on like this. Something has to change.

Another idiom from my mother. I read the words over and over. *Something has to change. Something has to change. Something has to change.*

'Can I get you another drink? Maybe a menu? Kitchen's open til nine tonight.'

The server had snuck up on me and stood beside the table, a tray of empty used glasses in her hand, dried beer clinging to the sides like cobwebs. She reached over and picked up my empty glass.

'Ah, no. I'm fine. Thanks.' My tummy rumbled and although the hot chips on the table nearby smelled amazing, I didn't have enough loose change to cover even a side serve.

'Okay.' She smiled, shrugged, and turned away, her fruity perfume lingering in a waft behind her. Another wave of tears overcame me, this time too quickly for me to stop them. I swiped at my cheeks and rummaged through my handbag for a tissue.

Something has to change.

If only I knew what needed to change. And how to change it.

When I glanced up, an elderly lady from the eightieth birthday table was walking my way. Her face was kind, her skin soft and wrinkled in all the right places, and she had a gentle smile on her lips. She stopped in front of me. 'Are you okay, love? I don't mean to intrude, but you look upset.' Her accent had a slight Kiwi lilt to it.

'Oh.' I forced a small laugh and waved my hand. 'I'm fine. You know ...'

The lady nodded and placed her hand upon mine with a light tap. 'It's okay to not be okay.'

It took every effort of my being not to dissolve into tears.

'You never know what's around the next corner.' Then she smiled gently, turned, and continued towards the ladies' toilets.

That was when it hit me. Maybe this was my catalyst moment?

Yes, something had to change, but I had to be the one to make sure it did.

ON THE DRIVE HOME, I was shivering, despite the warmth of my car. Maybe tonight's moment was simply the dark before the dawn? I had a meeting with my boss tomorrow, and I was fairly certain it would be the promotion she'd been hinting at. Or at least, I'd been hinting at wanting—okay, needing—for the past six months. Maybe that was the turning point, the *something to change* thing. I had to believe it was because otherwise, I wasn't sure if I had the courage to do anything else.

Nearing an intersection, I flicked the indicator and turned the corner. As I did, a loud thump knocked at the back of the car and edged me into the gutter. 'Jesus. What the hell?' I pulled over and stepped out of the car, hoping I hadn't hit a cat or a dog, or worse. With my hand, I shielded my eyes from the glare of the passing head-lights. Thankfully, no dead or injured animals. But the driver's side tyre was puckered and swollen at the base like a flabby muffin top.

The first spots of light rain landed on my eyelashes.

You've got to be kidding.

CHAPTER FIVE

The alarm jolted me from sleep, and I sat up in bed, my head fuzzy. It had been after midnight by the time I got home. The roadside assistance had taken forever, and then the guy bitched and moaned about having to change the tyre in the rain as if it was my fault. By the time I'd gotten home, Anthony was passed out on the couch, and Hayley and Coco were giggling from behind her closed bedroom door. I'd felt like I'd been on an epic journey fighting demons and dragons and had collapsed into bed without even getting changed.

With my body fighting the state of wake, I threw my legs over the edge of the bed. I had to suck it up. Today was the day I was getting a promotion. Today was the day things were going to change. I selected my best work suit and shiniest shoes, or the ones that were the least scuffed. After a quick shower, seven layers of make-up to hide my sagging eye sockets and hollow cheeks, and two Panadol, I eyed myself in the bedroom mirror. The pairing of the grey suit pants, navy blouse, and pointy black kitten heels was supposed to look simple yet sophisticated. It looked neither, but it would have to do. I pulled my hair back into a claw clip and headed downstairs to find

Hayley and Coco shovelling toast into their mouths while thumbing through their phones. Still giggling, of course.

'Morning.' I dropped a kiss on Hayley's head. 'Morning Coco.'

'Hi, Mrs Mendez,' Coco replied cheerfully.

I received a grunt from Hayley.

'How'd your presentation practice go?'

Hayley shrugged. 'Good.' Then she returned to her phone, nudging Coco and dissolving into giggles again.

I shoved two bits of bread into the toaster and noticed Anthony's feet hanging off the edge of the lounge. One shoe on the floor, one still on his foot. The washing still sat unfolded, and the coffee table had collected another cup and a bowl. My instinct was to wake Anthony and tidy up; instead, I returned to the toaster.

AFTER SEEING Hayley and Coco off and checking to make sure Anthony was still breathing, I was now battling the morning gridlock with thousands of other cars; engines idling, exhausts fuming, pollution being expelled into the environment. I checked my reflection in the rear-view mirror and smoothed out the skin under my eyes with my fingertips as if doing so would make the dark circles and fine lines disappear. I was tempted to get the eye drops out of my bag but instead made a mental note to do it when I got to the office.

The traffic began to crawl again, the green light up ahead ushering through car after car, until mine, of course. As I came to a stop again, an incoming call cut through the engine drone. A photo of Mum during her pink hair phase flashed on my screen. I let out an audible groan. The last thing I needed was to be stuck in traffic and have another exhaustive conversation with my mother. The last time she'd called, it was to tell me Dad had finally gotten around to cleaning out the garage and did I want my oil paints. I still couldn't bear to throw them out even though they would be as hard as rocks after almost twenty years in storage. Goosebumps crept up my forearms as my mind wandered back to a time when painting had been my solace. My escape. It had meant everything. Until it hadn't. In the end, I'd told Mum not to throw them out, much to her annoyance. I swear she must've been reading Marie Kondo with her regular clean-outs.

By the time I wrestled with the pros and cons of answering the phone, it had stopped ringing and I exhaled a sigh of relief. After the green light gods granted me motion, I veered off with three thousand other cars and crept towards the city, feeling just a pang of guilt for ignoring Mum's call. Another layer of guilt to lasagne on my chest. Guilt that I couldn't pull my life together, that I felt such an enormous pit of emptiness in my stomach. Guilt that I couldn't be the best mother. Guilt I was the worst daughter. Guilt I couldn't remember the last time I'd cooked vegetables that weren't from the freezer. Mum's ringtone startled me, and without another thought, I flicked the answer button on the steering wheel.

'Hi, Mum!' I turned on my 'I'm living the dream' voice to hide the fact I was living a fucking nightmare. Lying. Something else to feel guilty about.

'Oh, you are there, Emily! I rang earlier, but I don't know what happened. It just beeped at me, so I tried to leave a message, but it kept on beeping. I'll have to get your father to look at this phone. Ever since I switched to Samsung, I've had trouble. But you know your father, he swears by them. He's convinced Apple are taking over the world, one phone user at a time—'

'Mum,' I interrupted. 'You probably just hung up accidentally.'

'Well, yes. I suppose. Anyway, I'm ringing to tell you about Lucy.'

Of courses she was. Lucy was Mum's favourite topic of conversation. 'She's in business,' Mum proudly stated to anyone who would listen, as if Lucy was bloody Elon Musk or Richard Branson. She wasn't. Yes, she owned a small gift shop in Curlew Bay, but it was hardly the Tesla or the Virgin empires.

Mum continued, her voice beaming. 'She's been elected to council!'

Of course she had. Lucy won everything. Had done since she'd won a colouring contest at the age of seven. Even though I was only five, I distinctly remembered it. I thought her colouring was awful; she didn't even stay in the lines. Yet, my entry (in the lower age category) was meticulously within the lines, even if the cows were yellow —artist's integrity and all that. Anyway, that stupid colouring competition set the whole tone of Lucy's bloody life. And mine. Lucy the winner, me second place. Or last. I did a head check and changed lanes, silently cussing at the slow Camry in front of me.

'You there?' Mum's voice kept cutting in and out.

'Yes, Mum. I heard. That's great. Tell her I said so. Look, I'd better go; the traffic's crazy today.'

'Of course, darling. Say hello to Hayley for me.' She paused. 'And Anthony.' I can tell she's pursing her lips. 'Any luck on the job front?'

I hesitated. I didn't like lying to Mum, but I was finding it hard to keep propping Anthony up in a positive light, let alone telling her the events of the past twenty-four hours.

'Sorry, Mum, you're breaking up.' I ended the call, another weight of guilt crushing my chest. The lights changed, and for a split second, I wondered what would happen if, instead of braking, I planted my foot and reefed the steering wheel into the oncoming traffic. Instead, I braked and exhaled.

SOMEHOW, I was only five minutes late into the office. I shrugged off my coat while expertly balancing my travel mug of coffee.

'Hi, Tamika,' I whispered as I rushed past the receptionist, noticing my boss Megan wasn't at her desk.

'Morning, Em; Megan asked if you could wait in her office,' Tamika sang as I slunk past.

'Sure. I'll be there in a jiffy.'

In my office, I collapsed into my chair and plucked another Panadol from my handbag. The first two had done nothing for my throbbing head. I grabbed the eye drops from my bag and dripped one drop into each eye, blinking rapidly as my mind shifted to my original vision of a high-flying successful life as a lawyer and how I ended up in a B-grade PR agency, handling household brands. Falling pregnant at twenty-one, during my second year of law school, hadn't been part of the plan. But I already knew how plans didn't always go the way you wanted them to. And Anthony was over the moon when he'd found out. There wasn't an option to do anything else. So, I'd had Hayley at the tender age of twenty-two after dropping out of my third year, with full intent to return to my degree. It just never happened. Instead, Anthony wanted to support us. He'd just landed a junior partner position at a law firm and wanted to be the bread-winner. I was so tired from parenting that I hadn't really cared. It wasn't until Hayley started school that I made the decision not to return to uni. Instead, I landed a job in PR. It was only going to be temporary. Until it wasn't. And now, that was all I'd ever done. Anyway, I'd paid my dues for the past few years at this company, and the promotion was well overdue. I almost felt bad for calling Megan 'the boss from hell'. In my head, that was. Not to her face. Although, there were times when I had definitely been tempted. Sometimes Megan made Miranda Priestly from *The Devil Wears Prada* look like Pollyanna.

'Emily, did Tamika not tell you to wait in my office?' Megan's voice bellowed as she sashayed past my door.

I threw the eye drops back in my bag and followed Megan obediently to her office, taking a seat while she took residence in her executive leather chair and fluffed her platinum pixie cut.

'So, how was the traffic this morning?' she said in her plum-in-the-mouth voice. Totally a put-on. One of my colleagues once told me she'd known Megan back at uni and she had more Australian twang than Kylie Minogue in her *Neighbours* days.

'Bedlam.' I casually deflected the comment. 'Must be that road work on the new freeway link.'

'Yes, I know. It's why I always get in early, but this morning I had to stop by the drycleaners.' She mindlessly tapped at her phone before placing it on the desk and leaning back in her chair.

'You know the jade-coloured pant suit I wore yesterday?' She didn't wait for a response. 'Well, last night I spilled red wine on it. Well, technically I didn't; Jasper—my cat—bumped me while he was smooching my arm. I was so upset. Not at Jasper. He didn't mean it, of course. But it cost me a pretty penny for that outfit. Anyway, did you know you shouldn't try and rub wine stains out of pure wool?'

I shook my head, all the while wishing she would just get to the promotion.

'No, neither did I.' She sighed. 'The drycleaner can't promise anything. But ...'

My mind began to wander. Surely, Megan hadn't brought me in to chat about her stained pantsuit. I snuck a glance at my watch. Get to the promotion, I demanded in my head, outwardly nodding and smiling. I took advantage of a slight pause in her story to clear my throat. 'Mmmm, awful.' I was full of faux concern. 'Um, so what did you want to see me about?'

'Yes, let's get to that.' Megan leant forward and whispered, with a raised eyebrow, 'I'm sure you've heard well enough of my dry cleaning dilemmas.'

Indeed, I had. Enough to last me a lifetime, in fact.

'Right. Well, I'm not quite sure how to say this, so I'll get straight to the point.' She picked up a beige manilla folder and flicked through the contents.

It didn't sound like the beginning of a promotion chat, but knowing Megan, she'd take the long way round. I shifted forward, rehearsing my acceptance in my head. *This has come at the perfect time, Megan. Thank you. Of course, I accept! And I won't let you down.* For some odd reason, the voice in my head mimicked her plumb accent. I turned my focus back to what Megan was saying.

'The company is restructuring. The pandemic, of course, has made a lot of companies sit up and reassess. Our plan is to focus on higher-profile clientele—you know, celebrities, sports stars, influencers—the kind of people Anna and Serina deal with.'

Pandering to B-grade celebrities wasn't my cup of tea, but it sure beat representing vitamins and period underwear. The raise would make it worth the while. This was it, my chance to get us out of this mess. The change I needed. A glimmer of hope flickered in my chest, and I squeezed my hands together.

'So, we are going to whittle down our household brand portfolio, which means ...' Megan paused, then jutted her chin out. 'Unfortunately, your position has become redundant.'

The chatter, phone's ringing, and footsteps outside Megan's office disappeared into white noise as the word redundant echoed around my head. Redundant? My brain scrambled to make sense of what she was saying. She must've meant no one would be taking my old role. Okay, whatever.

'It's not reflective of your work commitment, simply a cost cutting measure. I'm sure you understand.'

Then it dawned on me. '*I'm* redundant?'

Megan nodded. 'I'm sorry, Emily. Really, I am.'

'What? No, you can't. I need this job.'

'I will give you a glowing reference—'

My mouth was suddenly sapped of moisture, and it was hard to push out the words. 'I don't want a glowing reference. I want this job. I need this job. You don't understand, Megan ... We've ... Anthony...' My head rushed with blood. 'Please, can't you reconsider?'

Megan rose to her feet and began shuffling files on her desk before pausing and catching my eyes. 'I'm sorry, Emily, the decision comes from above me, unfortunately.'

She gave a brief, thin-lipped smile as if that was enough consola-
tion for the news she'd delivered. 'I'll have Tamika finalise all the
details with you; your finish date, entitlements, and all that. Chin up;
you'll find something in no time. You are fabulous at what you do. I
mean that.' And with that, she grabbed her files and walked out,
leaving me frozen in the chair.

Redundant?

I grabbed the desk to steady myself as the room swayed. When it
came back into focus, my body froze with cold realisation. Something *had* changed. But in the worst possible way.

CHAPTER SIX

I'd feigned sickness after meeting with Megan and told Tamika I was going to work from home for the rest of the day, which of course, I had no intention of. I had almost five weeks of sick leave accrued, which apparently wasn't paid out, so I was damn well going to use it. In fact, who knew? I might just be sick for the next three weeks or however long it took me to 'tie up all my loose ends'.

When I arrived home, the house was eerily quiet. As it should be at five past one on a Thursday afternoon, Hayley at school, Anthony ... Well, my guess would be he was down at one of the pubs squeezing the very last bit of money from our already drained accounts. Maybe running up a tab, trying his luck on the pokies. The thought made me sick.

I lumped my bag on the kitchen counter. I was in the mind space to say fuck it to all those loose ends and walk away. Stuff everything, in fact. Years of working in a shitty job pandering to brands no one cared about, thinking I was clawing my way up to something when all I was doing was holding on so I didn't plummet down the metaphorical mineshaft of life. Not that I'd done a particularly good job at stopping myself. Look at where I was.

Standing in the middle of the kitchen staring at a half-eaten apple left on the counter, suddenly, everything became horribly clear. The life we'd tried to build, the life I'd tried to hold together. It seemed like one thing after another had compounded to where one lonely half-eaten apple left to brown on the kitchen bench was all too much. The thought of having to put it in the compost bin made me bone tired. Then I noticed the crinkled permission slip from Hayley's school lying beside the apple. I sped read down to the part requiring my signature and, of course, more money. You'd think the thousands of dollars we forked out in private school fees each year would cover such costs, but no, just another excuse to suck you dry under the guise of giving your child the 'best education possible and best pathway into future success'. A murderous rage overcame me, and I grabbed the note, scrunched it tight in my hands, and tossed it against the wall, letting out an almighty 'Uuuu-uuuuuurrrghh!'

My throat burnt from the guttural scream, and I bent down, grasped onto the kitchen bench, and leant my head against the cold cabinets. Thunderous, gut-wrenching sobs belched from me as if they'd been suppressed for years.

What the hell were we supposed to do now? We were in debt up to our eyeballs, and now both of us were unemployed. This wasn't how I'd pictured my life at this age. I was supposed to have my shit together by now, not be on the brink of losing everything.

My mind jumped from the half-eaten apple and scrunched up permission note to white beaches, oil paints, and the hum of music before being jolted back to the present as the front door creaked open, followed by the security door slamming shut.

Anthony's footsteps trod up the hallway. 'Em? You here?'

I frantically wiped my eyes with the back of my hands, stood up, and smoothed my hair back into place just as Anthony entered the kitchen with a furrowed brow, his eyes registering that something was wrong. Very wrong. 'Em? Are you okay?' He walked towards me, and I held my hands up in a 'back away' stance. The last thing I wanted right now was anyone touching me, most of all Anthony.

'Why are you home in the middle of the day?'

I took a deep breath. 'I just had my meeting with Megan.'

'Oh, right. How'd it go?'

'Turns out today was the day Megan was handing out redundancies, not promotions.'

'What?'

'Yep.'

Anthony leant against the counter and let out a long sigh, skimming his hand through his hair. He was still handsome in that mid-forties way men were allowed to be, the lines adding something to his face other than age. His dark hair was greying at the temples but was still thick and wavy on top. I remembered how he'd caught my eye at a party one night looking as handsome as Antonio Banderas, cheeky grin and all. But now, I saw past that. I saw what I didn't want to admit. What I hadn't wanted to admit for too long. Something had to change. I had to change. 'I can't do this anymore.' My voice was barely a whisper as if I was scared of the words.

Anthony's forehead creased. 'What do you mean?'

'I mean, I can't do this. Us. This. Everything.'

'Em—'

I shook my head, and suddenly, everything was clear. As if I'd just stepped off a precipice and been caught by the thermals with nothing to lose. 'We both know it's been broken for a long time.' I crossed my arms around my middle. The words tumbled out of me like clothes falling out of the dryer when you opened the door. 'I can't do it anymore. I can't pretend that everything is okay and that we're going to catch a break one day. That one day never comes. And even if it did ...' I wasn't able to finish the sentence. Us. We're too far gone. We were the camel. This moment was the straw.

'Em, you're not thinking straight. We can sort this out. Get through it.'

I shook my head, and we stood in silence. Anthony leaning against one bench, me the other. A whole lifetime of obstacles between.

'I'm going to take Hayley down to see my parents for the school holidays. We can leave tomorrow. Hayley finishes at two-thirty.'

'To Curlew Bay? For what? For how long?'

'I don't know. A week, maybe two. I don't know.'

I could almost see Anthony's thoughts scampering behind his eyes, trying to figure out what that meant. I didn't even know.

He shrugged a shoulder. 'Okay. Sure. It'll probably be good for you to ... take a breather. I can sort things out here. Talk to the bank. Get things sorted.'

I didn't have any fight left in me to argue that talking to the bank wasn't going to 'get things sorted'. Instead, I nodded and turned towards the hall.

'Em—'

'Don't.' I hesitated in the doorway, the tears itching in my eyes, my thoughts piling on top of each other. There was nothing left to say.

CHAPTER SEVEN

'We're almost there.' I glanced across at Hayley who was slouched down in the passenger seat staring out the window, earbuds nestled in her ears. She ignored me so I returned my focus to the road, flicked on the indicator, and veered from the winding coastal road. The drive had eased my tightened jaw and relaxed my knotted muscles. I don't know if it was leaving the city or the winding road along the coast, endless blue ocean on one side, dense national park on the other, but I somehow felt lighter.

My stomach fluttered as a glimpse of the Curlew Bay township came into view. The place where I grew up. Where rocky cliffs plummeted on one side, the river met the ocean on the other, and a sandy beach stretched along green parkland and across the town's esplanade and main shopping drag. Where my childhood and teenage memories danced along the beach, under the jetty, and up and down the streets I knew so well. Where summers were hot and punctuated by afternoon storms, and winters were grey with icy winds that cut right through to your bones.

Unlike Lorne and Torquay, the small inlet town of Curlew Bay along the Great Ocean Road on Victoria's southern coastline had somehow remained untouched by tourism. And that was the way the locals liked it. Quiet and unassuming.

Through the windshield, the grey July sky blanketed the horizon sending a knowing rush of goosebumps over my skin as the car wove around the small residential area lined with brick houses with tidy front yards and double garages. My parents still lived in my child-hood home. These streets as familiar to me as my own reflection. From the corner of my eye, I noticed Hayley sink further down into her seat. To say she wasn't impressed with our impromptu 'holiday', as I framed it, would be the understatement of the century.

At first, she had refused to go, shaken her head forcibly, tears welling in her eyes. Something about missing a party and all the other things she had planned for her holidays. I can't say I felt good telling her she didn't have a choice. She couldn't stay with Anthony. He was *supposedly* going to sort things out. The bank wasn't forgiving and with no way of making up the missed payments let alone any future payments we had no choice. We had to sell. Anthony was organising to get the valuers through the house and find a real estate agent. And whatever else needed to be done. I didn't want Hayley to see that. Not yet. I had to get things settled in my head before I sat her down and told her what was happening.

When she'd asked me why we were going and questioned if it had anything to do with running out of the supermarket the other day, I did what any decent mother would do. Deny. Deny. Deny. No use trying to explain things to her when I couldn't even explain them to myself.

A few moments later, I pulled into Mum and Dad's driveway. A quaint 1990s three-bedroom brick veneer of mottled red bricks, faded grey roof tiles, and striped pull-down awnings that were washed-out from years of sun exposure. The gardens, however, looked immaculate as usual, the lawn edged perfectly thanks to Dad's meticulous nature, while Mum's white iceberg roses were neatly pruned to knobbly sticks waiting out the winter in preparation for new season blooms.

As I switched off the engine, the wire door of the house swung open, and Mum popped out wearing blue jeans and a flowing floral top, a huge smile on her face. I was thankful her pink bob had returned to its natural blonde-grey state.

'Come on,' I said to Hayley. I feared I would have to drag her out of the car, but she rolled her eyes and unclicked her seatbelt.

'Oh, Hayley.' Mum raised an eyebrow as she saw her grandchild for the first time in six months. 'Look at you, sweetie. You've grown up, haven't you?'

The last time we were here, Hayley was a bubbly ball of love and cuddles. High on life and K-Pop. Yet, somewhere between fifteen and fifteen and a half, Hayley had suddenly grown up. Throw in having parents who hardly spoke to each other and a mother who was dragging her to 'some deadbeat small town' (her words, not mine) for the holidays, and she had morphed into a surly 90s supermodel: not a smile in sight.

'Hi, Grandma.' Hayley gave Mum a small embrace.

'Go on, honey. It's freezing out here. Second bedroom on the left, is all yours.'

Hayley dragged her suitcase inside, the wheels thwacking on each step before the wire door slammed shut behind her.

'Hi, Mum,' I said once Hayley had disappeared. 'Don't worry about her. She's in a mood. But she'll be okay.'

'Of course. Teenagers. I know.' Mum pulled me into her arms with a small, concerned tutting noise. The smell of her apple scented shampoo tickled at my nose. 'How are *you*?' she asked.

I'd given Mum a relatively limited briefing on our visit, leaving out all the dirty details. For now, at least. I knew she'd grill me the first chance she had. 'Well, you know.'

'Everything will be fine.' Mum rubbed my back so hard it felt like she was trying to convince herself more than she was me.

'Thanks for having us.' I looked up at the afternoon sky to dry my eyes before prying myself from Mum's vice-like hug.

'Don't be silly. Now, let's get you inside.'

I followed Mum up the front steps and into the hallway. The house smelt like figs. 'Something smells good.'

'Oh, isn't it gorgeous? It's my new candle—fig and cassis. I'll put the kettle on.' Mum continued to the kitchen while I made my way to my old bedroom. Tea was Mum's answer to everything. I prayed she understood this situation called for a hearty English Breakfast (preferably with a shot of whiskey), not one of those fancy berry ones she'd been telling me about. This was no time for some organic raspberry and ginger concoction.

I stood in the doorway of what was once my childhood bedroom. Of course, it looked nothing like it used to. Gone were the Savage Garden and Coldplay posters, replaced with mauve wallpaper covered in silver orchids. The double bed was packed with so many throw cushions in more than fifty shades of grey, I had no idea where I would put them to actually sleep in the bed.

Mum had turned into a mad decorator. My room stood untouched until about five years ago when she became obsessed with redecorating. I blamed all of those TV renovation shows. After each season, she transformed into redecorating mode, much to my father's dismay. Mum was so pleased with her latest efforts that she'd even posted photos to Instagram and actually tagged interior designer Shaynna Blayze, who'd been gracious enough to reply with a thumb's up emoji. The only odd piece in the room left over from my old things was the life-sized cut-out of Justin Timberlake I'd won in a competition at the local music store.

'Well, JT.' I plonked my suitcase against the wall and slumped onto the bed. 'Here we are again.' Justin's sugary smile didn't waver as all the throw cushions toppled on me.

'Tea's ready, Emily.'

I sat up with a sigh and caught my reflection in the mirrored robe doors. I almost expect to see my teenage self, but of course, almost two decades had passed, and I hardly recognised the person staring back at me. The woman who was naïve, ignorant, and pushed through each day with a mountain of coffee and wine, blissfully pretending she was working her way to success. That was the reality. But, staring at myself, I realised I had to face the fact that this was what my life now looked like. Once, I thought I was the *Titanic* destined for glory, but I'd hit an iceberg, and this, my childhood bedroom, was the bottom of the Atlantic Ocean.

AT THE KITCHEN TABLE, Mum pushed a steaming cup of tea towards me, an Earl Grey tea bag dangling. Not English Breakfast, but at least no fancy, schmancy elderberry and hibiscus.

'Where's Dad?' I blew on my steaming tea before taking a sip; it tasted like home. Instantly, my body relaxed.

'He's helping Bill at the golf club. Something to do with a new display rack or something.' Mum shrugged.

Since retiring from his forty-odd years as a plumber, Dad had taken to tinkering with woodwork in his shed. He'd joined the local Men's Shed and built numerous things, such as a spice rack for the pantry, a new mailbox, and free-hanging shelves for the spare room. Well, they were meant for the lounge room, but Mum took a dislike to them and relegated them to one of the spare rooms.

'So.' Mum placed her teacup down gently on the saucer.

Oh crap. Mum was onto me. Here I thought we would have a nice little catch-up discussing the weather.

'Are you going to tell me exactly what's going on?'

I let out a long breath as I studied Mum's expression. One eyebrow was raised ever so slightly, and the corner of her mouth was twitching rhythmically like a heartbeat. It was the look she gave me when she'd caught me sneaking a biscuit from the tin when I was a kid. The look that said, 'You thought you could hide from me, but I'm your mother.'

'You want the short version or the long version?'

'I want the honest version.'

I settled back in my chair and took another sip of warm tea to prepare. 'Okay.'

Five minutes later, our teacups were empty, and Mum's expression had softened, which I wasn't sure was out of pity or disappointment. Maybe I shouldn't have told her the full story.

'Oh, Emily.' She'd said that several times over the past few minutes. Which was odd for her; she was rarely lost for words.

'Yep. So here I am. Unemployed, my daughter hates me, and I think my marriage is broken. That pretty much sums it up. Oh and broke too, once my redundancy package is swallowed up by the debts we owe.'

'It's a blip in the road, darling. That's all.' Mum gave me a weak smile and patted my hand.

It made my heart tug to think that Mum could still come up with another one of her sayings at a time like this. 'I think it's slightly more than a blip, but thanks.'

'You know you can stay here as long as you want,' she continued, the worry lines on her forehead deepening. 'And whatever you need to get back on your feet ... However much you need, I'm sure your father and I—'

'Mum.'

'No, Emily. That's what family is for.'

'I appreciate it, I do. But we got into this mess; we have to get out of it.'

'Even if it's just a couple of mortgage payments to keep the bank happy. Surely—'

'Mum. No.'

Mum let out a disgruntled sigh through pursed lips. 'What about

Hayley?' she asked after a few moments of silence. 'Does she know what's going on?'

'She knows something's up, but no. We haven't told her much.'

Mum's eyes narrowed, and she straightened in her chair. 'You're best to be upfront with her. Perhaps not about everything, but at least let her know why you're here. And how long you're going to be here for. It's only fair. Kids are resilient, you know.'

I want to believe her, I do. But that mother's guilt was sitting squarely on my shoulders, whispering in my ear: *Teenagers need security. Stability. You've really stuffed this up.*

'What if it breaks her, Mum? What if she hates us? Turns to drugs?'

Mum frowned. 'Sorry?'

I wasn't making sense. My brain was jumping to worst-case-scenario conclusions, but I couldn't stop it from racing like a cassette tape caught on rewind, spewing everywhere. I concentrated on the flowers on the teacup, crimson and gold roses, their leaves and stems intertwining. As I blinked, a tumble of tears splashed on my cheek.

Mum reached over and placed her hand on mine, this time grasping it firmly. 'Oh, honey. Give it time. You will get through this.'

I nodded slowly, still unable to meet her eyes.

'It might not seem like it, but you will. I know you. You're as tough as nails.'

I forced myself to smile and remember she meant well.

As I wiped at my eyes, we both turned as the front door swung open in a flurry. I heard Lucy's voice before she'd even entered the kitchen.

'Sorry, Mum, I forgot all about dropping these off before—' She stopped midsentence when she saw me. 'Oh. Em. I thought that was your car. What are you doing here?' Her gaze flicked between Mum and me, searching for answers. 'Is everything okay?'

'It's a long story.' I tried to push my voice out brightly, but it came out in a squeak. Lucy raised her eyebrows. I cleared my throat. 'Hi, sis, by the way.'

'Oh, yeah, hi.' Lucy appeared to have lost her train of thought.

'The books?' Mum asked.

'The books? Oh, yes, the books.' Lucy dumped a calico bag on the end of the bench. 'Thanks for dropping these back at the library for me. I'm run off my feet at the moment with everything that's going on.'

'I probably won't get there 'til tomorrow morning. Is that okay?'

'Yeah. Fine. They're due back tomorrow. I'd take them, but we have Ethan's footy in Diamond Creek. Ungodly eight am start.' Lucy tapped the bench with her fingers as if still waiting for an explanation for my presence. She'd be bursting to ask Mum why she wasn't filled in on the details before my arrival. According to Lucy, Mum told her everything. Apparently not.

I smiled internally before deciding to put her out of her misery. 'I might be moving home. For a bit.'

'What? Why?'

I revelled in Lucy's eyes widening. 'Well, things with Anthony and I are ...' I scrunched my nose. '... And the bank is about to repossess the house; oh, and I was also made redundant yesterday.'

'Emily!' Mum tsked as she stood and collected our teacups to take to the sink.

'What? It's the truth!'

'I know, but you don't need to be so blunt about it.' She rinsed the teacups and dried her hands on the tea towel.

I glanced at Lucy, who still hadn't snapped out of the frozen look of surprise.

'Oh. Right. Okay,' Lucy finally replied, shifting on her feet. 'Um ... I'd stay, but I'm on my way to a meeting. Sorry.'

'It's fine. Go.' I didn't really want to get into things with Lucy. It was bad enough having Mum's pity, let alone Lucy's opinion. And there was no doubt she'd have a few of those if past experience was any indicator. Lucy and I didn't get along. Our teenage years were fraught with fights about everything and anything. Lucy always offering an unwanted opinion on what I was wearing, how long I spent in the bathroom, what I ate, what I watched on TV. Me always on the backfoot defensively. Okay, so it wasn't always her, I was as much to blame for our lack of synergy. And, our relationship as adults had developed more into a mutual truce laced with sarcastic comments through smiles. No, she didn't need to know any more than this. Not yet, anyway.

'Right. Well, I guess I'll get going.' Lucy moved towards the door slowly, as if waiting for me to add more details without asking.

'See you.' I fake-smiled so brightly my cheeks hurt.

When Lucy was gone, Mum shot me a look of disappointment; the one that said, Can't you two just get along? 'Why did you have to tell her like that?'

'Like what?' I shrugged, feigning innocence. Lucy craved gossip and details, and being the first to know about everything, she'd be dying to find out more. Especially now that she'd had a whiff that my life was imploding which would make her feel all the more superior. It surprised me she hadn't already texted Mum requesting a call.

'Well, then. This load of washing won't hang itself.' Mum interrupted my thoughts and pointed to a loaded laundry basket near the back door. 'Did you want to help me? Chat more?'

I shook my head. 'No, I think I'll just sit here and wallow a bit longer if that's alright.'

Mum gave me a sympathetic gaze and picked up the basket. 'Oh, and just so you know, Lucy, Gordon, and the kids are coming over Sunday lunch for a barbecue. Is that okay? I can cancel it. If you don't think you'll be up for a house full of visitors.'

'It'll be fine, Mum. It'll be good to see Chloe and Ethan. And Gordon. It's been ages.'

'Yes, they'll be excited to see Hayley too. Okay, I'll leave you to it.'

At least by Sunday, Lucy would've had time to process everything rather than hitting her with it at the barbecue. And it would be good for Hayley, too, to reconnect with her cousins. A stab of guilt hit me. I should have tried harder, visited more so she could have a familiar relationship with her family. But Lucy could have tried harder too. Anyway, I'd have to pry her out of her room first, which I suspected would be one of my biggest challenges over the next few days.

The front door rattled, and I leant back on my chair to see into the entry hall, half expecting Lucy's curiosity to have got the better of her, but it wasn't Lucy; it was Dad. He removed his jacket and hung it on the coat rack by the door. Another one of his 'Men's Shed' projects.

'Hi, Dad.'

'Ah, my Emily.' He rushed down the short passage, arms outstretched.

I stood to meet his embrace, his warm arms enveloping me; the familiar spicy-citrusy aroma of the Brut aftershave he'd worn forever was like a soothing balm.

'How are you, honey? How's Hayley?'

'We're okay. We're here.'

'And it's the best place for you.'

He released me and continued into the kitchen. 'Where's that granddaughter of mine, then?'

'Hauled up in the spare room. She's a bit upset.'

'Oh. Is she alright?' Dad took a can of beer from the fridge and cracked it open, nodding towards me.

'No thanks. Mum's already filled me up on tea. And yes, Hayley will be fine. You know teenagers. They don't do well with unexpected plans.' I sat down in my seat again.

'She'll come around. Now, where's your mother?'

'Hanging the washing.'

'She okay?'

I frowned. 'Mum? Yeah. I think so. Why?'

'Oh, nothing. She's most likely just worrying about you. I tell her not to worry. Anyway, want to talk about it?'

'No, not really. I'm sure Mum will fill you in. I've just got some things to sort out.'

Dad rested his hand on my shoulder. 'Of course. Well, I'll be in the shed. You know, if you need me.'

After Dad closed the back door, I sat for a few more moments and listened to the tick of the grandfather clock from the hallway. This house held so many memories. Good and bad. Good, because it was home. My safe place. Bad because it reminded me of how much I'd wanted to make my own life away from Curlew Bay. How I'd dreamed of something different. Bad, because the reason I'd left wasn't the reason I thought I'd leave. But that was all in the past. Where it needed to stay. Returning would test those waters, but nothing could be gained from revisiting the past. It was the now and the future I had to worry about. And that was going to take all the mental capacity I had.

CHAPTER EIGHT

Mary shook the wrinkles from the wet polo shirt and pegged it on the line. The sky was a sooty grey but the afternoon sun had poked through, the glare making her eyes water. Or maybe it was the situation. Poor Emily. Mary's heart grabbed. Emily always seemed like she had it all together. She was a go-getter, her Emily. Knew what she wanted, and even though life had thrown her a few curveballs, she'd always forged ahead. Mary had no clue that things had been this bad. Did that make her a terrible mother? Should she have known? Asked more? Taken more notice? She let out a small sigh as a willie wagtail flittered in the camellia bush nearby.

When did you stop worrying about your children? Emily was going on thirty-seven, and Lucy thirty-nine. And there wasn't a day that went by when she didn't think about them both at least once. But maybe that hadn't been enough. She made a mental note to call Lucy tonight and see if she was okay. She had seemed more stressed than usual. Rushing about from here to there, forgetting things. That wasn't like Lucy. She was normally on top of everything so effortlessly, but not lately.

Mary shook her head and pegged David's woolly socks on the

line. She was being silly. Of course, Lucy was okay. She'd just made her way onto council and had big ideas on how to improve Curlew Bay. Not that it needed improving. She enjoyed her down-to-earth and laid-back life in the sleepy little hamlet. But Lucy said they needed to tap into the tourist dollars. Mary supposed she was right. Lucy would know more about that kind of thing than she would. Lucy had her finger on the pulse. Whereas Mary just took one day at a time. Always had.

Mary's eyes glistened again. Oh, you silly thing. Her emotions had been all over the place lately. She'd feel perfectly fine one minute and then in an instant her mood would shift to that of a snappy Jack Russell. And she seemed to be so tired lately. Probably because she wasn't sleeping well. Even though she was tired when she went to bed, she'd often lay there for hours staring at the ceiling willing sleep to arrive and then worrying about how tired she would be when it didn't. It was a vicious cycle. Not even the mattress overlay she'd bought off the TV ad had helped. She hadn't been like this since going through menopause ten years earlier. No wonder David spent most of his days in his shed or on the golf course. She couldn't blame him. Yet sometimes she did. Or perhaps it wasn't blame but more a feeling of envy. He had his woodwork and his golf. What did Mary have?

Well, there was the book club she enjoyed each month—more for the gossip, wine, and sweet treats than the books sometimes, and then there was her yogalates, not that she could say she enjoyed that. Some of the positions the instructor expected her to get into were almost obscene. She was sixty three, for goodness' sake! She wasn't ready for the retirement village but she wasn't supple or balanced enough for that silly half-moon pose thing either.

And, recently her shoulder had been giving her trouble, and even her armpit had been tender for some strange reason. All these aches in silly places. She knew to expect a few aches and pains as she got older, but she didn't want to accept them. Then there were days she still felt young and spritely as if she could take on the world. She let out a muffled laugh. Take on the world? Really? As if she'd be taking on the world at her age? It wasn't like she could start a business or get a job.

Mary let her mind wander to a place she didn't often let it go. Travel. It was something she'd always longed to do. But David had never been the travelling type. He was more of a homebody.

A few years back, she saw a caravan for sale at the end of the street. She'd even enquired how much they were asking. Let herself imagine travelling across the Nullarbor, seeing Western Australia, maybe even the Red Centre, and up to Darwin. When she'd mentioned it to David as they walked past one evening, he chuckled as if she were joking. 'Us? Join the grey nomads?' He'd huffed dismissively. 'Couldn't think of anything worse than being cooped up in a house the size of a matchbox for months on end.' She'd not brought it up again.

With the washing hung, she bent down to pluck a few stray weeds from the rock garden, her thoughts still snagged on travel. Or the regret of not travelling more to the point.

When she was younger, she'd almost had the perfect chance. In her first job, after she'd worked her way up to secretary for the CFO of an electrical appliance company, she almost had her foot in the aeroplane. Her new promotion would see her accompanying the directors on their overseas trips which had delighted her wanderlust. Mary had prioritised her career up until that point and aspirations of flying to New York, London, and Paris were at the top of her list. But not long after her promotion, she'd met David. She was twenty-three and had fallen head over heels for him after they met at, of all things, a card night organised by a mutual friend. She was impressed at his manners and the shy way he scratched his cheek when he spoke. And, she was of course, impressed by his thick John Travoltarish hair and smile as warm as a fresh hot cross bun. And she loved hot cross buns.

Didn't know why people complained when they hit the shelves in January.

So, she'd fallen for David, followed him to Curlew Bay, and accordingly packed away her dreams of jet setting the globe in her discarded, brand-new suitcase that now sat gathering dust on the top shelf of their walk in robe. She'd replaced visions of drinking coffee in Paris and eating Bagel's in New York city with meat and three veg meal preparation and invoicing for David's new plumbing business.

Then came Lucy, followed by Emily, who filled her days with nap times, walks to the park, and sleepless nights. Then there was the volunteering at the school—back when mothers were around to volunteer—not like these days. And then, in the blink of an eye, Emily and Lucy were leaving home and making their way into the world.

And what had Mary done for the past twenty years? Not that she regretted any of it. Regret was such a dirty word, implying that the life led to that point had been a mistake. Not at all. She'd loved seeing her children forge their own lives and had been quite happy enjoying her days here and there and looking after the grandkids to help Lucy out in more recent years. But still, something itched inside her. Was it unfulfillment? Her stomach dropped. As admirable as it was being a mother, running a successful business with David, volunteering at the Red Cross Shop, and running around after Lucy, what had it really amounted to?

Mary rose gingerly, her legs unable to squat for very long these days. Pins and needles trickled down her calves. That annoying twinge was still in her knee. She really should stretch more like her yogalates instructor had told her to.

Throwing the weeds in the nearby green waste bin, she dusted the dirt off her hands, her mind still whirring. What was she supposed to do with the next twenty years until Emily and Lucy packed her and David off into a nursing home to play Scrabble and stare out the window at the birds?

Mary tutted as annoyance twinged inside her. 'Stop it, you old fool,' she muttered, noticing a shirt on the line had twisted in a gust of wind. She yanked it off before repegging it with more force than was needed. *The grass is always greener.* She should be grateful for the life she'd had. She'd done good things. Raised a beautiful family, made a beautiful home. There was no room for grand plans. Especially not at her age.

Mary huffed and turned from the washing line to see Hayley walk out the back door, phone in hand.

'Oh, Hayley.' Mary smiled, glad for the distraction from her maudlin thoughts. There was no use dillydallying in regrets and dreams. Regret was useless. Was it Marlon Brando who'd said that?

'Hi, Grandma,' Hayley said flatly, eyes still on the screen.

'Come, sit down. It's been so long since I've seen you.' Mary pulled out a chair from the outdoor setting and Hayley, reluctantly it appeared, sat down. Mary joined her across the table. 'You've shot up in the past six months, haven't you?'

Hayley shrugged, her eyes momentarily flicking up from the screen. 'I guess.'

Okay, so conversation wasn't going to be easy. Mary had to think outside the box. 'Is that the new iPhone?' Technology, that should get something out of her.

'It's not a new one. It's only an eleven. Mum says we can't afford a new phone. But anyway, the new one isn't much different. But has a better camera.'

Mary nodded. She didn't have any clue about what phones did these days, but she still found it odd how many photos everyone seemed to take. Back in her day, if you were lucky enough to have a camera, you were even luckier if you remembered to take it anywhere. Then remember to get the film developed at the chemist. If you could afford it. Anyway, at least she'd managed to get Hayley talking.

'You know your grandfather made me buy a Samsung. I hate it.'

'Urgh. No one has Samsungs.' Hayley screwed her face up like she'd sucked on a lemon.

'Yes, I can see why. So complicated. I can't for the life of me figure out how to text on it without it automatically correcting every word I type.'

Hayley dropped her eyes and began scrolling on her phone. Mary had lost her already with her tech-fail admission. Her heart sank. How was Hayley really feeling? What exactly had Emily told her? Poor Hayley. Mary wished she could say something, anything, to reassure her that things would be okay. But it wasn't her place.

'Have you made any plans for the holidays? It's probably too cool to swim, but the weather forecast is clear the next few days so you could head down to the beach.' Hayley's face darkened, and Mary realised she'd hit a sore point. 'It won't be all that bad. Maybe you could invite a friend from school for a day or so?'

Hayley was glued to her phone, but she'd stopped scrolling, her fingers hovering over the screen, and her eyes were filling with tears.

'Oh, darling.' Mary pushed back her chair, stood and opened her arms to invite her for a cuddle like she used to when she was younger. 'Come here.' Mary expected her to storm back inside and retreat to the bedroom, but to her surprise, Hayley stayed put and let the tears flow. Mary rushed around the table and held her tight, cradling her close as her body trembled.

'It's not fair, Grandma,' Hayley sobbed into her shoulder. 'I just want to be back home for the holidays. I miss my friends already.'

'I know you do, darling.' Mary stroked Hayley's hair. 'Everything will be back to normal soon.'

'Will it? I know Mum and Dad are fighting. What if they're getting a divorce? Then what?'

Oh dear. Mary wasn't equipped to answer such a question. Her innate response was to say something along the lines of 'It will be fine. Don't worry.' But what proof did she have to back that up? Instead, she tightened her hug and pressed a kiss to her crown.

'Why can't Mum and Dad just work it out?' Hayley pulled away from Mary and slammed back in her chair. 'That's what parents are supposed to do. Communicate and talk. Not fight and scream. And anyway, it's all Mum's fault. It is. I know it is. She was always too busy with work. Which is stupid because apparently, we have no money now.'

'Darling, I think it's a little more complicated than that.'

'They think I don't know. But I'm not a little girl. I hear their arguments. She's always blaming Dad!'

Tears continued to stream down Hayley's flushed cheeks, and she swiped at them with the sleeve of her jumper.

'Oh, Hayley.' Mary reached for her hand, but she yanked it away. Hayley possibly did know more than Emily and Anthony thought, but there was a lot she didn't know nor would understand at her tender age. Emily should've been more upfront with her. She was almost sixteen, not a child anymore. But it wasn't Mary's place to say anything, was it? Of course, it wasn't.

Hayley stood abruptly, the chair almost toppling over, and stormed back inside. The weight of everything suddenly made Mary's body feel heavy with tiredness. She rubbed her temples. She should talk to Emily more. Maybe she and David could take some money from their term deposit and loan it to Emily? She'd already offered, of course, but she could offer again. Emily would realise it was for the best. Or was it? Maybe Emily was best to get out of the city life. Maybe they could relocate and start fresh here in Curlew Bay. Mary had secretly wished she'd come home at some stage. Don't all parents wish their brood to return to the nest?

Mary sighed. It was all too much. Her head ached, her chest was heavy, and her armpit was throbbing again.

CHAPTER NINE

Sunday morning, I woke to the sounds of a thousand sparrows chirping and rustling in the tree outside my window. I used to be able to sleep through their morning song when I was a kid. I used to be able to sleep through the rumble of the garbage truck in the city on a Tuesday morning and even our neighbour's dog barking at three am. Lately, though, the sound of my breathing wakes me up.

After lying there for a few more minutes staring at the faded glow in the dark stars I'd stuck on the ceiling when I was nine, I remembered Lucy and the family were coming for lunch today. That would require a strong coffee (or two). And maybe even something stronger to help me deal with getting Hayley out of her bedroom. We'd tried yesterday, but she'd refused until dinner time. Mum's spaghetti napolitana eventually drew her out. It had the knack of doing that with its aroma of garlic and tomato. At least Hayley was eating. That was one less thing to worry about.

In the kitchen, Mum and Dad were already at the breakfast table. Early risers. Not because they had to be, just because they were. Best part of the day, Mum would always say. Mum poured black tea into her jade-coloured teacup, followed by a splash of milk, then drizzled honey over her hot crumpet. Dad was flicking through the local newspaper and sipping his coffee.

'Morning.' I headed straight for the kettle.

'Morning,' Mum and Dad chimed in unison.

'Don't forget Lucy's here for a barbecue lunch today,' Mum reminded me.

'Yeah, I remembered.'

The kettle didn't take long to boil, and I scooped instant coffee powder into a cup. It was going to taste like dirty dishwater, but it was caffeine.

I sat down at the table across from Mum. 'I think that mug has seen better days.' I nodded at Dad's coffee mug. Lucy and I had bought it for him from the Father's Day stall at school about thirty years ago. The 'best dad' writing was faded, and a large chip was missing on one side of the rim.

'This? No. This is my favourite mug. It's very sentimental,' Dad replied, admiring it like a family heirloom.

'I've tried to get him to retire it to the recycling bin, but he won't let me,' Mum added with a shake of her head.

'Here,' Dad mumbled through a mouthful of buttered toast, so burnt it looked like he had slathered Vegemite across it. 'Did you see this?' He pointed to an article in the paper.

Mum and I glanced down. The headline read: *Proposed Shore Front Development Causes a Wave*

'Oh yes.' Mum nodded. 'Lucy was telling me about it the other day. You know that vacant parkland with the grotty toilet block next to the inlet? Yes? Well, they want to turn it, along with the land that joins the inlet, into a resort-style complex, with accommodation and shops. Something like that.'

'Well, that'll be an eyesore,' Dad grumbled.

'That's what I thought.' Mum sat back in her chair.

I scraped butter on a piece of cold toast, one that was the least burnt. 'Maybe it will be good. Tidy up that end of the inlet, and you know, bring tourists and money.'

Mum tutted. 'We do alright without the massive tourist influx, thank you very much. All the rubbish they leave behind. There are plenty of other places along the way for them.'

'The Bay's getting by just fine,' Dad added. 'We have the curlews; we have the annual Snapper Fest; we are a scenic stop on the Great Ocean Road drive ... We have plenty to offer without being turned into another Lorne or Torquay.' Dad all but pointed a finger at me to get his point across.

'And if they go ahead, where will the curlews feed when they're here?' This from Mum. 'Remember you and Lucy used to love wading through the shallows, chasing the curlews, and twisting your feet in the sand in search of pipis?'

I smiled at the memory. 'Yeah, you taught us that, Dad.'

'Well, they can't let it get through. Lucy said she's looking into it to find out more about the environmental impact.'

'It'd be that bloody Hamil bloke going on with all that nonsense that Curlew Bay is struggling, and if we don't do something, we'll end up a ghost town. Rubbish. Lucy won't let it pass.' Dad turned the page with gusto.

I'd heard Mum speak of Terry Hamil. He'd turned up in the Bay a couple of years ago. A flashy businessman in his expensive grey suit and tie intent on making the Bay a 'destination'. Didn't even live here, but seemed to want to invest money in the place. No one had worked out if it was generosity or an ulterior motive of some sort. Although I did recall Mum telling me he was behind the new walking track.

'Isn't that the guy who helped fund the walking track and look-out?' I gulped some coffee (urgh) to help ease the dry toast down.

'Well, yes,' Mum replied.

'So isn't that a good thing?'

'But this is different.' Mum shook her head sharply, not adding anything further, and I backed off. Mum obviously had her view, and that was that. She was rather opinionated, much more than usual, and much more gruff than usual. Most unlike Mum.

'I'm off to the Men's Shed.' Dad left the table and stacked his mug and plate in the dishwasher, then dropped a kiss on Mum's head.

'Don't be too long. You've got to do the lamb,' Mum said.

'I know. The lamb's marinating already. I'll be back well before.' Dad's voice disappeared with him out the front door.

'What do you need me to help you with for the barbie?' I asked, finishing my coffee and glancing out the window. It was a glorious day, with wispy white clouds dancing across the sky, the sun reaching its morning tendrils through the window. No smog in sight.

'You can help with the salads and setting up the table. That sort of thing. I think Lucy's bringing a dessert, so that's covered.'

'Lucy? Baking?'

'Don't sound so surprised. Lucy bakes. When she has time. She's very busy, though, you know. Especially now she's on council.'

My left eyebrow raised slightly of its own volition, and I resisted the urge to comment, instead replying, 'I'll have a shower and be out soon.'

'What about Hayley?'

I collected my plate and cup and let out a long sigh. 'I'm sure she'll come out. She might be angry at me, but she knows better than to be rude.'

'Do you want me to coax her out?'

'No, she'll be fine.' I wasn't entirely confident, but at least I was hopeful.

CHAPTER TEN

Mum placed the salads down and sat at the outdoor table while I set down a pile of plates. While Mum wasn't looking, I quickly pinched a pasta spiral from the curried egg and pasta salad which had always been a favourite of mine. The grey skies from yesterday had opened to blue and the sun was warm on my back, although the air still had a wintery chill as it fluttered at the corner of the blue-and-white checked tablecloth. Dad was inspecting the joint of lamb in his beloved Weber, a satisfied grin on his face. Normally I would give in to the delicious smell of rosemary and garlic rising from the barbecue, but I'd lost my enthusiasm, my stomach knotted from the idea of seeing Lucy again. No doubt she'd come armed with a barrage of questions.

All sibling relationships were complicated, weren't they? Every family with multiple siblings has 'the favourite child', even though the favoured one and the parents will vehemently deny the fact despite it being glaringly obvious to one and all.

Lucy is what you'd call the golden child. At school, the teachers always emblazoned her report card with multiple As and comments such as: Lucy is a pleasure to teach, and Lucy is well beyond her years. The latter was a regular feature.

Then there was netball. When I started playing, my coach, who had coached Lucy a couple of years earlier, had expected me to be the star goal shooter like Lucy was. Needless to say, I wasn't the best goalie, but I was the best damn benchwarmer that team had seen in years.

The only thing I was remotely good at was art, but Lucy still came out golden, managing a blue ribbon at the local agricultural show one year. Probably because I was never confident enough to enter, but still.

Mum and Dad attempted to treat us equally, but there was no doubting the glint in Mum's eye when Lucy came home with gold star after gold star. Again. And again. When she finished her business degree with honours, it overshadowed my acceptance into law at Melbourne Uni, which I'd applied for but never intended to attend. And sure, it might've been a second-round offer after I'd done a year of a mediocre arts degree, but hello! Law! Apparently, business was where it was at, though. According to Mum, at least.

'Wait till you see how much Chloe and Ethan have grown.' Mum interrupted my thoughts. 'Chloe is captain of her netball team, you know. Just like Lucy was. And Ethan has just lost his first front tooth.'

Chloe was nine now, and Ethan had just turned seven. I did miss seeing them grow up, and Hayley had always loved cuddling and playing with them when they were little. She would've made a great big sister.

Seemingly happy with the meat, Dad walked past me, squeezing my shoulder affectionately before he sat down. I knew his action meant: 'Don't you worry about your big sister.' You see, Dad and I had this unspoken connection. Always had. Growing up, it almost seemed like Dad and I were on one team, Lucy and Mum on the other. Not that Dad was one to take sides or play favourites as openly as Mum did. But there were times when we were younger that he made me feel like his favourite. Like when he'd secretly slip me a square of Cadbury chocolate from the block he hid between the cushions of his recliner. It was like he saw how hard I struggled to live in the shadows of Lucy's success. It felt silly now. I was old enough not to worry about petty things like that. Besides, I had plenty else on my mind. Today would be fine. Positive thoughts. That was where I needed to focus.

A car pulled into the driveway, followed by a collection of slamming car doors and raised voices. Instantly, my insides flipped. Okay, seemed like my positive thoughts weren't working.

Footsteps echoed through the house and the back door swung open, bouncing off the back wall with a thwack.

'Easy now,' Dad said, faux gruffness in his voice.

'Aunty Emily!' I stood up just in time to save myself from being bowled over by Ethan. 'Look, I lost a tooth!' He squished his face into a grin, exposing his gummy smile, a cute little gap where his front tooth was missing.

'Oh wow! Look at that! Did the tooth fairy come?'

'Yes, but he only got a dollar,' stated Chloe emphatically as she followed up behind him in a calmer manner. 'I got two dollars for my first tooth.'

'Oh, you did not, Chloe,' Lucy interjected, rolling her eyes. 'Hey.' Lucy gave me a quick hug.

'Hi ya, Emily.' It was Gordon's turn to greet me, and he did so with a slightly awkward hug and slap on the shoulder like I was a long-lost mate. 'Great to see you.'

Gordon was built like a fullback, certainly not what you'd expect your average, down-to-earth accountant to look like, which is what he was. Relaxed and even keeled, that was Gordon. Unless you got him started on the state of the economy or tax, then he could get a little animated. But he was a good egg. And he put up with Lucy. That was an achievement in itself.

Chloe wrapped her arms around me. 'I've missed you, Aunty Emily.' All of a sudden, she seemed so mature, and a pang of guilt hit me. I should be a better aunty. I should be a better lot of things.

'Wow, missy. You've grown! How tall are you now?'

'One hundred and twenty-seven centimetres! I'm almost the tallest in my class. And the tallest in my netball team. That's why I play goal shooter.'

'Ooh, goal shooter. I'll have to come and watch you play one day.'

She gave me a proud grin. 'Where's Hayley?'

'She'll be out in a minute.' I ignored the heaviness of anticipation. Surely Hayley will leave her attitude behind for the barbecue, at least for Chloe and Ethan's sake.

The kids ran to the back lawn to play on the old trampoline that I was amazed was still in one piece, although the matt had been changed recently, by the looks of it. It surprised me Mum or Lucy hadn't insisted on installing the safety nets that came with the brand-spanking new ones these days.

'Is there anything I can do?' Lucy asked as Gordon joined Dad, who was back surveying the meat.

'No, it's all done. There's a gin and soda or a Corona in the esky if you'd like,' Mum replied. 'Lime's on the table.'

'Perfect.' Lucy grabbed a Corona, untwisted the top, and slid a wedge of lime inside the bottle. Then sat down with a sigh as if she had the weight of the world on her five-foot-nine frame.

'So, how are you, Em?' Lucy turned to me, sliding her sunglasses onto her face.

'Peachy. You?'

'You know. Same old, same old. Busy and all that.'

A huge elephant-shaped question was plonked right on the table in front of us. How long would it take Lucy to unveil it and revel in all its glory?

'I am sorry, you know,' she began. 'About, you know. Things.'

And there it was. But surprisingly not delivered with the sarcastic undertone I expected. She seemed genuine, and I was a tad suspicious. 'Ah, yeah. Thanks.' I shrugged as if it was nothing.

'How's Hayley?'

'Hayley's fine,' Mum interjected. 'She'll be fine.'

'Mmmmm. Maybe. Apart from the fact she hates me, hates life. You know. Normal teenage stuff multiplied by three thousand.' Better I tell the truth than sugar-coat the reality.

'Oh, Emily, she does not hate you.'

'I'm sure she'll be fine. Kids are resilient,' Lucy added. 'So, what's the plan?'

That was more like it. The probe disguised as an inquisitive question. What was it with Mum and Lucy and *plans*? As if it were that easy to sweep up your emotions and life into a dustbin and make a new life plan. If it were that easy, I would've made a better one that didn't involve hiding out and biding my time at my parents' house.

'I'm working on one.' Lie. I bit the inside of my cheek.

'You could always go back to uni and finish your degree?' Lucy took a swig of beer. 'You only have a year to go, don't you?'

'It's not as simple as that.'

'Why not?'

'First of all, I can't just hop back in. I'd have to apply all over again.'

'But you've already done three years.'

'Ah, two and a bit and that was moons ago. You can't just swing back in. Plus, I'd have to pay for it outright.'

'Mmmm,' Lucy pondered.

'And besides all that, I don't have the means to study. I need a job. Back in the city.'

'Are you sure that's what you want?' Mum tilted her head thoughtfully.

'What? To earn money?' I scoffed.

'To go back to the city.'

'It's where my life is, Mum.'

'Was,' Lucy added dryly.

'Maybe you can do something different?' This was from Mum, who was now busying herself, rearranging the plates and cutlery I'd laid out. She could never sit still. 'It's not like back in my day when you got a job and stuck with it pretty much for life. So many people change careers and directions these days,' Mum continued, aligning the salt and pepper shakers. 'Look at Amanda Willis' daughter, Imogen; remember her? She trained as a nurse but, after fifteen years, decided she wanted to study horticulture, of all things. Now she has her own nursery inland between Lorne and Torquay. Amanda tells me she's doing so well for herself and has never been happier.'

'I don't think Emily's cut out for gardening.' Lucy raised an eyebrow over her sunnies.

For once, I agreed with her. 'I'm as far from a green thumb as you can get.' A green thumb I was not.

'I don't mean that specifically, but something different. There's plenty you could do, Emily.'

'Teaching? Wedding planner?' Lucy chimed in. She was having fun with this.

'Oooh, interior design, like Shaynna Blaze!' Mum sported a childlike grin.

I sank back into my chair while my mother and sister ping-ponged back and forth with outrageous career options. Oh, the hilarity.

'Pet groomer! There's one in Apollo Bay. It's called Pup-a-licious. Isn't that adorable?' Lucy and Mum proceeded to have a good old chuckle.

'Somehow, I can't see Em having the patience for dog washing. Although I can picture her face when the dog shakes all over her,' Lucy added.

After the second round of laughter died, Mum's face became more serious. 'You could start your own business, Emily. There's a sense of pride and accountability running a business, isn't there, Lucy?'

'Of course.' Lucy straightened, looking like this was her topic of expertise. 'But it's not quite that simple. It takes a lot of hard work to get things up and running and make it viable. Patience too.' She pointed the top of her Corona towards me. 'Business isn't for everyone. And you need some capital behind you. I'm not sure Emily is in that position right now.'

'Oh, you don't think, Luce?' I said with a huge dollop of sarcasm. Lucy was right about one thing—my lack of patience. For this conversation!

'Settle down. I'm only stating the facts.'

'Well, thank you for pointing out how wonderful your life is compared to mine.'

'Now, you two ...' Mum pointed her finger between us as if we were kids again.

'I'm not saying that at all. You always take things the wrong way. When are you going to get that huge chip off your shoulder?'

As I was about to bite back at Lucy's snide remark, Dad and Gordon arrived at the table with a plate of piping hot lamb, charred sausages, and a mountain of oily onions. The smell was divine. I swallowed my retort and allowed it to simmer.

'Come and get it!' Dad called to the kids. 'Where's Hayley?'

I was about to get up and fetch her when she appeared at the back door, dressed in jeans and a hoodie. She'd even managed to brush her hair by the look of it.

'Ah, there she is!' Dad beamed.

After hugs from Gordon and Lucy, and more excited squeals from the cousins, we'd settled into devouring lunch, plates and cutlery clanging in between general chit chat. Personally, I was revelling in the succulent lamb and Hayley looked especially pleased when Dad served her up a veggie patty. In fact, Hayley was on her best behaviour. She was even having a lively conversation with Chloe about how lame *Frozen 2* was. I was surprised Hayley had even seen it, although perhaps she was pretending she had, for Chloe's sake. The thought made me warm and tingly. My little girl was still in there somewhere.

'Mum! Do I have to eat this?' Everyone turned to see Ethan with a smudge of tomato sauce on his cheek and a limp piece of rocket dangling from the edge of his fork.

'You have to eat your greens,' Lucy chided, and Ethan screwed up his nose.

'Hello?... Hello?'

A deep voice echoed from inside the house. Everyone paused. Hayley stopped with a fork of salad midway to her mouth.

I held my breath. I knew that voice.

What the hell was Anthony doing here?

CHAPTER ELEVEN

Everyone's eyes turned to me, except Hayley's. Instead, she jumped to her feet, the most animated I'd seen her in ages. My chest tightened with a mix of guilt and apprehension. It was the happiest she'd been all week.

'Dad!' She threw her arms around Anthony's waist as he appeared at the back door. Her smile as wide as Luna Park's.

'Hey there, pumpkin. I've missed you.' He returned the hug and pressed a kiss to her hair.

'I can't believe you're here.' Hayley's voice was muffled against Anthony's chest.

'Thought I'd surprise my favourite girls. And the in-laws.' He purposely avoided my eyes but nodded towards the rest of my family, who shifted in their seats unsure where to look. I clenched my fists under the table as Dad gave me a small nod and stood. He wasn't one for confrontation and despite his aversion to Anthony, (never thought he was good enough for his daughter), he stood up and held his hand out.

'Anthony. Good to see you.'

Anthony shook his hand with enthusiasm. 'You too, David.'

The ice was broken, and everyone suddenly pretended he was simply arriving late to a family barbecue. Everyone except me, that was. I remained seated, anger itching under my skin. I couldn't believe he'd turned up out of the blue like this. *And* was acting as if nothing was wrong. My shoulders stiffened. Mum noticed and mouthed 'You okay?' at me to which I shrugged. What else could I do? It wasn't like I was going to cause a scene right here, right now, was I? Especially with Hayley. No, I had to play it cool despite the fire raging inside.

Everyone took their seats again, shovelled more food on their plates, and began chatting.

Anthony's eyes rested on me. I ignored him.

'There's plenty here.' Gordon motioned towards the couple of plates left spare from the ones I'd brought out earlier.

'Yeah, come on, Dad.' Hayley grabbed Anthony's hand. 'You can sit next to me.' She pulled up a spare chair and made room for him to squeeze in next to her.

Everyone shuffled their chairs noisily, and Ethan took advantage of the situation and bellowed, 'I'm finished. Can I go and play?' Then, without waiting for an answer, he jumped up and ran to the trampoline, followed quickly by Chloe.

The conversation around the table was initially stilted but gradually relaxed. I chewed on my lamb much longer than necessary, just so I didn't have to involve myself in the façade of conversation. Gordon lazily plonked his arm around Lucy's chair, and she reached for his other hand on the table, snagging her fingers through his. I sank back into my seat, feeling as if a huge cloud had shadowed me. Lucy was right. I had a chip on my shoulder. She made everything look effortless. Whereas I was continually exhausted, frustrated, and miserable after years of trying to be that same effortless person. And now, seeing her gorgeous kids playing together and her hand intertwined with Gordon's, I realised I wasn't jealous. I was *envious*. Envious that she had things together. I'm sure her life wasn't perfect, but compared to mine, it was completely together. If our lives were sand-castles, Lucy's would be three layers tall, decorated with shells and a protective moat, whereas mine had collapsed and was about to be washed away into the ocean.

As everyone chattered away, plates and cutlery clanking and glasses being refilled, something finally became clear. It was the beauty in what Lucy had. A stable relationship. A stress-free life. A *happy* life. A simple life. Something I'd always wanted until ... until I hadn't. Until I was terrified of losing it before I had it. So, I'd gone and complicated things. Striving for something I didn't even want. My breath caught in my chest, that last thought almost winding me.

'Don't you, Emily?'

Mum's voice seeped into my ears. 'Sorry?'

'Your school reunion.' Mum placed her cutlery neatly on her empty plate.

'The good old school reunion, hey?' Gordon said. 'I remember mine a few years back. Had a blast seeing some of my mates again. Not much had changed in twenty-odd years. Just a few more wrinkles and beer bellies.' He laughed, taking a swig of his beer.

'You going? After all that went down back then?' Lucy's eyebrows raised and arched.

I shot her a look of daggers. I didn't even know one had been organised, but I had zero intention of going. There was no way I was exposing myself to a game of judgement from my high school peers, especially how things ended back then with Simon. And how messed up my current life was. As if I was going to subject myself to that scrutiny.

'You didn't go to the ten year one, did you?' Anthony chimed in, pulling me from my memories. 'We should go. When is it?'

Instantly, I recoiled at his shamelessness. Speaking if we were a happily married couple. A couple that went to school reunions together. The table was silent, and all eyes were on me, expecting a response. But it was the look on Hayley's face that nearly undid me.

Her doe-eyes pleading that things were okay enough that her parents would go to a school reunion together. As if that was a sign her life wasn't as off track as she thought.

I had two options. Play along nonchalantly and keep the calm? Or tell Anthony what I really thought about his idea of tagging along to my school reunion and pretending that we were the successful couple making it big in the city, still in love and winning at life. It was getting more difficult by the moment to keep this charade going. Anthony had to leave.

'Anthony.' I cleared my throat. 'Can I please talk to you?' My chair scraped along the pavers as I stood and motioned with my head towards the house.

'Sure.' His cheeks flushed. And Hayley looked at us suspiciously.

The table remained quiet as we left, their hot stares piercing my back, until Ethan broke the silence and squealed in delight from the garden.

'Look, Grandma! I found a worm!'

INSIDE, I rounded the kitchen bench, putting a barrier between us. He shoved his hands in his pockets, his mouth in a small thin line.

'What are you doing here?' I crossed my arms and stood tall.

'I know.' He held his palms up. 'I should've called first, but I just thought—'

'You thought what? You'd pretend like nothing's wrong.' Tears pricked at my eyes. There were a thousand things I wanted to say to him right now, like how dare he turn up here and put me on the spot like this. In front of my family. In front of Hayley. I could feel my ears heat and jaw tense as I reigned my thoughts in.

'I'm sorting things out, Em—'

'I don't want to hear it.'

'Hear me out. I have news.'

I lifted my chin, pressing my lips together.

'I met with the bank, and their valuer has been around with a real estate agent, and the agent is in talks with an overseas buyer he has on his book. They're moving to Melbourne for work and need something in the area asap. Reckons he'll get an offer out of them after they see the photos and video walk through.'

'An offer?'

'Yeah. I told him it's got to be enough to cover the mortgage and everything. Hopefully more. But, I guess we're not in a position to negotiate. The bank's only giving us so long. With all the interest rate rises, they're tightening everything right now.'

I rubbed at my ear, my thoughts scampering, trying to make sense of what he was saying and what it all meant. This was all happening so fast. This made it all so real. Too real.

'It's a good thing, Em. We'll be able to get a rental. Maybe not in the same area, but we can start fresh.' Anthony's brows formed an arrow of hope above his eyes. 'And,' he paused, bowing his head. 'I've signed up for AA meetings.'

'AA?'

'Alcoholics Anonymous.'

I knew what it meant; I was just shocked he'd done it.

'I know I have a problem, Em. I've known for a while and,' he shrugged and met my eyes. 'I should've done something sooner. I know.'

There was a beat and I took a shaky breath. The realisation unclouding my brain. Everything I'd tried to ignore for the past year. Ploughing forward, head down, hoping things would change once he got another job. I was as much to blame as he was really. Pretending everything was okay, not confronting the issues in our lives, our marriage. I wanted to burst into tears, but I didn't know why. Relief? Hope? Frustration? Helplessness? I swallowed back the lump in my throat. 'What about the job interview?'

'I'm waiting to hear.'

Anthony shifted on his feet, and all I could hear was the hushed chatter from everyone in the backyard. What I couldn't hear were my thoughts. Everything in my head was a loud rush. As if my thoughts were covered with a sepia filter like an old movie, the scenes and voices hard to decipher.

'I'm trying, Em. Trying to get things back on track. Trying to pull my shit together, you know?' He paused, shoving his hand through his mussed-up hair. 'I really stuffed up.'

'You think?' Understatement of the century.

'I'm trying to fix this. This can be,' he paused. 'Like a refresh on everything.'

I clenched my teeth as a sudden anger bubbled under the surface of my skin. 'You think it's as easy as that. Refreshing things. Starting over?'

Anthony looked at me as if I was stupid.

'Why now? Why not three months ago? Six months ago?' My voice caught, and I swallowed the irritation. My insides were twisted like a contortionist. It wasn't fair I was taking it out on him when I was as much to blame, but months of pent up frustration—years even—all came to a head.

'I thought you'd be happy. Isn't this what you wanted?'

'What I wanted was for this never to have happened.'

'I know that, but ...' Anthony puffed out a frustrated sigh and leant on the countertop, his hands splayed out like flat jellyfish. 'Look, I know this doesn't fix everything, but it's a start. We can do this. Come back with me and we'll start again. Do things better this time.'

I knew I should be happy. Happy that he was realised how serious things were. Had a wakeup call. Tried to fix things. But still, I couldn't shake this pent up fury wanting to escape from my insides. I wanted to scream. To run. To not have to deal with any of it. I just wanted it to be over. I sucked in a sharp breath.

'Em?'

It was as if a switch had flicked inside of me, my shoulders relaxed and the rage quietened. I met his eyes and I could see how sorry he was. The desperation reflected in his eyes; remorse carved into the frown lines on his face. And I realised something; I didn't want to go back. I didn't want to revisit something that clearly wasn't working on so many levels well before it all went to shit. It wasn't even about the house, or the drinking. Not even about the gambling. They were masking something I'd been ignoring for so long. For too long. The awareness stabbed me in the chest, almost enough to buckle me over. *I don't want to be with him. I don't want that life.* The thought of returning to the city made me physically feel ill, like someone was forcing me to jump out of a plane without a parachute. I rubbed my hands over my cheeks, pulling at my face, my eyes hot.

The silence had reached an awkward point, and Anthony cleared his throat. 'Look, you're right. I shouldn't have come back like this. Not without telling you.' He scratched at his stubbled chin. 'I could move in with Jamie. He has a spare room. You and Hayley could get a rental, and we'll take things slowly. See what happens with the house and then sort things out. One thing at a time, right?'

'Anthony ...' My voice splintered, and I clenched my abs to hold myself steady.

'Yeah.' His eyes widened, full of hope.

I almost changed my mind. Instead, I closed my eyes for a long moment before the clarity came. Then opened them and told him what I wanted. 'I need more time. More space. To figure things out. You're right. We need a fresh start. But I don't want to come back to the city. Not yet.' I paused, trying to order the new thoughts. 'I think Hayley and I need to stay here. Try a fresh start. Here.' The words fell out of my mouth, and I was almost as shocked as Anthony.

'A fresh start? As in ...'

I nodded.

'Here? In Curlew Bay? But what are you going to do? You've always told me how much you hated it here.'

'I don't know what I'm going to do. But I need space. From you.

From us. From everything. I know we need to deal with the house, the debts, and all that, but that's all I can deal with right now. I can't ... I can't deal with you, with us, as well.'

Anthony rubbed at the back of his neck. 'What about Hayley? Her friends? Her schooling? She won't want to stay here any longer than she has to. And there's her school formal. She won't miss that.' Anthony was pleading now.

'Well, sometimes you don't have a choice. And that sometimes is right now. She's resilient. She'll be fine.' Time to take a leaf out of Mum's book of positivity. 'And right now, seeing as we practically will have no place to live shortly, this is the best place for her. For us.'

'We can sort something out before then; come on, Em, you're being irrational.'

I gritted my teeth. If you ever wanted to evoke an evil spirit, the way to do it was by telling a woman she was being irrational. Just as I was about to explode again, the back door opened, and Hayley walked in, a worried look on her face.

'Dad? Mum?'

I threw a warning glance at Anthony, and he held my eyes. It was like the moment in a movie before the bomb goes off and everyone knows there's nothing they can do. Anthony turned to Hayley and threw on a winning smile. 'I have to head off, pumpkin.'

'Wait! I'm coming.' She paused when Anthony's eyes flicked to mine. 'You told Mum I was coming back to go to Coco's party tonight, right?'

I shook my head. The decision solidifying in my gut.

'I'll get my bag.' Hayley went to walk past me, but Anthony gently held her shoulder to stop her.

'Not this time, pumpkin. But soon, okay?'

'What? No. Not soon. I want to go home!' Hayley's voice cracked.

'We've still got things to sort out. Then we can think about it, okay?'

'What's going on?'

Hayley turned towards me, and I swallowed the bile in my throat. Of course it all came back to me being the big bad wolf.

'We're going to stay here a little longer than expected, honey,' I said as calmly as I could muster. My shoulders tensed, bracing for the repercussions.

'What?' Hayley's eyes widened and filled with tears. 'You can't make me stay here, Mum. I hate it! I want to see my friends. I have school to go back to. And what about Dad? Why can't you two just sort this out? You're supposed to be the adults!' Tears streamed down her face.

'Hayley,' I began, but it was fruitless. I exchanged a look with Anthony.

'This is all your fault!' Hayley screamed at me, then rushed past and thumped down the hall. 'I hate you!'

Anthony and I flinched as she slammed the door to her room.

'I'll talk to her.' Anthony made to follow her.

'No. Don't,' I managed. 'Just go. Please.'

His shoulders dropped. 'Em—'

'Don't. Not now.'

'When?'

'I don't know. Just please. Go.'

'Is this ... it? For us.'

'Anthony, please.'

He let out a gruff sigh, nodded, and turned towards the front door. As it shut behind him, the pain at the back of my throat ripped at me and swallowed a sob. The tick of the grandfather clock sounded like a jackhammer.

I'd just left my husband. And, I think I'd just broken my family.

CHAPTER TWELVE

'You okay?'

Lucy stuck her head out the front door where I was perched in an upcycled Adirondack chair. I wasn't sure how long I'd been sitting there; it must've been a while as the sun was casting long shadows across the front lawn. I'd been contemplating if Mum and Dad ever sat out here with a wine or a beer and enjoyed the breeze of an evening, as Mum said they would when she told me she'd found the chairs on Facebook marketplace and spent the weekend painting them. The paint still looked fresh. It was thinking about things like these that had been taking my mind off my problems.

'Em?'

'Yeah. I'm okay. I guess.' I turned to Lucy, and she handed me a balloon-shaped glass of red wine filled well over halfway.

'I'm guessing you need this.' The chair creaked as she sat down next to me.

'I probably don't, but thanks.' I took a large swill, expecting to enjoy the rush of the wine as it warmed through me, but instead, it only added to my nausea.

We sat for a few moments, the occasional car ambling by and the chatter of birds in the trees accompanying our silence. It wasn't awkward, but there was a heaviness between us, so much so that neither of us knew what to say. Without the insults and rudimentary insinuations, sitting here in a moment of rawness felt odd. Unchartered.

'Anything I can do?' Lucy's caring voice filled the silence. 'I could talk to Hayley?'

I shook my head. 'No. It's not going to help.'

'She'll be okay, you know? Eventually. I guess it's a lot for her to get her head around.'

My initial reaction was to snap. I certainly didn't need my sister, who has no experience with teenagers, broken marriages, *or* failed finances, to give me advice. But being reactive wasn't going to gain me anything. Plus, I was too bloody tired to bother, so instead, I sighed. 'Yeah. I hope so.'

'And so will you. Be okay. I mean.' Lucy took a drink.

'That, I'm not so sure of.' I wasn't. I was still trying to get my head around what I'd done. Right now, it seemed like a colossal mistake. One that couldn't be undone.

'Mum's right, you know.'

I switched my eyes from the wine in my glass to Lucy's as she slowly twirled the stem of the glass in her fingers. The afternoon sun caught the laugh lines on her face.

'About what?'

'About you needing a plan. You've always got a plan.'

'Yeah, well, I had a plan, and look how good it turned out.'

The silence returned, and I wondered if this was karma. Karma I'd created all those years ago by running away and becoming someone who chased success and validation. Someone who thrived on recognition. Some days I didn't know who I was anymore. I blinked away the last thought and put my wineglass on the wooden table between our chairs. I couldn't stomach any more.

Finally, after dismissing my thoughts, I turned to Lucy. 'Are you happy?' It was an odd question but a genuine one. I don't recall ever asking myself the same question and wondered if maybe I should have. Maybe if I had, I'd have recognised things were out of kilter a lot sooner and I wouldn't have let things escalate out of control.

'Sorry?'

'Are you happy?'

'As in, happy your life has been upturned?' She raised an eyebrow.

'No.' We exchanged a knowing smile. 'I mean, like *happy*. Happy with your life and how it's turned out.'

Lucy lifted a shoulder noncommittally. 'Yeah. I guess so, but I suppose it's not something I really think about. We're just living our life and seeing where it takes us. It's not like we have a formulated plan as such.'

'You just said *I* need a plan.'

'I said *you* need a plan because that's what you've always done. Ever since I can remember, you wanted to do this or that. Tunnel vision.'

'It wasn't tunnel vision. I think you need to have some sort of vision, foresight, that's all.'

'True. But if you have a goal, especially a big one, what have you got when it doesn't work out?' She paused. 'I guess what I'm saying is yeah, I have goals, but a lot of different, smaller ones. Not an overarching goal. And I lean into different things at different times.' Lucy was waving her hands about as she spoke, the wine sloshing in her glass. She was a hand talker. 'And yes,' she continued, 'sometimes that means going with the flow. Take the council position, for example. It wasn't on my plan. It came about because I cared about the community and wanted a say. The fact that I decided to run was more about feeling right than planning for it. Maybe you plan too much?'

'You just said—'

Lucy let out a deep laugh. 'I know.' Then her laugh faded. 'We do that, don't we? You and me? Go round in circles.'

'I suppose we do.'

A car glided by and gave its horn a small toot at the neighbour hosing their garden across the street. The man returned with a wave.

'Not everything's peachy keen behind closed doors, you know.'

Lucy made the statement with a tone I couldn't put my finger on. She sat still and twisted her mouth, biting the inside of her cheek. An old habit from way back, particularly when she was worried about something.

'Everything okay?' I asked.

Just as Lucy was about to speak, the front door burst open with Chloe and Ethan shooting out a break-neck speed.

'Give it back!' Ethan shouted, chasing Chloe down the front steps. She was holding a blue Zooper Dooper icy pole in one hand and an orange one in the other.

'You said you didn't want it, so Grandma said I could have it. It's mine now!' Chloe danced on the lawn, taking turns to suck both icy poles in between a cheeky grin.

'Muuuuuuuum!' Ethan burst into tears as Mum, Dad, and Gordon joined the commotion on the porch.

'It's true,' Mum said. 'Ethan said he didn't like orange, and it was the last one. I said Chloe might as well have it.'

Lucy exchanged a bewildered glance with Gordon. 'I think it's time we go.'

LATER THAT NIGHT, when the house was quiet and Mum and Dad were in the lounge room watching *60 Minutes*, I tentatively knocked on Hayley's door. I hadn't seen her since lunch and couldn't sleep until I talked to her. There was no answer, but I could see the dim light under the crack of her door, so I gently turned the door handle. 'Honey?' The sight of her made my heart break. She was curled up under her doona. The light of her phone highlighted her swollen red eyes.

'Can I come in?' Still nothing, so I padded into the room. 'I know this isn't the way you wanted things to work out.' I stood beside her bed resisting the urge to touch her. The last thing I wanted was a physical rejection. My heart broke at the hurt flashing through her eyes. 'And I'm sorry.'

'You're not sorry. If you were, we'd be going back home.' Hayley's voice was muffled by her doona, but the spite in her tone was still there.

'I wish it was as easy as that.'

Hayley sat up, pulling the doona tight around her shoulders, face flushed. 'Why isn't it? You don't tell me anything. I'm not a baby anymore, Mum.'

Tears welled as I watched her big, swollen, red eyes, her cheeks blemished with dried mascara. I so wished she was little again so I could hold her in my arms. I longed for those days when she'd look up at me with her big chocolate eyes filled with unconditional love and trust. When I could whisper, 'Everything will be okay.' Even if I knew it wouldn't, but she still believed. Still felt safe and loved. Why did they have to grow up?

'I know you're not a baby.' I picked up the throw cushion from the occasional chair in the corner of her room and sat down on the edge of the bed, hugging the cushion the way I wanted to hug her— tight and comforting. She was right. She wasn't a baby anymore, and I couldn't—shouldn't—hide things from her. Not everything anyway. 'Okay, so what's happening is, we ... your dad and I ...'

'Are you breaking up? Are you getting a divorce?' Tears trickled down her cheeks again.

'I don't know. I ...' Oh God, why was this so hard? I scrunched the corners of the cushion like it was a stress ball. 'We just need to be apart while we figure things out.'

'Is it because we're broke? And you lost your job?'

'Yes, all of that. And other things. There's been a lot going on for a while. Things we should've dealt with but ... And now we need to sell the house and then ...'

'Sell the house? Why?' Hayley's posture stiffened, her face stricken with disbelief.

Oh God. That was too much. Shit. 'It's complicated.' I held a hand up as she was about to protest. 'I know that sounds like a cop-out, but it's not. I'm not even sure what all this means. And that's the truth. While we're figuring it all out'—I took a deep breath—'we're going to stay here in Curlew Bay.'

'For how long?'

'I'm not sure. Just till we can get back on our feet.'

'What about school?' Hayley slammed her hands and slapped her legs making an imprint in the doona. 'I can't just take time off. I have exams next term and ... and I need to choose my subjects for next year. And then there's the basketball season and the formal.' She threw her hands to her head, shaking it in disbelief.

I briefly closed my eyes and mentally counted to ten. My gut twisted knowing what I was about to say would not go down well. 'We'll enrol you in the high school at Curlew Bay, just for the next term.'

Hayley's eyes widened. 'What? No!' She threw the doona off and jumped to her feet, her hands curling around the sleeves of her pyjama top. 'No! I won't. I can't leave all my friends! Please don't make me. I can stay with Dad.' Her voice was bordering on hysteria, hands fisted. 'I'll help him do whatever he needs. Mum, please! Don't do this to me.'

'Oh, honey. I wish it didn't have to be this way, and I'm sorry you're caught in the middle. But please, you need to trust me on this right now.'

Hayley shook her head. 'No! Mum, please!'

I rose and stepped towards her, expecting her to push me away, but she let me put my arms around her. Her body shook as she sobbed into my shoulder, tears falling down my own face. She felt like a fragile little bird in my arms. I had to make this right. I had to make sure this was the right decision. As easy as it would be to say to hell with it and make things work somehow, someway with Anthony, in my bones, deep down in the root of me, I knew I couldn't. I couldn't do it anymore. And no matter how hard it was, how much it hurt, I had to make this new start work. I was determined to. For Hayley. For me. For all of us. I just had to figure out exactly how. I had to be the strong one and get us through this.

CHAPTER THIRTEEN

The crisp morning air bit at my ears as I stretched out my hamstring on the front porch. I'd woken early again to the cacophony of sparrow tweets, but this time, something about the joyous nature of their twittering injected me with a burst of inspiration. I'd pulled on some activewear and sneakers and decided to go for a run. I wasn't a runner. Not in the slightest. But if I was going to make this new life work, I had to totally reinvent myself. So, running was my new thing. And why wouldn't you run when you had gorgeous, orange-skied sunrises to wake up to. Even if it were only nine degrees.

After a short warm-up walk to the end of the street, I turned the corner and began running—well, I wouldn't call it a run, more of a jog. Okay, it was a shuffle. A few minutes later, my mind cleared. I could do this. Not be a runner, well, I'd try, but I meant I could do this new life. I could make it work. Even though the Bay held some memories I'd run from, I was an almost forty-year-old woman, and I was old enough and should be wise enough to put things behind me and be my own person. Take charge. Be strong. Surely there was a podcast for that. A motivational podcast for the almost forty independent woman. I made a mental note to look one up for my next run. As I emerged from the residential roads—chest burning and legs like jelly, and a blister forming on my little toe—onto the beach road and down towards the esplanade, I noticed a woman carrying yoga mats onto the grassed area overlooking the beach. Another early riser. Good for her. Then, as I drew closer, she looked directly at me; she looked familiar.

'Emily!' She waved an enthusiastic hand over her head, juggling the yoga mats under her other arm.

I paused and used my hand to shadow the sun's glare as it lipped the coast to the east. Connie? It had to be. I'd recognise those strawberry spiral curls anywhere.

'Emily!' She dropped the mats and jogged towards me pulling me into a crushing hug. 'I heard you were back in town.'

Connie had moved to Curlew Bay when we were in year nine, and somehow, she'd ended up tagging along with me and my best friend Matilda. We used to call ourselves the three amigos. I couldn't remember the last time I spoke to Connie. It must've been about eight years ago when she was in Sydney. We'd reconnected on Instagram, began messaging, and spoke a handful of times. And then, life got busy, and we lost contact again. Such a lame excuse, *Life got busy*. I looked her up on Insta again a couple of years ago, but she hadn't updated her account for over a year.

'Wow! It's so great to see you.' I could barely speak from the heavy breathing, and my heart was racing.

We pulled away from the embrace, both with huge smiles. 'You do yoga?' I nodded towards the yoga mats she'd placed on the ground.

'Yep. Been teaching for about three years now, and it fits in nicely with the bookshop. Work-life balance. That's where it's at.' She grinned and looked so happy with the life she'd built.

'Mum told me you'd bought BookArt.'

'I know, crazy, right? Remember we used to go in there all the time? I'd go to the books, and you'd spend your time in the art section?'

I remembered fondly. Back when I thought I wanted to be an artist, I loved that place. 'Wow! That seems like a lifetime ago.' I shook my head and swiped a line of sweat from my hairline.

'Sure does. Hey, you staying for yoga?'

'Ah, no. I'm not a yoga person. I'm not really a running person either.' I shrugged, wishing I'd brought a water bottle.

'You should! You'd love it. Best thing I ever did. First session is on the house.'

I shook my head. 'Nah, I'll give it a miss. One new sporting activity is enough for me to deal with at the moment.'

'No worries, but you're going to the reunion, right?'

'Ah ... well ...'

'Come on, you have to! Twenty years, can you believe it? I didn't see your name in the Facebook group. Hang on, I'll friend you and add you to the group.' Connie dug into the pocket of her leggings to pull out her phone.

'Oh, I'm not on Facebook.'

'Ah, cool. Well, it's not this weekend, but next. We're all meeting for a school tour, and then there will be a BBQ on the grounds at five pm. After, we're heading up to The Commercial for drinks.'

'Um, I'm not sure ...' I gave a nervous laugh, all the while begging her in my mind not to ask me outright.

'Please come; it won't be the same without you there.'

Oh God, she said it. The thought of a school reunion was almost as bad as reliving that day in the supermarket or the bikini message debacle. Actually, it was probably worse.

All of a sudden, Connie's face fell, and she sucked in her top lip. 'Oh God. I'm so sorry. I didn't even think.' She palmed her forehead. 'Simon.'

A cold rush of embarrassment washed over my skin and I immediately felt clammy. 'It's fine.'

'Have you...? Do you...?'

I looked towards the ground to avoid her eyes. 'No, we haven't spoken in a while.' A long while. Like twenty-years-almost while.

'He probably won't even come, you know,' Connie said, flicking her hand to the sky.

'It's fine. We're both adults now. You know. Water under the bridge and all that.' I tried immensely to add a casual tone to my voice but my voice sounded more like a chipmunk.

'Of course. Anyway, you should really come. It will be fun. Like old times. I mean, well, you know what I mean.'

'Yeah, why not.' As I let the words fall out I was already thinking up excuses that I could come up with at the last minute so I didn't have to go. Maybe I could contract a contagious twenty-four-hour bug?

Connie's face erupted into a huge smile again. 'Brilliant! Look, I have to go.' She nodded to a few people mingling around the yoga mats, some already stretching. 'But I'll see you there. It's going to be so much fun. We have so much to catch up on.' She threw her arms around me, still bubbling like a can of soft drink after being shaken. 'So great to see you, Em.'

'You too,' I replied genuinely. It *was* great to see her. I hadn't realised how much I'd missed her. Old friends.

I waved to Connie and tried to get my now-stiff legs to shuffle along the esplanade path, my mind colliding into memories that were flooding back. As I approached the pier, an image of Connie holding me as I sobbed into her shoulder, wishing I could tell her what was wrong, stopped me in my tracks. Goosebumps pricked at my arms. It was as if the last twenty years had happened in a parallel universe, and Curlew Bay remained in 2003. I shook it away and turned to battle the headwind home.

. . .

I WALKED into the kitchen and Mum was sitting at the kitchen table with her fluffy pink dressing gown wrapped around her, sipping a cup of tea.

'Morning.' I caught my breath and poured a big glass of water.

'Morning to you. I see you've been out and about early.'

'Yep,' I replied between mouthfuls. 'It's the new me.'

Mum raised one eyebrow. 'Mmmm. The new you. What was wrong with the old you?'

'Funny. Is the kettle boiled?'

'Yes, just boiled.'

I popped a peppermint tea bag (yes, the new me) into a cup, poured the water from the kettle, then took it to the table to sit down.

'I expected you to be hiding in bed all morning after yesterday.' Mum didn't look up from flicking through the *New Idea*, no doubt searching for the crossword, which she liked to do daily. Said it kept her brain healthy. There was probably some truth to that.

'Nope.' My tone was matter-of-fact as I poured cornflakes into a bowl, followed by the milk. 'I told you. This is the new me. I'm done with moping around.'

'Well, that's good to hear.'

'Yep. I'm going to get a job.'

'A job? Good. I mean, yes, great idea.' Mum eyed me with a curious look.

'Do you know of anything?'

Mum hesitated, confused. 'Here? In Curlew Bay?'

'Yes, in Curlew Bay, I'm not commuting to the city from here every day, am I?'

Mum set her gaze back to the magazine, thumbing the pages, but I could tell her mind was whirring. 'So, you're staying? In the Bay?'

'For now. I realised after yesterday I need to make a proper go of it, don't I? Maybe Hayley and I can be happy here. Lucy and Gordon are, and you and Dad. Even Connie's back.'

The corner of Mum's mouth twitched into a small curve.

'Don't say anything.' I narrowed my eyes at her as I took a sip of tea, trying not to screw up my nose. Whoever thought hot minty water was a good idea?

'I wasn't going to say a word!'

'I know you want to think I'm back for good, but I don't know. I'm taking things one step at a time, that's all. I can't just sit around waiting for things to change. I have to be the change, isn't that one of your phrases?'

Mum nodded. 'Good for you, darling. You never know what can happen when you open the door to possibility.'

I rolled my eyes and continued crunching through my cornflakes. Confident. Forward-thinking. Go-getting. That was what I had to be. An independent woman for Hayley to be proud of. Showing her that when you were faced with challenges, you didn't curl up in a ball —or ignore things for years—you grabbed life by the horns and wrestled it into submission to your advantage. Made the best of the situation. And all that. Ooh, I was getting good at this positive self-talk.

Mum stopped flicking through the magazine at the crossword page and picked up her pen, tapping it on the table. 'Number one across: something that occurs unplanned in a happy or beneficial way.'

Her eyes glanced at mine before she pronounced. 'Serendipitous.' She beamed. 'Yes, that's it,' and then she wrote the word in big capital letters in the boxes at the top of the crossword.

I took another sip of my tea. Serendipitous? Maybe. Terrifying, yes.

CHAPTER FOURTEEN

By midmorning, Mum had left to visit a friend, and Hayley had, of her own volition, informed me she was going to walk to Lucy's to look after Chloe and Ethan. I gave a damn good performance pretending not to know Lucy had already asked me first.

With the day stretching out before me, I sat at the kitchen table, a half-cold cup of coffee (the peppermint tea went down the sink) to my left and laptop in front of me, the cursor blinking on an email from the real estate agent sent to Anthony and cc'd to me.

'Further to our previous email, we confirm that we have an interested party in your home at 18a Nash Street and are continuing to negotiate on your behalf to obtain the best price and conditions. The mortgagee is allowing us fourteen more days, and we will keep you informed of the process. Please keep in mind that with recent worldwide events and current interest rate rises, the market is quite volatile, but we are using our expertise to do our utmost and achieve the best possible result for you.'

It was hard not to feel deflated. That was our family home. We'd bought it when Hayley was only two years old. She'd spent the entire auction grizzling in her pram while I tried to soothe her, Anthony holding up the baton to bid at the right moment.

We'd spent the next eighteen months in renovation hell. I say hell because things did not go smoothly. It was one thing after another. First, the discovery of major white-ant damage, and then the realisation that our budget wasn't going to stretch as far as we first thought. Even though I told Anthony I'd return to work to help things out, he was adamant he could support us and the renovation.

Each week, each month, his hours increased until we barely saw each other. And when we did, we were both exhausted. Me from single parenting and managing a renovation, and Anthony from working eighty-plus hours a week. But we did it. We took that crumbling (literally) piece of property and transformed it into a beautiful three-bedroom family home with French shutters, landscaped gardens, and a designer kitchen that Nigella Lawson would be proud of.

We thought the strain on our budget would only be temporary, and with Anthony doing so well at work, we would recover in no time. Now, it all seemed so ... so arrogant. While we did get on top of things for a while, we never really caught up. And then when Anthony lost his job ...

It was the *if onlys* that were my constant nightly companion. *If only* I'd gone back to work earlier. *If only* I'd knuckled down and finished my degree. *If only* we hadn't desired to live above our means. *If only* I'd opened my eyes sooner. *If only* I hadn't fallen pregnant. *If only I hadn't run* ... I stopped my thoughts immediately. I couldn't think like that. This was my life. And I had to face the decisions I'd made that landed me back in Curlew Bay. I took a deep breath. This was a turning point. A pivot. A change.

I filed the email in the 'my life before now' folder and began trawling through online job listings, which admittedly didn't take long. Curlew Bay wasn't teaming with job opportunities. There were only two jobs in the area that were remotely suitable. The first was an office job at a car dealership in Lorne, and the second was an assistant property manager at the local real estate agent. I wasn't qualified or experienced for either, but they were vaguely in the realms of what I could do. At least that was what I was telling myself via my new positive mindset, aka *The New Emily Brown*.

There was a third job, a part-time reception/office role, but it was at Curlew Bay High. I was fairly sure that wouldn't go down well with Hayley, especially after I had just enrolled her there to start term four. And no, I hadn't told her yet.

Over the next hour, I pulled together a resume and emailed off the applications. I may have embellished here and there, but if I was good at anything, it was words and selling. As Mum would say, I could sell ice to an Eskimo. That done, I needed something in the interim to fill my days while waiting for the job offers to roll in. I hated sitting idle, so it was time for some drastic action. I reinstalled Facebook on my phone.

When I opened my account, the notifications tab glowed red with 172 unread notifications. With purpose, I clicked on the three little dots and selected 'mark all as read'. Immediately, the little red number disappeared, and my heart rate slowed. Then, I clicked the search bar and typed 'Curlew Bay Community Noticeboard'. There was bound to be a job or two posted there, something small to fill in my time until something more suitable came along. I found the group and saw it had 1,409 members, but I had to request to join. Well, there goes that idea. It would probably take the administrator days to respond. With a shrug of my shoulders, I clicked join and then quickly amended my Facebook profile, adjusting the 'lives' status from Melbourne to Curlew Bay. Then I began the mammoth task of unfriending a whole host of people, or so-called friends, all in the name of starting fresh.

The first one on my list was Sally Armitage ... I wracked my brain. Nope, no idea. Unfriend! Michaela Asquith ... Her daughter used to go to school with Hayley, I think, but if I recalled correctly, they'd moved to Queensland about two years ago. Unfriend! Samantha Baxter ... An acquaintance I met through Anthony's work. *When* he worked, that was. Unfriend! And so it went. Unfriending all these people I didn't really know was cathartic. Why was I even friends with them? It was a weird place we lived in. At its core, Facebook was simply a place where we spied on people we kind of knew. After all, didn't that guy originally set it up as a place to spy and rate on girlfriends? So cringeworthy, yet here we were, millions of people all over the world wasting countless hours envying others' seemingly picture-perfect lives, or on the other hand, revelling in our smugness that our life looked better than theirs. Or scrolling through ads to sell us on that perfect life so it looked that way from the outside. Urgh. As I continued contemplating Facebook and unfriending people, the ding of a notification stopped me, and I clicked it open without thinking. Ah-huh! I'd been approved for the noticeboard already! I clicked through to the group and began scrolling through the feed.

Someone was looking for the best car detailing place in Apollo Bay (probably cause there wasn't one in Curlew Bay). The following person complained about a cat jumping their fence at two am, which incited loads of comments about cat curfews. I scrolled quickly, not wanting to be drawn into the issue. Then there were a few photos of the curlews on the beach; these, interestingly enough, were from Simon. Further on, the local newsagent was advertising a special on greeting cards, and there was a post urging people to sign the petition against a proposed development for the foreshore. Lots of comments on that one. I made a mental note to go back and see what the general consensus was.

And then, a post caught my eye. It was from a lady named Doreen Sanders. The name rang a bell, but I couldn't place her from her tiny profile picture, which I then realised was of a dog. I read the post. She was seeking a dog walker for her basset hound named Fred. *Yes, I know, Fred.* At least she seemed to have a sense of humour. The dog on her profile picture must indeed be Fred.

Seeking someone to walk my beloved Fred while I recover from hip surgery. Once a day, seven days a week until I'm up and mobile again. Most of you know Fred; he's very friendly and a little overweight, so he needs the walks. Will pay $25 an hour, cash.

Twenty-five dollars for walking frumpy Fred for an hour each day? That was $175 a week. This job, well, okay, so it wasn't a job, but it was money, would be the perfect start to start my savings off until my redundancy payout came through. And I would be exercising at the same time. Surely, it was a win-win?

I clicked on Doreen's Facebook profile and tapped out a message. To my surprise, the response was immediate.

That would be wonderful. Fred and I would love to meet you. I'm out of hospital tomorrow, and then my son will be heading home over the weekend. Does next Monday 10 am suit?

I tapped out a reply, confirming it was perfect, and closed the laptop with a smile and a tingle of excitement in my fingertips. Finally, I had a purpose and forward motion. I checked the time: 11:15 am. Should I have another coffee? I glanced at the coffee canister on the kitchen bench. Nope. Not that instant rubbish; I needed a real coffee.

THE STRONG AROMA of coffee beans and a rush of noise assaulted me as I stepped inside Curlew Bay's most popular, and only, coffee shop: The Coffee Pot. Inside, the place was busier than I expected. The order line was five deep, with just as many in the pick-up line. I gauged many of them to be locals, but a few were obviously tourists. You could always tell the tourists with their three-quarter pants and sandals, even in winter, thick scarves tied around their necks as if that was enough to compensate for their freezing ankles.

I waited in line, resisting the urge to look at my phone and Facebook now that I'd reinstalled it.

'Next, thanks.'

I looked up to see a handsome barista smiling at me with dark eyes and black hair. He kind of reminded me of Anthony when he was younger. Apart from the man bun, that is. And the subtle stubble. Okay, so he wasn't quite like Anthony, but he was very easy on the eye. My bubble of excitement was hastily popped when I realised I was probably old enough to be his mother.

'Hi.' I smiled as my cheeks heated; thankful he couldn't read my thoughts. 'I'll have a double shot cappuccino, please.'

'Sure, have here or to go?'

'To go, thanks.'

'Do you have a keep cup?' the man child asked.

Oh God. Not only was I supposed to keep my life together, but I was also required to carry a keep cup at all times to save the environment. 'Sorry. It's at home.' I shrugged with a tight smile, to which he raised his eyebrow, cottoning onto my lie.

'Five dollars, fifty, thanks. Fifty cents extra 'cause you don't have a keep cup.'

Of course it was. I handed over the five dollars I'd scrounged from the centre console of the car and checked in both my leggings' pockets but came up empty. Great, this was going to be another repeat of the supermarket fiasco.

'Don't worry about it, Jay,' a voice said. 'She's right.'

The voice crashed me straight back to year twelve. *Simon*. A third wave of embarrassment flushed across my cheeks and over my ears. If I were in a cartoon I'd disappear into a puddle of sweat right now.

Holding my breath I cautiously looked up. Sure enough, standing to the left of the counter was Simon. Same but different. Gone was the smooth tanned skin of youth, replaced by unfamiliar crow's feet and laugh lines around his mouth. Lines that should've made him look his age, but instead, only made him more rugged and handsome. The sandy hair was still there, flopping to the side of his face like it always had, but now with a hint of grey at the temples. For so many years, I'd wondered what I ever saw in him. Especially after moving on with Anthony, who was very much the complete opposite of Simon. Simon was more Paul Rudd, Anthony more Antonio Banderas. But in the flash of two seconds, it was all back; no invitation, no probing the back alleys of my memory banks needed. Just a jolt of energy pulsing through me.

'Emily Brown.' His smile took over his entire face while the sound of his voice kicked open a barrage of recollections from the last few years of high school when all I'd needed to calm me was his smooth, soft tone.

'Simon Carter.' I cleared my throat, my mouth suddenly as dry as sand dunes. 'Ah, hi.'

He motioned to let the next customer in line order, and I stepped to the side. 'Thanks. I'll pay you back.' Averting my eyes, I tucked my hair behind my ears.

'Don't be silly. It's fifty cents. And I'm the boss; I can make up the rules as I go.'

'The boss?' I shot him a look of confusion.

'Yeah, I own this place.' He frowned. 'Took it over a few years ago. Surely your mum told you?'

'Oh, right. Yeah. Of course.' Of course I knew. I'd just conveniently forgotten in my desperate need for coffee. Damn caffeine addiction. 'Most of what Mum tells me goes in one ear out the other.' I laughed nervously. 'You know, gossip mill stuff. Mum loves it.'

'Mmmm, the Curlew Bay rumour mill. Always ticking over.'

It felt like Simon's eyes were all over me, shooting fiery flames and firing a burning sensation to every nerve ending. Without warning my brain transported me back to standing outside the school hall, my face bloated from crying. The conversation was as vivid as if it were yesterday. 'You think you're too good for us, don't you, Emily? Especially for me.' His voice had been thick with hurt. My stomach had clenched, unable to tell him, through the violent sobs caught in my throat that it wasn't it at all. I blinked rapidly to dismiss the memory.

'Emily! Double shot cap!' The barista boomed my name, and I almost jumped out of my skin.

'You okay?' Simon moved a step closer.

I stepped back reflexively. 'Yeah. Sure. Of course. Um, that's me!' I took my coffee, and the smell grounded me back in the present. Thank you caffeine. However, when I turned back around, Simon was still there.

'Want to grab a table?' He gestured to a very cosy two-seat table in the corner of the front window.

'Ah ...?' I should say no. Of course I should. But I'd never been good under pressure.

Simon nodded to the table again, and in an effort to not look like an idiot, I replied. 'Sure.'

We sat opposite each other, and I took a sip of coffee, avoiding his eyes. *Those* ocean blue eyes that could whisk me away in a glance. Thankfully the coffee tasted as good as it smelt and it eased my twitchy muscles as it slid down my throat.

'So, how long you up for?' Simon's tone was light. As if we were long-lost friends catching up over coffee. I suppose we were. If it weren't for everything else in our past that lingered between us.

'Oh, um, yeah, not sure. Really. I'm here with, um, my daughter Hayley.'

Simon's eye twitched for a split second. 'Great. And, your ...' He dragged the word out before adding, '... husband?'

I averted my eyes to my coffee, admiring the patterned logo of a coffee pot on the cup. 'Um, no. Not this time.'

When I looked back up, Simon's face told me he could still read me like a book, like he could all those years ago. Every miniscule movement, gesture, and tone of voice. It was an uncanny connection; avoiding eye contact was the only way to evade it.

'Things are a bit up in the air, actually.' The words blurted out before I could stop them.

'Oh, right. Sorry, I didn't mean—'

'No, it's fine.' I swatted away the words with my hand. 'Nothing really. You know. Just life. Work. All that stuff.' I gulped down another mouthful.

'Course.' Simon lifted his cup to his mouth, and my eyes made their way to his lips. The lips that had first met mine when we were barely sixteen, both combusting with a combination of nervous energy and lustful feelings we weren't sure the meaning of.

I glanced out the window, watching a combi with surfboards stacked on the roof racks pull into the park. The pressure to fill the silence itched at my skin. 'So, when did you come back? When you bought the café?'

'Yeah, four years ago now.' Simon tapped the side of his cup with his fingers. 'I came back when Dad got sick.'

Now I remembered Mum telling me. I'd meant to send a card, but ... God, you're a horrible person, Emily Brown. I fiddled with the sachets of sugar in the middle of the table. 'It was awful to hear about your dad. He was always so nice.' He carried his rosy cheeks and genuine smile everywhere, much like Simon.

'Cancer, hey.' Simon shrugged. 'At least I got to spend the last few months with him; now it's just Mum and me. Not that I live with her. I've got my own place.' He was quick to add that piece of information. 'But losing Dad made me realise a few home truths.'

My interest was piqued. Home truths? Catalyst moments? 'How do you mean?'

Simon shrugged. 'I guess I realised there was more to life than the nine to five. Or the six til eleven, more to the point. I'd been working a seventy-hour week in the financial sector and climbing the ladder to nowhere. My marriage broke up; thankfully, we didn't have any kids, but then I realised all my friends were her friends, and I didn't have anything left. All I had was my family back here.'

Something crashed behind the counter, and then there was laughter. Simon turned around.

'All good, boss!' one of the servers called out. Simon nodded and held up his hand in acknowledgement.

Meanwhile, I was trying to reconcile the Simon I knew with the one who ended up working a seventy-hour week. And I couldn't. 'That's never what you wanted? Working a regular job in the city?'

'Yeah, well. You know ... life.' He took a sip of coffee. 'Anyway, when Dad got sick and I came back here, I realised how happy he and Mum were. It reminded me of ...' He paused and turned to look out the window for a moment.

'Of what?'

'You know, the simple life ... like ...'

He turned back, our eyes meeting, and I knew exactly what he wanted to say. *The simple life we'd planned. Together.*

I was the first to look away, and Simon brushed over the moment, continuing to tell me how after his dad passed, he'd bought the coffee shop and now spent his days running the café and taking tourists on birdwatching tours when demand called for it.

'Bird watching?' I nearly knocked over my coffee. The Simon I remembered was into football and, well ... football. Certainly not birdwatching!

A flush reddened his cheeks, and Simon cast his eyes down. 'I always liked the curlews.'

Out of nowhere, a memory flashed of us sitting together on the inlet, me in low rise jeans and a cropped top thinking I looked like Britney Spears, Simon in his standard rip curl tee, watching the curlews wade through the shallows. My heart skipped, and I finished my coffee, wishing I'd bought a larger one to get through this awkward conversation. 'So, it's just you and your mum?'

Simon hesitated, his eyes darting. 'Yeah, I've got a girlfriend.'

'Oh.' I don't know why, but my face flushed. Whether or not he had a girlfriend was of no interest to me, but my body seemed to have a different idea. 'That's great.' Not that I'd asked, but he seemed to have made a point of telling me.

'Um, Tamara.'

I shrugged. 'Wonderful.' Of course he'd have a girlfriend. And what did it matter anyway? I glanced at the door of the café as a couple entered, glad for the rush of cool air as the door whooshed open.

'So, what's your story?' Simon asked, changing the topic. 'The real version.'

I was happy for the change of topic and swirled the last of my coffee in the cup. 'Like I said, just stuff. Things don't go to plan sometimes, that's all.'

Simon nodded slowly, but he knew I was hiding something. The problem was, I was hiding more than he realised.

'Well, be careful.' He held my eyes, the last twenty years dissolving into nothing making my skin hot. 'You might not want to go back.'

The air between us was electric, something magnetic making it impossible to turn away. Suddenly, I was claustrophobic and very aware of my heartbeat, and, oddly, the fact he had a girlfriend. I pulled my eyes away and glanced at my watch. 'Oh, wow. Is that the time?' I scrambled to my feet, knocking the table with my bag, causing the sugar satchels to tumble. I fumbled them back into their pot. 'Sorry, I promised Mum ... I'd bring back bread for lunch.' It was a pathetic lie, and I avoided his eyes.

'No drama.' Simon got to his feet.

'I guess I'll see you round.' I pushed my chair in and wiped my sweaty palms on my leggings.

'Hey ...' Simon began before pausing.

I met his eyes, and his face turned from thoughtful into a small smile. 'It was really good seeing you, Emi.'

Goosebumps danced up my arms. *Emi*. Nobody ever called me Emi. Except him.

I swallowed. 'Yeah, you too.' I turned, holding myself back from sprinting to the door.

Once outside, it wasn't until I rounded the corner in front of my parked car that I stopped and let out a shaky breath. I knew being here would dredge up the past, but I didn't realise it would feel like a sword had sliced my heart open. But we'd both moved on. We both had lives. His seemingly more together than mine, admittedly. But we were both adults. Everything would be fine. It would.

CHAPTER FIFTEEN

Mary checked her watch as she made her way down the last few stairs of the lookout. The waves crashed into the rocks below, white water flecking the surface. To her left the Curlew Bay lay splayed across the inlet, the small centre hub of shops like colourful Lego buildings. She'd made good time today. She always did when she had things on her mind. Which was more often than not these days. She checked her heart rate on her fancy smart watch Lucy had bought her last Christmas and slowed as she made her way downward towards the town centre.

Three months ago, her doctor told her she needed to increase her daily exercise. Turns out her bi-weekly yogalates sessions weren't enough to combat the changes her body was experiencing thanks to the ageing process. The *ageing* process. She scoffed. Today she felt good despite all the noise in her head and not having slept well last night with Emily and Hayley on her mind. All those hours of tossing and turning hadn't delivered any answers. Time. That's what was needed. And to busy herself. That was always a good thing to help pass the time, especially when things were out of her control. She needed something purposeful. But what?

She supposed she could redecorate the spare lounge room. The last time she did that was during the 2017 season of *The Block* when that young couple won. What were their names? She couldn't remember, but Sarah and Jason should've won. Their house was so much lighter and airier and such a better use of space. Mary had styled the second lounge room inspired by their vintage leather couches, navy and white cushions, and a blue-grey feature wall. It still looked classy. Not that anyone ever used that room.

Maybe it could do with a makeover. That minimal Scandi style was in vogue now. Wicker and jade greens. Maybe she should ask Emily what she thought. She was always good with colour, and maybe that could take her mind off things too, helping her redo the lounge room. Her chest snagged as she thought of Emily. If only she wasn't so stubborn and would just take the help she and David were offering. Especially now she'd decided to stay in the bay. A small smile graced Mary's lips.

Crossing the street, she passed Geoff Giddons striding past in his painting cover-alls.

'Afternoon, Mary.' He sung in a deep voice.

'Geoff.' Mary smiled brightly. Geoff had painted every room in their house at least once. Always for a good price too, although he was painfully slow. But that didn't matter, his work ethic was top notch which was hard to find these days.

Mary approached 'The Spotted Dove - Homewares & Gifts' and eyed off Lucy's new display in the window. Two blue-and-white Hampton-style table lamps stood on the white vintage dresser, which was adorned with recycled timber photo frames of all shapes and sizes. It looked lovely. Lucy really did have a flair for display. Must have got it from her. She spied Lucy at the counter, waved, and walked inside.

A rush of warm jasmine-scented air greeted her, along with the tinkle of soft classical music. She was so proud of Lucy and the business, which she'd grown from scratch while balancing motherhood and now a council position. But Lucy always exceeded expectations, even when she was a little girl excelling in school, sports, and everything in between.

'Hi, Mum.' Lucy smiled, put down the items she was unpacking, and rounded the counter. 'Good day to be out and about.'

'Hello, sweetie.' Mary savoured the quick embrace and Lucy's spicy perfume. 'You smell lovely.'

'A new fragrance from the Ashley Parker collection that came in yesterday. You like it? I think it's a little oriental, but I sold a bottle to Missy Nash, who seemed to like it.'

'It's nice. I quite like it myself.'

'Not that you'll ever change from your Estée Lauder *Beautiful*.' Lucy laughed before returning to her unpacking. She pulled out a beeswax candle and unwrapped it from the paper wrap 'What are you doing anyway? Out on your walk?'

'Yes, just giving Emily some space. She's had a hard trot.' Mary eyed Lucy's reaction and frowned. 'I saw that.'

'What?'

'That little eye roll.'

Lucy stifled a grin.

'She's your sister. I really wish you two got along better.'

'It's not that we don't get along. We have completely different lives. And she never comes back to the Bay. Only ever under sufferance. Plus, when was the last time she invited us to the city to stay?'

'Ah, there's been a little thing called—'

'A pandemic, yes, I know, but even before that, she was always so busy.'

'And so are you!'

Lucy shrugged and screwed up the paper, throwing it back into the box before lining up the candles next to wooden salad bowls she'd just unpacked.

'And anyway, she might be back for good.'

Lucy's head shot up. 'What?'

Mary picked up one of the candles and held it to her nose, the sweet smell greeting her senses. 'Might be. But it's not my place to say.'

'Oh, come on, Mum, don't give me that.'

Mary looked around to ensure no one was listening, but the shop was still empty. She shouldn't say anything. Really, she shouldn't. 'Her and Hayley are going to stay indefinitely.'

A rush of air filled the shop as the door swung open, the little bell jingling, and Mary hoped whoever it was hadn't heard what she said. She didn't recognise the woman.

'Hello,' Lucy called with a smile. 'Just browsing?'

'Yes, thank you,' came the reply.

Lucy turned her attention back to Mary, lowering her voice slightly. 'Don't get your hopes up, Mum. Emily might be all gung-ho now, but I give it a week before she's back in the city.'

Mary stiffened at Lucy's comment. Why were her children so judgemental of each other all the time? That wasn't how she raised them!

Lucy silently counted six candles and ticked hem off against the packaging slip. 'Like she always says, there's nothing for her here in the Bay.'

Mary's stomach twisted. She hated when Emily said that. And even more so when Lucy repeated it. She knew Emily didn't mean it the way it sounded, the way Lucy thought she meant it. Emily had simply meant her life was in Melbourne. Of course, there were things in Curlew Bay for her. Her family, for one. And she grew up here. Surely it would always hold a place in her heart. Just like Geelong, where Mary grew up and met David, would always be special to her. Although it'd been years since she'd been back there. She'd heard it was completely different nowadays. Probably wouldn't even recognise it. She made a mental note to see if David would venture for a day trip one day soon. Surely, he'd come at a day trip. They hadn't been anywhere in so long.

'It's always one drama after another with Emily. Always has been,' Lucy was saying.

'That's not true at all.'

Lucy shrugged.

'Don't be like that, Lucy. Emily needs her family right now. Anyway, I best be off. Don't want my heart rate to get too low.'

'Don't forget you volunteered for Little Ath's canteen on Friday.' Lucy stuck a price tag onto a wooden bowl. 'You said you'd help out with the canteen?'

'Is it still on in school holidays?'

'Yep. Remember, I asked you last week?'

'Of course I remember.' She didn't remember. Normally, she committed everything to memory without needing to write it down. Lately, though ... 'I'm looking forward to it.'

'See you Friday.'

MARY RETURNED HOME, taking the long route via the inlet path. She still couldn't shake the unease settling in her chest. It was a hollow feeling she couldn't quite pinpoint. Was it the fact that Lucy expected her to drop everything to help in the canteen? Again. Did Lucy not even consider maybe she'd like to watch their running races, or long jump, or whatever it was they did at Little Athletics these days?

As she crested a small rise, Mary let out a long sigh. Of course, she would help at the canteen, but sometimes she wanted the choice not to. She'd always been there for Lucy and the kids. Especially when they were babies. Free childcare it was when Lucy was working. And she'd often pick them up from school and take them to the playground or for an ice-cream until Gordon finished work or Lucy closed the shop. Had she been too available? What was it Dr Phil used to say? You teach people how to treat you? Yes, that was it. Without making a conscious choice, that's exactly what she'd done.

Continuing down the esplanade, even the picture-perfect winter day or the curlews wading in the shallows of the inlet couldn't improve her mood. It wasn't that she didn't want to be there for Lucy, or the kids, or David, even Emily and Hayley, for that matter. But where was the choice? It was almost an expectation. When did Mary finally get to have a say in her life? Or was this just the way it was? Turning towards home, the wind cool on her face, she let out a sigh. She was just feeling a little off today. Everything was upsetting her. You couldn't be spritely and happy every single day, could you? Especially not at her age.

CHAPTER SIXTEEN

Standing in front of the mirror in my bedroom, tugging at my clothes, I felt all of my self-conscious sixteen-year-old self again. The past week and a half, I'd applied for jobs I wouldn't get, further alienated Hayley by informing her she was starting at Curlew Bay High next week, and fielded messages from Anthony, who'd informed me he'd had a second interview for the new job, and the negotiations on the house were 'going well.' Whatever that meant. And now, here I was wrestling with the fact that I'd told Connie I'd go to this stupid reunion, all the while wanting nothing more than to get out of the bloody house and forget who I was for a while.

My watch buzzed on my wrist, alerting me that I had half an hour til I was supposed to meet everyone at the school for a nostalgic tour, but staring at myself, I highly doubted I'd make it. I had absolutely nothing to wear. The black jeans I'd chosen were passable, but I was seriously questioning the rust-coloured top and wooden beaded necklace. It all screamed MILF. And not the sexy one, more like the Mother I'd Like to Forget. The urge to change into something different was tugging at my gut, and I let out a defeated sigh. What was the point? *Accept it, Emily Brown. There's nothing wrong with owning who you are.* I straightened my shoulders. I could do this. But before I could take a step towards the door, I caved. I couldn't do it. Not like this.

I unclipped the necklace, pulled off the top and slipped into a sheer but not entirely see-through black collarless button-up shirt with billowing sleeves. Then I grabbed my loose hair and tied it into a messy bun, chucked in some dangly gold earrings, and changed my boots for simple but stylish heels. It wasn't much of a difference but at least an improvement, nonetheless. Black was definitely my friend. I wasn't ready to embrace the colourful freedom and confidence women of a certain age seemed to have with their bright, clashing patterns and funky, oversized earrings, no matter how much I was trying to reinvent myself. Or pink hair. Surely I was few years off that! I slung my handbag over my shoulder and left the room before I could change my mind again.

In the kitchen, Mum was busying herself at the counter surrounded by flour, eggs, and chocolate. The oven fan rumbled in the background.

'Emily, you look lovely,' she said as I entered the room. 'And you know what? I have a nice, bright necklace that could really take that outfit up a notch.' She wiped her hands on a tea towel. 'Just a jiffy, I'll grab it.' She whipped off to her bedroom, and I stuck my finger in the mixing bowl. The batter was sweet, chocolatey, and clung to my finger. I was impressed.

'Here.' Mum returned with the necklace. The long black cord was hanging off her hand, and three large fluorescent beads: pink, yellow, and orange, hung brightly at the bottom. It didn't look like it would be out of place in a Cyndi Lauper video clip from 1984. She slipped it over my head and spent a moment adjusting it around my neck. 'There you go. That brightens you up!' She smiled proudly. 'Oh, and what do you think of the brownie mix? It's a new recipe from Julie Goodwin. You know she was on *MasterChef*, again? She's great, isn't she?'

'The brownie's good,' I replied, fiddling with the necklace knowing I'd take it off as soon as I left the house.

Mum scraped the mixture into the pan, and we both looked up as Hayley appeared.

'Hayley honey, how lovely does your mum look?'

Hayley paused at the fridge and turned towards me. I struck a model-like pose, one hand on my hip and my lips pouted. Hayley wasn't impressed. She gave me a huge eye roll before asking, 'Where are you going?'

My mouth dropped open in shock. She was talking. Words. To me. And a question. This was progress.

'My school reunion.' I poured a glass of red wine from the bottle on top of the microwave.

'Why?'

This question was, in fact, the most intelligent thing Hayley had said in the past few weeks. Why *was* a great question.

'Because your grandmother is making me.' I poked my tongue out at Mum, who slid the brownie into the oven. She'd reminded me every day since I'd told her I'd run into Connie. She was like a count-down clock on crack.

'No,' Mum tutted. 'You are going because you need to get out of the house, and seeing all your friends will be lovely.'

Hayley nabbed a handful of strawberries from the fridge. 'Yeah, seeing friends would be great.' Then she slammed the fridge door shut and stormed off in yet another huff.

Mum glanced at me with a pained expression. 'I'm sorry, I wasn't thinking.'

'It's fine, Mum.' The cavern of guilt in my chest opened up a little further. I wished I could cocoon myself into bed for the night. But I couldn't. I had a reunion to attend.

. . .

THREE HOURS LATER, I was sitting at the bar on a sticky stool at The Commercial Hotel, finishing my second red wine as the reunion crowd trickled in. I'd ditched the school tour and BBQ (and Mum's necklace) instead opting for a drive reacquainting myself with the bay. I'd woven in and out of the residential areas, up along the bluff road and back down through the centre of town then along the esplanade before arriving about an hour and two wines ago. I was a little bit tipsy but needed all the Dutch courage I could muster to deal with the next few hours before I'd be able to think of a good excuse to leave early. I'd pushed Simon to the back of my mind. He'd hardly notice me if he did show up. He'd be with the boys, catching up on old times and momentous football wins. That was what I'd convinced myself, anyway.

I put my glass back on the bar and nodded to the bartender as if I was in some seedy whiskey bar. I waited for him to nod back. He promptly ignored me and served someone else, reinforcing the fact that I'd lost whatever charm or sex appeal I thought I'd had. I was invisible. It was a good thing. Simon would never see me.

'Emily!'

The sound of my name snapped me out of my pity-party and I turned to see Connie's animated smile heading towards me, her curls bouncing around her shoulders. She gave me another squishy hug. 'We missed you at the school tour!'

'Sorry, I lost track of time.' I waved my hand to give the impression of how busy and demanding my life was. 'But, I'm here now.'

'I'm so glad you are. Some of these people!' Connie raised her eyebrow, whispering, 'I can't believe we went to school with them.' She pulled up a stool next to me.

I laughed. It was good to know she was feeling the same as me.

More people streamed into the lounge area, laughing, and sharing anecdotes of those 'good ol' high school days.' It was funny, even though some of them looked vaguely familiar, I could barely put names to any of the faces. Hang on, was that Matilda? It couldn't be! Matilda was in Ireland? Had been since we finished school. Our eyes met, and we both grinned.

'Emily?' Her slight Irish lilt was articulate and delightful.

'Matilda? No way!'

Next, our arms were around each other, and we were jumping up and down like we were thirteen again.

'I can't believe you're here!' Matilda grabbed my arms and studied me. 'Wow, look at you.' Then she turned to Connie. 'Connie? Holy shit! You look bloody unbelievable!'

The three of us embraced, instantly transporting me back to 2003 as if no time had passed. Funny how old friends did that.

'I had no idea you were even coming. You weren't at the school tour,' Connie said.

'Nah, I ditched it. No need to see inside those boundaries again,' Matilda replied with a cheeky grin.

'True.' Connie slid back onto her stool. 'It wasn't all that exciting. Mrs Nunn, God bless her, gave the longest speech. I thought we were all going to fall asleep!'

Matilda shook her head with a knowing grin. 'Just like the old days.'

I grabbed a stool for Matilda, and we settled at the bar. Matilda had hardly changed. Her red hair was cropped shorter into a pixie cut that did wonders for her cheekbones, but she was still tall and skinny. 'How do you look so good after six kids?' I asked. 'It's six, isn't it?'

'Yep. Six of the suckers.' She eye rolled.

'Wowee!'

'You look amazing,' Connie added before ordering Matilda a glass of wine.

'It's the boob job.' Matilda proudly stuck out her assets.

I had to admit, they did look good. Round, perky, and a nice size without being in your face. 'They must've set you back,' I said, remembering a conversation with a school mum who had told me way too much about her recent boob job. When she told me how much they cost, I almost fell off my chair. I could think of much better things to do with a spare fifteen grand. A few debts instantly came to mind.

'It was my birthday present from Patrick,' Matilda continued matter-of-factly. 'He wanted another child, and I wanted new boobs. It was a compromise. I had Finn and after I finished feeding, and *voilà*, she announced with her hands as if presenting them as a prize on a game show.

'Nice.' I was suitably impressed. 'Anyway, enough of your boobs; what the hell are you doing here?'

'I came back for Sophie's wedding,' Matilda said. 'Her third wedding.'

'Sophie, your younger sister?'

'Yeah, she's been through two husbands already. Don't know how she managed to score another one. But she swears this is "the one".' She shook her head in disbelief. 'So, I told Paddy I had to come, and he had to stay with the kids. It's the middle of term over there and flying with six kids isn't in the least bit appealing. So, here I am. Best holiday ever! But don't tell the kids I said that. I fly back tomorrow night.' She took a sip of her wine. 'So, what's news with you guys? I can't believe we left this crap hole twenty years ago.'

Connie shared her news before I was forced, okay, not forced, but reluctantly shared my sordid life story. It felt good finally spilling the entire story to someone other than my family.

'Jesus Em. I can't believe you lasted so long.' Matilda took another swig of her wine and grimaced.

'I just thought things would get better.' I shrugged. 'I thought if he just got another job, he'd remember how much he loved being a lawyer and everything would be okay.'

'Did you confront him about any of it? Try and get him help?' Matilda asked.

'Sometimes it's not that easy.' Connie's voice was flat.

'Honestly, I was really good at pushing it aside. I wanted to get

Hayley through school and hoped everything would eventually fall into place. Guess that plan didn't work.'

'Wow. I'm sorry, Em. I wish we hadn't lost contact for all those years.' Matilda looked genuinely bereft, and my heart squeezed at the sight.

'Onward and upwards, right?' I drew from Mum's book of quotes.

'Oh geez, you're still in denial, aren't you?' Matilda shook her head, and Connie nodded hers in agreement.

'Scuse me?' Matilda waved her hand to the bartender, then leant forward, squishing her boobs to create a cleavage Dolly Parton would be proud of. Needless to say, the bartender was immediately attentive. 'This is rubbish.' She pushed her house white to the side. 'What we need is a bottle of your best bubbly, please.'

A few glasses of a local Prosecco later, the three of us were deep in reminiscing territory.

'What about the time in year ten when we skipped class and hid in the music room?' Matilda grinned that same mischievous grin she had back then.

The memory came flooding back, and I almost spat out my bubbles as I laughed.

'I don't remember!' Connie frowned as if raking through years of memories to find the right one.

'Remember? That day we skipped maths class and hid in the music room?' Matilda turned slightly on her stool. 'And we heard the door rattle, so we ducked behind the drum kit, and Miss Coulter and Mr Simpson came in?'

Connie's eyes widened. 'Oh my God. Yes! And they ...' Connie threw her hands over her face, and we all laughed.

Miss Coulter had been the new PE teacher. Fresh out of uni, she was tall, with long blonde hair and, of course, fit and lean. Mr Simpson was the music teacher and about ten years her senior, although, with his prematurely receding hairline, he looked much older.

We'd crouched down behind the drums and held our breath, hoping they were just coming in to get something, but then they moved dangerously close to each other before falling into a passionate and rather heated kiss. If we weren't so shocked, we would've surely giggled, but we kept as still as statues while we watched Mr Simpson's hands reach under Miss Coulter's tee-shirt and her hands squeeze his bum. Thank God the bell went because there was no way we wanted to see how far it would've gone.

'Remember we couldn't move for another five minutes after they left? Scarred for life, we were.'

'I know!' Matilda added. 'Didn't we get detention for being late to the next class?'

'That's right. We had to pick up rubbish during lunchtime the next day.' Connie scrunched up her face and shuddered.

The three of us dissolved into laughter, and it felt so good. So good to be here, reminiscing, as if no time had passed. As if we were the three simple teenagers navigating the ups and downs of high school. No responsibilities, a lifetime of dreams and hopes ahead of us. I took another sip of bubbles, and wiped the laughter tears from the corner of my eyes. Right now, there was no place I'd rather be.

TIME PASSED IN A DAZE. The alcohol we'd polished off had left me feeling happy and giddy. I was almost grateful Mum had made me come along. Not that I would give her the satisfaction of telling her that, of course.

Perched with Matilda, Connie, and a few others we'd been chatting with at a table now scattered with empty glasses and various bottles of plonk, I glanced up as the door swung open. As it did, a chorus of cheering arose from the guys milling at the bar. And then I saw him. Simon. My stomach clenched, the alcohol swirled around my gut, a hot flush crawled under my skin, and an unpleasant salty taste lingered under my tongue.

'I need some fresh air,' I said to Matilda, who was deep in conversation with Connie, oblivious to Simon's arrival and my reaction.

'Oh, you want us to come?'

'No, I'll be fine. Back in a minute.'

CHAPTER SEVENTEEN

Sitting on the deck, the cool air pricked at my skin, and I let out a ragged breath before gulping another one to quell the nausea. A couple leaning against the balcony ashed out their cigarettes and headed back inside, leaving me alone.

The crash of distant waves and the drone of noise seeping through the bar door gave me something else to focus on while trying to get myself together. Seeing Simon in the past few days had stirred up so many emotions. Emotions I thought I'd dealt with. Clearly, I hadn't.

I contemplated leaving, but the only way out was back through the lounge area where I'd be sure to run into Simon, let alone be unable to avoid Matilda and Connie's attention. And I didn't want to leave. I was having fun with Connie and Matilda, and for the first time in a while, I hadn't thought about my pathetic situation. But I couldn't go back in with Simon there. At least not until I controlled my emotions. It had been hard enough seeing him the other day and, in a way, I wish I hadn't. It brought back so many memories and feelings. Feelings I should be equipped to deal with by now. But then again, if I was planning on staying in the Bay, I'd have to get used to seeing him. And ... his girlfriend. It wasn't like I could avoid the coffee shop. Bloody hell. Why did he have to buy the coffee shop? Why not the bait and tackle shop old Mr Coles used to run? No chance we'd run into each other there. Urgh!

My mind whirred like an overheated computer with too many tabs open. I needed to hit control-alt-delete to reset myself. I was being ridiculous. What happened between us was so long ago. And hadn't I resolved to reinvent myself? Put the past behind and forge a new future? And new me? But being back here, seeing Connie and Matilda, reminiscing ... It had dredged up formative memories that flooded back, viscerally evident in the goosebumps on my arms. And no, the alcohol haze definitely wasn't helping.

Lost in my thoughts, it wasn't until someone pulled up a chair next to me that I realised I wasn't alone.

'I thought it was you.' Simon's voice was barely loud enough to hear over the din.

I opened my mouth to speak, but I couldn't seem to find the words.

'Sorry.' He went to stand. 'If you want to be alone ...'

'No, it's fine.' I waved my hand at him. 'I'm just getting some fresh air. You can sit.'

He sat back down, the corner of his mouth tugging upwards. 'Fresh air, or avoiding me?'

The corner of my lip twitched into a half smile. 'One and the same.'

'So.' Simon leant his elbows on his knees, tapping his fingers together.

We sat staring ahead into the dark sky while the breeze rustled a nearby tree, its branches scratching against the pub's roof. The hum of voices and thumping of music blended seamlessly into white noise and the smell of stale beer and cigarette butts hung in the air. While things were amicable at the café the other day, somehow, in the presence of our ex-school peers, an invisible wall had erected between us.

As if every emotion from that year had washed to the surface. I could tell Simon felt as uncomfortable as I did by the way he twisted his mouth. I desperately wanted to fill the silence but didn't know where to start. Small talk didn't seem right, yet anything else ...

'Look.' Simon spoke into the distance, avoiding my eyes. 'I know we've never really had the chance to talk about what happened back then. Between us. But I wanted to apologise.'

My thoughts drifted back to when I'd sit and admire Simon from a distance before we were together. He'd been a handsome kid. One of the boys, but despite his good looks, false bravado, and football prowess, he didn't really fit in with the popular wolf pack he hung out with. When we'd started seeing each other, he opened up about books he'd read, places he wanted to visit, and things on his mind. Stuff he'd never share when he was with the boys. It was like he was two different people. And, back then, I'd fallen for the quiet, unassuming guy he was when it was just the two of us. It was like I was the only one he'd let into his soul.

'Simon—' I rose to my feet and walked towards the balcony railing, praying the breeze would blow away the nostalgia the memory had dragged to the surface. 'We don't need to go there. That was twenty years ago.' And I was the one who needed to apologise. For so much more than he knew. But he couldn't know. I turned around, leant against the balcony and hugged my middle. 'We were kids trying to be adults and failing miserably. It wasn't important.'

Simon's face dropped as the words hit him, and my cheeks burnt with shame. It had been important. That was why I still felt like this. Why I could never tell him the whole truth. A heaviness descended under my ribcage. 'I'm sorry, I didn't mean it to come out like that.'

The reflection of the moon's soft glow graced the side of his face; the past twenty years were written in every line and shadow. I'd done that. Caused some of those pained creases.

'What? You didn't mean we weren't important?'

I hung my head.

'Or it wasn't important how you made me feel when you told me you'd changed your mind. About everything?'

The sting in Simon's words cut through my bravado, and something flickered in my brain, bringing to life the memory of us fighting outside this very pub on New Year's Eve. When I'd told him I didn't want to go travelling with him. When I told him I was moving to the city. The image of his crumpled face. How he'd somehow looked smaller. How he'd begged me to stay, to change my mind. How he'd dropped to one knee and asked me to marry him in a vain attempt to stop me from leaving. How my face had scorched in front of the small group of our peers that had gathered and hushed as if witnessing a real-life Shakespearean tragedy unfold as I turned him down and left him there. Leaving so much unsaid and the secret squeezing my chest like a corset I could never remove. I'd gone home and cried my eyes out because I'd wanted to tell him the truth. But I couldn't. I was too scared. Too stupid.

My eyes couldn't meet his. All I could do was whisper in a shaky voice, 'I'm sorry. I am.' It didn't sound like enough. It wasn't enough.

'Why did you do it? Change your mind about everything we had planned? I just don't get it. Something must've happened.'

My heart hammered. *Tell him. Tell him.* But I couldn't. It didn't matter now. It was too late. I let out a strained sigh as I forced myself to look at him. 'I don't know. It was just all too much. I was confused. Scared of making such a big decision.' I paused, twisting my fingers into knots, as my stomach did the same. 'It's been so many years. Can't we just leave it? I mean, what does it matter?'

'It matters to me.' Simon's eyebrows knitted together. 'Mattered to me. I thought we had our life mapped out?'

'*You* had it mapped out.'

'You never gave me any indication that you weren't on board with it.'

'I was.' I rubbed at my forehead, overwhelm itching behind my skull.

'But then all of a sudden you weren't? It's like you realised you were too good for our plans. Had to go and be a big shot in the city. When did you ever want that? How do you go from one day wanting to be a fancy-free artist with no ties to suddenly wanting to study at university? What changed?' Simon's voice prickled with frustration.

'I changed.' My voice caught in my throat.

'God, Emily!' He threw his head back.

'Simon, please. It was so long ago. Can't we just—'

'I really wanted to. When I saw you the other day, I was proud of myself for holding it together, but it dragged up so much. I just want to know you're sorry. That you give a shit.'

'I am. I do. But you weren't an angel either. You went off and kissed Tiffany Bloomfield. Why wouldn't I think it all didn't *matter* that much to you?'

Simon stood up, both hands flying to his head. 'I was angry!'

'And Tiffany just happened to be there.'

'It was New Year's Eve! "Auld Lang Syne" was playing and she grabbed me ...' He shook his head slowly. 'You know what? Don't worry about it.' He turned towards the door.

'Simon, I'm sorry.' My voice was barely audible over the noise inside. 'We were so young. Neither of us knew what we wanted.'

'I knew.'

'Really? You ended up in the city anyway?'

Simon turned back around to face me, hesitating before he spoke. 'I tried to go on our trip. Without you.' He smiled sadly. 'It never felt right.'

'Hey! Carter!'

We both turned to see the door fling open, and one of Simon's mates call out over the din of the crowd. 'Simon mate! Come here! You gotta see this. Mick's got a video of our footy grand final from 2003.'

Simon turned back to me, his shoulder's dropped, face crumpled with resignation.

'That's the one where you kicked nine goals?'

'You remember?'

I shrugged.

His mouth tugged slightly at the corner, and he hesitated a moment longer. 'I better go. Oh, and Emily, I don't have a girlfriend.'

'What do you mean, you don't have a girlfriend?'

'I lied.'

A relief of tension washed through my muscles. 'Why? Why would you do that?'

'Because I wanted you to think that ...' He paused then shrugged. 'That I had it all together.'

Simon turned and let the door close behind him as he vanished into the throng of old scholars. The tears I'd been holding back bit at the corner of my eyes before overflowing down my cheeks. I should never have come to this stupid reunion. I should never have come back to Curlew Bay. I swiped away the tears stinging my face in the cold. But this time, I didn't have the option of running away.

CHAPTER EIGHTEEN

'Hayley, I'm warning you, if you don't come out of your room in five minutes, I'm going to come in and drag you out.'

It was 8:15 am Monday, the start of the new school term. Mum, Dad, and I were standing impatiently outside Hayley's closed bedroom door, having tried almost every bribe and method known to coax a stubborn teen from their room.

We were due to meet with the principal of Curlew Bay High at eight thirty for Hayley's first day and, as expected, Hayley wasn't playing ball. Part of me didn't blame her. Changing schools three-quarters of the way through the year wouldn't have been my idea of fun either. Despite my guilt, I'd made my choice and had to face the consequences.

Dad cleared his throat and moved forward. 'Let me try.'

I had to smile. Dad was the most kind-hearted, gentle-souled person. His idea of getting Hayley out of the room would probably involve a short sentence with the word please at the end. I shrugged my shoulders and stepped aside.

'Hayley, come on, sweetie. It'll be fun. Think of how many new friends you'll have by the end of the day.'

'Dad! She's nearly sixteen, not four.'

He shrugged, oblivious to what he'd said wrong.

'Okay, that's it.' I took hold of the door handle. 'I'm coming in.'

'Are you sure that's a good idea?' Mum rested her hand on my arm, her tone laced with concern.

'Mum, please.'

She stepped away and motioned for Dad to follow her back to the kitchen.

'Okay, I'm coming in.' I paused for a few seconds then opened the door and found Hayley sitting on the end of the bed, eyes as stormy as an intense low pressure system. At least she was dressed in the second-hand uniform Lucy had sourced for me. The bottle green tartan dress and blazer were the same as I'd worn. I stifled a smile, remembering how much I'd hated green. I still disliked it today.

'I look like a piece of seaweed.'

'You don't, honey. You look fine.'

'Why do I have to go to school here anyway?'

'Because, as I explained, we're staying here for a little while until Dad and I sort things out.' The urge to hold her washed over me like a tidal wave, but I forced myself to remain hovering in the doorway.

'Well, if it's not for long, why can't I do remote learning or something? I survived that during Covid.'

'It's not as simple as that; now come on. Please don't make this harder than it already is.'

'Look at me, Mum! Look at this stupid uniform! I'm not going to fit in.'

'Everyone is going to be wearing the same thing. And, maybe, if you lightened your eye make-up a little ...'

'So that's your advice? To change who I am?' With that, Hayley grabbed her backpack. As she slung it over her shoulder she added under her breath, 'Dad would never be this mean.' Before she stormed from of the room, out the front and slammed the car door shut.

Great job, Emily. Back in the running for Mother of the Year, yet again.

MY ATTEMPTS at conversation with Hayley on the way to school were fruitless. She stared silently out the window. Her occasional forced huffs were to remind me she was profoundly unhappy. I slowed as we approached the forty-kilometre-per-hour school zone. Kids were making their way across the zebra crossing, bags slung on their backs, phones in hand, eyes glued to screens. A boy bounced a basketball in front of him, not a bad feat while watching his phone at the same time.

The school hadn't changed much. They'd repainted the basketball court lines, yet one of the backboards was broken. The portables were still walls of beige and faded olive green flat roofs. A sunken shade sail hung limply over the four-square courts.

My stomach flipped. It was a far cry from the shiny modern buildings and manicured ovals and gardens of Hayley's school back in Melbourne. Was I doing the right thing?

As I pulled the car into a park, Hayley's eyes stuck on the kids mingling around the front gate, huddled in groups, laughing and gossiping. She undid her seatbelt. 'I'll find my way.'

'No, we have to go to the office first and see Mrs Nunn. The principal. Come on.' I reached over and grabbed my handbag from the back seat. 'Don't want to be late on your first day.' Hayley glared at me as if I'd just asked her to walk naked over hot coals in front of the entire school.

'AH, MS BROWN.' A stern-looking lady in an ugly grey skirt suit greeted us as we entered the old red brick building housing the administration block. Hayley frowned and sent me a look, questioning why the lady had called me Ms Brown and not Mrs Mendez. I stuck my chin up, owning it.

'Principal Nunn, hello.' I extended my hand, and Mrs Nunn shook it briefly, albeit sturdily.

'This must be Hayley.'

Hayley's reply seemed caught in her throat, so I discreetly elbowed her in the ribs.

'Hi,' she replied, tight-lipped.

Principal Nunn settled us in her office, the furniture of which hadn't changed in the last two decades. The same worn wooden table and archaic filing cabinets, although the carpet did look new. Principal Nunn hadn't been Principal Nunn when I was here. She'd simply been Mrs Nunn and had taught maths and English.

'Welcome to Curlew Bay High.' Principal Nunn peered through bright red square spectacles, her grey bob brushing her chin. 'I see your grades are quite impressive, Hayley.'

It wasn't really a question, and Hayley looked as if she didn't know if she was supposed to reply, so she gave a shy smile.

'Hayley enjoys school,' I added on her behalf.

'Good to hear. I'm sure you will fit right in. We have a fantastic reputation here at Curlew High—as your mum knows, being a former pupil, going on to study law, wasn't it?'

I shifted in my seat and smiled briefly. What she didn't know …

'And, although we may not be as fancy as your last school'—Principal Nunn peered at Hayley over the top of her glasses— 'our curriculum is second to none, and we have a fantastic arts and music faculty.'

By faculty, she meant separate arts and music rooms, but I nodded enthusiastically anyway. Curlew Bay High was nothing like St Margaret's, and neither were the fees. Public schooling was even out of my budget, but Mum and Dad insisted they take care of things. For now. It was the only help I'd conceded to.

'She's looking forward to it.' I reached over to squeeze Hayley's hand before she pulled it away and crossed her arms.

'Lovely. Well, here's your timetable until you get familiar with the computerised system.' Mrs Nunn passed Hayley a printed sheet of paper. 'And Ms Nolan at the front desk will issue you a school laptop and then show you to your homeroom. The bell is about to go.'

Hayley squashed the timetable into her bag, and I bit my tongue.

In the foyer, Ms Nolan greeted us and asked Hayley to follow her to class.

'Have a good day, honey.' I pushed a brightness into my voice in the hope of hiding my unease.

'She'll be fine,' Principal Nunn said, with a knowing smile of someone who'd reassured hundreds of parents before.

'Oh, yeah. Of course she will.' I smiled hopefully. 'Hayley's her own kind of person. Very strong-willed. But also very lovely. Of course.' I was speaking in short sentences. Tacking on whatever came to mind to instil a sense of confidence that Hayley would be a model student. I had every faith in her ability to be; she enjoyed school, but my confidence since her dramatic change of attitude recently was undergoing serious reconsideration.

Mrs Nunn smiled politely. 'And, Hayley's cousins will love having her here. Although, we don't encourage the younger students to mix with the older students. But all the same.'

I smiled tightly at Mrs Nunn. 'Yes. Anyway, thank you for your time. I'm sure Hayley will love being here just as much as I did.'

As I left the school office, not an ounce of the confidence I'd exuded to Principal Nunn remained. It had all slipped through my fingers like grains of soft sand. Every decision I'd made, every which way my hand had been pushed, was questioned at this point in time. Doubt grew inside me like lichen on a rock. I wasn't the world's greatest mother, but I wanted to make everything okay for Hayley. If I had a fairy godmother, I'd ask her to ensure Hayley was okay. I'd find my own way to the ball.

CHAPTER NINETEEN

Mary crossed and uncrossed her legs, glancing at her watch. Almost twenty minutes she'd been waiting to see the doctor. Why did they always run late? It wasn't like the Curlew Bay clinic was overrun with people. There was only one other person in the waiting room and only two doctors and one receptionist on duty. Oh, and the nurse dishing out flu shots who seemed to walk past every few minutes as if she was run off her feet. Mary adjusted her mask, accidentally flicking the elastic against her ear. She rubbed it and tuned into the local radio station playing classic hits and read the notice board for the umpteenth time. "Have you had your flu shot? Book now at reception." "Did you know only 42% of people take the at-home screening test for bowel cancer?" "Strong thirst? Itchiness? Frequent urination? Have you been tested for type 2 diabetes?"

Her mind wandered to why Dr Schubert had wanted to see her. The receptionist wouldn't tell her when she rang to book the appointment, so Mary assumed it was most likely to check on her blood pressure. She'd been doing everything right; walking, watching her cholesterol. Although she couldn't come at eating that low cholesterol spread he'd suggested. Surely a little real butter on her toast wouldn't hurt. Her stress levels had been relatively low, or at least had been until Emily and Hayley arrived. With the events of the past few weeks, she would expect her blood pressure to be up a little.

'Mrs Brown.'

Dr Schubert's voice pulled her from her ponderings, and she looked up to find him standing in the doorway of his office. He motioned her in, and she followed his short, shuffling figure into the consulting room.

'Thanks for coming in, Mary.' He gestured for her to sit before lowering into his chair, which groaned under his weight.

'Before you take my blood pressure,' Mary started, 'I expect it to be a little high. I supposed you've heard Emily's back home.'

'I did hear, but this isn't about your blood pressure.'

'Oh?' Mary gripped her handbag.

Dr Schubert shuffled in his chair and swivelled to face her, looking over his half-rimmed glasses, which sat just above the bulb of his nose. 'Mary, we've had our attention drawn to an abnormality on your most recent mammogram.'

Mary frowned. 'I had that done over six months ago. Everything was fine. The report said so.'

'It was four months ago, but yes, you're right. The initial report was fine, but after a reporting issue, they've reviewed all the mammograms on that day and unfortunately discovered a slight abnormality on your scan.'

Mary went to speak, so many questions clouding her thoughts before Dr Schubert held up his hands.

'It's important to know most abnormal findings on mammograms aren't anything to worry about, so there's no need to be alarmed, but we will need to order further testing to investigate. Just to be sure.'

Mary's mouth had turned dry. She could use a glass of water right now. She glanced around the room, but there wasn't one of those water stations like the one in reception. She swallowed dryly and licked her lips.

'I'd like to refer you for an MRI rather than just an ultrasound.' Dr Schubert spun around to his desk and began tapping away on his computer. 'From there, we can determine what the mass is and if we need to biopsy—'

'So, it's a lump?' Mary interrupted at the mention of a biopsy. She automatically reached her hand to her chest. 'Which one?'

'Ah, it's not necessarily what we would term as a lump just yet, and it's your right breast.'

Mary's eyes welled with moisture, and she turned away.

'Mary, it's going to be okay. I'm sure it's nothing to worry about. It's just precautionary, that's all.'

'Of course.' Mary forced a smile and inhaled back the tears threatening to fall. 'Of course. Better to be safe than sorry, I always say.' But her voice wavered.

FIVE MINUTES LATER, Mary sat in her car outside the doctor's clinic, a radiology referral for Otway Health in her hand and an appointment for a week's time. It was probably nothing. Dr Schubert had told her so. Reinforcing the fact with a gentle touch on her shoulder as she left the room. But what if it wasn't? What if it was a lump? A cancerous lump. Her mind raced with thoughts of chemotherapy and mastectomies. Mary's hand reached to her breast and shuddered. She didn't want to think about it.

CHAPTER TWENTY

After driving aimlessly for forty-five minutes—twice past the coffee shop to see if Simon was there, hoping he wasn't so I could get a coffee but then chickening out anyway—I pulled the car to a stop at the front of Doreen's white weatherboard cottage.

The crisp breeze whipped at my jumper as I stepped out of the car and swung open the front gate, which creaked in need of a good oil. The front yard also needed attention. Weeds choked the bottom of the roses, and dandelions ran rampant in the overgrown lawn, their heads dancing in the breeze. Maybe I could help Doreen with the garden and lawns too? Sand and paint the faded blue timber windows? The dollar signs were adding up in my head. Maybe I could start my own 'Jill of all trades business'—Emily's Errands. That had a ring to it and wasn't as crazy as it sounded. And how proud would Mum be of me if I started my own business? I imagined her beaming as she told everyone about Emily's Errands.

At the front door, I looked around for a doorbell, but finding nothing, I opened the wire screen and knocked on the wooden door. A scratching of feet on floorboards on the other side of the door and then a deep, throaty bark made me jump. That must be Fred, and he didn't sound all too friendly. I hoped his bark was worse than his bite.

'Oh Fred, don't be daft, you silly old thing. Come on out of the way,' a voice that had to be Doreen's, huffed from behind the door. Fred continued to bark for what felt like an eternity until the door slowly swung open and a smiling Doreen, and Fred the basset hound, who stared at me with narrow eyes before letting out another almighty *rrrooooooof*, greeted me.

'Don't mind him.' Doreen leant on her walking frame. Her cropped silvery hair was tucked neatly behind her ears, deep laugh lines crinkling from her hazel eyes and around her cheeks. She shook her head. 'Silly old thing thinks he's a guard dog, but really, he's a big pussycat, aren't you?' She glanced at Fred, who quietened, and then back to me. 'You must be Emily.'

'Hi, Doreen,' I replied before bending down to Fred. I wasn't a dog person usually, but I figured I'd better pretend I was. I held my hand out to his nose. 'Hey, Fred, aren't you a beautiful boy?'

Fred regarded me with his long face and droopy eyes and gave a small growl.

'Oh, Fred! Enough!' Doreen snapped. 'Come in, Emily. Please.'

Fred turned and pattered down the hallway, and I followed Doreen as she shuffled slowly behind him, the walking frame squeaking on the boards. 'Don't mind me,' she said. 'I'm just getting used to this stupid thing. Six weeks, they say.'

'You look like you're moving pretty well for someone who's just had hip surgery,' I replied as Doreen offered me a seat in her lounge room. I sunk into the brown leather couch and took in the floral wallpaper and lace curtains. A bookcase packed tightly with fiction novels covered one wall entirely. Doreen lowered herself onto a floral recliner chair and, with a slight grimace, adjusted the pillows until she was comfy.

'It's been three weeks,' she sighed. 'Five days in hospital; then my son Benjamin was looking after Fred and me, but he's had to return to work in the city. The district nurse comes to check up on me daily, but poor Fred'—she patted his head as he sat quietly beside her, still giving me the eye— 'is going stir crazy. He misses his walks. Don't you, old boy?' At the mention of the word walk, his ears pricked.

'Well, I'd be more than happy to help.'

Doreen tilted her head. 'Emily Brown,' she pondered. 'Now, how do I know that name ... Oh, of course, you must be Mary and David's daughter? The one from the city?'

'Yep, that's me.'

'And you've moved back to the Bay?'

This was my first big test. I exhaled the words quickly. 'Yes, I have.'

'Good for you. I'm forever telling Benjamin he should get out of that rat race.' She tutted. 'Every time I see him, I swear he's a little greyer, although he is fifty-three now, so I suppose ...' she trailed off. 'Anyway, if you don't mind, I'd love you to start today. Fred has been sitting and staring out the front window all morning. Breaks my heart.'

It wasn't like I had a busy schedule, so I was all for starting straight away. Doreen directed me to Fred's lead, which I found in a basket on the sideboard in the kitchen.

'Oh, and don't forget the poop bags!' Doreen called out.

Mmmm. I forgot about that part. I secretly prayed Fred didn't need to do any sort of business while we were out.

When I returned to the living room with the lead and some bags shoved into the pocket of my leggings, Fred immediately jumped to attention and began dancing around in circles in front of Doreen's chair. 'Not me today, Freddy boy. Emily is going to take you.'

Fred stopped and looked at me as if he understood every one of Doreen's words. I was sure his eyes narrowed a fraction. I leant down tentatively and attached the clip to his collar.

'There's a good boy.' Doreen turned to me. 'He'll be fine. He's a good walker. Doesn't pull much, unless he gets a good whiff of something, but just tell him to "heel" and he'll be okay. And you can even walk him off the lead if you're going on the track. I don't go up that way much anymore, too hilly, but Fred used to love it.'

'We'll have a great time, won't we, Fred?'

Fred ignored me and jerked towards the hallway.

'Oh, and love?'

I pulled Fred back and stuck my head around the living room opening. Doreen's face was wrinkled in thought.

'Oh.' She shook her head. 'What was I going to say? I don't know, sorry, love, it's gone. Anyway, he'll be fine.' She waved us away with the flick of her hand.

'No problem, Doreen. We'll see you in about an hour.'

FOR THE MOST PART, the walk was uneventful. A chilly breeze whipped off the ocean, although the sun was warm on my face. It was quite cathartic walking a dog. Perhaps I could buy Hayley a dog? Something to take her mind off things. Of course, I'd have to run it past Mum and Dad, which could be an issue, they'd never been dog people. I remember Lucy had found a stray dog with matted grey fur one day when I was about seven. Mum almost had a conniption, promptly calling the dog catcher to collect it despite my and Lucy's protests. Apparently, it was claimed a few hours later by a worried owner three streets over. But perhaps Mum had mellowed in her old age and would agree we could save one from the pound. I made a mental note to file the idea away for later if things got more difficult with Hayley. I wasn't opposed to bribery.

Fred and I made our way up the track that led to the new look-out. About halfway to the top, I checked for other dogs and let Fred off the lead. He scampered a few metres ahead, sniffing grass and rocks, occasionally stopping to lift his leg. Thankfully, no number twos. Good boy, Fred. When we reached the top, Fred was huffing like a steam train.

'You okay, boy?'

I patted his head. He'd stopped to bury his nose in the long grass, which was good as I was huffing, too. The view from the top was gorgeous. The ocean lapped at the sand of a small bay to the right, the water turning from white to turquoise to deep azure blue as it stretched towards the horizon. Further on, coastal saltbush-covered cliffs dropped perilously sharply into rocks below.

As cliché as it sounded, I felt on top of the world. As if the breeze had picked up all my troubles, whisked them away, and scattered them across the ocean. I inhaled the sea air in a deep, cleansing breath before releasing it. 'Come on, Fred, let's go.'

Fred obeyed, and we kept a leisurely pace as we wound along the gravel path back down towards town. Fred tottered ahead, then stopped and began turning in a circle before pausing in a squatting position. Oh crap. Number twos. I looked around. If I grabbed a stick, I could probably flick it off the path, but my conscience had the better of me. When he'd finished, I pulled out the plastic bag and leant down to pick up after him. Oh lordy! The smell!

'What on earth does Doreen feed you, Fred?' I gasped, scrunching up my face to block my nose. It was like a mix between sour milk and rotting food. I'd never smelt something so awful. I cupped my spare hand to my mouth, gagging as I wrapped the bag around my other hand and picked up the warm, soggy deposit. 'Holy moly, Fred.' I choked. In this moment, twenty-five dollars an hour didn't seem quite enough for what this job entailed.

Once I finished collecting Fred's poop, I glanced up to see Fred had found a new lease on life. He'd taken off down the track at what seemed like a hundred miles an hour. Shit! Literally. I tied the bag to contain the foul odour, which didn't really have much effect, and then I took off after him. Fred was about fifty metres in front, but surely with his short little legs, he wouldn't be hard to catch before we reached the road.

'Fred! Here boy!' I called, jogging after him. Man, he was fast for an overweight hound! He reached the road, and I recalled what Doreen had said. 'Heel!' I called out.

Fred either hadn't heard or was completely ignoring me. Doreen obviously hadn't taken him to puppy school. By now, I was no longer jogging but running. In fact, full-on sprinting, yet, as he scampered across the road—thankfully no cars—I still didn't seem to be making ground. Now he was heading towards the jetty. I increased my speed, which I didn't think was possible, and the motion of my swinging arms was obviously too much for the flimsy poo bag and it broke open, flinging Fred's business all over the path and only narrowly missing my leg. But I didn't have time to be worried about it; Fred had made it to the jetty. I dropped the remnants of the bag and kept sprinting, even though my legs and chest were screaming in pain, promising I'd return later and pick it up.

Up ahead, Fred was galloping, beelining straight towards a woman strolling along the jetty minding her own business. Oh God! He was going to barrel her over. An image of her stumbling backwards off the pier's edge flashed before my eyes.

'Fred!!!' My throat was sore from screaming. To my shock, instead of taking her out, Fred put on the brakes and came to a sudden halt, dead in front of her. She bent down and patted him, scratching behind his ears as his tongue lolled out the side of his mouth. By the time I reached them—chest burning and legs like jelly —she had hold of his collar. I put my hands on my hips and sucked in some deep breaths. Fred was wheezing, drool dripping from his mouth forming in a puddle on the boardwalk.

'You really should have him on a lead, you know.' The woman's tone was as sharp as her judgy look.

'Thank ... you ...' I panted, now doubled over, hands on my knees. It seemed like it was taking far too long for the oxygen to reach my lungs and brain. 'He ... He just ... got away from me.'

The woman examined Fred's silver name tag on his collar. 'Is this Doreen's Fred?'

'Yes. I'm ... walking him ... while ... she recovers ... from—'

'From her hip surgery, yes.'

I nodded. My heart rate was finally slowing. I stood and dabbed some sweat from my forehead. Fred and I needed a moment here on the jetty to reflect on the morning's events before we headed home.

'Are you sure Doreen would want him off the lead? She loves this dog like nothing else. I can't imagine if anything happened to him.'

'It's fine. Doreen said he could go off-lead. I'll put him back on. He's had his adventure now.' I squatted to clip Fred, who was sniffing along the jetty's edge, back on his lead. 'Come on, Fred, time to go.' Again, Fred ignored me. There seemed to be a pattern to his behaviour towards me. I inched closer. He looked up at me, then to the water below, then back at me.

Surely, he wouldn't. Would he? Before I could contemplate the answer, Fred abruptly took a gigantic leap right off the edge of the jetty.

'Fred!' I yelled.

What happened next was like a slow-motion cartoon. The image of this round-bellied, short-legged dog sailing towards the water, floppy ears standing upright.

'Fred,' I gasped again.

Then came the splash.

The woman and I rushed to the edge and stared down into the ocean which was only about a metre or two below us, but a big drop for a basset hound. I expected to see him surface and then joyously doggie paddle to the shore, but much to my horror, Fred was still underwater.

'You'll have to get him!' the lady shrieked, clutching her chest.

'He'll be fine. He'll swim to the shore; it's only a few metres.' I mean, he was a dog. All dogs could swim, right?

'Basset hounds can't swim.' Distress was written all over the woman's face.

'What?' I looked down again and sure enough, Fred was still a big blob underwater, flailing about like a helpless baby.

'They can't swim,' the lady gasped. 'Their legs are too short. You have to save him!'

Before I knew it, I handed my phone to the lady, took a deep breath, and jumped off the edge. The icy water sent razors through me, but there was no time to think about it. I had to save this stupid dog. Luckily, I could just touch the sandy bottom and I grabbed hold of Fred, who was as heavy as a whale. I pulled his head out of the water and he gasped and spluttered, his little legs hanging limply underneath him. He was awkward to carry as he twisted and wriggled in my arms and I could barely see for all the water thrashing in my face. I managed to wade towards the shore in spite of my sopping clothes and waterlogged sneakers working against me. Somehow, my arms and legs found a strength I never knew they had.

Fred's breathing was heavy, and it sounded like he was full of water as he continued to splutter. By now, a small crowd had gathered, and as I reached the shallows, a couple of men strode out and took Fred from my hands.

'Jesus, mate. Basset hounds can't swim!' one of them huffed at me.

So everyone keeps telling me!

Fred had been laid down on the sand, his breathing laboured, his tongue hanging out the side of his mouth. The water pooled at my seaweed encrusted feet as I bent down towards him. 'Fred? Hey buddy.' His eyes were glassy.

People were muttering around us; all I could think about was Doreen. Oh, God. What had I done? Then, out of the corner of my eye, Simon appeared, jogging towards us. My cheeks heated.

'Emily?'

'He just jumped in. I ... I ...'

One of the men, who looked like he knew what he was doing, grabbed Fred by the hind legs and upended him.

'What are you doing?' I shrieked just before Fred expelled a large amount of liquid on the sand.

'That's Miles. He's the vet.' Simon came to a stop next to me, shrugging off his puffer jacket and placing it around my shoulders.

I accepted it and pulled it tight. 'Oh, right. Thank God for that.'

'You do know basset hounds can't swim, right?' Simon said rather bluntly.

Why, suddenly, was everyone an expert in the swimming expertise of basset hounds? It would've been useful information about three minutes ago.

'He's breathing.' The vet turned to me. 'He'll most likely be okay, but I'll need to take him back to the clinic to check him out. He might have water in his lungs, so I'll have to x-ray him and keep him on fluids and monitor him overnight. Is your car nearby? I'm on foot.'

'Ah, no. We were out walking … I …' I was shivering now.

'I'll take him in.' Simon pointed to his car in the parking bay, and before I knew it, he'd loaded Fred into his car. I climbed on the back seat on a thick blanket Simon had laid out next to a sodden Fred. He was panting heavily, and I was shaking with cold worry. How on earth was I going to face Doreen?

AFTER DROPPING Fred at the vet and being reassured he would be okay, although he did need to stay in overnight, Simon offered to drop me back at Doreen's. The vet had offered me a change of clothes—a scrubs suit—which I'd embarrassingly dressed into after peeling my saturated clothes from my freezing skin. I still had Simon's jacket and blanket wrapped around me—probably the only things saving me from hypothermia.

'Thanks.' My heart thundered as he pulled up out the front of her house. Doreen must be beside herself, wondering where we've been.

He nodded.

'I feel so awful ...'

'Luckily, he's going to be okay.' He blew out a breath between his lips. 'It would kill Doreen if anything happened to Fred.'

'I know. I don't know how to tell her.' I glanced at Simon, hoping for some sort of reassurance, but he continued to stare straight ahead.

'So, you're definitely staying here in Curlew Bay, I hear?'

I raised my eyebrow. Okay. Change of subject. 'Well, for now at least, although I haven't quite started off on the right foot, have I?'

Simon turned to me, and his lips parted as if he was about to speak before turning his eyes back ahead. 'I have to get to the café.' Simon moved the gear selector to the drive position. The message came through loud and clear: get out of the car.

'Yeah. Okay, well, thanks for this.'

He nodded curtly. I stepped out of the car, a heaviness in my stomach. I didn't know what was worse. That moment with Simon or now having to face Doreen with a plastic bag full of sopping clothes and no Fred.

CHAPTER TWENTY-ONE

As the sun rose in a brilliant ball of light over the horizon, I was impressed with my ability to hold the half-moon pose for more than three seconds. Connie had messaged me with yet another invitation to try yoga. After yesterday's adventures with Fred, I needed a good de-stress. Poor Doreen. Telling her what had happened had been one of the most shameful experiences of my life. When her face crumpled and tears sprung to her eyes, I, too, burst out crying, and we spent a few sorry minutes consoling each other. Her consoling me! Doreen was truly the most kind-hearted soul. Only after calling Miles and him confirming Fred would definitely be okay did I leave Doreen's. When I'd arrived home dressed in one of Doreen's fluffy winter dressing gowns which she insisted I put on over the scrubs, Mum and Dad found it highly amusing. And even though I crashed into bed exhausted last night, I'd hardly slept a wink.

I unwrapped myself from triangle pose to transform into mountain pose as Connie's voice drew me back to the present. As hard as I was trying, my mind wouldn't settle. It was like Groundhog Day up there replaying yesterday's events. I tried to focus on my breath as Connie had instructed. In two, three, four, out two, three, four. I was relieved when Connie gently led us towards the end of our practice with a head bow and a soft *namaste.*

'You okay?' Connie helped me gather my mat and towel. 'You seemed a little distracted this morning.'

'I was. I am.'

'Want to grab a quick juice?' Connie motioned up the esplanade to the health food store.

'Sure, sounds great.'

TEN MINUTES LATER, Connie and I sat on the plastic chairs, sipping our juices outside the shop. 'So, what's up?' Connie slurped on a carrot, kale, and ginger juice that, if I was honest, looked a little like baby vomit.

'You mean you haven't heard?' I relayed the entire Fred encounter, much to Connie's amusement. She tightened her lips to hold back her laughter.

'Go on, laugh. Mock me. I deserve it.'

'I'm sorry,' Connie said, recovering from a subdued fit of the giggles. 'I do hope he's okay. Poor Fred.'

'Oh God. Me too. If anything happens to him, I don't think I could ever live with myself. I'm going to see Doreen after we finish here. I'll take her some flowers.'

'I'm sure he'll be fine. Miles is a great vet. And I'm sure Fred is tough. And as for Doreen, she's so lovely. I promise she won't hold a grudge.'

I stretched my neck to release the tension that had formed again. So much for yoga. 'I hope not. But I don't think I'll be offering my dog-walking skills to anyone else anytime soon.' I took a mouthful of my more-subdued plain orange juice that Connie had shouted me. 'Enough of me though. What's going on with you? Why are you back in the Bay anyway?'

Connie's face darkened, and I sensed maybe the topic was off limits.

'It's okay. You don't have to tell me.'

'Nah. It's okay.' She sighed heavily, twisting one of her curls around her finger. 'It was a guy, of course.'

'You followed a guy to Curlew Bay? Who?'

'No. The opposite.' Her small laugh was more of a resigned sigh. 'I moved here to get away from one.'

'Oh.'

'There was a guy in Sydney. We were together for about five years, but ...' Connie took a sip of her juice and swirled the straw in thought. 'Let's just say it wasn't a great relationship, and by the time I realised it was all one way—his way—things turned ugly.'

'What happened?' I replied, thinking the worst.

'He wasn't too happy about the break-up. He accused me of cheating on him, lying, using him ... yeah, it got pretty rough. He wouldn't leave me alone. That's why I went back to Melbourne. And then, when he discovered where I was, he turned up on Mum's doorstep.'

'What?'

'Yeah. I had to get a restraining order, and Mum moved to a different apartment, but I couldn't shake the feeling he would turn up again. I didn't want Mum worrying about me, and I didn't want him to turn up and confront Mum if I wasn't home. Mum didn't want to move again, so I moved back here. It's the only place he wouldn't think of looking. I'd never told him I'd lived here.' A ute rumbled by slowly and a man waved, Connie waved back.

'Oh, Con. Did he threaten you?'

'Verbally, but he never physically hurt me. I can't believe it took me so long to realise he emotionally abused me during our entire relationship. I was just too dumb to see it.'

'Not too dumb.' I reached my hand over to hers. 'Sometimes we don't see things because we don't want to. That's what it was like with Anthony and me. We had troubles years ago, even before he lost his job. I just didn't want to admit it or face it. It was much easier to stick my head in the sand and push things aside, hoping they'd get better.'

Connie nodded. 'Men, huh?'

'He hasn't bothered you again?'

'No. Thank God. But that's the last of it. No more relationships for me. I am one hundred percent happy on my own.'

'Not even the guy in the ute? He was kind of cute?'

She slapped her hands on the table and laughed. 'Crimmo? As if! Anyway, enough of that. Notice anything different?' She gave me a pouty smile.

'Apart from the fact that you haven't aged and are still drop-dead gorgeous?'

'Flattery will get you everywhere. But seriously. Look.'

I scanned Connie and noticed her skin did seem rather fresh. 'Have you done something to your skin? It looks like it's glowing. I'd ask if you were pregnant if I didn't know better.'

Connie almost choked on her juice. 'Definitely not pregnant!'

'Botox then?'

'Nope.' She frowned. 'Not that there's anything wrong with that. But no. Here, I'll show you.' She reached into her bag. 'It's this.' She slid a thin tube across the table.

'Face Freeze?' I eyed the pink tube.

'It's a face lift in a cream!' Connie sported a proud grin. 'Without being Botox. One of my mum's friend's daughters in Melbourne is a rep for the brand. Apparently, she's making a mint as a consultant. Only started six months ago and has already left her job and is doing it full time. This product has only been approved for use in Australia recently, but they've been using it in France for years. This'—she tapped on the tube—'is why French women have amazing skin!'

I wasn't really sure if French women had amazing skin or not. It was the part about the consultant leaving her job because the income was so good that caught my attention. 'So is it like a multi-level marking thing?'

'Something like that, but not the dodgy kind. It's legit. She's doing really well and bought a brand-new car recently, Mum said. Maybe you could get into it? The range is only new, so not many people are doing it. You could make a heap of money.'

'Me? I don't think so. Beauty's not really my thing.' My skin routine consisted of splashing my face with water, a lick of moisturiser, and SPF. I'd never been one to spend money on fancy products that made outrageous claims. Although, remembering my reflection in the mirror lately, maybe I should have.

'What's the difference between PR and selling a brand? Isn't that basically what PR is?' Connie continued.

She had a point. And I *could* do with the money. Even if I only did it for a few months until I found something else. Perhaps it was worth looking into.

'And just think of the discounted products you'd get!' Connie added as if reading my mind.

'I don't want to step on your toes.'

'Oh God no. I'm not selling it. Between BookArt and my yoga classes I don't have time.'

I twisted my lips, and Connie's face erupted into a cheeky grin. 'I'll message you the website.'

I shrugged. I couldn't see myself as a skincare consultant, but my dog-walking foray hadn't turned out, so I guess I needed to keep my options open.

AFTER FINISHING my juice and saying goodbye to Connie, I called into the florist and picked up a bunch of flowers for Doreen. A posy of colour to brighten her day, hopefully.

'Hi, Doreen,' I said sheepishly when she answered the door.

'Oh, love. You didn't have to.' Doreen shuffled in the doorway. 'They're lovely. Would you mind putting them in water for me?'

In the kitchen, Doreen directed me to a vase and filled me in on Fred, who was sitting on his dog bed near the table. His eyes flicked up to me and narrowed.

'Miles dropped him off about ten minutes ago. You just missed him. He assured me Fred would be fine.' Doreen's eyes were a little glassy. 'He took in a bit of water, but his lungs are clear, and he's been eating and drinking. He won't be himself for a few days, that's all. Will you, Fred?' Fred slumped his head back down with a groan. Obviously meant with full effect to make me feel bad again.

I filled the vase and placed the flowers on the table. 'I'm so sorry, Doreen. I feel awful about what happened.'

'It's okay, love. These things happen. The main thing is he'll be fine.'

'Once he's fully recovered, I'll walk him for you, Doreen. Free of charge.'

Doreen's mouth twitched with concern for a split second.

'On the lead the whole way, and we'll avoid water and the jetty,' I added quickly to reassure her.

'Okay.' Her shoulder's relaxed. 'That would be nice; he does need his walk.'

I nodded and noticed an invoice on the table from the vet. 'And I will be paying this for you.' I picked it up and folded it in half. 'You won't have to worry about a thing.'

'Oh, Emily, no—'

I held my palm up. 'No, I insist. It's the least I can do.'

Doreen's eyes welled, and I gave her a quick hug before giving Fred a quick rub on the head—to which he managed a tired growl—and bid my farewell. As I headed down the path, I unfolded the vet invoice and inhaled sharply. 'Nine hundred and sixty-three dollars!' Looked like I'd be taking a hard look at that website Connie was going to send me.

· · ·

LATER THAT NIGHT, I swallowed my pride and signed up as a 'Maisy May' skincare consultant. It wasn't like I had other options. And it didn't sound all that bad. Touted—unofficially, of course—as Botox in a tube, it was apparently the chosen skincare of some of the most famous women in the world—although none were named because, you know, they didn't want to share their secret. Or so the website said.

The products were natural, organic, and all the 'friendlies'— vegan, animal, eco, planet. I had to admit, the copywriting was very convincing. I had no idea if it worked, but after paying my $175 consultant joining fee, I now had a truckload of PDFs to read, which would tell me all about the products and how they worked their magic. My consult pack and products were being express shipped, and in the meantime, all I had to do was complete a series of seven videos on how to successfully sell Maisy May, and then boom, I was a certified Maisy May consultant.

I closed the laptop and switched off the light. Selling skincare had never been on my wildest dreams radar but neither had dog walking. And although it wouldn't make me a millionaire, it would at least help me pay Fred's vet bill and maybe even tide me over until another job presented itself. And what was the worst that could happen? It wasn't like there were any dogs I could harm, and at the very least, I'd get some free skincare and a few less wrinkles.

CHAPTER TWENTY-TWO

Mary arrived in the car park of Otway Health, switched off the car engine, and riffled through her handbag for the referral. David had wanted to come, but there was no use worrying him if it were nothing. Like Dr Schubert said, it was just a precaution. That was what she kept telling herself, although it hadn't settled her restlessness for the past few days.

She'd barely slept a wink last night. Stupid little thoughts. Like her life was flashing in front of her eyes, not with all the things she'd done, but with all the things she *hadn't*.

The folded referral slip was wedged in the side pocket; she yanked it out and shook her head, again annoyed at her overthinking. She'd never been one of *those* people. Worrying about things out of her control. And she wasn't going to start now. She'd always been a 'focus on the now' person. No sense in dwelling on the past or worrying about the future. Mary adjusted the collar of her shirt and stuck out her chin. Time to get this over and done with.

. . .

MARY EMERGED from the hospital feeling like she'd spent the last hour on a construction site with jackhammers next to her head. The MRI machine had been louder than she'd expected, and even the headphones filling her ears with soothing music didn't help. A metallic taste remained in her mouth from the contrast dye, and a headache had set in. She rubbed at the injection site on her arm where they'd put the needle. Going to the linen store was the last thing she felt like doing, but she was too rattled to drive home. The sun was high in the sky and warm on her back as she strolled along the main street, admiring shop window displays and seeking a café that looked welcoming for an early lunch and a strong tea.

The smell of jasmine and roses from the sidewalk florist and fresh food made her feel a little better. Her thoughts turned to Emily. What to do, what to do. She didn't know how to help her, apart from financially, which she and David had offered many times. They didn't have much but had enough to help their daughter. As they would for Lucy if she ever needed it. Which was never likely to happen. But you never knew. But Emily, in her ever-stubborn self, had repeatedly refused. She'd also been quiet since the school reunion, leaving Mary to wonder if something had happened.

It reminded Mary of how Emily was in those final days of school, through exams, and into Christmas. How she'd changed from carefree to anxious. And then she suddenly took a second round university place in an arts degree that they'd offered her. Which she ended up transferring into law, of all things! That was a turnaround of sorts. Of big sorts. But Mary had been happy for her. She'd never been sure of her eighteen-year-old daughter gallivanting around the countryside in a combi van. Not that she didn't trust, Simon, but it hadn't been long since that English backpacker had been shot and his girlfriend terrorised.

'Mary? Is that you?'

A familiar voice broke her train of thought.

'It is you!'

'Susan?' Gosh, she hadn't seen her in, what, two, maybe three years. No, it had to be longer than that, but despite her now silver hair and heavy laugh lines around her eyes, she recognised her in an instant. She still had that warm smile and lust for life that lit up her eyes.

'Hello, you.' Susan reached out and embraced Mary. 'You're looking great. What are you doing here in Apollo Bay?'

Mary hesitated, the words pooling under her tongue. She was never great at keeping secrets or lying. It went against every one of her principles. And Mary knew it was principles that kept the world in order. Even white lies were hard for Mary to tell. 'I'm ... I'm here for an appointment.' At least it wasn't a lie.

'Do you have time for lunch? I was just on the way to the post office.' Susan juggled a small square package in her arms. 'I'd love to catch up. It's been too long.'

'Oh, I don't want to hold you up.'

Susan swatted away the comment. 'Don't be silly. Come on, this place has great focaccias.' She motioned to the café one shop ahead.

'Okay, then,' Mary said, relaxing. 'Why not?'

A FEW MINUTES LATER, Mary was seated across from Susan at a table inside the café. The open bi-fold doors let the warm sunshine flow in and settle on their legs.

'I can't believe it's been almost five years,' Susan began, taking a sip of her coffee that had just arrived.

'I know. I thought maybe two or three. But five? You know what they say, time flies ...' Time had flown. The last time Mary spoke to Susan, she'd felt rather envious of her upcoming three-month trek to Canada with her husband, Sam. In fact, Susan hadn't shut up about the trip for the few months leading up to it.

'Gosh, that must've been before we went to Canada. Or was it after?'

'Before.'

'That's right. We tried catching up a few times when I returned, but I think that was when you were looking after Lucy's kids for the week. She and Gordon were at a gift fair or something?'

This surprised Mary. Susan had a watertight memory. It had been a good excuse for her to avoid catching up straight after Susan returned. It wasn't that she didn't want to see her; she just wanted to give it a few weeks so she wouldn't have to hear all about the trip. But then weeks turned into months, and before long, it became too awkward to pick up the phone. Shame rested on Mary's shoulders. They only lived half an hour away, and Susan had been a good friend. It was Mary who hadn't. 'Yes. It was a busy time.' Mary jiggled the tea bag in her Earl Grey, watching the water darken. 'I'm really sorry we lost touch, Susan.'

'Me too. But the past is the past, isn't it? Not much we can do about it, and here we are now.' There was such warmth in her smile.

A server delivered their lunch, and Mary's stomach rumbled at the sight of the golden vegetarian focaccia she'd ordered and the smell of freshly roasted capsicum. And, for the first time in such a long time, Mary felt like someone. Not a wife, not a mother. Like a lady who lunched. She almost giggled under her breath. So contrite, but it felt nice to feel like her own self.

Mary chatted with Susan over lunch, and it wasn't long before the five years seemed to dissolve and it was like they hadn't lost all that time.

'So what appointment did you have?' Susan patted her mouth with a napkin and placed it on her empty plate.

Mary's breath caught a little, and before she knew it, her eyes filled with unexpected tears. She inhaled a deep breath and tried to disguise her unusual display of emotion with a cough. 'Oh, it was nothing.'

Mary could tell Susan didn't believe that for a second.

'Is everything okay, Mare?' Susan reached her hand to Mary's.

That was it. A rogue tear dared to escape, and Mary quickly wiped it away with her napkin. 'Really, it's probably nothing.' She cleared her throat. 'I had to have a follow-up breast MRI after they found an abnormality on my last mammogram. Just routine, Dr Schubert said. You know.'

Susan's face softened further. 'Oh, Mare. I'm sure it's nothing. I had to have one a couple of years back, too.'

'You did?'

'Yeah. Bloody loud, uncomfortable experience it was.'

Mary let out a small laugh. 'So loud!'

'I'm sure it will be nothing. And if it's not, well, we can deal with that then, right?'

Mary nodded, her eyes filling once more. It was good to have a friend to talk to again. Not that Mary had been lonely. She had David and Lucy, her book club ladies, and now Emily and Hayley were home. But no one that she could've ever confided in like this. Susan had been that person. A warmth of gratitude swelled in her chest.

Mary's shoulder's relaxed, and she lost herself in Susan's company, intrigued about Susan's latest travel plans to the Northern Territory.

'We're not sure if we should do the Kimberley tour from Broome to Darwin in style with luxury accommodation and coach transfers or more of a laid-back camping style itinerary.'

Mary instantly thought the luxury option sounded better. 'Camping as in tents? In the outback?'

'It's more like glamping, I believe. I don't think we'll be roughing it in swags.' Susan let out a throaty laugh.

After lunch, Mary farewelled Susan, and they planned to catch up again in a couple of weeks. Susan would come to Curlew Bay for lunch.

Mary returned to the car with a mix of emotions, slumping back in the seat with a sigh, feeling wrung out like washing on the fast spin cycle. The stress of the MRI, the surprise at seeing Susan, and how relaxed she felt in her company chatting with an old friend. Mary was exhausted. She turned over the ignition and was glad to end the day on a lighter note. Maybe if anything good were to come out of this, it was reigniting old friendships. She hoped so.

CHAPTER TWENTY-THREE

'Come on,' Mum said after I'd literally pushed Hayley out the front door to school.

'Come on what?'

'I thought it would be nice for you to see Lucy at the shop,' she replied, tying her shoelaces.

I finished washing the last of the breakfast dishes and pulled the plug out, the water rushing out with a gurgle. 'Why?'

'Why not?' Mum stood. 'When was the last time you saw the shop?'

I pulled an 'I don't know' face.

'Exactly.'

'What about Fred? Doreen's expecting me?'

'Perfect. We'll walk past and get him on the way.'

After collecting Fred, Mum and I walked into the main shopping drag. Fred wasn't up to his normal pace, but he trotted alongside happily. Mum hadn't stopped talking since we left home, rabbiting on about the weather and the coffee table Dad was making. It was hard to get a word in.

The smell of freshly baked bread wafted out as we passed the bakery. 'Maybe we should get a donut?' I suggested. A freshly baked iced donut was the one treat Mum used to spoil Lucy and me with on a Saturday morning after netball. I could almost taste the sweetness of the soft dough and the chocolate icing. Lucy always went for strawberry.

Mum shook her head. 'No donuts. We're on a walk.'

I scoffed. 'Oh, a new health kick, is it?'

Mum tutted. 'Emily, you should look after yourself more; you don't want to get to my age and'—she paused—'and regret the decisions you've made.'

Okay, so that was weird. 'I don't think one donut is going to ruin my life. And besides, I've been jogging and doing yoga.'

Mum ignored me and focused on the footpath.

'Is there something wrong, Mum?' My gut told me there was more to Mum worrying about a donut than met the eye.

'Here we are! You can tie Fred up on that little pole thing there.' Mum pushed open the door to open and disappeared inside.

'You behave, Fred,' I commanded, double-checking the knot. The last thing I needed was him wandering off again.

A lofty hit of warm lemon-scented air greeted me when I stepped inside; Lucy waved from the counter before returning to the woman she was serving. Mum was smelling the various oil burners and candles, so I wandered over to join her. Lucy had done a nice job with the shop. I had to give her credit for that. There were trinkets and homewares, throw cushions, baskets, photo frames, and jewellery boxes. An eclectic assortment, to say the least.

'Thanks, Mrs Ashley, see you again.' Lucy sounded bright and chirpy, happy and in her element. Always so self-assured and confident within herself. It came naturally to her. Whereas I'd always felt I was wearing a mask, a persona that I had to take on in order to prove myself.

'Yes, see you dear.'

'Shop's looking good,' I called to Lucy, who was tidying up the wrapping paper and ribbon she'd just used.

'Yeah, thanks.'

A look transposed between Mum and Lucy. I'd been brought here for a reason. Oh God. Lucy wasn't going to offer me a job, was she? Could you imagine us working together? My mind scrambled for excuses to come up with. I couldn't wrap presents. Christmas and birthday gifts were always delivered in gift bags instead. I had no idea about interior decoration. Again, true. I didn't want to work with Lucy. True, but probably not something to voice aloud.

'I feel like there's a reason you brought me here.' I caught Mum's eye and held her gaze, challenging her to tell the truth, something she always bangs on about.

'I thought you'd like to see Lucy's shop. It's been a while since you've been here.'

'Nothing's changed much.' Lucy straightened the candles Mum had displaced. 'Unless you know how to get more customers?'

'Don't be silly, Lucy,' Mum scoffed. 'You have a roaring trade.'

I glanced around the shop, which was empty apart from the three of us, but held my tongue.

Lucy rolled her eyes, then turned to me. 'Actually, I am glad you dropped by.'

Ah, there it was.

'I wanted to ask you something.'

Mum looked at me expectantly, confirming my fears—I'd been set up.

'Mmm-hmm,' I replied. 'What is it?'

'Well, you know Snapper Fest is coming up, and well, I was wondering if you'd be interested in joining the committee.'

'Oh yes! What a wonderful opportunity, Emily.' Mum's smile was wide and knowing. 'Don't you think?'

Snapper Fest was a big deal in Curlew Bay. Held at the end of every September, it brought swarms of tourists to the town for the market stalls, to see who could haul in the biggest snapper, and then have it prepared by a celebrity chef at the night market. There were craft stalls, food vans, and live music. I fondly remembered Snapper Fest as a kid, running around barefoot, and hiding with my friends in unseen places as a teen. Lucy had been on the organising committee for the past ten years—of course she had.

'It's only eight weeks away,' I said. 'Aren't you all organised?'

'Sandy's just left for England. Her daughter's pregnant and has just been diagnosed with pre-eclampsia. She's heading over to help her out in her last weeks.'

'And it's the 75th anniversary this year,' Mum added with a firm nod. 'It has to be super-duper. They really do need all the help they can get.'

I vaguely remembered it was supposed to be last year, but with Covid running rampant, they had to cancel it. Lucy must be under enormous pressure to pull off a successful event. Lucy and Mum were staring expectantly at me, waiting for my answer; there was no getting out of it. What excuse did I have?

'I suppose I can. I won't be a great help, but—'

'Oh, Em. That would be amazing.' Lucy placed her hand on my arm, to which I gave her a look to indicate this was not the time for faux sisterly love. She quickly removed it. 'We have a meeting on Monday night. If you're free.'

'Well, actually, I did have plans.' It irritated me they assumed I had nothing better to do. Places to go and people to see and all that. Who was I kidding?

Lucy and Mum both eyed me with surprise.

'Okay, I don't, but you shouldn't assume.'

'No, I didn't. I mean—'

'It's fine, Lucy,' I sighed. 'What time?'

'Six o'clock at The Coffee Pot.'

'The Coffee Pot? They don't open at night.'

'Simon lets us hold our meetings there.'

'Fine.'

Again, Lucy and Mum exchanged a glance and I had another sinking feeling there was something else and was just about to question them when Fred barked, signalling he'd had enough waiting. 'Come on, Mum, let's go. Fred's waiting.'

MUM and I parted ways so she could go home and I could walk back to Doreen's. As we reached her gate, I unclipped Fred's leash, and he trotted ahead. He seemed to be putting up with me. It was like we had an unspoken mutual agreement. As long as I took him for his daily walk, I was in his good books. Although he still narrowed his eyes at me, once I pulled out his lead, it didn't take long before he turned on the charm. Who knows? Maybe we'd even be friends one day.

'Oh, you're back already?' Doreen shuffled into the kitchen.

'It was a full hour.' I put Fred's collar on the table, and he made a beeline for his water bowl, splashing it on the floor as he lapped it up.

'Gosh, it only felt like half that. How was my Freddy boy today?' She bent down to give Fred an ear rub. She was moving better every day.

'He's fine. We're a team now, aren't we, Fred?' Fred glared at me as if to say, 'I wouldn't go that far,' and then retreated to his bed, turning in circles three times and plonking down with a muffled grunt. The kettle whistled in the background. 'I'll make tea for you before I go.'

'Oh, that would be wonderful.' Doreen hobbled into the lounge room and lowered herself into her chair. 'My hip's a bit achy this morning. Must be rain coming. You have a cuppa too, won't you love?'

A few minutes later, I handed Doreen her tea and sat on the couch, cradling mine in a faded, rose-coloured cup.

'Ah, just what the doctor ordered.' Doreen smiled serenely after she took a mouthful of the sweet brew. 'So, Miss Emily, how are things with you? How's your mum?'

'She's doing okay. Mum's mum. Always busy doing something.'

'Yes, she's always out and about. Tried to get me along to do some exercise class with her before I did my hip. Maybe if I were a few years younger, I'd join her. But, anyway, she must be glad to have you back. You staying for good?'

'Well, for good is a long time. Let's just say I'm here til I sort a few things out.' I hadn't told Doreen much of my situation, but I could see her brain ticking over.

'Your husband coming?'

Yep, she was a smart one. And a nosey one. A well-meaning nosey one. I took a sip of tea to disguise my smile. 'Mm-hmm. That's what needs sorting.'

'Ah, I see. Yes, well, I can't offer much advice on that front. I lost my Wally when Ben was only thirteen. We were going to spend forever together.' Doreen looked wistfully at a black-and-white framed wedding photo on the mantle above the gas heater. Her dress was high neck with long sleeves and intricate detail along the bodice. Doreen was looking directly at the camera, a smile of complete and utter joy radiating across her face, and Wally, with his slick-backed hair and sideburns, looked at her as if she was the only thing that mattered in the whole world. 'I guess, in some strange way, we are,' she said with a glassy-eyed smile.

I took another sip of tea. It didn't seem appropriate to say anything, so we sat in comfortable silence, deep in our thoughts.

'But,' Doreen continued, 'you know what he said to me before the cancer took him? He said, "Doreen, live your life from the heart. Do what you want to do and don't let anyone tell you otherwise."'

I nodded. It was sage advice. But I couldn't see how Doreen had done that. As far as I knew, she'd lived in the Bay her whole life.

'So, I did. I have. Every day is a blessing, and apart from this problematic hip, I still am.' Doreen shot me a look accompanied by a wry smile. 'I know what you're thinking: But Doreen, what have you done? I know I've lived a small life. But that's exactly what I wanted. Wally and I were never ones for fancy things, travelling or fast cars, or big houses. And we were okay with that. Ben, on the other hand.' Doreen shook her head. 'My Ben. He went chasing all of that. But there was no talking him out of it. That was what he wanted. And I suppose he's happy enough. Although, I wonder sometimes.'

Doreen was wistful, and I could see in her eyes she wished Ben had been able to appreciate the smaller things like she did. Take one day at a time and not worry about the stress of money or the want of bigger things. Though I couldn't see how it was possible in today's fast-paced world where everyone was striving for faster, bigger, better, and social media constantly bombarded us with what a successful life supposedly looked like: fast cars, big houses, perfect clothes, filtered faces. Where was the slowdown button on the mouse-wheel of life so you could pause and consider jumping off? There wasn't one.

'One day you'll understand, dear. I think we all understand the meaning of life in the end, no matter what we've done or where we've been.' Doreen's smile, and the genuine warmth it contained, reached me like a warm hug. The back of my nose stung, and a small tear escaped one of my eyes. I wiped it away.

'Oh, look at me doddering on like an old fuddy-duddy. I'm sorry. I didn't mean to upset you.'

'Don't be silly. You're fine. I ... It's just been a rough few weeks, that's all.'

'I'm sure it has.'

I took the last sip of my tea and stood. 'Thank you for the tea. I'd better get home.'

'Of course. You'll be back tomorrow? For Fred?' Doreen handed me her teacup.

'Absolutely. Wouldn't miss it for the world.' I glanced at Fred, who was sound asleep, his back leg twitching, and I almost felt a stab of love for the hound. Almost.

CHAPTER TWENTY-FOUR

The second I walked in the front door, my phone started ringing.

'Ms Brown? It's Adele here from Curlew Bay High.'

'Oh, hi. Is everything okay?'

'I'm afraid there's been an incident involving Hayley—'

'Oh my God! Is she okay?'

'Yes, she's fine, but I need you to come straight to the school if possible. Principal Nunn will fill you in when you get here.'

'Of course. Yes, I'm coming now.'

By the time I reached the school, I'd worked through myriad scenarios as to why Principal Nunn wanted to see me: Hayley had been bullied. Hayley was bullying someone. She'd broken down in class or locked herself in the toilets; she'd stolen something. A ball of tension had formed between my shoulder blades. It was like I'd been opened up and filled with rapid-set concrete.

It was home time, so I had to navigate the flurry and excitement of teenagers heading home. I swung open the door to the office and stormed to the counter.

'Hi.' The rushing had left me out of breath.

'Afternoon, Ms Brown.' The lady's name tag read 'Adele' in bold letters. 'I'll let Principal Nunn know you're here.' She picked up the phone and motioned for me to sit in the plastic chairs by the front windows, which I did.

Whatever Hayley had done was all my fault. How did I think ripping her away from school, away from her friends, her home, was a good idea? But the choice was well and truly taken out of my hands. I tried to remind myself of this, but it was futile. My mind rebuked that line of thought. What if there were other options? As my mind wrestled with its thoughts, the door to Principal Nunn's office opened, and out walked Hayley, her lips twisted in a pissed-off scowl.

'Hayley! Are you okay?' I went to reach for her but stood tall when Principal Nunn appeared behind her.

'Ms Brown, if I could have a moment, please?' She summoned me into her office while Hayley plonked herself down on the chair where I'd been sitting.

Inside the office, Principal Nunn settled behind her desk, and I sat on the other side, on the edge of the chair.

'Now, I'm sure you want to know what all this is about?'

Ah, yeah? I nodded.

'So, Hayley was sent to my office during English this afternoon after repeatedly being rude and arguing with her teacher.'

My eyes widened. 'What?'

Principal Nunn pursed her lips in disapproval.

'I'm really sorry, Mrs Nunn, this is so out of character for Hayley—'

She held up a hand to silence me. 'It seems Hayley isn't too pleased with the curriculum at Curlew Bay High, particularly the English text they are studying.'

'How?'

'It seems Hayley has had much to say about Romeo and Juliet. I'm sure she will tell you about her thoughts on the way home, but she certainly made her views quite clear to Miss Chen who, I might add, was quite upset after the outbursts from your daughter.'

'Look, of course I don't condone Hayley speaking out of turn; she's going through a bit right now—'

'I understand that, Ms Brown, which is why I am giving you the name and contact details for our school counsellor. Have you considered having Hayley talk to someone about her situation?'

'It's not something I thought was necessary.' Was the principal reprimanding me? Heat rushed to my cheeks.

'Well, I think it's possibly something you do need to think about.' Mrs Nunn handed me a card across the desk, leant back, and removed her glasses. 'I like to think I run a pretty tight ship here, but I also like to think I'm in touch with the younger generation and what they're going through. Parents who are never home, social media influences, divorce ...' she trailed off before continuing. 'Anyway, I'll leave things with you, and if you need any further assistance, please let me know. I hope this is the last time I have to call you in here.'

'Of course. Yes. I promise this is a one-off.' I got to my feet, hoping with all my heart it was.

ONCE WE WERE in the car, I asked Hayley what she had said.

'It doesn't matter,' she grunted, staring out the window.

'It does matter, and you need to tell me.'

Hayley sat stiffly and clenched her jaw so tight I was worried she might crack a tooth. 'I told her Romeo and Juliet is an outdated piece of crap.'

'Hayley! Language!'

'What? It is! Do you know how old Juliet was? Thirteen! Thirteen and she's off having sex and then killing herself for a boy! How is that teaching us anything good?'

'Well, I don't know if they were off having sex willy-nilly.'

'She's thirteen, Mum! Oh, so you'd be happy if I was off having sex right now? I bet Dad wouldn't be.'

I ignored the barb and took a deep breath. 'Neither of us would be, but I don't think—'

'See!'

'I'm not saying I don't agree with you in that context, but I'm sure whatever the teachers are focusing on is important to learn. You know, language, themes, that kind of thing.'

Hayley glared at me and then slumped in her seat, returning her stare out the window. 'So, I guess I'm grounded?'

I sighed. I had two options: ground her and piss her off even further, or let it go and hope she takes it as a peace offering and just bloody behaved. The latter had more appeal.

'No, you're not grounded. I just want you to promise that if you have issues with anything at school, you will bring them up in a respectful manner in future, okay?'

Hayley's face flickered with confusion but only for a second, being quickly replaced by another frown. 'Whatever.' She slammed the car door shut and thumped into the house, leaving me in the car for a few quiet moments. I had to admit she had a point. Studying a text so out of date and context with today's teens wasn't teaching them anything, but there was no way I condoned her behaviour. Just another thing to chalk up on the 'I failed at parenting board'.

'KNOCK, KNOCK. CAN I COME IN?' I'd finally plucked up the courage to knock on Hayley's door. It was nearly bedtime, and I wouldn't be able to sleep if I didn't at least try and smooth things over.

I waited a beat.

'Yeah.'

When I opened the door, Hayley was leaning up against the wardrobe, laptop resting on her knees.

'We really need to get you a desk in here,' I said, sitting on the end of her unmade bed.

She shrugged, and her eyes went to the plate I was holding.

'Thought you might like this.' I held it out to her. 'It's lemon slice. Your favourite.'

Hayley twisted her mouth, and I tried not to smile. There was no way she'd be able to resist lemon slice. No matter how foul a mood she was in.

'Where's it from?'

'The Coffee Pot.'

Hayley put her laptop down and reached for the plate.

'So, doing homework?'

She shrugged as she chewed, little bits of coconut clinging to her lip. 'An assignment.'

'What subject?'

'Environmental studies.'

I crossed my legs and shimmied back on the bed. 'Oooh, you love that, don't you?'

Hayley finished her mouthful and shrugged. At least she was talking to me. And I didn't care in the slightest if the lemon slice was the reason why. Bribery worked, and that was where we were at. Whatever it took.

'I have to research an endangered species and do like a report thing.' She shoved the last piece into her mouth.

'Hey, you know what?' I said, gauging the conversation was progressing well. 'Simon at the café, where I got the slice, he's into the curlews. You know, the birds?'

'I know what curlews are.' She didn't need to add the 'derrr' at the end of the statement as she inferred it loud and clear.

'Well, he knows a lot about them; maybe, you should talk to him.

I think he's even part of a preservation society or something. Does birdwatching tours. He'd be a great source of knowledge.'

'How do you know?'

I stiffened slightly. 'We ... I ... We went to school together.' She didn't need to know our history. 'You should go and see him.'

Hayley shrugged. 'Yeah, maybe.'

'Great. Okay.' I took a deep breath. This was progress. An actual conversation that didn't end in an argument or a snide remark. As much as I wanted to bring up what had happened earlier, I needed to let it go. If I'd learnt one thing about teenagers—especially teenagers who hated you—it was not to push too hard. I stood up. Best to leave on a good—goodish—note. 'Right, I'll leave you to it.'

CHAPTER TWENTY-FIVE

'What on earth is all that?' Mary closed the back door behind her and surveyed the mess. It looked like the beauty aisle at the local chemist had exploded on her kitchen table. Tubes, bottles, and sample pouches in an array of pastel colours.

'Mother dearest! Come. Sit.' Emily's voice was theatrical, channelling her best version of Dame Edna, rest her soul. She ushered Mary into one of the chairs. 'Let me share with you the magic of Maisy May skincare.'

'Maisy May skincare?' Mary had never heard of it. What had ever happened to Avon?

'Yes, direct from Paris.' Emily had screwed the lid off a pale pink tube, smoothing some of the cream over the back of one of Mary's hands.

'Oooh, that feels nice.'

'It's their fabulous hand cream from the premium collection.' Emily kept rubbing her hand. 'Just a small amount rubbed in each night, and you will wake up with hands as smooth as a baby's bottom.'

When Emily finished, Mary lifted her hand to her nose.

'Mmmm, it smells'—she sniffed the back of her hand—'like marshmallow.'

'It's lovely, isn't it?'

'Just the thing to make me feel better.'

'Why? What's up?' Emily screwed the lid back on, leaving Mary wishing she hadn't made the comment.

'Oh, nothing. You know, just feeling a bit off today,' Mary replied before brightening, rubbing her hands. 'Oh, my hands feel like satin!'

'It feels nice, doesn't it?'

'Are you one of those ... what do you call it?'

'Consultant. Yes. I've just signed on. But it's not about the money; it's because I believe in the products.'

Mary jutted her head back with a questioning look, to which Emily gave a one-shoulder shrug.

'Okay, I admit it. I'm doing it for the money. But'—she held up a finger—'they are great products.'

'Well, I think it's a lovely idea.' Mary's mind raced. Then she had a brilliant idea. 'You should have one of those parties. Like a Tupperware party.'

'Yep, that's the idea, Mum.'

'Oh, I know! Our book club is next week, and it's my turn to host.'

'Are you still in that book club?'

'Yes. Although we don't read many books. It's more about the wine and cheese.' Well, the wine mostly. 'We had a lot of discussions after we read *Fifty Shades of Grey*, though.' Mary remembered that one like it was yesterday. 'That was an interesting evening. Did you know Beth and Peter Bright are into bondage?!'

Emily held up my hands. 'Oh God, Mum. No! And I don't want to know!'

Mary chuckled at her daughter's outburst. 'Anyway, there's about eight of us in the book club and a few ladies who like to spend, if you know what I mean.' Mary raised her eyebrows. Nola was exceptionally frivolous with her money. Always said there was no way her kids were getting hold of it when she'd spent her whole life working for it.

'Well, if you think they'd like it, maybe I could do a short presentation after you discuss your book?'

'That will be perfect.' Mary rose to her feet to find her phone. 'I'll text the others now and let them know.'

She left Emily to pack up her products and went to find her phone, which she found on her bedside table. She squinted at the missed call on the screen. She knew that number and quickly dialled.

'Curlew Bay Clinic. This is Simone.'

Mary cleared her throat. 'Oh, hello, Simone. It's Mary. Mary Brown. I think—'

'Oh yes, Mary. Dr Schubert was looking for you. Just a moment; I'll see if he's free.'

Mary's chest tightened. It had to be bad news from her MRI. Doctors only called personally if it was bad news. If it was nothing, the receptionist would have simply relayed a message. Mary swallowed and sat down on the edge of her bed.

'Mary. Hello,' Dr. Schubert began. 'Thanks for calling me back. How are you?'

How was she? How was she supposed to answer that? 'Well, thank you, Dr Schubert.'

Mary wished she was in his consulting room so she could ascertain what he was about to say from his body language and facial expression, but instead, she closed her eyes and waited for the bad news.

'Good. Good. Now, I'm sure you know why I'm calling, and yes, the results from the MRI have come back.'

Mary held her breath.

'Unfortunately—'

Oh God. Mary's shoulders dropped.

'—the MRI was inconclusive.'

'Inconclusive?' What did that mean?

'Yes, but there is a very small mass showing, so we need to do a biopsy to be sure it's nothing nefarious.'

'But I can't even feel anything.' Mary had checked her breast at least a hundred times a day since her last visit with Dr Schubert and still couldn't feel any lumps. It was the only thought that had kept her sane.

'It's possible that it feels normal and hasn't grown large enough for you to notice any difference. And that's also a good thing. It means treatment—if needed—will be effective.'

Treatment? Mary felt as if the wind had been knocked out of her. Did that mean it was ...? 'So ... it's cancerous?'

'No, that's not what I'm saying. This is all precautionary. There's no need to be alarmed. I would rather be overconcerned and it be nothing, than to let things go. I know that's not reassuring, and you will, of course, think the worst, but don't. Let's take things one step at a time, okay?'

Mary clenched her spare hand, which had begun to shake. She knew Dr Schubert was trying to sound reassuring, but her brain was convincing her to prepare for the worst. *Prepare for the worst, hope for the best.* It was one of the quotes she'd only recently pinned to her Pinterest board. But thinking of it only made her feel ill. It was a tumour. Even though he hadn't used that word, she knew. She just knew. The lawn mower whirring next door began to grate on her nerves. She hadn't noticed it until now; it seemed someone had turned the volume up on everything.

'Mary, please don't overthink this. You're going to be fine.'

Mary nodded, even though the words didn't calm her. He didn't know that for sure. If he did, she wouldn't need a biopsy. No, he was saying those words to make her feel better. But they didn't.

'Of course.' Mary concentrated on keeping the waver out of her voice as the first pinpricks of tears itched at the corner of her eyes. Dr Schubert had been her doctor for years. Delivered both her children and helped her through menopause. She trusted him implicitly. But still, she didn't want to hear anymore. Instead, she had an overwhelming urge to hang the phone up without saying goodbye.

'I'll have my receptionist confer with Otway Health for an appointment and let you know when it is. And I'll be in touch as soon as we have the results.'

'Thank you, Dr Schubert.'

Mary sat on the bed, cradling her phone. A biopsy. A lump. Her mind raced forward to losing her hair and days in bed recovering from chemotherapy. How would she tell David? Who would help Lucy with the kids? And she didn't want to burden Emily and poor Hayley. Feeling like they had to look after her. Mary shuddered in a deep breath and wiped at her cheeks. No. She had to pull herself together. Like Dr Schubert said, it was probably nothing. She sent a quick group message to her book club about Emily's presentation and convinced herself everything would be fine. She'd have the stupid biopsy without anyone knowing. What would be the point in worrying everyone? It was going to be nothing.

CHAPTER TWENTY-SIX

'So, the first item of business is the marquee layout,' Lucy announced at the committee meeting. I was sure she could feel my eyes burning into her soul. The one thing she'd neglected to tell me about being on the committee was that Simon was also a member. If I'd known, there was no way I would've agreed.

'Simon? You've finished the layout for the stallholders?'

'Sure have. Here's a copy for everyone.' He handed a copy to the six of us sitting at the table. I took mine without meeting his eyes.

'I think it gives everyone enough space, and I've put the food vendors together and the crafts and everything else down the other end. Then we have the space in the middle of the park for the tables and chairs and the band and dancefloor as per usual. I don't think I've missed anyone.'

'This looks great, Simon,' Verity, one of the committee members, I think she was the secretary, said. 'Yes, perfect. Motion to accept.'

Everyone raised their hands.

'Fabulous.' Verity shuffled through the papers. 'I'll email a copy to all the vendors and stall holders.'

The meeting continued for another fifteen minutes, discussing agenda items such as insurance, temporary fencing, and Facebook marketing. They didn't need another committee member; with the festival only a matter of weeks away, everything seemed under control.

'And, to the last item of business, unfortunately, the celebrity chef Sandy had lined up has pulled out as he's been offered a job overseas.'

'Can he do that? I mean, don't we have contracts in place?' This from Tony, an older guy with the longest eyelashes I've ever seen.

'Technically, no, but I don't think we want to be "that festival" that's not accommodating to extraneous circumstances.'

There was a consensus of nodding around the table.

'So, what now?' Simon asked.

'Well, maybe Emily has some suggestions.' Lucy turned to me. 'Do you have any contacts within the industry through your PR role?'

Simon scoffed. Not loud enough for everyone to notice, but I did. I shifted in my seat as all eyes were on me. 'Ah, well. No, not personally.'

'Maybe one of your colleagues has contacts?' Lucy continued. 'All they have to judge is the best snapper dish. They don't even have to cook if they don't want to. Of course, all the other judges have had their own stall and cooked up a fancy snapper dish, but I suppose they don't have to. We have a room at the motel booked and a small budget for travel costs and time.'

'What do you classify as a small budget?' I didn't think the Snapper Fest budget would extend too much.

'Fifteen hundred dollars.'

'Are you kidding? You expect to score a celebrity chef judge for a measly fifteen hundred dollars?'

'Last year, well, before Covid, we had Gabriele Bisset, and the year before that, Andre Grotto.' Tony folded his arms across his chest most defiantly. 'They were more than happy with that amount and our hospitality, I might add.'

I had never heard of either of those so-called 'celebrity' chefs but imagined they were more celebrity in their own minds than in reality.

'Go on, Emily, with all your PR connections I'm sure you could source someone. And, you have plenty of time on your hands,' Simon added.

I shifted uncomfortably in my seat. Why was Simon being like this? And why the hell was Lucy throwing me in the deep end? I was being attacked at all angles.

'I suppose we might be able to stretch the budget a little.' Verity tapped away on her iPad. 'Maybe a couple of hundred extra.'

Lucy nodded. 'We could manage that.'

'You're not in the city anymore,' Simon added.

What was he playing at? Was he upset at me after what happened with Fred? 'What's that supposed to mean?' I turned to Simon.

'It's not supposed to mean anything other than you might be used to throwing around money and "celebrities"'—he motioned air quotes around the word—'but here we're about what's important ... people.'

Lucy cleared her throat, clearly sensing the tension between Simon and me. She took control. 'So, Emily, what do you say?'

I turned away from Simon, unable to marry his words with the look of contempt he was displaying. The fridge motor kicked over the silence, prompting me to reply. 'Well, there is someone who might be interested.'

'Who do you have in mind?' Eva (the last committee member) had a twinkle in her eye, eager for celebrity gossip.

'Well, this person has had bad press in the last twelve months, fall from grace sort of thing, so they might be open to some good PR. I could frame it as doing a community service and helping out for the love of food and community. Back to his roots, kind of thing.'

'Who is it?' Eva leant forward in her chair.

'I'm not making any promises ... but Oliver Barnard.'

Eva's eyes widened to dinner plate size. 'Get out!' she said, reminding me of Elaine from *Seinfeld*.

'Who is Oliver Barnard?' Lucy's brows pinched together.

'You know that judge on the TV show *Show Me the Food!*' Eva looked like she was going to wet her pants; she was that excited.

'Oh, yes. He is rather handsome, with those big blue eyes and curly brown hair that flops over his ears.' A blush crossed Verity's cheeks. 'He always wears the top button of his shirt undone and has that little sprinkling of hair poking out.'

'Didn't he get kicked off the show because he was secretly banging a contestant, and then one of the chefs at his Melbourne restaurant accused him of not paying overtime for three years?' Tony piped up.

Tony didn't strike me as the reality TV type, but whatever floats your boat. 'Yep, that's the one!'

'You really think you can get him?' Eva was still on the edge of her seat.

'I can't promise anything, but maybe.' It was a possibility. A long shot, but a possibility. 'Maddy, his publicist, owes me a favour.'

'If you can keep your promise.' Again, Simon's snide remark was meant only for me, but instead of pissing me off, it gave me the urge to make sure I fulfilled this. Maddy owed me a favour, and I'd make sure she'd pull through—at the very least, just to annoy Simon.

'If you pull this off, I will owe you forever!' Lucy beamed in an unusual show of emotion.

I returned the smile. And having Lucy indebted to me forever would also be a great motivator.

THANKFULLY, after another half hour of discussion and debate on the finer details of the event, the meeting ended, and I said my good-byes with a to-do list on my phone's note app.

'Emily?'

It was that familiar voice again. Our eyes met over the top of my car.

'What do you want, Simon?' I stopped, keys in hand. 'Got some more snide remarks to make?'

'Not snide. Just truth.'

I shook my head and opened the door, but Simon wasn't done.

'Just don't ruin it. Snapper Fest is a big deal around here. It might seem like a fun little time filler for you to be on this committee and throw your weight around with celebrity offerings, but these people matter. This town matters. It's time you started treating things seriously and growing up.'

'Are you kidding? Growing up? I'm not the one who's been acting as if I was the town enemy. And felt the need to lie to me about your girlfriend.' I wrapped air quotes around the word. 'You know what? I was trying to be civil and put everything behind us, like adults. But clearly, I'm not the one who needs to grow up here.'

I stormed into the car, slammed the door, started the engine, and threw it into reverse. My eyes darted to Simon visible in the rear-view mirror, standing there dumbfounded.

It wasn't until I got home that I realised how much I was shaking.

CHAPTER TWENTY-SEVEN

The alarm buzzed and groaned as I rolled over to shut it off. These early morning running and yoga commitments were a drag. I think I'd taken the reinvention of Emily Brown a level too far. Forcing myself from the bed, eyes still half shut, I pulled on my sneakers, threw my hair into a loose ponytail, and willed my body to a state of wakefulness. As my feet pounded the bitumen, my legs screamed with every stride. My mind, though, had woken and was now reminding me of the encounter with Simon from yesterday. What a pompous pig he'd been! Here I was trying to put things behind us and he was now acting like a two-year old.

The anger in my stomach motivated me to run faster as I wondered what I ever saw in him. Yeah, things had been awkward between us. Understandably so, but I thought after the reunion, we might've said all that needed to be said and could move on. Especially when he'd helped me with Fred. Instead, he was being a real dick about things. For no reason. Well, I suppose he had a reason, but ... Urgh! He made me so mad.

Along the esplanade I slowed to a walk in order to catch my breath and let my flaming red cheeks calm before I reached yoga. My phone buzzed against my leg and I slipped it out of the pocket. It was Anthony. I paused to read the message.

'Offer in. $1.1 mil. All furnishings too. Call me.'

I stopped and stared at the number. That would only just cover the mortgage. My chest tightened and I steadied myself on the bus stop shelter. Everything we'd ever worked for. Gone. Just like that. I closed my eyes and focused on my breathing.

'You alright, love?'

My eyes sprang open to a burly guy with a newspaper under his arm standing in front of me. I turned on a huge smile.

'Yeah. Just ran too hard.' I forced a smile.

He let out a belly-laugh. 'That's why I don't run. Could kill ya!' And he strode off.

I looked back at the phone in my hand and tapped out a message. 'We have to take it.'

The reply was instant, as if Anthony had been waiting. 'Okay. I'll get it done.'

I pressed the two side buttons to turn my phone off and instantly my body eased. It was a strange mix of emotions. Shame, regret, anger, but most of all relief. Like the first glimpse of light over the horizon. I slid the phone back into my pocket.

By the time I reached the green overlooking the beach, Connie was calling everyone to their mats. Decked out in a pale, pink-coloured matching crop top-legging combo that made her look like a musk stick—a seriously good-looking musk stick—Connie motioned to a mat for me before addressing the class.

Forty minutes later, and after twisting into positions I never thought possible, I was amazed at how much better I felt compared to when I first arrived. Zen even.

'You're really getting the hang of this.' Connie wiped the sheen of sweat from her brow.

'I'm not sure about that,' I replied. 'I'm amazed my body hasn't snapped in two, to be honest.'

'Up for a walk, to stretch out the kinks then?'

The breeze had picked up, and a walk sounded blissful compared to my original plan of running home. 'Sure.'

'So, how's things?' Connie asked as we headed to the shoreline and walked towards the jetty.

The cold water was like little knives jabbing at my toes, so I edged slightly towards drier sand. 'You know, getting there.' I sighed. 'Looks like we've sold the house.'

Connie smiled. 'That's great! I mean, it is, right?'

I shrugged. 'Yeah. Hopefully it will cover all our debts but, yeah, it is what it is.'

'I'm so sorry, Em. I can't imagine how tough this is for you.'

My feet sank into the wet sand as the low tide lapped at shore. 'I still battle daily with whether I've made the right decision staying here. Not that I have a choice at the moment, but still. Hayley isn't adapting. You know she got kicked out of class the other day?'

'What for?'

'Arguing with the teacher about the appropriateness of Romeo and Juliet being taught in today's schools.'

'Shakespeare is classic literature. Very important,' Connie said with purpose, before adding, 'Although I get it. I didn't appreciate it when I was fifteen either.'

'Yeah, well ... anyway, so she's pushing boundaries. And I still think Anthony believes we'll start over when everything's sorted.'

'And you won't?'

For the first time since this shitstorm started, I was clear and determined. I shook my head. 'I'm sure of one thing; I can't go back to that life.' The more I said it, the more I'd believe it, right?

'Why do you have to? I was like you when I first came back. I never thought I'd adjust to living the slower life, especially here in the Bay, but after a while, you realise how much calmer you feel, and you slip into the lifestyle and wonder why you didn't do it sooner. I'm so much happier.'

I was dubious, especially after the incident with Simon, but I had to credit Connie for how much she loved life after years in the corporate world and breaking up with her toxic ex.

'How is your mum?' I asked, steering the conversation away from myself.

Connie's dad left when she was younger, and it had always been her and her mum; they were very close. It surprised me when she high-footed it to Sydney after school finished.

'She's ...' Connie's expression saddened and she sucked in her bottom lip as if she was about to cry.

I stopped walking and put my hand on her arm. 'What is it?'

'I think Mum ... I don't know ... she might have early onset dementia.'

'Oh, Connie. I'm so sorry.' I wrapped my arms around her.

After a moment, she pulled back and wiped her eyes. 'It started with her memory going, just short-term things. Like conversations we'd had or appointments she'd made and then forgotten about.' We began walking again. 'And then she stopped volunteering at the food bank, which she's done for years. I think she'd become embarrassed not remembering things and faces, which is why she stopped. Then Jill, her best friend, called me a couple of weeks ago saying she'd had a conversation with Mum, and it was like it was twenty years ago. She was talking about me moving to Sydney.'

'Oh, Con. Has she been to see a doctor?'

'That's the thing. She's refusing to see anyone. But I'm going to have to make an appointment for her and get Jill to help me get her there under false pretences or something. I'm worried about her. She's on her own, and I'm here.'

'Would she ever move back to the Bay?'

Connie shook her head. 'Nope. She loves her little apartment, and I don't think a big upheaval would help. She'd be more confused. Jill's checking on her daily, but I feel so hopeless. With the shop and everything, it's hard for me to get away.'

We'd reached the jetty and turned around as a rambunctious border collie bounded towards us, sidestepping at the last minute.

'Banjo!' the owner yelled, jogging past. 'Sorry.'

'Is there someone that can look after the bookshop for you?' I asked as we headed back towards the car park. 'You know, so you could spend time with her and figure things out.'

'I've been closing on Wednesdays to visit her. I mean, it's not like I'm hectically busy, but I have my regulars, and the local art groups get their supplies through me, too. I couldn't manage if I closed the store for another day, but no one would want a day or two of work. It's not like it's great money. Or even that riveting if you're not into books or art.' Connie stopped walking and turned towards me, her eyes wide. 'I know ... What about you?'

'Me?'

'You need a job, right? I need someone to look after the shop. Even if it were to cover my Wednesday and half of Thursday so I can spend the night with Mum. You'd be perfect! You're into art—'

'Was,' I corrected her. 'I haven't painted since high school.'

'But you still have all that knowledge! And you were really good. What do you say?' Connie's eyes were bright, buoyed by the prospect.

'Um ... I ...'

'It's fine.' She shook her head and waved me away. 'This isn't your problem, and you need more hours anyway. I'll figure something out.'

No, it wasn't my problem, but Connie was my friend, and there was no way I would let a friend down when I could help.

'Of course I'll do it. It'll be fun. Maybe I'll even take up painting again.' I smiled excitedly, and an unexpected quiver jolted through me.

'Really?' Relief washed across Connie's face. 'Are you sure?'

'One hundred percent.'

She threw her arms around me. 'Em! Thank you so much. It'll

give me a chance to spend a night each week with Mum and make sure she's okay. Help her with things. Get her to appointments and get to the bottom of it.'

A thought crossed my mind. 'What about your ex? Are you okay with being back there and him finding out?'

Connie shook her head. 'I don't know for sure, but hopefully he's moved on. It's Mum that matters now anyway.'

I nodded and squeezed Connie's hand. 'I'm here for whatever you need.'

AN HOUR LATER, I walked out of the bookshop with a tote bag of books and a new job. And, although the pay rate wasn't great, all I had to do was watch the shop, dust the shelves, unpack a few books now and again, and top up the art supplies from the stock out the back. It was better than nothing. It meant I could slowly pay Fred's vet bill, finally afford a coffee, and of course pay my way at Mum and Dad's a bit more. And, to be honest, I was secretly looking forward to reacquainting myself with the smell of oil paints and canvas.

On the way home, I stopped in the park to give my shoulder a break from the weight of the books. I needed to ring Maddy again about Oliver Barnard. I'd left her a message the other day, but she hadn't replied. It wasn't unusual; that was Maddy for you.

'Maddy!' I sat on the wooden bench under a large sheoak and stretched my legs in the sun.

'Hey. Hey, Ems. Soooo sorry I haven't rung you back. You were on my list, promise. Anyway, long time no hear! I've been under the pump here. So much going on. What are you up to?'

'Oh, you know,' I replied. 'This and that?'

'And why on earth didn't you tell me you'd quit?' Maddy added quickly. She was like an Energizer Bunny. Go, go, go. Barely stopping to breathe, flitting from one thing to another. It was always hard to get a word in edgeways.

'I didn't quit. I got fired.'

'What the? No way! Bloody Megan. Trust her to throw it back on you to make her come off unscathed. Anyway, I've been telling people there's no way you would quit. But you've moved back home, I hear. Curlew Bay, isn't it?'

'Good news travels fast.'

'I can't believe she fired you. She won't last much longer anyway. Apparently, her head's on the table from further up. Or so I hear.'

Listening to Maddy, I was surprised I didn't have a pang for my old life. In fact, I was secretly smiling inside knowing I didn't have to deal with that crap anymore. Although, I did miss the gossip. Just a little.

'Anyway, I haven't got long,' Maddy continued. 'I need to ask you a favour.'

'Me a favour? I rang you for a favour.'

Maddy let out a lively laugh. 'Oh yeah. Well, you first, then.'

'Well, my sister is organising this Snapper Fest thing in Curlew Bay.'

'Ah-huh. And?'

'Long story short, they have a celebrity chef attend every year, but this year it's fallen through, so Lucy asked if I knew anyone with any contacts and I immediately thought of you and Oliver Barnard.'

'Bloody Oliver. He's doing my head in right now. He should seriously stick to cooking and get someone to run the business side of things. And keep his bloody dick in his pants.'

I giggled. I didn't want to know.

'So, you reckon Oliver for this gig?'

'That's what I was thinking.' I waved to a mother who followed a little boy into the park, making a beeline for the swings.

'Mmmm, it could work. He could do with some good publicity. At the rate he's travelling, I'm almost ready to dump him.'

'Well, this could be his opportunity.'

'And you're willing to take the risk?'

'Come on Mads. If anyone can keep him in line, it's you. All he has to do is turn up, pick the best-looking snapper winner, and cook it. Surely he can't get into too much trouble doing that?'

'You'd be surprised. But, yep. Okay. What's on offer?'

The million-dollar (or lack thereof) question. 'That's the thing. Their budget isn't much.'

'Three, four kay?'

'More like two. Maybe a bit less.'

'Bloody hell, Ems. He wouldn't pull on his boxer shorts for that. But you know what? I'm not gonna give him a choice. This could be just the thing to get him back in people's good books. Community service and all that. Mingling with the people. And, I'll tell him he has to do it or find a new publicist and believe me, there won't be anyone jumping up to take him on at the moment. Leave it with me.'

'Really? You're a lifesaver.'

'Don't speak too soon. My turn now.'

'Of course. Anything.'

'It's funny; my favour involves Curlew Bay too.'

'You're kidding? How?'

'You know the proposed development of the foreshore?'

'Yep. Not getting a great response down here.'

'Exactly. The thing is, my brother works for the developer, and they're keen to get it through. It's a huge contract, and they need it. If you know what I mean. He asked if I could find someone to help throw some good spin on it, you know, to convince the locals.'

'Mmmm. I don't know—'

'Of course, I can't do it, too close and all that, but then I thought of you.'

'Me?' I knew what was coming.

'Yep. It'd be perfect. All you have to do is come up with some positives, present them at the council meeting and that's it. As long as it looks like you've come up with some great points and tried and sway the councillors, that's all you have to do. It's different from what you're used to, of course, but if anyone can do it, you can with your smarts. They're offering five grand. And your fee isn't dependent on the outcome. Even if council doesn't give it the green light, you get paid. I mean, they'll appeal and probably use you again at the tribunal hearing; anyway, it's a win-win!'

Five thousand dollars?

'I know what you're thinking; what do you know about development shit—'

Okay, not exactly, but ...

'It's their last-ditch effort. They know things aren't looking good, but the development meets all the regulations and everything, and they reckon with a bit of good press and especially from a local like you—'

'I haven't been a local for years—'

'You have family there, close enough. Come on, Ems, it's easy cabbage.'

'Oh, Mads, I don't know.' Simon's comment from yesterday revisited me, '...these people matter. This town matters.' and made me feel uneasy inside.

'Look, I'll give you a few days to mull it over, okay?'

'Okay.'

'But you know I won't take no for an answer!' Maddy laughed. 'Look, gotta scoot; I'll get onto Oliver. Lock it in. Text me the deets, and I'll make it happen. I'll call you in a few days. Cheers.'

And just like the Maddy whirlwind, she was gone.

Five thousand dollars. The figure snagged in my head. That could get me and Hayley a place of our own. Bond, rent in advance for a few months at least. Plenty enough to get us set up. And pay that vet bill in one fell swoop.

A boy on the swing glided through the air, a huge grin on his face, the blue sky silhouetting him. Not a care in the world. Life was so much simpler here; that was why people stayed. They didn't want the hustle and bustle of a city life or the influx of tourists that a development like this would bring. Could I really try and convince them otherwise? Did I want to? But five grand? And then there was Lucy on the council, would she be for this? The little boy jumped off the swing as it passed the ground with a big leap and squeal of joy. Nope. I couldn't do it. At least I had a few days to figure out how to tell Maddy.

CHAPTER TWENTY-EIGHT

Thursday brought blue skies with only a whisper of white clouds and the perfect opportunity for Mary to bring her cup of tea and magazine into the garden and sit on the wooden bench seat in the sunshine. David wasn't due back from golf for another half hour or so, and she'd already organised the finger food for tonight's book club, making sure she set aside some homemade sausage rolls for David. All she had left for the day was to make a lasagne for Lucy for the scout meeting they had tonight.

Mary loosened her scarf around her neck as the sun warmed her face and opened up the latest *Better Homes and Gardens* and flicked through the first few pages until she found the section titled '7 laundry renovations that will make you want to do the washing'. She didn't imagine anyone would ever *want* to do the washing—including herself—but her laundry room could do with a makeover. The stainless steel trough was dull and scratched, and the laminated bench top was chipped in places, not that she knew how that had happened. Nonetheless, she'd love a new bench top, maybe some shelving, and one of those fancy accordion drying racks would be nice. And a new laundry basket, maybe one of those linen lined wicker ones to tie it all in, possibly some new taps? Probably new tiles while she was at it. All she needed was some inspiration for designs and colour schemes.

Taking a sip of her tea, she perused the first renovation with white subway tiles, timber bench tops, and a charcoal linen basket. It was a little too clinical. The next one was more her style. Sage green cabinetry, white benches, wicker baskets, and one of those American-farm style laundry troughs that sat prominently out from the cabinetry which she'd always admired.

Mary took another sip of tea and her mind snagged. What was the point of doing the laundry? What if she wasn't even around to enjoy the makeover? Doctor Schubert's rooms had rung earlier to tell her the date for the biopsy. Another trip to Apollo Bay, but not for two weeks. Two weeks? Shouldn't she be a priority patient? How much could cancer spread in two weeks? It could be the difference ... Mary stopped herself. She wasn't ready to die. She couldn't leave David, Lucy, and the kids. And Emily needed her more than ever. Whatever would they do? And she had so much she still wanted to do with her life. Much more than the laundry. She brushed away a tear, but still, her mind raced, hurtling back to her conversation with Susan and the discussion about travelling to the Northern Territory.

Mary had surprised herself by how interested she was in Susan's ramblings the other week. She'd even contemplated how wonderful the camping option could be. Getting close to nature, but not too close. Glamping, she could manage. Could she and David do that? Maybe. She swallowed. No, she didn't have time for that dreaded C word or ... or worse.

'Great day for it, love.'

David's voice startled Mary so much that she spilled the last of her tea on the open magazine. She quickly put the cup down and brushed away the spots of tea now staining her coveted laundry trough.

'Sorry, love. Didn't mean to sneak up on you.' David chuckled as he sat down next to her giving her a quick peck on the cheek. Mary remembered her tears and was glad David hadn't noticed. 'I didn't hear you come in. How was golf?'

'Mmmm. Not so good today. Three bogeys. Shoulder's a bit stiff.' He rolled his shoulder as if relieving tension.

Mary didn't know much about golf, but she knew a bogey was something about being over par which wasn't good.

'The beer was cold, though.'

Mary tried to brave a smile, but seeing David's and his gentle grey eyes made her well up again.

'You alright?' David asked, turning his body towards Mary.

She shook her head. 'Oh, I'm fine.' Mary leaned and placed her teacup onto the stone table beside her, still clutching the magazine.

'You're not fine. You've been out of sorts all week. What is it?'

It was hard to hide things from David, that wasn't how their relationship worked. They'd always shared things, even if David was a man of few words most of the time. But, honesty had always been the strong foundation of their marriage. Mary was torn between wanting to ignore it all and soldiering on, telling David, and sobbing.

'Mary?'

'It's ... I ...' Mary tried to wrap her tongue around the words to say out loud. Susan had been the only person she'd told, and that was before she knew she needed a biopsy. But telling David? Her hands clenched at the corner of the magazine. 'I have to have a biopsy.'

'A biopsy? What for?' David's eyebrows rose into an inverted V above his nose, his face etched with worry. 'Dr Schubert found something in my breast, and I had an MRI, and now I need a biopsy.'

'A lump?'

'Not a lump, an abnormality. That's what Dr Schubert said. An abnormality.'

David reached his hand over and cupped Mary's which clung to the magazine. 'Oh, love.'

'It's probably nothing. He said it's probably nothing, but he wants to be sure,' Mary replied quickly to quell David's worries. 'But I ... I can't help but ... I'm worried, David.'

David's mouth twitched like it did when he didn't know what to say. 'When?'

'Two weeks.'

David let out a sigh, and the washing on the clothesline flapped in the breeze. Mary squeezed David's hand back, her chest tight.

'No use worrying about it, really. Not until ...' Mary trailed off.

'Yes. You're right. We can cross that bridge when we come to it.' He stroked the back of her hand with his thumb.

Mary did feel better telling him. David was a man of few words. It was his gestures that said the most. 'Right, well, Lucy will be here any minute to drop off the groceries. She's on her lunch break.' She got up and collected her teacup and magazine.

'You sure you're okay, Mare?'

'I am. Just need to keep busy.'

A FEW MOMENTS LATER, Lucy arrived through the front door in a flurry, hands laden with two paper shopping bags. 'Hi, Mum,' she bellowed as Mary put her teacup in the sink. 'Here's the ingredients for the lasagne.' Lucy unpacked pasta sheets, tomatoes, cheese, and mince from the shopping bags. 'They didn't have a mixed mince, and I didn't have time to call by the butcher, so it's just beef.'

'Mmmm. Lasagne for dinner?' Emily appeared from the lounge room.

'No, not for you. Mum's making it for our scout meeting tonight.'

'Why couldn't you just make it?' Emily screwed up her nose.

Lucy scowled back. 'Because I'm busy.'

Mary listened as her daughters bickered yet again. 'Please, will you just ...' Her voice came out harsher and louder than expected.

Loud enough to silence them both. Mary's eyes betrayed her yet again.

'Mum?' Emily said, with knitted brows.

Lucy too, questioned her. 'Mum? What is it?'

'It's nothing.'

'It must be something,' Lucy said, placing her palms on the bench and leaning forward. 'What is it?'

The back door opened, and David entered. 'It's nothing. Leave your mother be.'

The gruff but concerned tone of David's voice undid Mary. Her hand shot to her mouth as she tried to swallow a sob. Lucy and Emily both moved towards her, bumping into each other as they did.

'Hang on!' David held his hands up and pushed through to Mary first, placing his hand on her arm. 'You should tell them, love,' he whispered.

Mary's eyes dipped to the floor; she didn't want to tell them like this. She didn't want to tell them at all, but now look what she'd gone and done.

'What is it?' Emily asked again.

David cast his arm back over Mary's shoulders, pulling her to his side. 'It'll be fine, Mare.'

'For God's sake! Will someone please tell me what's going on?' Lucy threw her hands in the air.

'I have to have a biopsy.' Mary rushed the words as if saying them at speed would make less of an impact.

'A biopsy?' Emily questioned.

'What?' Lucy's voice was a bare whisper.

'Don't you all go and get bothered about something that might be nothing,' David said with an authoritative tone.

'I have a lump.' Mary shrugged out of David's arms. He was trying to reassure her, but right now, she didn't want anyone to touch her. She reached for the chopping board and then pulled out a knife from the knife block before beginning to chop the tomatoes

Lucy had bought. 'Well, not a lump. A something. An abnormality. In my breast.' She cut the tomato with a little too much force and ended up squashing it, tomato juice and seeds squirting onto her jumper.

'Do they ...' Lucy began, sitting down slowly at the table. She didn't finish the question, but Mary knew what she was going to ask.

'Dr Schubert said the scan was inconclusive, so they want to take a bit and test it,' Mary said, patting at her jumper with a paper towel.

'It's probably not anything to worry about.' David joined Mary in the kitchen, taking over chopping the tomatoes. 'Let's just wait and see.'

'Exactly.' Mary plastered a fake smile on her face. 'No use worrying about things, right? Like I always say, worry is like a rocking chair; it gives you something to do but gets you nowhere.'

The room was silent.

'Now'—Mary turned to face Lucy— 'what time did will you be back for the lasagne?'

'It's fine, Mum. Don't worry about it.'

'I can do it.' Emily stepped forward, determination in her eyes.

'Don't be silly. All of you.' She took the knife from David and returned to chopping. 'I'm not dead yet,' she quipped, but the joke fell flat.

CHAPTER TWENTY-NINE

I'd offered to drop the lasagne Mum had made—no, she didn't let me help, although I did hang about and annoyed her by making light conversation—over to Lucy's.

'Knock, knock!' I tapped my foot on the front door, my hands full with one of the biggest lasagnes ever seen.

'Come in,' Lucy's voice bellowed from within.

'I actually can't!' I sang back. 'Hands full.'

A moment later, the front door flung open. Ethan flashed past and disappeared around the corner at lightning speed.

'Slow down in the house!' Lucy called out, followed by 'Oh, thanks,' as I plonked the baking dish onto the kitchen bench. The kitchen was littered with the detritus of life. School bags and shoes were on the floor. The drying rack on the sink was piled with clean dishes longing to be put away. Lucy was frantically tossing together a green salad amongst matchbox cars, crayons, empty coffee cups and, weirdly, a car battery.

'Are you feeding a whole footy team or something?'

'It's Ethan's scout break-up tonight, and we're on mains.' Lucy piled the salad into a large Tupperware container. 'Well, Gordon is on mains. Scouts are his domain, but you know, it all falls to me.'

'And what's with the battery?' I nodded towards the black box on the counter edge.

'Gordon's car battery died.' She rolled her eyes. 'I have no idea why it's on the bench.'

Lucy was still in her work clothes. A slightly rumpled navy pant suit. Hair unusually out of place. A smudge of mascara under her eyes.

'And, I've got a meeting at council'—Lucy looked at her watch—'in approximately seventeen minutes.'

'Want me to do anything?' Part of me was enjoying seeing Lucy in this flustered, dishevelled state. She'd dropped the ball a little since I was here last.

'Could you? Chloe doesn't want to go to the scout thing. Do you think maybe you could take her back to Mum's? She could hang out with Hayley. I could pick her up after my meeting?'

'Muuuumm.' Chloe's whining voice rang from down the hall-way. 'Do I have to goooooo?' Chloe appeared at the door in her pyjamas. 'Hi, Aunty Emily! Look, Mum, I'm in my PJs already. I seriously can't go in my PJs!'

'Lucky for you Aunty Emily will take you back to Grandma's. You can hang with Hayley.'

Chloe's face erupted into a huge smile, and she fist pumped. 'Yaaass,' then thew her arms around me.

Gordon was next to appear, pulling on a jumper over slightly wet hair. 'Oh, hiya Em. How's things? Come on, Ethan! We'll be late!'

'Good. Things are hectic here.' I stepped back to get out of the way, resting my butt on a stool.

'Always the same.'

'Here's the lasagne and the salad. Make sure the container and baking dish come back. Especially the dish. It's Mum's.' Lucy pushed them towards Gordon. 'And can you get rid of that battery?'

'I'll do it when I get home.' Gordon collected the food, stuffed his wallet in his pocket, and called out to Ethan again, who came running dressed in his navy scout uniform and hat.

'Let's go!'

'Well, that was a whirlwind.' With two fewer people in the kitchen, I edged off the stool. 'You ready, miss?'

'Can I bring my magic kit to show Hayley?'

'Course you can.'

Chloe ran towards the bedroom, and Lucy grabbed her handbag off the bench before turning to me with a small smile. 'Thanks, Em.'

I shrugged. 'Sure.'

'How's Mum?'

'She seems fine. Acting like normal after today.'

Lucy shook her head. 'I just don't know what to think. It's out of the blue.'

'She told me she had a mammogram a few months ago, and then the doctor called to schedule an MRI as there was an inconsistency.' I tapped the bench. 'I hope it's nothing.'

'God, me too. I just can't ...' Lucy shook her head.

'She does a lot for you.'

Lucy's head jutted back in defence. 'What's that supposed to mean?'

'Nothing. Just ... maybe she needs a bit of a break.'

'Typical of you.'

'What?'

Lucy flicked her hand above her head. 'All judgemental. Mum offers to do this stuff. And if I want anything done, I ask. She can say no. But it gives her something to do. What else would she be doing? Sitting at home? She'd be bored.'

'No need to be defensive. I was just saying. Maybe she wants to do her own thing. Maybe she feels like she can't say no.'

Lucy stiffened. 'I bet you haven't lifted a finger since lobbing up on her doorstep!' she snapped before her shoulders dropped, and she quickly added, 'I'm sorry, Em.' She blew out a breath. 'Things are just ... crazy at the moment.'

'Is everything okay?'

'Here it is!' Chloe appeared with a black velvet box and top hat.

'Awesome! Go jump in the car. I'll be out in a tick.'

'Luce?'

'It's fine.' Lucy picked up the toy cars from the bench and threw them into a plastic tub on the floor. 'There's just a lot going on right now. Juggling council and the shop, and Gordon's flat out at work.' She sighed. 'It's fine. Thanks for taking Clo.'

'If you need a hand, I'll help you know. Not that you'd ask, but ...' I shrugged.

Lucy adjusted her bag on her shoulder as we walked to the door. 'Call me when you win the lotto.'

ON THE DRIVE BACK HOME, Chloe chatted endlessly about all the magic tricks she was going to show us, but my mind was elsewhere. I couldn't shake the feeling Lucy was hiding something. Or maybe it was just the shock of everything with Mum. Or maybe it was just Lucy being Lucy.

CHAPTER THIRTY

'It's not too late to cancel, Mum?' I glanced at my watch as I finished setting up my Maisy May display. 'It's still only half past seven.'

'Of course not. It'll get my mind off things,' Mum replied, carrying another dining chair into the lounge room. 'Besides, I've been looking forward to this all week. I'll be your guinea pig. You know, you can give me a facial or something.'

I laughed. 'Of course.' Mum would need more than a facial to make her feel better, but it was the least I could do.

An hour later, I was smiling through the book club discussion of the latest award-winning literary fiction novel.

'Well, I don't know about you, but I struggled to get past the first chapter. All that description about the clouds and the sky! I mean, how many ways is it possible to describe white, wispy clouds?' Liz said, waving around her wineglass.

'About forty, according to this author,' replied Jane.

The room filled with laughter, and I stretched my neck. I suppose I should've read the book. Mum had offered it to me; in fact, it had sat untouched on my bedroom table all week. I nodded along anyway, hoping I wouldn't get asked for my opinion.

'Anyway, enough book chat for now.' Mum rose to her feet. 'As promised, I have a special surprise for you all this week. Emily is going to share with us her new business venture!'

'It's not really a business, Mum—'

'Of course it is, darling. Anyway, over to you.'

I stood up and whipped the pink satin cloth away to unveil the display on the table, knocking over the display signage in the process. It landed with a clunk and cracked the Perspex.

'Okay, well, that wasn't meant to happen.' I fake-laughed, fumbling to set things straight again. The room was eerily silent, and I turned to find nine pairs of eyes staring intently at me in anticipation.

'Right, so ...' I scrambled nervously, searching for the introductory notes I'd memorised. Ah, there they were!

'Okay, remember that peaches and cream glow of youthful skin?' Everyone nodded. 'Well, what if I told you it was possible to regain that fresh-faced, firm, fantastic skin you thought time had stolen?'

'And gravity!' Judy quipped, prompting a raft of giggles.

Thankfully, it broke the ice, and I continued with my spiel. 'Introducing Maisy May Skincare direct from Paris and brand new to Australia. For years the French have known the secret to flawless, glowing skin, but now, thanks to Maisy May, their secret is out.' I passed around different jars and tubes to collective 'oohs and aahs'.

Fifteen minutes later, I'd shown the ladies the core products—cleansers, toners, moisturisers, and masks—and they were all busily making notes on their order forms. It was working! Well, I'll be! Now, it was time for the power product—or so Maisy called it—the amazing YouthGlow serum.

'Now, ladies, if I can have your attention.' The chatter paused, and everyone edged a little further forward on their seats. Wafts of patchouli and vanilla hung in the air.

I presented the small tube of serum in my hands as if it were a rare diamond. 'Don't let size deceive you!'

'Oh, don't worry, love, it's not the size, it's the way you use it.' This from Beth Bright. Yes, *that* Beth Bright, or *Bondage Beth* as I'd nicknamed her in my head. The room dissolved into fits of giggles. They were worse than a roomful of hormonal teens. But I forged on, certain this product would knock their socks off. And open their wallets.

'This, ladies,' I continued, pushing aside the horrifying image of Bondage Beth from my mind, 'is our most prized product. Our YouthGlow serum. One small drop, and when I say small, I mean the size of a pea, on freshly cleansed skin in the morning and your skin will instantly tighten and firm right before your eyes, reducing the appearance of even the deepest wrinkles and diminishing age spots and smoothing uneven skin tone and dark circles. Your skin will glow all day long.'

'Here! I want to try it!' Mum jumped up and sat in the chair we'd set aside for this purpose.

I washed her face with cleanser, warm water, and a waffle cloth. 'You have to buy this waffle cloth, ladies; it is amazing! So smooth, and helps exfoliate all that dry, old skin as you cleanse.' I was fully committed to the role now, almost impressing myself.

'Okay, ladies. As I said, one small drop ...' I squeezed a pea size amount on my palm and showed the ladies. 'That's all you need. And now, this is probably the most important thing to note. You must apply it to clean, dry skin. There can't be any other product residue like creams or make-up on your skin before using the YouthGlow serum; it's very powerful and may be reactive to products until fully absorbed. This is why it's important to apply it in the morning and let it soak into the skin before you apply your moisturiser, suncream, or make-up.' Everyone nodded, wide-eyed.

'Okay,' I turned back to Mum, who had a jar of face cream in her hands. 'You didn't put that on, did you?'

She quickly relidded the jar. 'Oh, no, I ... I was just smelling it.' She returned it to the table. 'They really do smell lovely, don't they?'

'I love the jasmine smell in the hand cream,' Lena replied. 'It reminds me of George. He loved jasmine. I haven't been able to get that jasmine on my fence to flower since ... well ... you know.' A melancholy look crossed her face, and Beth patted her on the knee.

'Okay, so this one small amount will do your entire face.' I dotted the tiny bit of cream over Mum's face. 'Are you sure you didn't put any cream on, Mum?'

She shook her head, and I continued to smooth the cream over her face.

'Okay, so we just dot the cream on with the pads of our ring fingers, then smooth it over very gently. There we go. Now, we just wait a few moments for it to do its magic. It's important at this point to keep your face expressionless for three minutes. You'll begin to notice the skin around the jawline'—I patted Mum's skin softly like I was a pro on the cosmetics counter of David Jones—'under the eyes, the smile lines and the creases between the brown all begin to firm and tighten.' The product did work. I'd tried it myself. And while it wasn't a miracle-sent-from-the-heavens cream, it had improved my skin tone and lessened some of my wrinkles.

Everyone had shuffled forward on their seats in hushed anticipation, all eyes eagerly on Mum's face.

'Is it meant to tingle, darling?' Mum mumbled, trying not to move her mouth.

'A little tingling is fine,' I assured her. 'And sssh, you have to keep your face still.'

'What about burning? Is burning okay? Just here on my cheeks, they feel, well, a little warm.'

I bent down to inspect; Mum's skin was quite red. Then, before my eyes, her cheeks developed an angry red glow. My eyes widened.

'Darling, it really is hurting now.'

'Oh Mary, your face is quite red,' Mrs Jenkins added, her face etched with concern.

'Is it meant to do that, Emily? It doesn't look quite right.' Beth's eyes were wide.

I held my breath. What was happening? This certainly wasn't in the PDFs or the videos. It was supposed to firm the skin and fill the wrinkles right before your eyes, like in the videos. There was nothing about redness.

'You're not allergic to anything, are you, Mum?'

Mum shook her head. 'No, not that I know of.'

And then I froze. 'You didn't put *that* cream on your face, did you?' I pointed to the Active Skin Renewal cream she'd been holding.

'Well, maybe just a little!'

My hands flew to my head. 'Oh my God, Mum! Didn't you hear me say it had to be applied to clean skin? No other products? I asked you!'

'Not really. When did you say that? Ouch! I really need to get this off.' Mum patted her cheeks and then fanned them.

I grabbed her by the arm and hurried her to the bathroom, leaving a hushed murmur of concern in the lounge room. Then, I shoved her head towards the basin, splashed cold water onto her face, and rubbed manically with a face cloth.

'Emily! Em—'

'Close your mouth, Mum! Just let me do this.'

By now, water was splashing over the vanity. Mum's top and my jeans were completely soaked, water pooling on the tiles.

She pushed back from the vanity, water dripping in streams down her face. 'I think that's enough!'

'Here!' I handed her a towel. 'Is it still hurting?'

She covered her face with the towel and muffled a reply. 'No, it's just a little tingly now.'

When she pulled the towel away from her face, my mouth fell open.

'What is it?' Mum turned to look in the mirror.

'Oh my gosh, Emily! What have you done?'

'What have I done? I told you. I was very clear about how important it was to apply this to clean, product-free skin. Otherwise, the ingredients may react with each other.'

We both stared silently at Mum's reflection. She looked like she'd had an allergic reaction to a bee sting. Her eyes squinted above puffy red cheeks glowing like toffee apples. If it wasn't so shocking, it would be hilarious.

'Oh, Mum!' My eyes filled with tears. 'I'm so sorry!'

Mum slowly turned from her hideous reflection and hugged me. 'It's okay, darling, I'm sure the puffiness will go down, and then I'll have that youthful glow, right?'

LATER THAT EVENING, I stared at the pile of Maisy May products I'd thrown into the corner of my room. Needless to say, no one ordered anything. Oh, apart from Beth, who bought a tube of hand cream, I'm sure, just to be polite. I gave her two sample bottles for free. It wasn't like I'd need them anymore. My days as a Maisy May consultant were done and dusted. I considered a lawsuit against them. I mean, if the products can react so badly with each other, how on earth did they get cosmetic approval from the TGA? But that line of thought exhausted me.

As I was chalking the experience up as yet another thing to add to my growing list of failures, there was a soft knock at the door. 'Honey? Can I come in?'

'Yeah.'

Mum opened the door. Her face wasn't as angry red as it was a couple of hours ago. Now, instead, it was glistening with a wet sheen.

'Oh my God! Is your face weeping?'

'Oh no, it's aloe vera gel. It's helping.' Mum waved her hand at me and sat on the end of the bed. 'I'm sure it will be fine by morning.' There was a waver of unsureness in her voice.

'I'm so sorry, Mum.'

'Don't be silly, darling. It was my fault. As you said, I should've told you I put that cream on. I don't even remember doing it, really; it was only a tiny bit ...'

'It's all a load of rubbish anyway. Overpriced rubbish that smells good.'

'You tried your best. That's what matters. I tried to get everyone to buy something, at least one item. Maybe not the YouthGlow, but something. But, well, you know ...'

'It's fine, Mum. Really. I just ... I just wanted to make some more money. You don't know how hard it is to save while I'm still paying off bills I thought were taken care of, and then there's all the stress with the house.' I covered my eyes. 'Oh God. How did things get this bad?' It was a rhetorical question. One that had been on constant repeat in my head for weeks now.

'Things will work out. They always do.' Mum patted my leg; what a selfish, self-centred cow I was being. Here I was, worrying about my stuff and Mum was possibly facing a battle *for* her life.

'Oh God. I'm sorry. You've got enough to worry about without worrying about me. Are you okay? I wish there was something I could do.' My eyes filled with tears and I wiped them away with my fingertips.

'I'm fine. Really. I just have to climb each mountain as it presents itself. Like your father said, there's no use worrying about something before you need to.'

'But you must be scared?'

Mum shifted on the bed. 'You know what? I was, but then I got angry, thinking, why me? Then I thought, why not me? I'm strong. I'm not going to let some silly lump beat me.'

'You've always been strong, Mum. I wish I had half your strength.'

'It's okay to put yourself first, you know.'

The words were like sandpaper jarring against my morals.

'It's something I never did. And it's something I regret,' Mum continued with a faraway look.

'But you had a family to look after. Like I've got Hayley to look after. It's what's expected. We do what we have to do.'

'Yes, true. But things are different now. For you. It was expected of me to be the homemaker, and look, I'm not saying I wouldn't choose to do that again. I'd just do it differently. You have that chance.'

'I did have that chance, and I blew it.'

Mum scoffed. 'Hardly. But it's okay to change your mind too. There's no shame in that. In fact, I'd say you're a bigger person for admitting it.'

I bit the inside of my lip. I didn't want to cry. Didn't want to acknowledge she might be right. I wasn't ready. Up until now, I'd been faking it til I made it, in so many ways. Even now, I was faking I could make a life in Curlew Bay work. But I wasn't ready to admit to anything.

'And you know what? Once this, this thing—I'm not going to say the C word—is over and done with. I'm going to change a few things around here.'

'What do you mean?'

'I'm going to put me first too.' Mum's smile broadened, and then she grimaced.

'Oh God, Mum, I'm so sorry!'

'I'm fine. I am. Apart from looking like a soggy sunburnt tomato.' Mum stood up. 'Anyway, you know I said you can stay for as long as you need, and I meant it. Look, honey'—Mum cupped my hand —'you will be fine. Something else will come up, and things will turn around. You'll see. Maybe just stay away from the beauty products.'

CHAPTER THIRTY-ONE

Fred and I walked along the beach towards the inlet. When I say walked, I mean plodded. Fred was dragging his heels today, and he seemed to be limping slightly. I tugged on his lead, and he stopped dead in his tracks. I bent to check out his paws.

'Ah, there we go. That must've been hurting.' I dislodged a prickle stuck between the pads of one of his paws.

'Hey, Emi!'

When I stood up, Simon was waving to me in the distance, trying to catch my attention. Great. Just what I needed, another encounter like the committee meeting.

I gave a small wave and was about to turn back towards Doreen's when Simon began jogging towards me, clutching his camera to stop it from swaying around his neck. I stopped. *Take a deep breath. And don't be defensive.*

'I thought it was you.' Simon leant down and patted Fred on the head. 'G'day mate, good to see you're not swimming today.'

I ignored the barb. And Simon kept patting Fred's head for the longest of times. I think even Fred was getting annoyed about it from the way he kept eyeing me.

After an eternity, Simon stood up, his eyes still on Fred, his hands wrapped around his camera. 'I'm sorry about the other day. You're right. I was being ... a prick.' He looked at me, his eyes full of remorse. 'I'm sorry.'

'It's—' I held my hand up, palm out, and shook my head. 'It's fine. Let's just forget it all.' I really did want to forget it all. Try and be ... friends.

Simon nodded. 'You're right. Done. Forgotten.' He waved a hand in a strike-out fashion.

'Taking photos?' I asked to lighten the mood.

Simon held up his camera. 'Yeah, the curlews.' He pointed to the birds wading in the shallows. 'Hang on.'

He crouched down, brought his camera to his face with one hand, and fiddled with the zoom lens with the other. A pair of curlews had stopped and were stabbing their long, curved beaks into the sand. Simon's camera clicked a few times before he stood, tapped the viewfinder of his camera, and held it towards me. The image was surprisingly clear, the curlew in sharp focus, with the sand and water in the background. The image was so crisp I could make out the individual feathers and the beautiful pink tinge to the underside of its long, curved beak. It almost looked like it was posing for the camera. 'Wow! I didn't know you were into photography.'

Simon shrugged. 'I wasn't until I moved back. Dad left me his old Nikon FA. It was one of his prized possessions. I used it a few times and even developed my own photos for a while. But then the bug hit, and I splurged on this.' He held up the camera. 'Digital is so much easier. Dad would probably roll over in his grave, though.' He chuckled.

It felt nice to hear him laugh. Like the old days where we could just ... be.

'You're really invested in these birds, aren't you?' I said.

'I guess I just needed something to take photos of and then I became fascinated by them. We really should've learnt about them at school.'

'Mmmm, I guess. I don't remember if we did or not. All I know is that's why the town is called Curlew Bay—after the birds. And there's the picture on the welcome board coming into town.'

'You know how far these guys fly when they migrate north?' Simon snapped another photo as a group of curlews landed on the flats. 'Over ten thousand kays!'

'Seriously?'

'Yep. They migrate to China and Siberia around March where they breed and feed and then make their way back here this time of year to hang out for the warmer months.'

'Wow!' I was genuinely impressed. 'That is kind of cool.'

'Their internal organs shrivel up for the journey so they can focus all their energy on flying the distance.'

Okay, so that fact was a little weird, but still.

'Sorry.' Simon's cheeks blushed slightly. 'Stupid getting excited over birds.'

'Not at all. More people should know this. How many of them fly down?'

'I'm not sure of the exact numbers, but we know their numbers are dropping rapidly—supposedly have dropped over eighty percent over the past thirty years. They're endangered. Habitats along their migration path are being built on and destroyed. I guess that's why I'm so invested in them.'

Fred let out a bark, and we began walking again.

Simon told me more about the curlews and some other migra-tory birds and how he was now president of the wetlands committee that offered birdwatching and curlew information tours. He snapped more photos, and I was surprisingly interested in the topic. Maybe it was the fact that Simon's passion was infec-tious or just the warmth of the sun rising above the ocean and reaching its rays towards me, but I had a warm, fuzzy feeling of calm that I hadn't felt in such a long time. That I hadn't thought I'd feel next to Simon again. And then, when his hand brushed mine, goosebumps tickled over me. It jolted me into a bundle of nerves.

'I s'pose I'd better get Fred back. Doreen might think I've tried to drown him again.'

'Yeah, sure. I might stay a bit longer. See if I can get some more photos for the newspaper. They promised to do a story for me on how the development will impact the curlews.'

Simon and I stood arm's length in a weird sort of standoff as if we were both waiting for the other to say goodbye first. An energy rippled between us, and just as he was about to speak, a flock of seagulls came into land behind us, breaking the moment.

'Okay, I'll see you at the next committee meeting, I guess.' Simon held his hands out to his side then slapped his palms together, wringing his hands together.

'Yeah. See you then.' I headed back up towards the dunes with Fred trotting along beside me. It was nothing but old feelings. That was all. Feelings long lost and not to be revisited. Fred eyed me sideways. 'Don't give me that look. It's nothing.'

Fred and I cut back to the Esplanade, and my mind was awash with what Simon had said about the curlews. They weren't the prettiest birds with their plain brown plumage, but there was a simplicity about them carrying on their days, not caring if they were the best-looking bird on the shore. A simplicity not unlike Simon. He was like that in high school. Even though he was in the popular group and captain of the footy team, he was never flashy or cocky. He was the quiet one of the group. Until he started showing interest in me, I hadn't thought much about him. He was awkward around me at first, particularly in a group setting. Being a teenager was awkward. There were so many social dos and don'ts to follow. So many moments were walking on a precipice between social acceptance and social suicide. Only when we were alone did I get to know the real

Simon. Caring, soft, funny, and not fussed about what other people were doing.

How we ended things back then wasn't good. So much anger, so many misunderstandings. I should've told him the truth. But how? How could I admit to doing something so stupid and wrecking everything we'd ever had? Ever could have had. I couldn't. I was too embarrassed. The shame etched into my heart had grown over with scar tissue many years ago. There was no point in scratching at it.

I didn't realise I was crying until my cheek itched from the tears. I brushed them away and inhaled the salt air as a heaviness lodged itself behind my ribcage. 'It's ancient history, Fred,' I said aloud. Fred ignored me, as per usual and we continued on, reassuring myself nothing good ever came from reliving history.

CHAPTER THIRTY-TWO

'We'll call you when the book comes in,' I said to Mrs Jenkins, making a note in Connie's order book.

'Thank you, Emily. And say hello to your mum for me.'

It was just after midday and my first shift at BookArt. Connie had run through things with me before she left for Melbourne, and so far the day had gone smoothly. I'd finished unpacking the books that had arrived, contacted the people who'd ordered, and tidied up the oil paints.

I headed back to my easel and canvas Connie had set up by the front window overlooking the esplanade. What looked like a mother's group sat on picnic blankets in the parkland across the road juggling babies in their arms or rocking prams. The beach and ocean sat in the distance against a backdrop of an inky sky with dark clouds lingering on the horizon indicating an afternoon change might be on the way. A few people wandered past the window every now and then running daily errands or exploring the esplanade. Connie was convinced it was a great idea to have me set up in the window with a canvas so people could see a real artist at work. A real artist! I shook my head. As if. The closest I'd been to a real artist was when my year twelve teacher offered to purchase my final assessment piece. It was a piece I'd painted of the jetty, looking straight along it and out to sea, where a pink and orange flamed sun rose against a midnight blue sea. Mum wouldn't let me sell it and used to have it sitting above the mantlepiece in the lounge room, but since she'd 'Shaynna Blaze'd' the living room, it was now in Lucy's old room, now Hayley's. I wondered if she even knew I'd painted it.

I picked up the palate on which I'd spurted blues, yellows, black, and white oil paints and continued with my painting. I hadn't sketched anything. I was taking a more abstract approach. It had been so long since I'd felt the gentle weight of a paintbrush in my hand, so I let muscle memory take over, swirling colours here, blending colours there.

Today's image was beginning to take the form of rolling waves splashing into a stormy, dark sky. They say you paint best when you simply let your mind guide your paintbrush without too much thought. Overthinking kills a painting. I allowed my hand to glide over the canvas, feeling its subtle resistance beneath the brush, the smell of the paints acting like a cleanser purifying my mind. I hadn't felt so calm for years, and it was almost as if I was a child again. Carefree and innocent.

After what felt like a few moments, but was in reality almost forty minutes, I stepped back from the canvas and let the painting come into focus. I added a few gentle splodges of white to the crests of the waves to add depth and texture. It wasn't great—in fact, it was far from great—but it was something. It had been so long since I'd felt such a sense of satisfaction. The bell on the door chimed, and I wiped my hands on my paint-splattered apron. 'Hello,' I called to the woman and young girl entering.

The young girl, who looked around ten years old, ran over to me, wide-eyed. 'Are you an artist?'

'Maya,' the mum called out.

'Hello,' I replied.

'Did you do that?'

'I sure did.'

'Wow!' The little girl's eyes glowed as she studied the painting.

'Don't touch it, sweetie; it still looks wet,' said her mum.

'I've only just finished it. It will take a few days to dry properly.'

'Really?' The little girl looked up at me with a frown as if what I'd said was ridiculous.

'You see'—I held the palate towards her, showing her the oil paints—'these are oil paints, and you layer them on the canvas over each other until you get the look you're after. So, yes, it can take a lot longer to dry than normal watercolours. Do you like to paint?'

'Ah-huh. I love to paint. I have that.' She pointed towards an elaborate watercolour palette and brush set on a nearby shelf.

'She loves painting,' added the mum. 'Much better than TV or iPads.'

'Very much.' I nodded in agreement. 'Maybe one day you could try oil painting.'

'Would you like that, Maya?'

The little girl's eyes brightened. 'Yeah!'

'We have a great little starter kit I could show you. Maybe not to buy today'—I looked up at the mum and smiled—'but when you're ready.' I showed her the set comprising a wooden palette, four oil colours, two paintbrushes, linseed oil, and an A4 pack of canvas paper. 'It's seventy-five dollars so maybe for your birthday or Christmas?'

'Wow!' The little girl's mouth formed a perfect circle as her eyes darted over the pack.

'Maybe we could get it today instead of the book you were after?' Her mum inspected the set, turning it over in her hands.

'Really?'

Her mum nodded, and Maya gave her an enthusiastic hug, arms tight around her waist. 'Thanks, Mum. I'll do the dishes for you tonight, okay?'

I laughed, and a tinge of sadness washed through me. Hayley would throw her arms around me like that when she was younger. It hadn't happened in a while. And the way things were going, it probably wouldn't happen for a long while to come.

'We'll grab this, then. Thanks.' The mum wandered to the counter while Maya disappeared into the junior book section. 'Connie not here today?'

'No, she's with her mum in Melbourne for the day.'

'Oh, that's right. I heard she was unwell. I'm Kate, by the way. We only moved her a few months back, and Connie has been so great getting in books for us and, of course, the art supplies. We love this shop.'

'Curlew Bay's definitely lucky to have a place like this.' I smiled and bagged up the paint set while Kate tapped her credit card. My phone buzzed in my bag, and I made a mental note to check it when they left.

'You don't by chance do art lessons?' Kate nodded towards my painting. 'Maya would love some tips on painting. She's actually quite good. Seems to have a bit of a knack for it.'

'No, it's just a hobby. It's the first time I've picked up a paintbrush in years, actually.'

'Oh, you'd never know it. That painting is amazing. All the textures and swirls, it's like it's moving.'

My cheeks flushed.

'Well, if you know of someone or change your mind, let us know. We're in here all the time, so no doubt I'll run into you again. C'mon, Maya. We'd better go and pick up Matty.'

'Thank you!' Maya sang as she grabbed her parcel.

'Enjoy your painting.' I waved goodbye, and feel-good warmth rushed through me at seeing the joy on the little girl's face. Childhood innocence. When everything seemed so wondrous and amazing. Those were the days. Oh, God. I sounded like my mother. Next, I'd be sprouting clichéd quotes from Pinterest.

When I finished cleaning my brushes, it was almost closing time. I ran through the close-up checklist, then grabbed my bag and keys. Then I remembered my phone had buzzed while I was serving Kate and Maya. I pulled it out, and my heart stopped.

It was Hayley's school.

I ENTERED the school reception area to find Hayley slumped on a chair. Déjà vu I wasn't enjoying.

'Hayley?'

She looked up at me with glassy eyes but didn't answer. She was close to tears, and my heart snagged. This must be a hell of a lot more serious than questioning classic literature. My gaze shifted to Principal Nunn as she appeared from behind the mirrored window of her office.

'Ms Brown.' She clasped her hands in front of her. 'I see you finally got my message.'

'I'm sorry. I was at work.'

'Seems your husband is hard to get hold of too.'

I tensed at the mention of Anthony before regaining my composure. 'I'm Hayley's next of kin while we're here,' I said, purposely avoiding Hayley's stare which burned through me.

She pursed her lips and gestured for me to head into her office. 'Please wait here, Hayley.' She closed the door behind us.

'What's happened?' The message she'd left had been vague, just that there had been a 'serious incident' at the school and Hayley would need to be collected as soon as possible.

'Hayley wasn't present in class this afternoon.' Principal Nunn met my eyes.

'As in, she skipped class?' Hayley had never skipped class. Well, at least not that I knew of.

'Yes. We found her and another couple of students behind the gum trees at the far end of the oval when they should've been in English.'

I let out an exasperated sigh. 'I'm sorry. This is so out of character—'

The principal held up her hand to cut me off. 'They were smoking'—she paused for theatrics— 'marijuana.'

My mouth dropped open. 'What?'

Principal Nunn tilted her head back, the disapproval evident in her stern expression.

Pot? What the hell? I shook my head. What could I say to make this better? Nothing. Embarrassment, shame, worry, and anger roiled within me. There were too many emotions for my body to process. I took a breath to quell the rising sensations.

'So, in this instance, we will deal with each child separately. And, with Hayley being new to the school, we've decided not to expel her, but we will be suspending her for the rest of the week.'

'There's got to be some mistake.' My head continued to shake with disbelief. 'Hayley would never—'

'I'm sorry, Ms Brown, there has been no mistake. I'd also like to strongly suggest you take up our offer of counselling. We have a wonderful school counsellor she can see during or after class.'

'But was Hayley actually smoking it? Or was she just with the others who were?'

'Whether she was smoking it or not is something you can discuss with her. Our issue is that she should've been in class. Instead, she was involved in the activity in one form or another. In this instance, the police have not been involved but we will certainly make no exceptions should this happen again. We have zero tolerance for drug use and smoking, and it goes against all my beliefs to let this incident slide as much as I have. But I assure you, if something like this happens again, I will take the appropriate measures. Now, if you will excuse me, I have a lot of paperwork to complete. Please take Hayley with you; she is not permitted to return until next week. Her teachers will email the work that she needs to complete at home.'

I rose from the chair and nodded. Unable to say anything. What could I say, 'Thank you'? 'It won't happen again?' What was appropriate to say in situations like this? I had no idea.

Hayley started making excuses as soon as the car pulled away from school. 'I wasn't smoking it. I didn't even know Tyler had it until he brought it out. He offered me some, but I said no. I promise.' There was a pleading edge to her voice, her hands wringing together on her lap.

Hearing that made me feel a little better, but still the anger was bubbling in my stomach. I took one hand off the steering wheel and held it up. 'Don't. I can't talk to you about this right now. I'm too upset.'

The silence lingered, and you could cut the tension with a butter knife. How could she do this? I mean, I was no angel in my youth, there'd been times when yes, maybe, I'd had a drag on a joint or two, drank a few bundy and cokes underage, but at parties away from the unseeing eyes of parents and adults. This was at school! And skipping class in the first place? She'd never done anything like this. I couldn't let it rest. 'Why Hayley? Why do this? Why skip class? I know you hate it here. I know it's been tough for you, but I'm trying everything possible to make this work.'

'I don't want it to work,' Hayley hissed.

'It's not like your dad left us in a position where we had options. I'm doing the best I can!' By this time, my voice had cracked, and tears pricked at the corners of my eyes. 'I'm just asking you to be patient. To make the best of this situation. Why can't you do that?'

Hayley didn't answer, and I glanced from the road for a second; tears were streaming down her face. Fuck! Parenting fail 398.

'I can't let this slide. You know that. You're suspended from school and grounded for the week. Maybe that'll give you some time to think about things. And, you'll probably have to see that counsellor.'

'Counsellor?' Hayley turned swiftly in her seat. 'No way. You can't make me.'

'What choice do I have, Hayley? You won't talk to me and obviously there are things you need to talk about—'

'I don't need to talk to anyone! I just need to go home. To Melbourne. To my friends.' Hayley's voice wavered and she turned away to look out the window.

It was times like these I wished for a parenting manual. I didn't know how to handle my shit, let alone deal with this. I didn't want to come down hard on her, but letting things slide wasn't the answer either. And maybe it would do her good to get things off her chest to someone else. Although, apart from dragging her there by the earlobe I couldn't see how on earth I'd get her there. A problem for another day, no doubt.

The rest of the drive home was excruciating. Neither of us wanted to be in the car together. When we pulled up, I turned to Hayley. 'Honey.' I reached my hand over to her, but instead, she ripped it away, threw open the door, and ran inside. I closed my eyes and let the tears free, sobbing into the steering wheel, feeling as if my life had unravelled just a little further. I wasn't sure how much unravelling I could take until there was nothing more to unravel.

THAT NIGHT, I crawled into bed. It had felt like the longest day ever, and it still wasn't over. I wriggled to get comfortable against the pillow and pulled up my phone contacts, my finger hovering over Anthony's name. Without further hesitation, I tapped out a text outlining the need-to-know points, finishing by assuring I had it all under control. Which, of course, was a lie, but only a white one. I would have it all under control. Soon. Within seconds, my phone rang. Anthony's smiling face lighting up the screen instantly raising my hackles. That smile. I used to love that smile. But now all it made me feel was resentment. And weariness. I was so tired. Of it all. Of everything.

'Hey.' How could he sound so calm? 'What's going on?' he said, his voice light. How the hell could he be calm right now?

I let out a frustrated sigh. 'I've told you everything. There's nothing more to tell.'

'I'll talk to her. She's rebelling, that's all. It was bound to happen eventually. She's a teenager.'

She's a teenager? That's it? I refrained from throwing my phone across the bedroom and regained my composure with a calm, 'Ah-huh.'

'Look,' Anthony continued. 'I'm sorry you have to deal with this right now, but I promise it won't be long. Things are looking up here.'

Well, good for him.

'I've been seeing a drug and alcohol counsellor and stopped drinking. I think this was the shake-up I needed.'

'Shake-up?' I snapped. 'You think us losing everything and me leaving you was a *shake-up*?' There went my composure.

'You know what I mean. It was what I needed to realise how selfish and lost I'd been.'

'Oh please!'

'I know, I know. You don't want to hear it, and I don't expect you to. I deserve that. I'm feeling good about things, Em. And I haven't felt good about anything for a while.'

At that point, my eyes decided to betray me and filled with tears. We filled the next few moments with silence. Every time we spoke it felt like we were going around in circles. Him telling me he was fixing things, me not wanting to hear it.

'Hun—' Anthony began.

'No! You don't get to call me hun anymore!'

'Okay, okay. I'm sorry.'

'I don't want to hear it, Anthony. I only texted to tell you about your daughter. The principal has suggested counselling.'

'Counselling?' Anthony scoffed. 'I don't think we need to fill her head with things like that. It's a phase. And with everything she's going through... New school. Not knowing what's going on...'

I tensed at the insinuation in his voice. 'So it's my fault, is it?'

There was a long pause before Anthony continued. 'It's the situation. That's all. I think we need to keep her hopeful, you know, that everything will be okay, will get worked out.'

'Hopeful? Right. Hopeful. I'll keep that in mind while I'm living in my old bedroom, dealing with a *rebellious* teen, and trying to pull our lives together.' I paused and bit the inside of my lip.

'Okay. I'm sorry. I'll talk to Hayley, okay?'

'Fine.' And without a goodbye, I swiped his face away, turned my phone off, and chucked it on the bedside table. He'd talk to her. Fat lot of good that would probably do. But at least he was still in her good books, so maybe it would. Me, I was the problem. Or at least Hayley saw it that way. I turned off my light and pulled the doona over my head.

CHAPTER THIRTY-THREE

At the next Snapper Fest committee meeting, everyone was thrilled with the news about Oliver. I'd presented the contract, which I'd emailed Maddy earlier that day and she'd quick-smart returned it signed and sealed. I finally felt like I'd accomplished something.

'Thanks for organising Oliver,' Lucy said when the others had filed out and Simon had disappeared into the bowels of the café.

I shrugged my bag on my shoulder. 'Glad I could help.'

'Well, it's taken a load off. At this rate, I think this will be the best Snapper Fest yet.'

My phone pinged.

'Anyway, I'll see you later. Say hi to Mum and Dad for me. And Hayley.' Lucy started towards the door but pulled up and turned back. 'How is Hayley? Settling in?'

I rolled my eyes. 'Don't ask.'

Lucy grinned. 'She'll come round. See ya.'

I checked my phone, tensing as I pulled it out of my bag. Every time it made a noise these days, it seemed it was bad news. I breathed a sigh of relief when Maddy's name appeared on the screen.

Maddy: *Now I've delivered Oliver, what do you say about the project we discussed?*

'Oh, you're still here.' Simon popped up from behind the counter like a jack-in-the-box.

I slotted my phone back into my bag. Maddy could wait. 'Just leaving, sorry.'

'No drama. Hey, want some of this?' Simon offered a plate of what looked like apple pie.

My stomach growled. Served me right for picking at my dinner. 'Sure. Why not?'

Simon disappeared into the back kitchen, returning with two plates of reheated apple pie topped with dollops of cream. We sat at one of the tables, and I shovelled hot apple pie into my mouth, the scent of cinnamon and cloves wafting in puffs of steam. The pastry was decadent and buttery; the apple filling a perfect balance of sweet and tart. It was a feast for my senses. 'Wow!' I licked the sweet, cinnamony my goodness from the back of my spoon. 'This is delicious. Where's it from?'

'My kitchen.' There was a hint of a proud smile on Simon's lips.

I tilted my head. 'As in, you made it?'

Simon nodded, a slight flush across his cheeks.

I tried not to let the surprise show, but wow. When did this happen? Simon hadn't stopped ceasing to surprise me since I'd returned. 'Since when could you cook?'

'Dad was a great cook, and my uncle—Dad's brother—was a chef. He came around when I was younger, and he and Dad used to bake stuff. I liked watching. But never thought more of it until a couple of years ago when I found one of his recipe books and started making some things. I enjoyed it, and it reminded me of Dad. Then, I started bringing the food here to see if it would sell, and it seemed to go alright, so I got my kitchen registered and I make a few different things now.'

'Like?'

'Well, those sugar cookies are mine.'

'No!'

Simon laughed. 'Yep. And the carrot cake. The lemon slice. Sometimes I make an apple cinnamon tea cake. That's popular with the oldies.'

'And no one knows you make them?'

Simon shrugged.

'Why keep it a secret?'

'It's not like I'm a pastry chef or anything. And it's not even that it's a secret, just no one has asked.'

'Well, I think you should be out and proud. This is bloody amazing.'

Simon shrugged again.

'I'm surprised you find the time to bake. You have so much on your plate, pardon the pun, what with the café, birdwatching tours, the curlews.'

'And I play badminton twice a week. I'm president of the club.'

My eyebrows rose, and I shook my head, feeling a little outdone.

'I guess with Dad dying so young, it was a wake-up call. I'd done nothing but work sixteen-hour days, and yeah, I made good money, but I had no life, and then when I moved back, I realised everything I'd been missing out on by being in the city and doing nothing but eating, sleeping, and working.' He finished the last of his pie. 'I mightn't make as much money now, but I'm happier.'

He did seem happy. Like the Simon when it was just the two of us. Carefree and easy going.

'Did you see this?' Simon interrupted my thoughts, reaching for the newspaper on the nearby rack. He unfolded it and pointed to an article regarding the development.

My face heated, so I put the last of my pie in my mouth to hide it. Simon's carefree face had now creased into a frown.

'Yeah, Mum and Dad have told me about it.'

'You know they want to build this thing alongside where the curlews nest and feed?'

'Surely they'll have an environmental impact plan or something, though, to ensure they're protected.'

Simon grunted. 'Yeah, it will be all bullshit, though. From the plans, it doesn't seem to impact the area, but it's more the impact on the foraging areas than the nesting. If they feel threatened, they move on, and they won't come back. That's why they're so vulnerable. Habitat destruction along the coastline with projects like these.' He shook his head, wearing his passion for these birds like an open book. 'We need to protect species like these; before we know it, they'll be gone. Not that it seems many around here care.'

'I think they do. Dad doesn't think it will get through council.'

'I hope you're right. Council have recently passed a new by-law, meaning it has to go to a council vote before the planning department can even consider it. So that's something, at least. Anyway, I'll be putting forward my thoughts at the meeting as I'm sure the rest of the town will.'

I shifted in my seat, remembering the message from Maddy. There was no way I could agree to help her. Not knowing how it will affect the curlews. I placed my spoon on the plate. There goes the five grand. But it wasn't about money. It couldn't be. Even though that money could pay for bond on a rental, furniture to get set up... get Hayley and I into our own place, our own space...

'Sorry.' Simon folded the paper and returned it to the stand. 'I didn't mean to put a dampener on the day.'

I waved away his concern. 'It's fine. It's good to be passionate about something. Those birds are lucky to have you.' Our gaze caught, and a sudden warmth ran through my body. That feeling that flips your stomach and makes your toes curl all at once. I had to get out of there. 'Right, better get home.' I jumped to my feet.

'No worries. I'll lock the door behind you.'

'Thanks for the pie.' I grabbed my bag off the back of the chair and headed towards the front door, my body ever conscious of Simon right behind me. He leant over to open the door while I fumbled in my bag for my car keys, locating them before clumsily letting them slip through my hand and crash on the tiled floor. We both leant down at the same time to pick them up, knocking heads in the process before Simon handed me the keys.

'You okay?' Simon skimmed my forehead; the heat from his finger pads sent my nervous system into overdrive. Our eyes locked again. His hand lingered and then slowly traced along my cheekbone; before I knew it, his lips were on mine. Gentle at first, tentative and then deepening, wanting. His hands reached around the back of my head, his fingers through my hair. The familiarity of his touch sent a shot of warm desire through me and I fell into the kiss, whisked away to a place where it was just the two of us and nothing else mattered. Until my brain donkey kicked me back to the present and I pulled away, inhaling sharply.

'I ... I'm sorry.' Simon took a step backwards.

I swallowed hard. 'It's fine.' My heart thumped against my ribcage so hard I thought it would burst through my chest. 'I ...' I gestured to the door, avoiding his eyes. 'I should go.'

'Yeah, course.'

Simon pulled the door open and let me through. Our bodies brushing, mine tingling all over so much it was almost painful.

'Thanks again. For the pie.'

I rushed out the door, head down, my face and body on fire. What the hell had just happened?

CHAPTER THIRTY-FOUR

Snapper Fest arrived along with a brilliant spring morning. The last few weeks had passed mostly uneventfully, apart from Hayley's suspension. She'd refused to see a counsellor and Anthony had been no help, telling her if she could improve her behaviour we'd hold off. I wasn't impressed but had been pushed into a corner. Thankfully Hayley was playing along. Tolerably. Going to school, doing her homework, she'd even taken to going on afternoon walks down to the beach. I was taking each day at a time, it was all I could do.

As for Simon and me, we'd managed to reach a mutual ignorance of *that kiss*, which meant we both pretended it had never happened. I enjoyed walking Fred, chatting with Doreen, and looking after the bookshop. I'd even done a few more paintings. Maybe things were going to be okay.

Bright and early, at 7:30 am on the dot, I stepped out the front door with Mum and Dad in tow. Mother Nature was playing her part with cloudless blue skies and only the slightest of breezes. Last night I'd confirmed Maddy was still on track with Oliver Barnard, and now all I had to do was make it to the end of the day without a hitch. My primary job was making sure Oliver Barnard was happy, but apart from that, I was looking forward to scouring the stalls and sampling the fresh seafood.

'What a ripper of a day.' Dad linked his fingers through Mum's as we walked towards the pier. Childhood me cringed at my parents holding hands in public, but adult me smiled inwardly that they still wanted to hold each other's hands after all these years. I guessed the events of the past few weeks had helped them realise what was important.

'When do you get the results?' I asked. Mum had been for the biopsy yesterday but hadn't really spoken about it.

'Not for a few weeks,' she replied after a glance from Dad. 'But I'm not thinking about that today. Today is all about this wonderful festival.' She threw me a bit of a smile, but it wasn't very convincing. I could tell she was worried, probably trying to hold it together for the rest of us. That's what Mum did. That's what *mums* did, wasn't it?

'Everyone is excited to hear who the judge is.' Dad was good at changing the subject.

'Yes! I can't believe you haven't told us yet.'

'All will be revealed.' It had been the talk of the town, and it had taken a mammoth effort on my part not to spill the beans. I hadn't even told Connie, who tried to get it out of me nearly every time we spoke about Snapper Fest. And the last person I would have told was my mother, who couldn't keep a secret to save herself.

A crowd of people were already milling near the pier, the chatter growing louder as we got closer. It was tradition for everyone to send off the anglers at eight am on their day-long quest to capture the biggest snapper. About twenty or thirty boats were moored near the pier, all bobbing rhythmically with the gentle tide. An infectious buzz of excitement hung in the fresh morning, elbowing my nostalgia for Snapper Fests of the past.

'Is Hayley coming?' Mum asked.

'Not to the send-off. She's a teenager and won't be out of bed before lunch on a Saturday. She promised to come down to the market this afternoon and meet for dinner.'

'Oh, good,' Mum replied before spying someone in the distance. 'Oh, there's Milly and Dale!'

My phone buzzed and I stopped to pull it out of my pocket. 'I'll catch up.' I saw Maddy's name gracing the screen as it buzzed again. Seeing her name made every muscle in my body freeze. No. Stay calm. She probably wanted to check the final details or something. I took a deep breath and answered with faux cheeriness. 'Hey Maddy!'

'Emily, there's a problem.' Her voice was sharp and low.

No! There wasn't a problem. There couldn't be.

'Please tell me this is your deluded sense of humour on show right now?'

'Sorry, Ems. It's bloody Oliver. He won't be making it to Snapper Fest.'

'What? No! He has to come. He signed a contract.'

'Yes, and the contract had an out clause for extraneous circumstances beyond our control.'

'Extraneous circumstances?'

'Let's just say he's been unexpectedly detained. It's not something he can, well, get out of.'

'What are you talking about?'

Maddy let out a long sigh. 'He was arrested last night for drink driving.'

'What?' Drink driving. So what? Pay a fine, whatever.

As if reading my thoughts, Maddy continued, 'And it gets worse. He crashed into a car while he was under the influence. An undercover cop car. And then he tried to evade arrest by running off through a nearby park. It's a bloody mess, Ems. This is the last straw; I'm dumping him. He's out of control.'

The frustration in Maddy's voice was apparent, and as much as I wanted to rant and scream, it wouldn't do her or me any good.

'Fuck,' was the only word I could manage as my body filled with dread.

'I know. I am so sorry, Ems. I know you had a lot riding on this. Look, I've got to run. Another call coming in. I'll talk to you later. And really, I'm sorry.'

I blinked slowly. What the hell was I going to do now? Lucy was going to kill me. The committee was going to kill me. The *whole town* was going to kill me. I shook my head. Simon was right. I couldn't be counted on.

I could see my tombstone now: Here Lies Emily Brown. The Queen of Failure since 1985.

My stomach churned like the ocean on a stormy day.

'Hey.' Simon appeared beside me; hands shoved in his pockets. 'Today's the day! Can't wait for the big reveal. Finally.' He grinned, oblivious to how the world was crumbling around me.

I remained frozen. My brain a scrambled mess like the eggs Mum made this morning. I'd forgotten how to form words and send them to my mouth.

'Emi?' Simon frowned. 'Are you okay? You look like you've seen a ghost.'

'I have.' My face remained set. 'My own.'

'What?' Simon let out half a chuckle.

'He's not coming.'

'Who's not coming?'

I grabbed Simon's elbow to steady myself; my head was spinning.

'Whoa. Come here.'

Simon led me to a nearby park bench away from the noise of the pier and sat down beside me.

'I think I'm going to throw up.' I propped my head up in my hands. 'What the hell am I going to do? There's no way I can find anyone else at this late notice. Lucy's going to hate me. Everyone's going to hate me. I've ruined Snapper Fest!' I threw my hands in the air.

'Emily, what are you talking about?'

'Oliver! He's not coming!'

'What? Why not?'

'Oh God. You were right. I can't do anything without messing it up.' I threw my head back in my hands.

'C'mon, I'm sure we can figure something out.' He rubbed my leg with his palm.

'Nope. This is just another thing I've stuffed up. Just like the skincare thing, just like poor Fred. My marriage. Being a mother. The story of my life. I stuff everything up.'

'Don't be like that. Every problem has a solution.'

I looked at him, deflated. 'I love your optimism, Simon, but unless you're secretly related to Jamie Oliver or Manu Feildel, and have them on standby, then I'm truly fucked. Pardon my French.'

Simon gave me a small, sympathetic smile, and I stared into the distance as if the answer lay beyond the stark white boats in the deep blue sea.

'Well, there may be someone.' Simon clicked his tongue. 'My uncle.'

'I was kidding, Simon. And as amazing as your uncle is, I'm pretty sure he's—no offence—not in the same league as Oliver Barnard.'

'Probably not in the same league now, but he was a famous TV chef back in the 80s and early 90s.'

I threw Simon a sharp look. 'What?'

'He was one of the very first celebrity chefs in Australia. Before 'celebrity chef' was even a thing. He had a show on ABC.'

'Who is it?' When Simon told me his uncle was a chef, he omitted to tell me he was famous.

'Harry Clarke.'

'Fair dinkum beaut?' If I was right, that was his famous catchphrase.

'That's the one.'

I vaguely remembered the show from when I was a kid. He was popular for his nasally twang, scruffy beard, and love of Australian colloquialisms. 'He's your uncle? What? Where is he?'

'He lives inland at Snake Creek. He was fifteen years older than Dad and is pretty much a recluse. Has been for about twenty years since Aunty Marilyn passed away, and since Dad died, he rarely comes into town.'

'Gosh, he must be, what eighty odd by now?'

'Late seventies, I think. But look, I haven't seen him for'—he raised his eyebrow—'ages. He took Dad's passing pretty hard. Last time I spoke to him, he said he'd never head back to the spotlight, so I don't like our chances.'

'But it's worth a shot!'

'A long shot.'

I turned to Simon with my best Puss-in-Boots sad eyes. 'There is no one else, Simon. You know that as well as I do. No way I could scrounge someone of any calibre up in eight hours. Come on, we have to try. Please!'

'I don't know.'

'Call him. What's the worst that can happen? He can say no, and we'll be no worse off.'

'He never answers his phone.'

'Then take me to him. I'll talk him around. I can be very convincing, you know?'

Simon's mouth upturned. 'I know you can be.'

My insides fluttered. I ignored them. This wasn't the time. 'Come on, this is my only chance. Please.'

Simon let out a long breath. 'You really want to do this?'

'I don't have a choice.'

CHAPTER THIRTY-FIVE

After seeing the boats off, Mary and David strolled along the path towards the green where the market stalls were setting up for the day. The smell of the salty sea air was tainted with oil and engine smoke which cleared away quickly on the gentle breeze, replaced by the warm scents of fresh baked goods and scented candles. The craft and farmers' market was a highlight of the festival for Mary and she was looking forward to selecting some homemade raspberry jam from Mrs Crippes and honey from the local Beez-Kneez apiary. And maybe one of Avis' famous orange and poppyseed muffins. She subconsciously patted her cheeks, checking she'd put sun cream on before she left the house. They were still a little red after the beauty cream debacle and she didn't want them getting too much sun.

'I might just duck over and say hi to the fellas.' David motioned to the information stall the Men's Shed had set up. Mary gave Roger and Phil a wave.

'Okay, then. I'll just have a wander. I'm sure Gordon and the kids will be around somewhere.'

David gave her a sad look. It was only for a split second, and no one would've noticed the slight squeeze he gave her arm. She had to blink away the tears. No time for that nonsense. Today was a good day. It was Snapper Fest and not to be ruined by 'what-if' scenarios. It was bad enough she had to round up those wild types of thoughts countless times a day, but she refused to let them overwhelm her today.

For the next hour, Mary traipsed up and down the makeshift aisles and stopped at every stall to check out the wares, filling her hamper with goodies. Amazing places these markets were and so many young people taking up craft again. Gabby with her resin earrings, Karly with her crocheted pieces, and Jeremy with his hand-turned wooden wares. She bought a lemongrass candle from Jemima and admired the cupcakes her thirteen-year-old daughter Imogen was selling. She promised to come back for one a little later.

As she continued past the last few stalls, Mary began to feel a little useless. Even the kids had their creative outlets these days and turned them into micro-businesses. Not that Mary wanted to get into craft. She sighed, resigned. It was too much to think about at the moment. She wasn't herself, that was all. And understandably so. Once this ... condition ... of hers was sorted, she'd return to feeling her normal self and stop worrying about what she was missing out on.

Just as she slipped the paper bag with the pot of honey inside the hamper, Mary looked up to see Susan purchasing a pot herself. 'Oh Susan, hello, I was wondering if you'd be down for the fest.'

Susan looked up with a bright smile. 'Mary! I was hoping I'd run into you. Hang on a minute.' Susan took the change and it popped into her purse. 'Don't worry about a bag, John. It'll fit in here.' She popped the honey into a wicker basket she was carrying. She turned to Mary. 'How are you? I've been thinking about you.' She leant in a little closer and whispered, 'Any news?'

''Fraid not, yet. But Dr Schubert says that's a good thing. If it were concerning, they'd be onto it straight away.'

'Of course. Of course. Where's David?'

Mary glanced over her shoulder where David was still chatting. He'd found a chair and pulled up behind the desk, making himself right at home. 'Talking with the boys.' Mary gave a playful eye roll.

'I couldn't convince Sam to come. Wanted to get the lettuce and spinach planted, so I left him to it.' Susan laughed. 'Anyway, you want to grab a coffee? I saw The Coffee Pot had their little caravan set up over with the food stalls.'

'Sure. That'd be great.'

A few minutes later, Mary and Susan were sitting at a white plastic table with steaming coffees in hand.

'Mmmm.' Susan closed her eyes and released a sigh. 'Needed that.'

'Me too.' Mary enjoyed the creaminess of her latte. She usually preferred tea, but today the latte was doing just nicely.

'So, how did your MRI go?'

Mary took a deep breath. 'I had to have a biopsy.'

'Oh, Mary.' Susan's brow wrinkled.

The biopsy hadn't been painful as such, but she'd felt violated, which was silly. It was a biopsy! Women had been through much worse. But still, the day's emotion had churned in Mary's stomach all the while they poked and prodded at her. And they'd expected her to stay perfectly still. She wished they'd have put her to sleep. In fact, she longed to sleep a long, interrupted, peaceful sleep from which she woke up and everything was different. 'Just to be sure it's nothing.' Mary picked at the plastic cup lid. 'Well, that's what we're hoping.'

Susan reached her hand across and gave Mary's a squeeze. 'I hope so too, Mare. But if you need anything, I'm only a phone call away; you know that.'

Mary nodded. Susan was a good friend. One she would make time to appreciate more.

'So.' Mary needed to change the subject. 'How's the planning for your Northern Territory trip coming along?'

Susan raised her eyebrows and let out a defeated sigh. 'We've had to put plans on hold as Sam needs knee surgery.'

'Oh, is he okay?'

'He's fine. An old footy injury from years back. Should've stopped playing long before he did, and now he's paying for it. You know men.' She rolled her eyes. 'So, yes, it's on the backburner. Sam says I should go with his sister Trish ... Did you ever meet Trish?'

Mary shook her head.

'Look, I love her to death, but the idea of spending a couple of weeks with her ...' She shook her head. 'Ah, no.'

'Oh, that's a shame. You were looking forward to it.'

'Yeah. I was. I suppose we can delay until later next year, but we wanted to get to New Zealand then.' She leant back in her chair. 'Mmmm. I don't know.'

Mary took another sip of her latte and waved to Lucy who was forging towards her on a mission.

'Mum!' Lucy chimed. 'Have you seen Emily?'

Mary gave Lucy a little glare that said, 'Excuse me, please mind your manners.' Lucy got the message.

'Oh, sorry. Hi ...' She glanced at Susan. 'Oh! Susan. How nice to see you! It's been ages.'

'It has. How are you, Lucy? You still on the organising committee?'

'Yes, which is why, I'm sorry, I'm a little flustered. I've been trying to get hold of my sister, but she's not answering her phone.' Lucy said the last sentence through gritted teeth and looked at Mary as if she had a crystal ball and knew Emily's exact whereabouts.

'I have no idea where she is.' Mary scanned the crowd and came up blank. 'She was here earlier. I'm sure she's busy sorting out the surprise chef.' Mary straightened in her chair with pride that both her daughters were part of organising the fantastic Snapper Fest.

Lucy bent down towards Mary's ear. 'That's the thing. The'— she quietened her voice—'chef hasn't turned up.'

'Oh. Well, I'm sure she's got it under control.'

Lucy rubbed her forehead and tapped the iPad she was holding. 'Right.' Then she gave Susan a quick smile and said, 'Sorry, Susan, got to run. Great to see you again.' Lucy turned to Mary and gave a thin-lipped smile before storming off in the direction she came.

'Daughters.' Susan shook her head with a smile.

'Yes, tell me about it. They're well and truly grown-ups, yet I still feel like pulling my hair out with them sometimes.'

'It must be good to have Emily back.'

Mary smiled wistfully. 'It is, and she's trying. But I still worry about her. And Hayley. She's almost sixteen; it must be so hard for her. I've tried to talk to her, but she doesn't want her silly old grand-mother trying to give her advice.' Mary gave a throaty laugh. 'Emily doesn't want me giving *her* advice most of the time.'

'I'm sure she does. She just won't let on. Ours are the same. And Lucy, Lucy's doing so well for herself.'

'She is. She's on council now,' Mary said proudly before a shadow crossed her face. 'But I still worry about her. Something's not right. She's on edge more than usual. Normally she's so, well, so organised and in control. I always said she could run the country one day, but lately.' She shook her head. 'I don't know. I think some-thing's up.'

'We do have that intuition. I totally believe it. When Jessie was in that minor car crash—she was alright, nothing serious—but I knew. I rang her only minutes after it happened. I just knew something was wrong.'

'I'm glad she was okay, but yes. You're right, we know.' Mary finished the last of her drink, unable to shake the feeling something was wrong. She made a mental note to talk to Lucy. After Snapper Fest, though, when she had a little less on her plate.

'You look like you have the weight of the world on your shoul-ders, Mary. You need a holiday.'

Mary let out a harrumph. 'Holiday? What's that?'

Susan's eyes widened. 'That's it!'

'What's it?'

'You should come on a holiday with me!'

Mary frowned as Susan leant across the table and squeezed her hand.

'Come with me to the Territory. We'd have a ball, Mare. You've always wanted to travel—'

'Yes, but Dav—'

Susan waved her hand. 'Don't worry about David; he'll cope by himself for a couple of weeks.'

'Well, yes, but I haven't got the results back yet, and Emily and Hayley ... Lucy ...'

Susan sat up straight; her expression had turned to something rather serious as if she meant business. 'Mary, come with me. It will do you the world of good to get away and do something for yourself. You deserve it. Everyone will survive without you. And when was the last time you did something on your own, for yourself?'

Mary sat back in her chair and rubbed at her fingernails. This was exactly what she'd been dreaming of, but ... She didn't want to answer. She'd never done anything for herself. Not really. You couldn't count the redecorating as for herself. Maybe her yogalates, but ... Could she? What about David? An odd sensation fluttered in the pit of her stomach. Was that excitement?

'Look,' Susan interrupted her thoughts. 'You don't have to commit right now. But give it a good thought, okay? We'd have so much fun riding camels, sipping on sunset cocktails, sunbaking with crocs.'

'Sunbaking with ...' Mary let out a giggle, and Susan threw her head back in a throaty laugh. Before she knew it, Mary was laughing so hard she felt like a teenager. And it felt damn good.

CHAPTER THIRTY-SIX

Simon and I drove slowly towards the outskirts of Snake Creek, on the eastern edge of the Great Otway National Park, about thirty kays inland from Curlew Bay. As the car slowed, and I glanced around at the ghost-like town. A small single-pump petrol station sat deserted with dry weeds poking up through the cracked concrete. A dilapidated shack that appeared to have once been a general store by the look of the faded Coca-Cola sign above the doorway had its windows boarded up. I wouldn't have been surprised to see tumbleweed blow down the road.

As we approached an old milk can letterbox on the side of the road, Simon flicked on his indicator, and we turned down a dirt road flanked by thick bushland. The scent of eucalyptus wafted into the car as branches scraped the roof.

'Are you sure this is it?' I asked Simon as we bumped along the potholed road.

'I think so. It's been a while since I've been here.'

'Looks like a good place for a serial killer to live.' My pulse quickened as the words left my mouth.

'He's a little eccentric, but a serial killer he is not,' Simon replied before adding, 'Although there was that woman who went missing bushwalking in this area earlier this year.'

I shot a wide-eyed look at Simon who sported a shrewd smirk.

'I'm kidding!' He laughed, and I whacked him on the arm.

A few minutes later, an old cottage with peeling white paint came into view. On the veranda was one of the biggest collections of pot plants I'd ever seen. There must've been over a hundred pots of different shapes filled with lush, green foliage, some with bright flowers, others tumbling over the edge of the veranda. Seems old Harry had a bit of a green thumb.

'You ready to meet Uncle Harry?' Simon pulled to a stop and switched off the engine.

Not entirely sure what I'd gotten myself into, I swallowed back my uncertainty. Considering no other options were available, it wasn't like I had a choice. And we were here now. I raised my eyebrows. 'Right. Let's go meet the famous Uncle Harry.'

Simon knocked on the door and walked inside before Harry answered or opened it, calling his name. As we entered the hallway, a raspy voice called, 'Who is it?' followed by heavy footsteps. 'Zat you Simon?'

'Yes, Harry. It's me.'

Harry appeared from the hallway. 'Well, I never!' He gave Simon a brief, manly pat on the back.

He differed somewhat from my vague memory of him from TV, but somehow the same too. Strands of wispy white hair floated atop his balding head, but the bushy beard was still there, although it was now as white as snow. His lined face could tell a thousand stories.

'And who's this sight for sore eyes, then?' Harry eyed me with suspicion.

'Hi Harry, I'm Emily. Emily Brown.' I held out my hand.

'Well, the pleasure is all mine.' Harry nodded and shook my hand. He turned to Simon and gave a wink. I giggled under my breath.

Harry invited us into the kitchen, which smelt like bacon and burnt toast. I expected it to be a mess of old pots and dirty dishes, but to my surprise, apart from the well-worn cupboards and bench-tops, it was spotless. We took a seat at the Formica table.

'What brings you all the way out here?' Harry said after offering us both a cup of tea. He fiddled with the gas stove before placing an old-style kettle on top. 'Or should I say, what do you want?' Harry's shoulders shook as he laughed. 'No one comes out here unless they want somethin' these days.'

Simon nodded to me, and I cleared my throat. Harry seemed like a straight shooter, so I got straight to the point.

'Well, it's Snapper Fest today,' I began.

Harry glanced over at a calendar hanging on the fridge. 'Ah, so it is. Haven't been down to the Bay for years, let alone the festival. Good to see it's still on.'

'Yes, but we have a little problem.'

I informed Harry of the morning's chain of events as the kettle boiled with a whistle and he poured our teas. He nodded with a wry smile.

'And where do I fit into this, then, missy?'

I exchanged a nervous look with Simon who gave me a small nod to go ahead. 'I know you were the guest chef for the fiftieth anniversary of Snapper Fest.' (I'd discovered this on the way in the car, thanks, Google.) 'And, I thought, in light of things, with this year being the delayed seventy-fifth anniversary, maybe you'd like to ...' I paused for dramatic effect.

'You thought I'd like to be the guest chef again, huh?'

The breath I'd been holding slipped through my lips as I tried to smile my most convincing smile. 'Something like that.'

'I'm sure everyone in the Bay would love to see you again, Uncle Harry,' Simon added.

The kitchen was silent apart from the rustle of branches against the window pane and the old iron roof creaking under the morning sun. Harry leant back in his chair and stroked his beard. His eyes were hard to read. Was that a flicker of excitement? Reluctancy?

'I totally understand if you don't want to.' His hesitation was palpable as he fidgeted with his mug.

'Well, it's sure been a while since I've whipped up tucker for anyone but meself. Not sure I'm up to it.'

Harry was fishing for a compliment, so I obliged. 'A talented chef never loses his touch, I'm sure.'

Harry let out an enormous sigh and shook his head. 'I'm sorry, love, I just don't think I can do it.'

'Oh.' The tension grabbed my shoulder blades again. What now? 'It's fine. I know it was a big ask to expect you to agree at the last minute.'

'It's not that. It's ...' Harry and Simon exchanged a look that I didn't understand. As if they knew something I didn't. Something big. I gripped my coffee cup tightly.

'Harry hasn't been down to the Bay much since Dad passed,' Simon said.

'Oh. I'm sorry.'

'He was my best mate.' Harry's eyes were suddenly glassy, and he pulled a scrunched handkerchief from his shirt pocket. 'My little brother.'

Sadness crossed Simon's face, and there was a stillness in his body.

'Should've been me going first. Not him.'

'Harry—' Simon began.

'And I know I should've been there for you more. Stepped in when ... But ...'

Simon patted Harry on the shoulder. 'It's okay, Uncle Harry. It was a hard time for all of us.'

'And now it's been so long ... I'm embarrassed. Embarrassed to face your mum more than anything.'

'She understands, Harry. And she'd love nothing more than to see you again.'

I shifted in my seat, feeling like I was intruding on an intimate and private family conversation. It was a bad idea coming here. Look what I'd done.

Silence hung heavily in the room. Then, a big cheesy grin the size of Luna Park suddenly erupted from Harry. His face lit up as he slammed his hands down on the table with determination. I jumped and let out a small yelp

'Alright,' he said with resolute firmness. 'I'll do it.'

'Are you sure?' A sizzle of excitement started forming in my chest. And relief, pure relief. 'Please don't think you have to; we can find someone else.' Not likely, but ...

'Not someone like me.' Harry was still grinning as he pushed back the kitchen chair as he stood. 'Now, where are my chef whites?'

We waited in the car while Harry changed into something other than the stained and torn overalls he'd greeted us in. 'Thank you, Simon. You saved my butt.'

Simon shrugged and drummed his fingers on the steering wheel. 'I've got to admit,' he said. 'You've still got it.'

'Got what?'

'That thing where anyone finds it hard to say no to you.'

I looked away to hide the blush creeping up my neck and across my cheeks, recalling the moment we found ourselves in recently. The heat settled on my ears. 'Are you sure he's on board? I don't want to make him feel like he has to.'

Simon chuckled, deep and throaty, and I had to remember that I was here on business. 'Believe me, Harry doesn't do things he doesn't want to. I'm glad he agreed. It'll be the best thing for him. And Mum will be stoked to see him.'

'He seems pretty lonely out here. I mean, if he fell and hurt himself ...'

'Yeah, I know. He won't listen to anyone, though. He's a stubborn bugger.'

The cottage's front door swung open, and Harry walked out with a spring in his step, decked out in chef's whites tinged with yellow. In his hand, he carried a blue-and-white striped apron. He'd combed back his wispy white hair and tied his signature Australian flag scarf around his neck. I smiled at Simon. 'He looks a treat!'

Harry slid into the back seat with a slight groan. 'Alright you ankle biters, let's hit the frog and toad!'

CHAPTER THIRTY-SEVEN

'Here's to Emily.' Lucy raised her eco-friendly plastic wineglass towards the stars. 'You nailed it with Harry! He's been the star of the show.'

'To Emily.' Everyone cheered.

I sat alongside Hayley, Simon, Mum and Dad, Lucy, Gordon, Mum's friend Susan, and a few others around a large oval plastic table as twilight descended. Fairy lights hung between trees and wove around light poles dotted throughout Ocean View Park, crowded with people chatting, laughing, and dancing to the duo performing on the mini stage. Food stalls were pumping out fried snapper, chips, and all manner of cuisines and the salty aroma of seafood lingered on the air.

Harry was in the distance, surrounded by a large group of people each of them hanging on his next word. He looked right at home with the crowd cast under his spell. He gesticulated abruptly before everyone roared with laughter. I couldn't help but smile, the relief of a successful day sweet in my bones. I took another mouthful of crisp white wine.

The day had been a tremendous success. *Harry* had been a

success. At the reveal, the crowd gasped before letting out a huge cheer, and it was at that moment I finally exhaled and let go of all the tension that had caused me endless nerves all day long. I'd done it. Well, Simon had.

'It was nothing.' I peeked at Simon from the corner of my eye. Only the committee knew about the Oliver/Harry debacle—Eva had been most upset. But, it had all worked out in the end, and that was all that mattered. And now, Lucy owed me big-time gratitude. I fingered a handful of hot chips; I'd hardly eaten all day, and my stomach was pinching and making noises that, thankfully, no one could hear.

'I'm going.' Hayley stood up and slung a small handbag crosswise over her chest.

'Are you sure you don't want to stay a bit longer? Maybe catch up with your friends?' I asked. 'I saw you hanging out with a few of them earlier. Looked like you were enjoying yourself.'

'They've gone.' Hayley's reply was curt and to the point.

'I'll walk you back.' I stood, too, placing the chair under the table, and took another big gulp of wine.

'I'm not five.' And with that, she stormed off into the crowd.

Simon put his hand on my arm as I went to call her back. 'She'll be fine.'

'Leave her be,' Mum added. 'It's not dark yet; she'll be home in a few minutes.'

I wasn't sure about letting her go off into the night by herself, even though it was only a short walk back to Mum and Dads. I'd have much rather she stayed here, enjoyed the night with us, but everyone had kept telling me to give her time and space. I rubbed the back of my neck, sat back down. I only wish I knew how much time and space she needed. Glancing around, seeing everyone laughing, chatting, enjoying the night, I realised I could really see myself and Hayley here. A renewed sense of peace washed over me. We could be happy. If only she'd give it a try. In time, I reminded myself. In time.

'She'll be okay. Come on, let's go for a wander.' Simon nudged me as if reading my thoughts. It was uncanny how small gestures spun me back twenty years.

I nodded and we walked to the edge of the park away from the lights and noise. 'Surely you remember what it's like to be a teenager? All that angst,' Simon said as he shoved his hands in his pockets.

'I don't remember being angsty. I was loving life.' Mostly.

'Not when we used to fight.'

'We didn't fight that much, did we?' I didn't think we did; nothing big anyway. Stupid things like, why didn't you call me last night when you said you would?

'Not really. We were good together. Until ...'

'Until I stuffed it up.'

'I didn't mean that.'

'You did. It's okay. You're right. I was selfish and scared.'

'Scared of what?'

I shrugged, my mind skirting around the truth. 'I don't know. Missing out on life. On being something. Someone.'

Even though he nodded, I could tell by the way his mouth twisted that he was torn between thoughts.

'Anyway, it doesn't matter. That's ancient history. I appreciate how you helped me out with Harry. It's you we should be cheering for.'

A loud cheer erupted from the crowd as the duo struck up a well-known song. We stopped and looked over to see the makeshift dance floor flooding with people.

Simon nodded, pointing to my parents. Mum was dragging a reluctant Dad to the edge of the dancefloor.

'Oh, god.' I let out a laugh. 'Dad hates dancing!'

Simon turned to me, and his eyes staring straight into mine send ripples of energy through me. 'You want to dance?' he said, softly. 'For old times' sake?'

My head was light from too much wine and not enough food,

and a wave of weird emotions I wasn't sure I wanted to feel were swirling through my body. All of sudden dancing felt like the only thing I wanted to do. At the very least to break this lock of our eyes. 'Sure.' I shrugged. 'Not that I remember us dancing much,' I added as Simon grabbed my hand and weaved our way to the dancefloor.

'Come on, you must remember the year eleven ball?' Simon yelled over the music as we shimmied into a small space and began moving.

Memories of a bright blue strapless dress and strobe lighting flooded my mind along with downing a six-pack of Ruski Lemon in the toilets, Sophie Ellis-Bextor's "Murder on the dancefloor" rumbling from the dodgy Soundsystem. I threw my head back. 'Oh God! Now that was a night!'

Simon laughed and his hands slipped around the small of my back, my body relaxing into his.

I WASN'T sure how long we'd been dancing for but it felt good to let go of the stress of the day and the past few months. The crowd had thinned, and the food stalls were packing up for the night. The music switched from upbeat to a more subdued tempo with a cover of Dan + Shay's 'Tequila', and Simon pulled me in again, wrapping his arms around my waist. Ignoring the warning in my head, I let my arms fall loosely around his neck as we swayed from side to side. The air was warm, and the inky sky was dotted with a million stars as we moved together. I could feel the movement of his shoulder muscles and his hips press into mine, muscle memory taking over.

'What's the smile for?'

I didn't realise I was smiling. 'It's been a good day. An eventful one, but a good one.'

'I'd have to say it was the best Snapper Fest yet.'

'Wow, that's a big call.'

'Maybe, but from where I'm standing, there's only one way it could be even better.' Simon's eyes bored into mine, and he shifted closer. Ripples of energy moved in the limited space between us. A magnetic pull as my body drew even closer. Our lips only a whisper away.

'How?' I murmured, biting gently on my bottom lip with a fire erupting deep in my groin.

'This.' Simon leant down; his lips enveloped mine, and I lost all sense of the present moment. I didn't know if it was the wine, the elation and relief of the day, or simply the moment, but everything faded into background noise. It was a quick, fervent kiss, not long enough to draw attention, but my body was certainly aware of it.

'Come home with me,' Simon whispered, the inside of his palm skimming my cheek. My mind skipped to Hayley. To Anthony. The stress of everything that had happened in the past few months. I wanted nothing more than to escape. To be selfish, just this once. To be free of expectation and responsibility, even if only for a night.

Before I could overthink it any further, I nodded, by breath quickening. 'Okay.'

CHAPTER THIRTY-EIGHT

The clock on Simon's bedside table read 6:04 am, and I turned over to see a bare-chested Simon asleep on his back. He was snoring softly, and tingles of warmth swept through my body remembering what we'd done only a few hours earlier. The tenderness of his lips on my neck. His kisses moving over my breasts and stomach. The weight of his body on mine. It differed from our experiences when we were younger. More mature, more sensual. Being so close to him and the desire was almost too much to bear before giving in to him completely. I inhaled quickly, my body reliving the moment.

Simon's eyes flickered open. 'Hey.' His morning voice was sleepy with a sexy huskiness that made my stomach backflip.

'Hey.'

He reached over and landed a gentle kiss on my lips, his hands wandering under the sheet, down my back. There was a throb between my legs. A wanting convincing me to stay.

'I should go.'

'No, stay.' This time his hand skimmed over my butt.

'I can't. I ...' The attraction and pull towards Simon deepened in my body. It would be so easy to roll over and give in to the need, the want. But the realisation of what I was feeling had settled in. What it meant. What it couldn't mean. Within seconds, tears gathered and spilled down my cheeks.

Simon sat up and pushed my hair behind my ear, swiping the tears away with his knuckles. Such a tender touch. 'What is it?'

My heart thumped, and I pressed my hand over my chest and drew in the deepest breath before it released in a rugged sigh. I couldn't hold it in any longer. Now was the time. 'There's something I need to tell you.'

'You can tell me anything.' He pressed a kiss to my temple. My heart sank. There'd be no more kisses after this.

I sat up straight and pulled the sheet up to cover myself.

'What is it?'

The words were hard to force out, but I had to. I couldn't keep it any longer, and if I was going to stay in Curlew Bay, if anything was going to come of us, even if it was just a friendship, I had to go forward with honesty rather than this secret. 'I didn't leave you because I didn't want to travel around Australia.' There, I'd said it. Well, half of it. My chest immediately felt a little lighter.

Simon's forehead creased. 'What do you mean?'

I averted my eyes to the rumpled white sheets. 'I ... I was pregnant. Well, I thought I was pregnant.'

Simon's voice came out in a gasp. I couldn't meet his eyes; instead, I knotted the sheet, squeezing it tightly.

'I'd changed to a new contraceptive pill, and my hormones were all over the place. I'd missed two periods but was too scared to tell Mum.'

Simon shoved a hand through his messed-up bed hair. 'Jesus, Emi. Why didn't you tell me?'

'I was petrified. We'd already spoken about not wanting kids. At least not for a long time—and ...'

'So ... you just ... what? Up and left? Had an abortion?' Simon's voice was getting louder and louder.

'No!' I forced myself to look at him. To look into his eyes which were full of despair and distaste. 'That wasn't it. I was scared, so I made up the story about going to uni. When I got to the city, I was planning to ... but ... when I went to the clinic, they took another test and ... and it was negative. I wasn't pregnant. It was the new pill. It had been reported as commonly giving false pregnancy results. I was never pregnant.'

Simon's forehead was etched in a deep frown, and he rubbed at his temples. 'So ... why didn't you just come back? Tell me?'

'I don't know. Like I said, I was scared.' I shrugged. 'And embarrassed. I thought you hated me. Of course you hated me. I'd ruined everything.' Fresh tears were threatening now. This wasn't how I wanted this to go. I shouldn't have told him. I didn't know how to say the right thing. Explain my feelings. He was right. It felt so lame. So wrong. Why didn't I just go back and tell him? Funny how twenty years of life experience allows you to view things through an adult lens. 'I'm sorry. I know. I was wrong. The irony of hindsight.'

Simon's face crumbled before he tensed his shoulders. 'I think you should leave.' And he turned his back on me.

'Simon, please ...' I rested a hand on his bare shoulder.

He pulled away, grabbed his tee-shirt, slid it over his body, then pulled on his pants, ignoring me.

I stood with the sheet wrapped around my nakedness, walked around the bed, and reached for his hand, but he recoiled as if he couldn't bear to touch me. 'Emi, please. I can't deal with this right now.'

The front door slammed. I peered around the edge of the blind as Simon slunk down the driveway and into the predawn. I'd just stuffed everything up. Again.

My clothes were still strewn across the bedroom floor. I dressed as fast as I could, not worrying about my bra, splashed cold water over my face, and scurried home. Streetlamps flickered off as the dawn gave way to light, but all I could think about was how much I'd hurt Simon yet again. I thought telling him was the right thing to do. But now, now I knew it was the worst thing. I swallowed back the barely there contents of my stomach.

I was rummaging in my handbag for the front door keys when my foot knocked over the pot plant. It landed with a crash, which at 6:30 am in the morning—when the only other sounds were quiet morning birdsong and a gentle lapping breeze—sounded like the clashing of cymbals. I froze for a moment, half expecting Dad to open the door with a rush, cricket bat in hand. But, after a few moments of continued silence, I bent down and picked it up, sweeping the dirt into my hands and righting the pot.

Finally finding my keys, I unlocked the door and tiptoed down the hall towards my bedroom, consciously avoiding the creaky floorboard. As I raised my hand to my bedroom doorknob, Hayley's door swung open, and she stepped out into the hall in her pyjamas, rubbing her eyes before noticing me, frozen to the spot.

'Mum?' She looked me up and down, the recognition of seeing I was still in my clothes from the night before registering on her face in the form of narrowing eyes and a deepening frown.

'Morning!' I chimed as if nothing was out of kilter. Yet here I was, a grown woman, sprung doing the walk of shame by her teenage daughter.

Hayley let out a grunt of disgust. 'Did you? Oh my God, Mum! I can't believe you!' She threw me a look of disgust and thumped across to the bathroom, slamming the door behind her.

'Hayley!' I whispered. 'Let me explain!' I don't know why I let those words come from my mouth. I was a grown woman; I didn't need to explain anything. I waited a few moments, wanting to clear the air. Make sure she didn't jump to conclusions. Which, of course, she'd be right in doing, but ... Oh God! What had I done? My body flooded with heat, and I retreated to my bedroom, ripped my pillow off my bed, smothered my face into it and let out an almighty rasping scream.

CHAPTER THIRTY-NINE

It was after eleven before I emerged from my bedroom, desperate to avoid Hayley but in need of coffee. After flicking on the kettle, I went outside where Mum and Dad were sitting in the sun working on the newspaper crossword and chatting about Snapper Fest.

'Ah, here she is. The lady of the hour.' Dad beamed as though I'd won a Logie.

'You look like you could use a coffee.' Mum eyed me curiously.

'Morning.' I pulled out a deck chair. The mirror hadn't lied when I braved a quick glance as I walked past the bathroom—I looked like crap. My eyes were grainy and looked like I'd been knocked out by Mike Tyson they were that swollen. Where were my sunnies when I needed them?

'Are you okay?' Mum rested her pen on the newspaper.

'Yeah. Just tired.'

'Dilapidated!' Dad announced with a grin.

'What are you on about, David?' Mum tutted

'Dilapidated. Number four down "tired and run down".'

'Oh yes, you're right.' Mum penned in the letters.

'Has Hayley been up yet?' I asked, stretching my neck.

'Can't say I've seen her.' Mum tapped on the newspaper. 'What do you think seven across is?'

'What's the clue?' Dad leant in and pushed his glasses up his nose.

'Something waiting to happen.'

'Anyone want a coffee?' I asked, getting to my feet.

'No thanks,' they both chimed before Mum said, 'Disaster!'

INSIDE, I spooned some instant coffee into a mug. Disaster. Yep, word of the day. No, word of the year. I leant against the counter as the kettle grew louder, and all I could see behind my eyes was the look on Simon's face. It was as if I'd slapped him. I'd hurt him all over again, probably more than I had the first time. Then Hayley's face flashed at me. I'd really stuffed things up and I had no idea how to fix either of these disasters. Maybe I'd overexaggerated Hayley's reaction. She was half asleep when I'd run into her, maybe she wouldn't even remember.

Before I poured the water, I knocked on Hayley's door. Nothing.

'Hayley?' I called out, knocking a little harder this time. When there was still no answer, I opened the door and stuck my head in. As my eyes adjusted to the darkened room, her bed came into focus. It was empty. The covers were thrown back, the pillow with only an indent of where her head had rested. A dank combination of body spray and shoes hung in the room. I pulled back the curtains and slid open the window to let some fresh air in. When I turned back to her bed with the idea of stripping the sheets and throwing them in the washing machine, I stopped dead in my tracks.

The wardrobe door was wide open, and most of Hayley's clothes were gone. I looked around her room: no phone, no laptop, no chargers. Her jewellery box was not on her bedside table, and her school bag wasn't anywhere to be seen. I opened the other side of the robe; her suitcase was gone. My hand flew to my mouth. 'Oh God,

Hayley,' I whispered and then shouted, 'Hayley!' I ran to the front door and flung it open. It slammed against the meter box with a thud. 'Hayley?' I screamed again and ran to the road, looking up and down the empty thoroughfare. I don't know what I expected to see. She was probably long gone.

'Emily?' Mum appeared at the front door, followed by Dad. 'What is it?'

I turned and looked helplessly at my parents, the realisation slamming into my chest. 'It's Hayley. She's gone.'

CHAPTER FORTY

'I'm sure it's not what you think,' Mum said as I paced the kitchen, redialling Hayley's number in case she'd switched it on in the past thirty seconds. It went straight to voicemail again.

'Hayley, please call me back and let me know where you are. And that you're okay. We can work it out. I promise.' My voice broke, and Mum held my shoulders.

'She'll be okay,' she said, rubbing my back as I collapsed into her. 'She's tough, our Hayley. She's probably at one of her friends' houses.'

'Have you tried Anthony?' Dad asked.

I pulled away from Mum's embrace. Anthony. Of course. But how would she have gotten there? Buses don't run from the Bay on Sundays. I blocked thoughts of hows and whys and brought up Anthony's number. Voicemail. I slammed the phone on the table, and Mum shot me a look questioning how slamming my phone was going to help the situation.

'Sorry.' I rubbed my forehead. 'I ... Oh God. I can't believe she would do this.'

Mum flicked the kettle on, and Dad removed three cups from the overhead cupboard, pushing aside the cup I'd set out for my earlier coffee.

'Why would she do this? I know she's been struggling, but ... to run away? I just don't understand.' My hands started to tremble as thoughts of her hitchhiking and being picked up by someone with evil on their mind flashed through my visions. 'Oh God. I have to call the police. God knows where she could be. Who she's with.'

I went to grab my phone, but Dad's hand reached it first. 'I'll do it, love. You sit down.'

'I don't want to sit down!' I yelled, throwing my hands up to my head. 'I want to find Hayley. Sitting down and cups of tea aren't going to find her.'

'I know,' Dad said placing his hand on my shoulder.

I sucked in my bottom lip to stop it shaking. 'I'm sorry...I...'

'It's fine, love, here.' He pulled the chair out and guided me into it.

My breathing started to calm, my thoughts still racing.

'Is there anywhere else she might have gone?' Mum asked, bringing over a cup of tea. 'A new school friend maybe?'

I shook my head. 'I don't think so. I mean, she did mention Amber. I think.'

'Amber? As in Amber Smith? I'm sure that's Richelle and Mick's daughter. Mick works with Gordon.'

'I don't know. Maybe.' I swallowed hard, tears pricking at my eyes. I should know. I should know who she's made friends with, but I'd been too preoccupied with my own life, trying to make a new life that I'd totally dropped the ball when it came to Hayley.

Mum strode over to the landline. 'I'll call Lucy.'

I nodded and reached for my phone, willing Anthony to call or respond. Instead, I dialled in Coco's mum's number.

'Hello?'

Milla answered in record time as if she'd been sitting on her phone. 'Oh, Milla, sorry, it's Emily. Hayley's mum—'

'Oh, Emily! Hello,' she replied in a friendly tone. 'It's been so long. Coco told me you were taking an extended holiday. Up in, ah, Apollo Bay was it?'

'Curlew Bay.' I stood up and wrapped my free arm around my middle.

'Oh yes, that's right, well—'

'Milla, I'm sorry to interrupt but, um, is Coco with you? I mean. Has she heard from Hayley?'

'Oh, um...' I could hear the frown of confusion set in on Milla's face. 'Hang on a tick, Coco's in the next room. Still in her pyjamas watching Netflix. Teens, right?'

Impatience itched under my skin as I urged her silently to hurry up.

'Coco. Have you heard from Hayley? I've got her mum on her phone.'

I heard a mumble from Coco but couldn't make out the words.

'Right... Emily, you there, no, Coco hasn't since last night. Why is there a problem?'

I closed my eyes. 'I... she... I'm just not sure where she is.'

'Oh, right. Well, is there anything I can do? I mean, well, not from here, but if Coco—'

A thought crossed my mind. Hayley was always checking on her phone to see where her friends were. Some location app or feature on Snapchat, maybe. It seemed ludicrous to Emily knowing where everyone was all the time. Her and Anthony had been staunch refusers of putting any type of location app on Hayley, or each other, like so many did. It felt intrusive. Untrusting. But right now she wished she'd not been so 1995 about it. 'Milla, do you think Coco could check on her Snapchat thing if she can see Hayley's location?'

'Yes, what a great idea. Coco, honey? Can you look up on that app thingy and see if you can see where Hayley is?'

Another mumble and then a rustle. Now Milla's voice was muffled as if she was covering the mouthpiece of the mobile. I grew even more frustrated shifting from foot to foot unable to hear the conversation. I glanced at Dad pacing the kitchen.

'Emily? Sorry. No, it seems like she's offline.'

'It's not turned on!' I heard Coco call out in annoyance.

'Not turned on, Coco says.'

'Okay, well, thanks anyway.'

'I'll see if Coco can chase her up with her other friends, maybe they've heard. I'm so sorry, Emily. You must be sick with worry. I'm sure—'

'Thank you. I really appreciate it.' I swiped at her phone to end the call, not feeling a shred of guilt about cutting Milla off. She would do the same if the situation was reversed.

'Any luck?' Dad asked, stopping and leaning on the bench.

'No.'

'No luck with the Smith's either,' Mum added walking back into the kitchen. 'Lucy texted Richelle while I was on the phone with her.'

'Well, we have to do something. I can't just stand around here. We have to go and look.' I grabbed my car keys off the side table.

'Here, I'll drive.' Dad held his hands out for the keys and I passed them to him.

'I'll stay here in case she comes back. And ring around a bit more. I suppose...' Mum paused. 'I suppose we should call the police.'

Dad instinctively put his arm around me and nodded. 'Yes. Yes, you call them Mary, tell them we're out looking.'

I inhaled a shaky breath. My Hayley. Out there. Alone. I squeezed my eyes shut. All I wanted to do was hug her. Tell her I was sorry. That I'd fix everything. Dad pulled me into his arms and patted my back. 'Come on,' he said softly. 'We'll find her.'

I removed myself from Dad's embrace and reached for my phone on the table just as Anthony's face lit up the screen.

I let out a gasp. Mum and Dad froze.

'Anthony!' I said, snatching the phone. 'Is Hayley with you?

She's gone. I don't know where. I don't know when. God! She could be anywhere—'

'Emily,' Anthony said calmly. 'She's here. She just turned up on my doorstep.'

My heart hammered to a sudden stop and I slumped down in the kitchen chair bursting into tears of relief. 'She's there,' I sobbed glancing between Mum and Dad. 'At Anthony's. She's okay.' Mum's hand shot to her heart and Dad's shoulders relaxed. 'Put her on,' I continued, pulling myself together with a deep breath.

'Look, maybe not.' There was hesitation in Anthony's tone and a chill swept over me. Oh, God. Something was wrong. She was hurt.

'What? Why not? Oh God, is she okay?'

'Em, she's fine but doesn't want to speak to you right now.'

'What? What do you mean she doesn't want to speak with me? She's just given me the fright of my life; I want to speak to her!' My knuckles were white from strangling the phone. I could strangle someone else about now.

'Em, please. She ... she doesn't want to speak to you. She doesn't want to go back to Curlew Bay.'

CHAPTER FORTY-ONE

The drive down to Melbourne was a blur. My mind constantly on repeat of Anthony's words, '*Hayley wants to stay with me.*' Stay with him? Where? On the sofa at his mates' place? What the fuck? I shook away the anger. I needed to calm down. Barging in like Mike Tyson with a baseball bat wouldn't get me anywhere. I needed to listen, then state the facts and make them realise Hayley couldn't stay with Anthony, as good an idea as it sounded.

The GPS directed me to turn into a narrow street in Box Hill, where Anthony was staying with his mate Jamie. I stopped in front of a two-storey brown brick apartment block with a row of carports off to the side. At least there were some green shrubs out the front to hide the 1960s facade and faded paint.

I patted my cheeks to inject colour and looked in the rear-view mirror. I looked like shit but didn't care. I wasn't here to impress anyone. I just wanted to get this over with and get Hayley back to Curlew Bay.

Before I had the chance to knock, the ground-floor apartment door swung open. Anthony greeted me with a thin-lipped smile. He was clean-shaven and wearing a button-up shirt. 'Thanks for coming. You okay?'

'I'm fine. Where's Hayley?' My voice betrayed my bravado.

Anthony opened the door wider; I spied Hayley leaning against the bench in the tiny kitchen, chewing on the side of her mouth. I rushed and wrapped my arms around her, squeezing like I never wanted to let go. Ever. She hung like a rag doll in my arms. 'Thank God you're okay,' I mumbled into her hair, smelling like it had just been washed. After a moment, I unwrapped my arms, stepped back, and composed myself.

'Hayley,' Anthony said, still standing in the lounge room. 'Do you want to ...'

'Yes, grab your bags. I'll talk to your dad,' I said quickly.

'Dad?' Hayley turned to Anthony, her face pleading before he motioned with his head for her to leave the room. Hayley rolled her eyes and disappeared into what I guessed was a bedroom.

I turned to Anthony. 'I have no idea why she did this. It's so not like her. I'm just glad she's okay.'

'Me too.'

'How did she get here?'

'You don't want to know.'

Fear gripped my chest, and I closed my eyes. 'Jesus.'

'Thankfully, it was a young mother who picked her up. Said she knew what it was like to run away from home and didn't want her on the streets like she'd once been. Thank God for that.'

I scrubbed at my face, squeezing all the alternative scenarios from my mind.

Anthony stuck his hands in his jean pockets. 'Em—'

I knew exactly what he was going to say, so I beat him to it. 'She can't stay here. You know that. What? You both going to share a cushion on the couch?' It was hard not to fire angry sarcasm.

Anthony didn't react to my fury, simply remained standing calmly in the middle of the tiny room. 'Jamie's gone overseas for six months. Got a contract in Tokyo. I'm subletting the place. And it's two bedrooms. Hayley will have her own room.'

I shook my head defiantly.

'That's why she ran, Em. She doesn't want to be in Curlew Bay. She wants to be back in the city. With her friends, at her old school.'

'Well, of course she does,' I snapped. 'But you don't always get what you want. I'm doing my best to make it work for her. For us both.'

'There's no reason she can't stay with me until you return. She can catch the bus to her old school; it's only three extra stops. I've got a job now too, so the house sale is final, we can'—he shrugged—'find something new. For the three of us. Or you could even move in here? Til Jamie's back and—'

'Move in here? What the hell, Anthony?' I took a step backwards feeling as if I'd walked into a trap. Had they figured all of this out and just thought I'd go along with it?

'I'm working hard to fix this, Em.'

'It can't be fixed. It's done.' A concoction of anger bubbled and threatened spill over. My eyes pricked, and my jaw tightened. Fuck you! Anthony. Fuck you!

Anthony took a step towards me to put his hand on my shoulder, but I flinched away, crossing my arms to hide how much I was shaking.

'You've made your point,' Anthony continued. 'And it was the wake up call I needed, we needed. We've got a chance to really get it right this time, Em. For Hayley.'

'Make my point?' My face scrunched up incredulously. 'It wasn't a point Anthony, I didn't have a choice. We were about to get kicked out of our house, neither of us had any money coming in. It wasn't a point!'

'Things are different now. Like I said, we can start over. Running away isn't—'

'Running away?'

'It's what you do, Em.' Anthony shrugged. 'Like you ran away from Curlew Bay in the first place.'

I froze, as if he'd just slapped me in the face. 'What?'

'I'm sorry. I didn't—'

Anthony had been the only one I'd told the truth as to how I ended up studying in the city. Fighting my way to get into law. One night after we'd drank too much and I'd let my defences down for the first time since leaving the Bay. Now, all that seemed like a rose-coloured haze and here he was throwing it back in my face.

'Emily, come on.' Anthony put his hands on his hips, a smarmy smile on his face like he was right and I was wrong. It was in that moment I knew the truth. I'd known it for a while. Maybe all along. But never been strong enough to admit it. I didn't love him. Long before the shit-show that had land slipped our life over the past year. Long before he lost his job. I think I'd been grieving it over the past years without fronting up to it. But I wasn't running away. I just wasn't going to stick my head in the sand for another minute longer. Now, I was going to face it.

I straightened and cleared my throat. 'I'm happy for you. That you've got a job, a place to live. I really am. But I'm not coming back to you.' I shook my head.

'Em...' He went to reach for me before thinking better of it and rubbing his palms over his stubbled chin.

'It's over, and we have to move forward. For Hayley's sake.'

Anthony's face fell, realisation in his eyes. He nodded slowly but didn't say anything. I had to give him credit for getting his life together and thinking he could make everything right. But he couldn't. I couldn't. Not together. We could only make things right for ourselves. Apart. Separately.

Hayley appeared from the bedroom door, her arms wrapped around herself, black mascara stained on her cheeks. She looked broken, and guilt suddenly crashed over me again. I couldn't force her to come back. It would only make things worse. I had to give her time. All of us time to work out what things would look like going forward and the best place for Hayley was somewhere familiar. With friends, school, normality. I didn't want to leave her with Anthony, but he was her father. As much as we'd been through, I trusted him with her.

'It's okay.' I gently pulled her in for a hug, rubbing her back like I did when she was a toddler and she fell over and scraped her knee. Reconnecting with the memory of when she trusted me. When I could hold her soft cheek against mine and stop her tears. But she wasn't a baby anymore. She was a young woman.

Hayley tentatively put one arm around my waist, and she shuddered ever so slightly. I sucked in a breath so as not to collapse into a mess of tears and beg her to come with me. Then I let her go. 'Are you sure this is what you want?'

Hayley stared at her feet, bottom lip pinched between her teeth and nodded.

I lifted her chin so her eyes met mine. 'Okay. You can stay here till we work it out.' What the answer to *it* was, I had no idea. 'I love you; you know that?'

I felt her tense, but she didn't say anything. It was too soon. She'd been through a lot and I took solace in the fact she was actually listening to me and not telling me what a horrible mum I was. I didn't want to push her anymore. I rubbed my thumb across her cheek to remove the still-moist mascara and then pressed a kiss to her forehead. 'We'll talk soon.' I turned to the door, and Anthony followed me to the curb.

'So?' Anthony began.

'So, she stays here. For now. Until we work things out.'

'Look, Em—'

I turned back to Anthony. 'Don't make this any harder than it is.' He stepped back, hands held in the surrender, then I opened the car door, got into the car and drove around the corner, where I pulled over and cried.

THAT NIGHT, I sat on the front porch of Mum and Dad's, staring into the blackness of the sky, the stars hidden by a thick layer of clouds, and an unseasonal humidity sticking on my skin. The heaviness fitted my mood. I'd failed. When I didn't think I could fail any harder, I managed it. Because in hindsight, I'd been failing at adulthood since I left home. And that was a bloody long time ago. No wonder I was exhausted. And when I thought I was getting it all sorted, I went and messed it all up. It was like the universe was tormenting me. Punishing me. I deserved it.

The front wire door squeaked open, and Dad poked his head out. 'You coming in, love? It's getting on.'

'I'll be in soon.'

Not one to be dissuaded, Dad closed the door behind him and sat down in the spare Adirondack chair with a sigh. 'Bloody chairs,' he muffled under his breath. 'Your mother thought they'd be relaxing, but they're the most uncomfortable bloody things.'

I gave a small smile, and Dad joined me, staring out at nothing. I clenched my jaw so as not to crumble into sobs.

These front steps had been a place of solace when I was a teenager. After Mum and I had a huge fight—I can't remember what it was about, probably Lucy—Dad came out and sat with me. He didn't say anything, but he didn't have to; his presence was enough to make me feel better. Another wave of guilt washed over me. My parents were good people. They deserved to live out their retirement in peace. Not worrying about their stupid daughter and her tumbleweed of a life. I sucked in a sob that rudely escaped.

'You'll work through this, love,' Dad said ever so quietly.

I nodded in acknowledgement. Not because I agreed with him but because what was there to say? But how was I going to work through this? I'd all but lost my daughter to my alcoholic, gambling, soon-to-be ex-husband. Okay, so that was a bit harsh. Anthony was a good person, and he'd worked hard over the past few months. Who was I to think I was any better than him? I clearly wasn't. But how would this ever work with me being here and them being there? That was one problem I couldn't see a solution to.

'Whatever you decide to do, we will support you.' He squeezed my hand that was resting on the chair's arm.

I threw Dad a look with raised eyebrows. Whatever I decide?

'You know,' he replied, reading my mind. 'If you need to go back or anything. Don't think you have to stay here because you set out to do so. Or, you know, because of your mother. She'll be fine. She's your mother; she's tough.'

That was what undid me, and the tears spilled down my cheeks. Here I was selfishly consumed with my life dramas and my mother could have breast cancer. How does someone who has only ever put everyone else first deserve that?

'I'm sorry, Dad,' I babbled, shaking my head. I was sorry for everything. For being a shit daughter, a crap sister, a rubbish mother. But most of all, sorry that my parents had to go through this.

'Nothing to be sorry about, love. Your mum will be okay. And so will you.' Dad, ever the optimist. 'As your mum would say, "Life throws us curve balls. It's all about either dodging them or facing up to them."'

That was one I hadn't heard before. A hint of a smile flicked the corner of my lips, and then out of nowhere, my shoulders started shaking, and a giggle escaped my lips. Before I knew it, I was laughing, a full belly laugh, my eyes leaking with tears. I wasn't quite sure whether they were actual tears or laughing tears. Probably both.

I looked at Dad. His face had cracked into a smile, then a laugh. 'Tough times never last, but tough people do,' he added.

'We can't change the cards we're dealt, just how we play the hand,' I said through fits of laughter.

'I can hear you two, you know!' Mum's voice came through the lounge room window. 'Laugh all you want!'

Dad and I did. And I was completely overwhelmed with love for them. Dad had done it again. He'd made me feel better, even if only for the briefest of moments.

CHAPTER FORTY-TWO

After a night of tossing and turning and hardly any sleep, I dragged myself out of bed. It was barely six am, and as I power walked down the esplanade, AirPods delivering a podcast from Glennon Doyle about doing hard things. The horizon cracked with an orange glow and a garbage truck rumbled in the distance. The only place open was the newsagent where the owner was piling up the day's newspapers on the shelf.

When I reached the end of the jetty, I sat, concentrating on the gentle lapping of the tide and the sound of a car passing by. A few hours ago in between wakefulness and dozing, I'd come to a decision: I couldn't stay here while Hayley was in the city. I had to swallow my pride and admit that, while I'd tried, a life in Curlew Bay wasn't going to work out for us. There wasn't anything here for me, only trips down memory lane, which I couldn't keep reliving.

I'd thought I'd done the right thing by telling Simon. I don't know what I thought his reaction would be. I guess I expected him to understand, for it all to make sense. But that was a childish thought, just as my actions were back then. I needed to step up and be an

adult. I belonged in the city. It wasn't that I was running away back
to the city. That thought had snagged me all night after Anthony's
throwaway comment. I wasn't. In fact, it would probably be easier
staying here in the Bay. Going back to face a divorce and what that
looked like was scarier than staying here. Knowing feelings that
should've kept me and Anthony together were long gone and we had
to make things work separately was going to be tough. But he was
Hayley's dad. He'd always be in my life. And he was right about one
thing. I needed to move back and find a job. Perhaps this was the fork
in the road and I needed to face the fact I didn't have to reinvent
myself; I just needed to be better at life. And the life I needed to be
better at was in the city. Simple as that.

It was half past seven by the time I made my way home. I paused
on the driveway and dialled Anthony's number. He answered immediately.

'Em, hey.'

'Hi. Sorry, I didn't wake you, did I?'

'Nope. I've just stepped out of the shower. And, before you say
anything, I've spoken to Hayley and made it clear she's not allowed
to shut you out of her life. She'll probably need a little time, though.'

Last night, I'd sent her a message before bed, saying I was there
for her, loved her, and already missed her. As expected, she hadn't
responded.

'It's fine. I know she will when she's ready. But that's not why
I'm calling.'

'Oh?' There was concern in Anthony's tone. 'Is everything okay?'

'I'm coming back to the city.' I quickly continued before he
could jump to conclusions. 'Not to be with you. So we can work out
things properly. Separately. For Hayley.'

'Oh, right, but—'

'Look, Anthony, we had something great once. But somewhere
along the way, we lost each other, and I don't know if it was meant to

be that way ... or ... Anyway, I'm ... it can't ... I'm not in love with you anymore.' It was both hard to say and a relief to say it. 'And not because of the past few years,' I continued. 'I mean, it didn't help, of course ... but I think we'll be better people, better parents when we're apart.'

'Don't say that, Em. Don't—'

'But we do have a beautiful daughter together. One that needs both her mother and her father, so I'm coming back to the city. I'm coming back for Hayley, and we'll figure out how to co-parent and everything else that goes with it. You have to stand on your own two feet, and I have to stand on mine. For Hayley.'

The radio crackled in the background, and Anthony's breathing was heavy until he finally replied, 'Okay. I get it.'

I wasn't sure if he fully understood; I wasn't sure if I fully understood what the future held for us, but this was what I had to do. Even though nausea churned in my stomach at the thought. And there was something I had to do, that would make it possible for me to get back to the city.

I swallowed hard and typed out a message to Maddy.

If it's not too late, I'll do the PR for the development in Curlew Bay.

She responded immediately with a breathless voice message, pop music blaring in the background. 'Talk about leaving it to the last minute. Council meeting's in two weeks. But I know you'll be all over it. I'm just at the gym right now. Spin class is killing me! I'll get them to call you. So hang tight. Cheers. You'll smash this, and you've saved face with my brother too! Talk later.'

Two weeks. I'd have to work fast. But I had no choice. This was the only way I could make things work. There was no way I was borrowing money from my parents, and this five grand would tide me over with rent and bond until I found a job.

Climbing the steps to the front door, I pushed all thoughts of how to tell my parents aside. And then there was Connie. How would I tell her she'd have to find someone else to cover the bookshop? But I had to. I had to let these people down because I was doing this for Hayley.

And as for Simon. He'd be one person glad I was leaving the Bay.

CHAPTER FORTY-THREE

The next morning, I skipped yoga, had a coffee and crumpet for breakfast, gathered my laptop, and planned to head to the library, where I'd booked a private study room. The library was the only place I'd be able to tackle the project without anyone asking questions. I'd have to come clean to Mum and Dad, and Lucy, but that would come. Right now, I just had to get on with it.

Maddy's contact called me yesterday and, after a brief discussion, emailed approximately seventeen hundred documents to pore through to prepare my presentation. I'd almost thrown it in when I'd begun reading through the information last night in bed. I had to distance myself from the situation and remember why I was doing it. For Hayley.

'Where are you off to in such a rush?' Mum walked into the kitchen, tying her dressing gown around her waist.

'I'm not in a rush, but I'm going to the library. I've ... um, got some prep work for a project I've picked up through one of my old work contacts. Might lead to a job back in the city, so I'll be working on it for the next couple of weeks.' There you go. Not completely a lie.

'Back to the city?'

'Yeah, I need to be there. For Hayley.'

Mum nodded with a sad smile, then flicked the kettle on and removed a cup from the top rack of the dishwasher. 'You're sure about this? I know Hayley needs you, but is it the best thing for you?'

I zipped up my laptop bag and slung it over my shoulder. 'You're a Mum, you'd have done exactly the same thing.'

'Yes, I suppose you're right. I just worry about you, Emily. Is there more to it?'

'More to what?'

'I thought things were going so well with you here. You were working at the bookshop, helping Doreen with Fred, getting along well with Simon, and you were key to Snapper Fest's success. I just felt you were fitting back in so well.'

An enormous lump of guilt lodged in my throat, and I couldn't swallow it. Things had been going well. *Had*. I let out a sigh. 'Things change.'

Mum opened the fridge and paused momentarily, her hand resting on the handle as if she was about to say something.

'I've gotta go, Mum. Want me to pick anything up for dinner?'

Mum had more to say, but it was clear she was resigned to the fact that I wouldn't change my mind. 'Could you grab some burger buns on your way home? I'm cooking Korean chicken burgers for dinner.' She grabbed the milk and shut the fridge. 'Actually, maybe get them on your way in case they run out.'

'Sure.'

CHAPTER FORTY-FOUR

After stopping in at the bakery, I passed the bookstore on my way to the car, pausing out the front. Now seemed like a good time to tell Connie.

'Hey, Con.' I walked towards the counter, and the door jingled closed behind me.

'Oh, Em. Hey.' Connie quickly looked around without her usual effervescent enthusiasm, then turned back to a small parcel of books.

'So, I have to give notice.' Short and sharp. To the point. I felt a little better until Connie spun around; her usually bright eyes were rimmed red.

'Con? Is everything okay?' I placed the bag of buns and my keys on the counter.

She shook her head and promptly burst into tears.

'What is it?' I wrapped my arms around her and then passed her a tissue to wipe her eyes.

'It's Mum. She's getting worse.'

'Oh honey. I'm so sorry.' My eyes welled up, and I grabbed a tissue as well.

Connie blew her nose before throwing it in the bin and sanitising her hands. 'Mum walked out her front door last night at two in the morning.'

'What?'

'Luckily her neighbour is a shift worker and spotted her walking down the middle of the road in her nightie. She had no idea where she was.'

'Oh, Con.'

'She's okay. Physically. They admitted her to hospital because she was dehydrated, but she can't go back home. She's going to have to go into a care facility.' Connie's voice cracked, and I hugged her again. 'I'm going to have to go to Melbourne and sort it all out ... until ...'

'Of course. You have to.' I plucked another tissue from the box under the counter and passed it to her.

'I was wondering if—' Connie looked down at her feet. 'If you wanted to run this place while I was away. Full time.'

'Oh Con ...'

'I know it's a lot to ask and wouldn't be a great income for you, but I don't know what else to do. I'll probably have to sell the place. But I don't want to. Or maybe I do. I don't know. I can't seem to make any decisions right now.' She covered her face with her hands and started crying again.

A dull ache hit the side of my temples. 'Of course you can't make decisions right now.' I chewed on my top lip. This was harder than I thought. 'But, um ...'

'Oh God, you just gave notice.' She waves her hand at me. 'It's fine.'

'Connie, it's okay—'

'No. It's fine. I'm sure the shop will be okay if I close up for a little while, at least until I decide what I want to do.'

'I really want to help you, but Hayley ran away on the weekend. Back to Melbourne.'

'What! Is she okay?'

I nodded. 'Yeah, she's fine. She's staying with Anthony, and I'm ... I've got to go back to the city.'

'Of course you do! Don't worry; I'll be fine.'

We were both crying now. What a great pair we were.

'Things are really shit right now, aren't they?' she mumbled as she passed me a tissue this time.

'Yeah, they are.' A heaviness settled deep in my chest.

'It's okay, Em.' Connie rubbed my arm. 'We'll get through it. Somehow.'

I hoped she was right.

CHAPTER FORTY-FIVE

I took my eyes off the bright computer screen and allowed them to adjust to the low evening light of the bookshop. Today would be my last day at the shop and, as Connie was in Melbourne for the foreseeable future, the sign was already on the door informing customers that the shop would be closed for the next little while.

It was almost eight pm, and I'd lost three hours working on the PR project, but I was happy with how it was coming together. I'd spent every spare moment working on the right angle for the development. I'd already sent out a press release to the local paper that'd run a story, and I'd commented without mentioning my name, instead referencing 'the company's PR representative'. The community group on Facebook and the local newspaper's Facebook page had gone off with comments, but surprisingly, they weren't all bad. Okay, so most of them were, but it seemed some had taken on board the points I'd made about the boost to jobs and the economy and the company's one hundred percent dedication to their environment policy and protecting the curlews and inlet.

From what I could see, the development wouldn't encroach on the inlet or the habitat but would sit in the pocket behind. It looked legit. Or at least, that's what I'd convinced myself. I had to. And I had to keep remembering why I was doing it. It would be a hard task to convince the councillors to vote for it, but I had to do my job. That's all it was, a job. A means to an end. Money in my pocket. Hayley's future.

It was time to call it a night. I got up from the stool and stretched my back before ducking out to the kitchen to turn off the light and lock the rear door. As I walked back towards the shop's front, I was sure I heard footsteps. I paused, straining to hear it again to be sure. The hairs immediately pricked on my arms.

'Hello?' I sounded more confident than I felt sticking my head around the corner. Simon was standing at the desk, the glow of the laptop lighting up his face.

'Geez.' I released my breath. 'You scared the life out of me.' My heart began to slow down.

'What's this?' Simon pointed to the laptop.

My eyes flicked to the computer, and cold washed over me.

'Are you working for the development company?'

'No. Well, yes. Not really. I can explain.'

Simon took a step back, shook his head, and let out a disgusted snort. 'Wow. Just wow. You know, I saw you in here as I walked past before and kept walking. I couldn't face you. And then I thought, hey, we're both adults. We should be able to talk about things. We've changed. Grown up. We aren't who we were twenty years ago. But ...' He shook his head. 'I can see you haven't changed a bit.'

'I have—'

'Then how could you do this? You know everyone is against this development. The whole town. I thought you cared about the Bay, about the curlews.'

'You don't understand. I need the money. I have to get back to the city. Hayley's back there and I need to be there.'

'Convenient.'

'What's that supposed to mean?'

'Convenient that you choose to run away again.'

'I'm not running away. And it's not my choice.'

'I thought maybe we could work things out. I wanted to try and understand why you did what you did and didn't tell me. Do you know how much it hurt to find that out? It was ten times the pain of thinking you just left because you changed your mind.'

Tears sprung to my eyes as I saw Simon's pain, the pain I'd inflicted, drawn deep in his eyes. 'Simon, stop. Please.'

'Stop? Why? Because you don't like hearing the truth?' Simon paused, his breathing heavy, and then he seemed to lose all resolve; the tension slipped away from his shoulders as his posture slackened. He sighed. 'How can you come back here and do it all again? Let me believe that we could have something?'

'I'm sorry. I shouldn't have let it happen. My life is a mess—'

'And now so is mine. The sooner you're gone ... probably for the better.'

Simon turned to leave, arms hanging limply by his sides.

'Wait, Simon, can we just talk about it?'

But he didn't stop. He didn't turn around. He simply opened the door and disappeared into the night.

I wanted to run after him, to make him listen. Make him understand. But maybe he was right. He was right. The sooner I was out of here, the better.

CHAPTER FORTY-SIX

Mary poured the tea from the teapot into her cup and then David's. It wasn't often she made a full pot of tea, but this morning called for one. She'd woken with a few aches and pains, but that was nothing on how she felt after checking her Facebook notifications.

'That's right,' Simon had written on the community page. *'Emily Brown is running the campaign to try and convince us that PropCo's development will be good for the town. Was it all an act helping at Snapper Fest, BookArt, getting to know everyone in order to get us on side so she can push her hidden agenda? It sure looks that way. But we aren't going to be bullied by Emily or by PropCo. We know what's good for this town and we will protect the curlews. The council meeting is less than two weeks away, and we will make our presence felt. Who's with me?'*

'I'm sure she has her reasons,' David said, taking a sip of his tea.

'I'm sure she does. But there isn't a good one I can think of,' Mary responded bluntly. Gosh she was upset with Emily. After all her efforts to make Curlew Bay her home. Her work at the bookstore, Snapper Fest, she was beginning to fit in. Get back on her feet. Or had Mary dreamed up how well things were going? Sure she'd let her mind jump ahead a few more months with Emily and Hayley having their own place. Jenny Rippens' tenants were moving out of that lovely two-bedroom cottage on Major Street. Mary believed there was even a small view of the beach from the front porch. It would be a lovely spot for them. Mary imagined visiting and having them around for family dinners with Lucy, Gordon, and the kids.

David scribbled on his Sudoku, the pen scratching on Mary's nerves.

So, maybe she'd jumped a little far ahead. But how could Emily possibly think that siding with the development was a good thing? She didn't understand her daughter at all.

A moment later, the front door swung open, and in waltzed Emily in her exercise getup, face flushed.

'Morning,' she sang, pouring herself a glass of water.

Mary glanced at David, who slightly raised his eyes. He knew better than to tell her not to say anything. Of course, she was going to.

'What's going on?' Emily cocked her hip against the counter.

'That's what I was going to ask you, Emily,' Mary said through pursed lips. 'Please tell me it's not true.'

'What's not true?'

'You're the one behind this new PR campaign doing the rounds for the proposed waterfront development.'

She didn't need to answer. Emily's slightly open mouth and stiffened shoulders confirmed her guilt. David clicked his tongue.

'How did you find out?' Emily asked.

'It's all over the Facebook.' Mary swiped and tapped her screen to load the offending page and held it up for Emily to see. 'Is it true? What Simon is saying? If this is about money, we could've helped you.'

'Of course, love. All you had to do was ask,' David added. 'And we've offered many times.'

Emily's gaze scanned over the Facebook post, a red bloom tinging her cheeks. She closed and then opened her eyes, and Mary noticed the tears. 'I need to do this on my own,' Emily said, before adding in a softer tone, 'Moving back here was the wrong choice. I have to fix it. I have failed at everything I've ever tried—'

'Oh, Emily—' Mary's heart panged for her daughter, but she was getting too old for dramatics.

'I have! It took me two attempts to get into law school, and then I fell pregnant and couldn't even finish! And for the past ten years, I've been trying to make something of my life and hold my family together. Look how that turned out! I can't even walk a bloody dog without almost killing it! Or sell skincare without endangering someone's life. This is my chance to prove I can get back on my feet all by myself and stop getting walked over rather than be a failure.'

'None of that is failure, love.' David twirled the pen in his hand.

'No? Well, tell that to Hayley.'

Mary didn't know what to say. She couldn't grasp why Emily felt this way. As far as she was concerned, Emily had always tried her best. That was all that mattered. A lesser person would've given up, but not her Emily. It seemed she'd always been trying to prove something and Mary could never figure out why. Frankly, both her children left her bewildered many a time.

'Anyway,' Emily continued. 'I need the money. I need to get back to the city. To Hayley. That's why I'm doing this. And if a few locals aren't happy about it, I'm sorry. I really am.'

'This isn't the way to go about it, Emily. I'm disappointed,' Mary replied.

'Well, that's no different to usual, is it?'

'Emily!' Mary and David responded in unison, their different tones blending into one.

'I'm more upset that you lied to us,' Mary added.

'I didn't lie to you; I just didn't tell you about it because I knew you would overreact.'

'I don't think we are overreacting—'

Mary's comment was silenced as the front door swung open, and Lucy strode into the kitchen looking flustered. 'Sorry, Mum, I would've called first, but—' She paused and glanced around the room, sensing something was off. 'What's going on?'

Mary and David again exchanged glances before Mary began. 'Emily is helping with the development.'

Lucy's eyes shot to Emily, her face flushing. 'Oh. As in?'

'As in she's helping them get it through council,' Mary confirmed.

'I'm just putting forward a positive proposal, that's all. I can't make it get through council any more than you can.'

'Well, typical, I suppose.' Lucy raised an eyebrow.

'Lucy.' There was a warning in David's tone that Lucy didn't heed.

'You come back here thinking you're it and a bit. Why wouldn't you do something like that?' Lucy's hands were firmly planted on her hips.

'I'm not doing anything. And by the way, have you actually ever considered that this development could be beneficial to the Bay? Have you even sat down and analysed it properly? I mean, of all people, Lucy, I would expect you to have some sort of objective thinking about it. Aren't you supposed to be growing and supporting the town?'

Lucy's eyes narrowed as she spoke. 'You think you know it all, don't you? Unbelievable.'

'Lucy.' It was time for Mary to interject before things were said that couldn't be unsaid. 'I think perhaps we need to calm down a little. We're all upset. Maybe a cup of tea—'

'No!' Lucy and Emily chimed together, and Mary put down the teapot.

'No, Mum, a cup of tea isn't going to fix this.' Lucy was more measured this time. She turned to Emily to say something and then seemed to think better of it, turning back to Mary. 'Sorry, Mum, I'll call you later.' And with that, she departed out the front door.

Breaking the uncomfortable silence after Lucy's car roared off in the distance, Emily cleared her throat. 'Even if the development gets accepted at the council meeting.' She fingered at a small scratch on the kitchen table. 'It doesn't mean it will be approved once it hits planning. It's only the first step. That's all I'm helping with. After that, it has nothing to do with me.'

Mary turned her teacup around and around on the saucer. There was nothing left to say.

'Mum?' Emily said.

'What's done is done.' It was too late now. Emily's bed had been made, and now she had to lie in it.

CHAPTER FORTY-SEVEN

Keeping a low profile in a town the size of Curlew Bay wasn't an easy task. But over the past few days, I'd managed surprisingly well. In the private study room at the library, no one interrupted me, and even if the library staff wouldn't give me the time of day, they couldn't ban me. Well, I suppose they could, but they hadn't gone that far. I'd sheepishly slink in each day, go to my room, and keep my head down. And, in a mere twenty-four hours, it would be all over. The meeting would be done and dusted, and no matter the outcome, I would've fulfilled the contract.

Maddy had kept her ears open for further opportunities, and already within days, she'd come through, lining me up for an interview next week with a small press publisher as a publicist. Not that I knew a lot about the publishing industry, but surely my, albeit short, experience at the bookshop would count for something.

I packed up my laptop, slung it over my shoulder, and headed out the library door before it closed. I had a meeting around the corner at the Sailor's Arms Motel, where I was to meet with Terry Hamil, my contact from the development company. *The* Terry Hamil everyone seemed to be wary of. We were going to run through the last few details and finer points of the presentation.

Terry's room was on the first-floor balcony, room 17. It didn't sit well that we were meeting in his room, but he was the one handing over the cash. I didn't really have a choice. I didn't get good vibes from Terry; he was a short man with an air of arrogance and dark, beady eyes that seemed to stare straight through you. I think people were right to be unsure of him. Not that it mattered. I didn't have to like him. All I had to do was the job I was being paid for.

Head down, I traipsed up the stairs one by one, and at the top of the landing, I noticed someone leaving Terry's room. I blinked. What? But my eyes weren't deceiving me. Lucy had walked out of Terry's room. What the ...?

With her head down, Lucy rummaged through her handbag and then, as I approached, looked up. Her face immediately lost all colour.

'What are you doing here?' I couldn't keep the accusation out of my voice.

'Ah ...' Lucy looked around as if she was in a thriller movie and the bad guy could appear at any moment. 'It's not what you think.'

'Really?' Truthfully, I didn't know what I was thinking. Was she having *an affair* with Terry Hamil?

'I can explain.'

I shook my head and held up a hand. This was none of my business. If Lucy had issues in her marriage, it wasn't for me to judge. Well, it possibly was, but I wasn't going to. Not right now. 'No need. But really, Terry Hamil? How do you even know him?'

Lucy jutted her head back.

I shrugged. 'I just never thought you'd do something like this. Not to Gordon.'

Lucy's eyes widened, and she let out a gasp. 'Emily! God no! I am not having an affair with him!' Her voice came out in a rushed whisper.

'Right. Well, what are you doing here?'

Lucy's eyes flitted from side to side. She grabbed me by the elbow and ushered me to the dead side of the stairwell. 'I can't tell you.'

'What do you mean you can't tell me?'

'Ssshh! For Christ's sake, keep your voice down.'

I was completely confused. Was she having an affair and trying to throw me off the scent?

'It helps you anyway, so it doesn't matter. Just leave it and pretend you never saw me here.'

'What are you talking about?' I wriggled my elbow out of her steely grip, wondering what that menacing look in Lucy's eyes was.

'Let's just say my vote will help your cause.'

'What?' And then it hit me. Was Terry Hamil *paying* Lucy for her vote? In a rush, all the air escaped from my lungs. Lucy was taking bribes? 'What the hell? This goes against everything you stand for. I don't get it.'

'Of course, you don't get it, Emily, because it doesn't involve you. You're always so self-centred, but the world doesn't revolve around you. Other people have problems too. Other people are dealing with shit that you wouldn't even understand.' Lucy spoke through gritted teeth; her face was flushed.

'Are you in financial trouble?'

'If I was, you'd be the last person I'd tell.'

'Why?'

'Why wouldn't I tell you? Because you'd love it, that's why?'

'Of course I wouldn't—'

'Of course you would. You've been waiting your whole life for something in my life to go wrong. You think my life is perfect. Well, it's not. The shop hasn't recovered after all those bloody lockdowns. Tourists aren't coming, and I can't keep pumping into it without return.'

'What about Gordon?'

Lucy's head dropped. 'Gordon doesn't know.'

'But he handles the books? He's an accountant.'

'We kept the business separate. I wanted it to be my own thing, not rely on Gordon. He understood that.'

'But surely if things aren't—'

'Don't start with all your self-righteous crap,' Lucy hissed. 'You aren't the only one who wants to be something.'

For a split moment, there was silence, and although Lucy turned her face away, I'd seen the tears. A saltiness gathered under my tongue, my stomach swirling.

Lucy tugged at her jacket. 'Anyway, this helps you. You don't need to sway my vote at the meeting tomorrow. They've already got it. And a couple of others too. This makes your job easier. Or, I suppose you could use it against me.'

'What?'

'I'm sure you'd love to stand up in front of everyone and out me? You've always wanted to beat me at something. This could be your chance. Expose me for the liar and the cheat that I am. I'll be booted off council, lose my job, my business, probably my marriage. There'd be criminal consequences. You could floor me in one fell swoop.' Lucy fingered her wedding ring as she spoke.

I didn't know what to say. Was that what she really thought I'd do?

'Anyway, do what you will.' Lucy turned and headed down the stairs.

'Lucy, wait,' I called, leaning over the balcony.

But she ignored me, got in her car, and drove off.

I STAYED GLUED to the ground, hanging onto the handrail. How could I have not put two and two together? I knew something was up with Lucy. Why hadn't I tried to get her to tell me something was wrong? Been there for her. Like sisters should. They were right. Lucy, Simon. I was so caught up in my mess of a life I'd never given thought to anyone else. A door opened, and I spun around.

'Oh, Emily, there you are. Come on in.'

I swallowed and, on the surface, pulled myself together. 'Hi Terry.' Yet, on the inside, I was reeling.

CHAPTER FORTY-EIGHT

Things had remained tense in the house since our little run-in, so the morning of the council meeting, I left the house early to avoid Mum and Dad. I filled in time with a walk along the beach and then past the shops on the esplanade. The lights were off in BookArt, and leaves and debris had gathered against the door. My heart tugged. Poor Connie.

I tapped out a message:

Hey Connie, how's your mum? I hope you're both doing okay. Call me.

I should've called long before now. I was a terrible friend. Yet another person I'd let down.

I tried not to let my thoughts turn to Lucy. I'd already spent the night feeling like the worst sister in the world. I had so many questions. Why hadn't she gone to Mum and Dad for help? To Gordon? How had I been such a crap sister and not been there for her?

But of course, I had no answers.

Crossing the jetty car park, I spied Doreen walking slowly with Fred plodding along by her side, sniffing the odd pole or two.

'Hi, Doreen,' I called out with a wave. She was only about twenty metres away but didn't hear me, so I jogged up to her.

'Hi Doreen. Hey Fred!' I bent down to pat Fred. He stopped and looked up at me, considering whether or not he should let me pat him but then complied. 'Sorry I haven't been around to walk Fred lately.'

'As I said, we're fine now, thank you.' Doreen's answer was short, her tone sharp. 'Come on Fred, let's go.' She tugged at Fred's lead and then stopped and turned back. 'Everyone's disappointed in you, Emily,' she finally said. My face flushed.

'I think it's time you went back to the city. Maybe these sorts of shenanigans work in the big smoke, but here we look after people. And our animals. Furred or feathered,' she added with a slight eyebrow raise. 'Come on, Fred.'

She was right. Not about the 'shenanigans' or whatever she meant, but right that I didn't belong here. Even if I wanted to stay, I couldn't. I'd burnt too many bridges. And with what I knew about Lucy ... I swallowed back the guilt in my throat.

I spent the next couple of hours reviewing my presentation in the library before it was time to head to the council building. On the way, Maddy rang.

'It's the big day,' she chimed. 'You ready?'

'Ready as I'll ever be.'

'Don't sweat it. You'll phone it in.'

'I don't know about that. I'm going up against a hostile crowd.'

'So no luck swaying the public, then?'

'Not really. Maybe one or two.' There had been a couple of positive comments on one of the Facebook group posts, but they were few and far between and rarely commented twice after being ripped apart by those against the development.

'Well, you never know. And who knows? You only have to sway a councillor or two for it to get to the next stage. And anyway, your job is done. Win or lose. My brother says they're pleased with the presentation you gave them last week.'

I thought back to last Thursday when I gave the presentation to the developers over Zoom. I'd bumbled my way through, but they seemed to like it. Either way, as Maddy said, in just over forty-five minutes, my job would be done.

'Alright, chick, gotta scoot. Let's catch up when you get back to the city. I can't wait to hear how you go with Yellow Press.'

I was so close to the end. So close to getting back to the city. A turning point where things might actually pull together. A fresh start. Not a reinvention. Just a better version of who I was supposed to be. Me and Hayley. Co-parenting with Anthony. I had to keep all of that front and centre. Things were so close I could touch them. So why did I feel like the worst person in the world?

CHAPTER FORTY-NINE

Mary stepped out into the crisp morning and slipped on her gardening gloves. Picking up her trowel, she began turning over the soil, its rich, earthy smell reminding her of freshly mowed grass and sun showers. David had recently built her a raised veggie garden from left over timber he had in his shed. 'No more stiff back and achy knees, love,' he'd said as he'd stepped back, crossed his arms, and smiled proudly. Mary's nose tingled at the memory and before she knew it tears had formed in her eyes. She shook them away. There she went again with her overactive emotions, although she could hardly be blamed. She still hadn't heard from Dr Schubert and she wasn't sure if that was a good or bad sign, in fact, she'd tried not to think anything at all. And, then of course, today was the day of the council meeting.

She'd heard Emily creep out of the house earlier and she'd let out a sigh of relief at not having to face her, which had filled her with shame. It had become the elephant in the room, this development business. All of them walking around each other at a distance so not to bring it up. Bah! It was ridiculous. Emily was doing what she thought was right. The fact that Mary—or the rest of the Bay—

didn't agree was simply a matter of opinion. Mary picked up the plastic tub of lettuce seedlings and tapped the bottom so they fell out gently ready for her to plant in the holes she'd just dug. She knew it wasn't just opinion, though. Deep down no-one wanted or needed this hideous development. She'd been so angry with Emily, but she felt like she should be supporting her daughter at the same time. The juxtaposition of the two emotions split her insides in half. It was like being torn apart like the roots of the lettuce.

She patted the soil around the seedlings and stepped around the other side of the garden bed to prepare the holes for the cucumber seedlings. Anyway, what would be, would be. That was what she always liked to say. Although, it was much more difficult in practice to live by that theory.

'Mary?'

Mary looked up and saw David emerging from the house looking like he was on a mission. And then she saw the phone in his hand.

Mary's mouth fell open as David rushed towards her, his eyes wide, brow creased.

'It's the doctor,' he whispered with one hand over the mouthpiece of their portable landline phone.

Mary shook her head. She couldn't do it. She didn't want to hear the bad news. No. She would just keep on living day by day with whatever it was. Ignorance was bliss.

David reached out a hand and placed it softly on her arm, its warmth immediately calmed her. 'It's okay, Mare. I'm here.' With the other hand he held out the phone.

Swallowing back the bile that had risen from her curdling stomach, Mary took the phone and David led her to the garden seat where they sat down, his arm placed supportively on her knee.

She cleared her throat. 'Hello? Dr Schubert? It's Mary.'

CHAPTER FIFTY

The council chambers were on the main road, a three-minute drive from the library. I parked a block away and walked the rest to clear my head, get the blood pumping, and do a mental checklist to ensure I hadn't forgotten anything. The presentation was on my laptop, with a USB for backup, and a spare report, which councillors already had copies of, was in my satchel. Everything else was in my head. I knew the proposal back-to-front. Knew the main things to mention to appease the councillors' questions and knew what to skim over, giving just enough detail without inciting any negative comments. There were eight councillors, and I only needed five for it to be passed and accepted through to planning. Well, four. They already had Lucy. Not that the votes mattered; I would be paid either way. But in a way, it did too. I didn't like failing. The development addressed all the planning clauses, so there was no reason council could obstruct it from going to planning if they voted in the majority.

As I rounded the corner to the council offices, a group of locals milled about the entrance. I stopped. So many of those faces I knew. I didn't want to have to face them out here. A car pulled up, and two councillors stepped out. The group surged forward.

'Save our curlews. Save our bay. Save our curlews. Save our bay.'

Their chant repeated on a loop. Some even held up hand-painted signs. Some with 'No development at Curlew Bay' and others with 'Say no to PropCo'. The group's chants grew louder, and they converged on the councillors, who dodged their way into the front door.

The protesters would greet my arrival in much the same way, so I decided to check for a rear entrance. With one last glance at the crowd before heading down the side of the building, my gaze caught on someone holding a 'Save the curlews' sign. I gasped. It was Hayley.

CHAPTER FIFTY-ONE

My heart leapt into my throat as she waved the sign in rhythm with the chant. What was she doing here? And then I saw Anthony standing back from the crowd, leaning against the old oak tree on the public green adjacent to the building. Alongside him were Mum, Dad, Gordon, and a few others I recognised by face but not name. I shuffled sideways and ducked behind the building, peeking around the corner so I could still see them.

'Listen up!' a loud voice exclaimed from the entrance to the building, and a hush descended. 'If you're here for the council meeting, you'd better take your seats. There won't be enough in the chamber, but we've set up the Perry Room with additional seating and a TV with a live link for you to view.' With that, the official turned back inside and everyone pushed towards the doors in a wave. I turned away and bit back the fight-or-flight response flooding through me. It was 99% flight. I waited a few moments to regain my composure before going inside.

By the time I navigated the winding maze of corridors to find the chambers, the room was full. I hung outside the door until Terry

Hamil caught my eye. He smiled and walked towards me, arm outstretched.

'You ready?' he asked with a firm handshake.

'Ready as I'll ever be.'

'Let's do this.' He gestured for me to walk in first. Maybe I could feign a sudden onset of food poisoning. The sweat on my forehead was a genuine touch. But there was no time; he ushered me through the doorway. A low hum of voices circulated the timber-lined walls, and it was obvious from the crossed arms and narrowed eyes that the atmosphere was tense. With my chest tight and head down, I steadied myself and walked past the first row of people, Terry shadowing me.

'You should be ashamed of yourself, Emily Brown,' a female voice whispered as I passed. I didn't dare look up to see who it was. Instead, an official-looking woman drew my attention and nodded for us to follow her to our allocated seats. I blocked out the low rumble of comments behind me as the councillors filed in and took their seats.

Mayor Henry Jacobs, whose belt looked like it was straining to keep his stomach in, sat in the centre of the long table with an oomph. 'You can plug in your device to the lectern,' the official said, gesturing to the lectern next to the board table. 'It will automatically connect to the screens. Any trouble, give me a yell.' She turned away and took her seat.

'Tough crowd,' he leant in and whispered.

He had no idea.

Thankfully, within thirty seconds—although it felt like an eternity—the mayor cleared his throat and switched his microphone on. A high-pitched squeal echoed through the speakers, and everyone groaned and covered their ears.

'Sorry 'bout that.' He adjusted the microphone. 'Don't usually need this thing on for our regular meetings, but today is an exception with so many of you here.' He let out a small chuckle and adjusted the glasses on his nose. 'Right, thank you, everyone, for coming; we will begin with the Acknowledgement of Country.'

Henry's voice turned to a dull drone as my thoughts took over. My stomach churned like waves smashing into Curlew Cliffs on a winter's day, yet the stickiness would have you think it was forty degrees. Was the air conditioner even on in here? I glanced around; there was a lonely fan turning at low speed with a wonky tilt. My mouth was like sandpaper. I needed water. Or better still, whiskey. I didn't even like whiskey, but right now, it felt like the perfect thing to quell this horrendous feeling in my gut and loosen my constricting throat.

'Right,' the mayor continued. 'As this is a special meeting and not a general meeting, there is no general business to attend to. So, we will move onto the only item on the agenda: the proposed development on Beach Road put forward by PropCo, which is what you are all here for.'

'Too right, Henry,' a male voice echoed from behind me, which led to a quiet murmur of agreement.

I took a deep breath, focusing on inhaling and exhaling, just like Connie had shown us at yoga. This was it. I glanced over to where Mum, Dad, Hayley, and Anthony were seated in the second row on my right. Then my eyes darted to Lucy alongside the mayor. Nervousness flickered in her eyes. Did she really think I was going to out her? I had thought about it fleetingly. But I never wanted to win at all costs. Not at someone else's expense, especially my sister's. I might be selfish and self-centred, but I wasn't evil. Lucy had her battles to fight. Maybe we could now have a mutual respect for how hard we've been fighting our whole lives? Maybe we weren't so different after all. I offered her a small smile, and she looked away to rummage through her paperwork. Maybe it was a truce. I turned back to Mum, and she gave me a sad 'why are you doing this?' look. Then it was my turn to look away. The scrutiny was too much to bear.

The mayor was prattling off the development and application details, as well as the process set out in the council by-laws. I tuned back in. '... protects the strong community values and morals which Curlew Bay residents deem important and critical to a successful community-driven council ...' Apart from Henry's voice, shifting of feet, and the wonky fan, the room was silent. It was as if everyone was holding their breath on the edge of their seat, waiting for the moment they could free their opinions. On me.

'So, keeping all that in mind,' Henry continued. 'Let's strive for the respect and high values that we hold strong and give Emily Brown, on behalf of PropCo, the chance to address council on the issue at hand.'

I felt all eyes immediately turn to me. Each piercing into my back like little daggers, actually, make that pitch forks. For a moment, I was frozen in my seat. It was like my legs were detached from my body, unable to get the instruction from my brain to move. Terry nudged me with his elbow, and I sprung to my feet, hoping my legs would hold me steady as I walked to the lectern with my laptop. With a shaky hand, I fumbled to plug the laptop into the Smart Lectern and waited for it to connect.

A bellow of contempt rose from the audience as the laptop fired to life.

A security guard standing on the door stepped forward and announced in a deep, firm voice, 'Can we keep this orderly please.' The crowd murmured and shuffled and I tried to block them out as I fingered the touchpad to bring the presentation to the screen. With every nanosecond, my face flamed a little hotter. 'Sorry, ah, won't be a moment.' My voice crackled over the microphone.

'Just skip to the vote, honey. That's all we're here for!' It was the same heckler as before. I ignored them.

'Quiet, please,' Mayor Henry said. 'There will be a time and a place for questions, and we will make it orderly. Got it?' He nodded at me to begin.

For the first time since taking the lectern, my eyes met the crowd. My stomach did a back flip, threatening to escape out of my throat. I swallowed, staring into the abyss of mostly familiar faces which I'd either known for years or had gotten to know recently. But they were no longer the friendly, smiling faces I'd encountered around town. Instead, mouths were drawn tight, eyes were narrowed, arms were crossed, and small whispers and shaking heads met my view.

Dad's head was down, either embarrassed or ashamed; I didn't know which one was worse. Mum, despite her previously vocal disagreement with the situation, looked like she wanted to rescue me. Her eyes were soft and under an inverted V-shaped brow. Then there was Hayley. The sign was at her feet, and she held a small stuffed curlew, like the ones sold at the gift store next to the café, in her hands. She couldn't look at me either. My heart wrenched. I wanted her to understand the only reason I was doing this was for her. Everything I'd ever done had been for her. I clenched my teeth to stifle the emotion. Then I noticed Simon seated directly behind Hayley. He inhaled and exhaled as if exhausted, but the look on his face wasn't the one of anger or disagreement I expected. He offered me a half smile. Which, to me, felt like a final goodbye. The end. As if what I was about to say would spell the end of everything we'd ever shared, before, now, and in the future. A sadness for all we'd lost. All I'd lost.

'Everything okay, Ms Brown?' Henry's voice startled me. I blinked slowly and nodded. Took a shaky mouthful of water from the glass on the table. Then with one last glance around the room, everything didn't seem so complicated anymore. As if a filter had been lifted. An unexpected calm washed over me, cooling my face, warming my muscles, and drying the stickiness on my fingertips. And despite the shallowness of my breath and the thickness in my throat, I began to speak.

'I came here today to present the reasons why PropCo's proposed development of the lot at the end of the esplanade, or Beach Road, would be a great investment for Curlew Bay.'

A rumble began in the crowd. Feet shifted. Arms uncrossed and re-crossed.

I cleared my throat and continued. 'I came to tell you about the financial benefits to the community and, in particular, tourism. The dollar values that would benefit Curlew Bay. That would see property values increase, provide more opportunity for local businesses, create jobs for locals, and bring more people to our beautiful corner of the world.'

'It's not your Curlew Bay. It's ours! Hands off!' A voice yelled out.

'Hear! Hear!'

'Damn straight.'

'Go back to the city!'

The security guard stepped forward again, arms crossed across his buffed chest. Henry looked over his bifocals and gave him a small shake of the head and he stepped back to his post.

I raised the volume of my voice as I gained confidence. 'I came to tell you how PropCo plans to protect Curlew Bay, the habitat of the curlews, and limit the environmental impact of the proposed development by meeting and exceeding'—I emphasised the words—'certain criteria.'

'Rubbish!' Another grumble from the crowd.

My eyes flicked over all the faces, not landing on anyone in particular until they landed on Terry. His brow was furrowed, and he opened his hands in a 'what are you doing?' gesture.

'And—' I didn't get a chance to finish my sentence.

'I have to remove myself.' All eyes turned to the council bench. Lucy had risen to her feet. Her face flushed. Eyes darting about. 'I can't serve this council.' Her voice wavered, then she rushed off.

'Lucy?' Henry cupped the microphone and gave her a questioning look, to which she shook her head and hurried out of the chambers. 'I'm sorry folks, this is rather unusual,' he said, looking flustered. 'Please excuse me a moment.'

A murmur developed over the crowd. Dad's brow was furrowed, and Mum looked positively panic-stricken. Even Gordon looked bewildered. Without thinking, I rushed to where Lucy and Henry had disappeared, finding them in one of the offices.

'No!' I said breathlessly. 'Wait.'

Lucy and Henry both turned to the doorway. I hoped Lucy hadn't implicated herself.

'Sorry, Mr Jacobs, but could I possibly have a moment with my sister?'

Henry looked at me and then back to Lucy. 'Can it wait a moment? Lucy needs to speak with me. And we have a crowd of people waiting to continue a meeting.'

'I know. I'm sorry. I promise it won't take long.' I gently guided Henry by the arm and led him out the door before closing it behind him, leaving Lucy staring at me.

'What are you doing?' she said, holding her arms out in a shrug, eyebrows squished together.

'What are *you* doing?'

Lucy's face tightened. 'I can't do it. I can't lie. It was wrong to accept the bribes. I have to come clean. And I can't have you expose me in front of everyone.' Lucy's eyes filled with tears.

'You really think I was going to do that?'

'Why wouldn't you?'

'Because you're my sister.'

'More like because it would jeopardise your role.'

'It's not even that. I know we aren't the best of sisters, but you don't have to do this. And I'm not going to out you. I get that you're feeling guilty, but don't do it like this. Don't jeopardise everything you've worked hard for, Lucy, for a moment of weakness. For being human.'

'I have to come clean. I can't lie.'

'I know, but not now. We can work something out.'

'What? How can this possibly be "worked out"?'

I placed my hands on the back of a chair, my brain in thinking mode. I swear I could hear the cogs churning. 'I don't know ... yet.'

'Why are you doing this? Helping me?'

I bit my lip as a plan formed. 'Because family is more important than success. Just leave it to me. I have a plan.'

A knock sounded at the door, and Henry stuck his head in. 'I'm sorry to interrupt your sisterly discussion, but I have to resume this council meeting. Now, Lucy, what was it you needed to tell me?'

I shot a look at pleading look at Lucy, and she looked at me before swallowing. 'Sorry, Henry, it can wait.'

Henry looked as confused as ever and let out a frustrated sigh. 'Righto then. Come on, let's get back to it.'

Lucy and I followed him back into the room of eager bodies, and I gave her hand a quick squeeze before heading to the lectern, my heart thumping in my ears, my skin prickling. What I was about to do was going to change everything.

CHAPTER FIFTY-TWO

'Alright, alright. Quiet, please. Apologies for the interruption.' The mayor squeezed back into his seat. Lucy took her place at the table, and I stood at the lectern. 'Thank you Emily, please continue.'

The entire room, including the councillors, exchanged puzzled glances and continued murmuring, so I tapped the microphone. 'As I was saying ...'

The room finally quietened, and all eyes turned back to me.

'As I was saying, I *was* going to tell you all of those things ... but I can't.' My eyes flicked to Terry. 'I can't stand up here and support this proposal ...' I paused for effect. 'Because it's wrong!'

Terry jumped to his feet. 'What are you doing?' he whispered, the vein at his temple bulging.

A murmur of confusion filled the room before half of the crowd rose to their feet. Laughter. Voices. Clapping.

'Please,' Henry called over the noise. 'Please take your seats. And let Emily finish.'

Everyone slowly returned to their seats, and a hush fell over the room as if the initial surprise and elation had worn off and they needed to hear what else I had to say.

'I can't support this proposal because Curlew Bay is a special place. Barely touched by development, we have a strong community passionate about the Bay and each other.' Simon gave me a questioning look when our eyes met.

'People here are genuine. They look you in the eye. They call you by name. They ask how you are, and they want to know the answer. And all this is something I've only just realised is what's missing in the big cities, where life passes you by and leaves you exhausted and broken.' I blinked back the tears. 'But not in Curlew Bay. We appreciate the beauty on our front doorstep and don't take it for granted. We respect the environment and care for those bloody curlew birds, which I'd never given a thought to until recently. But you all have. And you're all here to protect them. To protect their home. To protect your home. And there is no way I can try and convince you that this proposed development, in any way, shape, or form, will be a good thing for this town.'

Cheers and clapping again filled the room; there was even a wolf whistle. I held up my hands to silence them. I wasn't done.

'And I have proof that PropCo secretly paid at least one councillor for their vote.'

A sharp intake of breath seemed to suck all the oxygen from the crowd before they exhaled and erupted with out-of-control jeers. Terry sank into his seat; his face was as white as the breaking waves.

'And,' my voice strained over the noise. 'And, the councillor who never planned to take the bribes but instead use them against the company, is willing to show proof of this and expose them for who they really are!'

I stepped down from the lectern as chaos ensued from the bench of councillors. Henry looked in shock as anyone. I headed towards Terry, who jumped to his feet, his face bright red, eyes narrowed, veins pulsing as if he was about to blow a gasket. If those beady eyes could shoot bullets, I'd be long gone.

'What the fuck!' he said through gritted teeth.

'I'm not even sorry.' I went to walk past him but he grabbed my elbow almost unbalancing me. I turned back and stared at him. The old Emily would have crumbled. Worrying too much about failing and not proving herself. But I wasn't that Emily anymore. I knew in my gut what I'd done was for the right reasons, no matter how it made me look. No matter what the consequences on my career, or bank balance.

'Get your hands off me.' I shook my elbow out of his grip right as the security guard appeared, his imposing six foot or more frame stepping between Terry and myself.

'I think you should leave,' he said firmly to Terry.

'Alright.' Terry stepped back, hands in the air, then, with an arrogant smile he adjusted his tie, 'Don't think you'll see any money from us. And I'll make it my business to see your name is tarnished beyond repair. You'll never get another job.'

'Do what you have to.' I pushed past Terry and nodded a thanks to the guard and powered towards the door, my heart racing. A slow clap began from the back of the audience, which quickly elevated into a momentous chorus of applause. I stopped and turned around.

Hayley rushed towards me and threw her arms around my neck. 'Thank you, Mum,' she sobbed. 'And I'm sorry. Sorry for everything. I love you.'

'You have nothing to be sorry about. It's me who should be sorry.'

'Excuse me! Excuse me!' Mayor Henry's voice cut through the commotion, firmer and gruffer than before. 'I need to ask you all to sit down and be quiet. This is still a council meeting, not a social event.'

'Come on,' I whispered to Hayley, linking our fingers. 'Let's get out of here.'

CHAPTER FIFTY-THREE

Hayley and I stopped out the front of the council building on the lawn under the oak tree. We weren't the only ones who had left the meeting; it was half the room. We were flooded with people patting me on the back, offering to shake my hand, thanking me, and telling me how sorry they were for doubting me. My neck flushed with heat and all tension from the past few weeks rapidly flushed from my body leaving me a little breathless. Then, Mum and Dad appeared, their faces wide with beaming smiles.

'I'm proud of you, love.' Dad planted a kiss on my forehead.

'Me too, darling. Me too,' Mum added before pulling me in for a hug.

'Where's Lucy?' I asked.

'Still inside.' Mum pointed towards the chambers, her eyebrows knitted. 'Was she ...?'

'It's fine, Mum. Don't worry about anything. It's all going to be okay.'

I wasn't entirely sure of that statement, but a weight had been lifted, and despite the fact I'd completely stuffed any chance of my plan to get back to the city, and I had no idea what was going to happen moving forward, I knew that the people I loved most in the world were here, and that was all that mattered. I'd done the right thing. And for once, I had no regrets.

'I have some other news.' Mum grinned like a Cheshire cat. Dad wrapped his arm around her shoulders. My heart skipped a beat. 'Dr Schubert called. My biopsy was clear.'

My hands rushed to my mouth. 'What? Really?'

'Yes.' Mum's eyes were weepy. 'Just a stubborn ball of breast tissue, probably scar tissue or something.'

I threw my arms around Mum and felt the lightness of relief wash through me.

'That is the best news!' Hayley said, who was also hugging us.

'And'—Mum wriggled out of the four-way hug—'I'm going to the Northern Territory!'

'Sorry?' I shot a questioning look at Dad.

'Not with your father. With Susan. We're going on a fourteen-day camping tour from Broome to Darwin!'

'You, camping?' Images of Mum in a swag didn't flow freely into my mind.

'I know! Won't it be fantastic?' She clapped her hands like an excited child receiving a bag of mixed lollies.

Dad smiled with a shrug of his shoulders.

'That's awesome, Grandma! You'll be able to see all the Indigenous art and the gorges. You'll even see some crocodiles!'

Mum gave a shaky smile, obviously unsure about the crocs, but she continued telling us the complete itinerary. I didn't think I'd ever seen Mum as excited as she was right now. I even had the feeling Dad was looking forward to some time out while she was away. Not that he'd ever admit it.

As we waited for Lucy to emerge from the chambers, I chanced a look around the swelling crowd for Simon. Maybe he was still inside. Or had he left without saying anything? Not that I'd blame him. If it were me, I probably would've left. I'd violated his trust and kindness.

And even though he'd turned the town against me with his Facebook rant, I knew I'd deserved it. He was hurt and was hitting back. But it was me who'd hurt him the most. I wasn't proud of myself. In a way, I hoped after today's events, I'd made amends in some small way. I did still owe him an explanation and apology, though. Not that he'd want to hear it.

Just then, as my thoughts about Simon were tangling like fishing line, the council building door flew open and the rest of the crowd spilled out into the sunshine in a jubilant rush of noise and colour.

A wave of unexpected emotion rushed through me and I tipped my head back to the sky, letting the tears fall. I'd done this. I'd finally done the right thing. I hadn't run away or pushed aside my gut feeling. I'd trusted myself and did what was right. I felt freer than I had in my entire lifetime.

CHAPTER FIFTY-FOUR

The Commercial Hotel was heaving under the weight of almost all the residents of Curlew Bay later that night. Beer and wine were flowing freely; kids were clambering over the playroom in a free-for-all, and from the smiles and merry conversations, you'd think someone had just won the $50 million Powerball jackpot. Although, for the residents of Curlew Bay, the day's outcome was just as good. There was one notable absentee in Terry Hamil. No doubt he'd slunk back to the city to lick his wounds. He'd texted using some rather colourful language, which I ignored. Another noticeable absentee, though, was Simon. I glanced around the room to see if he was hauled up in the crowd, but he was nowhere to be seen.

'There you are! I've been looking everywhere for you.' Connie sidled up and threw her arms around my shoulders, pulling me in for a hug. 'You did a good thing today.'

'You were there?'

'Made it at the end, just in time to see all the action. I knew you'd do the right thing.'

We clinked glasses. 'How's your mum?'

'She's doing okay. Has more bad days than good. It was killing me thinking of her alone in the nursing home, but now I see her every day. And even though I know she will recognise me less each day, I want to be there for her.'

'Look Con—'

'It's okay, Em. You don't need to say anything.'

'I was going to ask you if the offer to run BookArt was still on the table.'

Connie tilted her head. 'What?'

I glanced around the room at the smiling faces, the feel of community. Something I'd never appreciated until now. 'I'm going to hang around for a bit.'

'In the Bay? But what about Hayley and Melbourne?'

I let out a long sigh. 'I haven't figured that part out yet, and I have to speak with Hayley and Anthony about it, but ...' I shrugged. 'I need to be here. For a lot of reasons.' I had no idea if it was the right thing, but for the first time in my adult life, it felt like it was, right down to my core. Curlew Bay had nudged its way under my skin and shown me so much in the past few months. And now I needed to trust my gut that it would all work out.

'Of course, the offer's still on the table. I think you belong here, Em. I really do.'

I hoped she was right.

JUST AFTER NINE, the crowd dwindled as people waved their farewells and wrangled sleepy kids out the door. A few stragglers were still at the table where I was sitting with Mum and Dad. I stifled a yawn, my eyes so heavy I could barely keep them open. It had been a big day. A big few months, really.

I felt a tap on my shoulder and Lucy sided up to me. She motioned and I followed her over to a quiet corner of the room where Ethan lay fast asleep across two chairs pulled together.

'I remember us doing that when we were little.' I smiled.

'Yeah, we did, didn't we?'

'Where's Chloe?'

'Went home with Tayah. I'll get her in the morning.'

Lucy sunk her hands into the pockets of her jeans. 'Look, I wanted to thank you,' she said, her foot nudging the carpet.

'You don't have to—'

'I do. I've been a pretty shit sister most of the time.'

I shook my head. 'I think we were equal on that one.'

She shrugged. 'Maybe. Anyway, I could never have done what you did. Any of it. Having the strength to leave Anthony, start again, stand up for the Bay,' she paused. 'For me.'

There was a small commotion at the bar as a glass was knocked to the floor, shattering the quiet din. 'Taxi!' someone yelled, before a rise of laughter.

'Anyway, I just want you to know you didn't have to. I'm going to resign from council.'

'Do you have to?'

'I spoke with Henry and because I hadn't banked any of the cash Terry gave me they can, as you said, argue that I was planning to expose his bribery, but it could be complicated. He said they'd support me, but I think it's for the best. I've got things I need to sort out for myself anyway...' She glanced around the room before returning her eyes back to me. 'You and Mum have shown me that I need take a long hard look at myself. Come clean to Gordon about the money situation. Sort things out. The right way.' She jutted her chin forward, swallowing back tears.

'Gordon will have your back. And so will we.' I leaned forward and put my arms around Lucy. She gingerly hugged me before pulling away and wiping her face.

'Yeah, I know. Thanks.'

Ethan stirred and attempted to turn over, both Lucy and I bent down quickly to right him before he rolled off the chairs.

'I think this one's ready for bed,' I said with a small giggle. 'I'll get

Gordon.' I gave Lucy a quick hug—which was weird, but nice—before spying Gordon at the bar chatting with Anthony and wandered over. 'Hey.' I leant up against the bar. 'Think you better help Luce with that one.' I motioned over to where Lucy was attempting to heave a sleepy Ethan onto his feet.

'I think you're right.' Gordon nodded with a wink. 'Good to see you, mate.' He patted Anthony on the shoulder before jogging over and whisking Ethan up in one motion onto his hip.

'It's soda water,' Anthony said, nodding towards his half-empty glass on the bar.

'I didn't...!'

He nudged my arm playfully. 'I know.'

I wasn't sure if were at that level of light-hearted banter yet, but I smiled and let the muscles in my jaw relax.

'Thanks for bringing Hayley down.' I pulled up a stool and slid onto it.

'I didn't have a choice. She's been chewing my ear off about these damn curlew birds all week. Said she'd hitchhike if I wasn't going to bring her.'

I rolled my eyes. 'That's our daughter.'

'Yeah. She's very much like her mother.'

'Mmmm. Is that a good thing or a bad thing?'

'A good thing. She's determined, strong-willed, and passionate. All the things ...' he trailed off and stared at the cardboard drinks coaster he was fiddling with. 'I am sorry things turned out like this.'

'Me too.' I tapped my fingers on the bar, knowing now was the moment I had to tell him.

'You're not coming back to Melbourne, are you?'

I raised my eyebrows and let out a small laugh.

'What? It's obvious you're happy here.'

'Yeah. It feels right. I don't know why. It could be a huge mistake.' I shrugged, jittery. 'Won't be the first one I've ever made.'

'It's okay, you know.'

'What?'

'That you're happy. I know you used to say how much you hated it here and you couldn't wait to get out, but I don't think it was the Bay you were running from. I think it was yourself.'

I hung my head, sucking back a shaky breath. The weight of carrying the secret had affected my present each and every day ever since. And it was true. Simon had said it. Even Anthony knew. And, deep down I knew. I had been running from myself.

'No more running, okay?' He nudged me with his elbow.

I nodded. The look of truce between us made me realise every-thing was going to be okay.

'Anyway,' Anthony said, before throwing back the last of his drink. 'I guess we have to sort things out with our daughter.'

'I don't know what to do. Hayley won't dream of coming back here.' I rubbed the back of my neck, the tension building again.

'Maybe she doesn't need to. It's time for you to put yourself first, Em. You pretend you're always working towards making something of yourself, but you always put Hayley and me above your own needs and happiness. And I'm ashamed to say I took that for granted. If you do what's best for you, it will be best for Hayley too.'

'But she needs me. I'm her mum. I can't just walk away from her.'

'And you won't be. She wants to study environmental science. Says there's this 'Rewild' program or something at her school that allows her to do a vocational education where she studies two days a week in the field. She wants to do that in Curlew Bay. Study the curlews. Apparently, the guy at the café here had been telling her about them, and she's interested in their preservation. The program forms part of her university pathway. Gives her credits or something.' He shrugged.

Hayley had mentioned something earlier when we had a chance to chat alone. She told me her interest in the curlews came from the beach walks where she'd run into Simon. At first, I wasn't sure how to react—her and Simon? Chatting?—but the big smile on her face made it clear she was fascinated. She'd also mentioned the program but amidst all the action of the day, I hadn't realised how serious she was. 'So, she'd spend time here and in Melbourne?'

'Apparently. Anyway, we'll talk have to sit down with the school and figure it out.' Anthony reached his hand to mine. 'And we will. Figure it out. Whatever that looks like.'

For the first time in years, I remembered how good a person Anthony was. And how lucky Hayley was to have him as her father. And now, how lucky I was going to be to co-parent with him.

I WAS bone weary by the time Mum, Dad and I wandered into the carpark.

'You okay, Emily?'

'Yeah, I am. I mean, I'm exhausted but I'm okay.'

'I'll bring the car round.' Dad motioned for us to stay where we were and he strode off to get the car.

'I'm proud of you, Emily,' Mum said, using her serious voice. She grabbed my hand. 'That showed true character today. But—'

'There's a but?'

'But I've always been proud of you. I may not have told you or shown you often enough, but I—we, your dad and I—are both very proud of you. You're a strong, intelligent woman who is selfless, and it's about time you were happy.'

'I don't feel selfless,' I said, staring into the starry night. 'You don't think I'm being selfish, staying here?'

Mum squeezed my hand. 'Not at all. I made the mistake of always putting everyone else first for a very long time. It catches up with you. Then one day you realise life has almost slipped you by.' Mum sucked in her bottom lip.

'Oh, Mum.'

'Don't get me wrong. If I had my time over I wouldn't change anything. Only that I looked after myself a bit better. Treated my needs. You can't always be filling everyone else's cup without filling your own.'

Tears welled in my eyes and I squeezed Mum's hand back.

'Anyway, just remember, you don't have to live up to anyone's expectations. Not mine. Not your fathers. And certainly not society's. I couldn't be prouder of you Emily Jane.'

I pulled mum in for a hug and her warmth radiated into me. 'I love you so much, Mum. And I couldn't have a better person as a role model.'

Dad approached with the car and pulled up in front of us, before hopping out and rounding the front as Mum and I separated from the hug.

'All okay?'

Mum straightened her shoulders. 'Couldn't be better.' She smiled and Dad walked her towards the passenger seat door. I paused, a swell of love in my chest I watched my parents. They'd been together for so long, been through so much and yet the affection and care for each other was more powerful than ever. I longed for that in a relationship. That rock that held you up when you needed it most. Even when you didn't know you needed it.

'What are you doing, love?' Dad said glancing back at me, as he opened the passenger door for Mum. 'Hopping in?'

I looked over my shoulder as the last few stragglers chatted outside the front door.

'I didn't see him all night,' Mum said quietly. 'Simon, I mean.'

I nodded, my stomach sinking.

'Mum!' I spun around to see Hayley and Anthony striding out the door.

'Oh, I thought you two had already gone?'

'Can I stay at Grandma's tonight?' Hayley said, bouncing on her toes.

'Of course you can!'

'Yes, of course, honey,' Mum added. 'You don't have to ask; your bedroom will always be ready for you, and you can stay whenever you want.'

Hayley did a mini fist pump. 'Thank you, Grandma. But you might regret that when I'm here every week.'

Hayley jumped in the back seat and Mum looked at me curiously. 'I'll explain later,' I said with a grin.

Mum turned to Anthony who was standing on the curb, hands pressed into this pockets. 'You're welcome to stay too, Anthony. Of course, you don't mind, Emily? But you'll have to take the couch.'

'Oh no, Mary. It's fine. I'm right to drive back.'

'You sure?' I studied Anthony for signs of fatigue, but he looked fresh, his face free of the worry and stress I'd come to recognise every day for so long.

'Yeah. Course.'

'I can drive you back to your dad's tomorrow morning,' I said to Hayley, sliding in next to her.

'Tomorrow afternoon? Maybe we could, I dunno, do yoga or go for a walk tomorrow, maybe see the curlews?' Hayley shrugged.

I squeezed Hayley tight. 'Of course we can.'

'But not too early. I'm sleeping in until at least ten.'

CHAPTER FIFTY-FIVE

When the sun broke through the blinds the following morning, I was already awake. Although I mainly felt light and relieved, a heaviness still weighed on me. Simon. I'd never be able to fix or change my past actions, but I wanted to apologise. I wanted him to know I was sorry. For everything. For then, for now. Everything. I didn't expect him to forgive me. Hell, I expected him to tell me to piss off, but I needed at least to try. It was early so I had plenty of time for a walk to clear my head before Hayley would be out of bed.

When I made it down to the beach, shades of orange and violet streaked across the sky. Seagulls screeched overhead, greeting the morning. Thinking this would be my life from now on felt a little surreal. A routine involving getting up early, exercising on the beach, and breathing in the salt air was far more invigorating than battling smog and horns in peak-hour traffic. And while I wouldn't be living the lavish life in a big house and endless social and shopping options, I didn't care. I didn't have anything to prove to anyone.

After ten minutes of brisk walking, I found myself at the inlet mouth, watching the ocean gently lap at the shore and the curlews wade through the shallows as the sunrise threw dappled light onto the water. The breeze flicked at my hair.

In the distance, someone was crouching down with a camera. Simon. His lens pointed at a curlew preening its feathers.

'I wondered if I'd find you here,' I said, walking up the wet sand towards him.

He rose to his feet, his face a little surprised. 'Hey.' His voice was so soft it barely caught on the breeze and only just touched my ears. 'I like this time of day,' he continued, more loudly this time. 'The lighting's good for photos.' He crouched to take another picture. And I watched, still, as he patiently and silently waited for the right shot before clicking away.

'I didn't see you at the pub last night,' I said sliding my hands into the side pockets of my leggings.

A curlew plunged its long beak into the sand and poked around. Simon's camera clicked again rapidly.

'I'm sorry.' My voice caught on the breeze and seemed to still the air.

Simon stood slowly, and fiddled with his camera, avoiding my eyes.

'I know it's a cop-out.' My mouth was suddenly dry, but I needed to get the words out. 'But if I had my time again, I'd do it differently. Everything. Sorry doesn't even half cut it. I know that.'

The curlew took flight, scooting upwards their wings beating in rhythm. We watched as they resettled further down the beach.

'So, when do you head back to the city?' Simon kept his eyes fixed on the curlew.

'Well.' I exhaled a long breath. 'I'm not.'

Simon's eyes met mine. His brow wrinkled.

'Yeah. I ... I'm staying in Curlew Bay.'

'Oh. Right.'

'I'm going to look after the shop for Connie so she can be with her mum.' I forced a lightness into my voice.

'Well, that's good for Connie. And for you.' He nudged a shell with his foot. 'What about Hayley? I saw her at the meeting yesterday. I presume that was her dad with her.'

'Yeah. We're okay. I have you to thank for that, mostly.'

'Me?' Simon scratched his chin.

'Yeah. Apparently, you spurred her interest in the curlews, and she's talking about studying a credit program for uni. It means she can spend her time between here and Melbourne. While she's here, she'll study coastal habitats and wildlife. Mainly the curlews.'

'Wow! That's great. She has a genuine interest in it. She was like a little sponge when I was telling her about them.'

It was as animated as I've seen Simon for a while. He seemed embarrassed at his enthusiastic response and kicked at the ground again.

'She's always had a thing for animals. I guess this is her calling. For now, anyway. She is still a teenager.' I wrapped my arms around my body as the breeze picked up again.

'I'm happy for you. Both. And,' he paused, his teeth pressing into his bottom lip. 'I'm sorry for well, turning the town on you like I did. It was uncalled for.'

I shook my head. 'No, it was perfectly warranted.'

A waved crashed behind us and we scampered to avoid our feet being soaked.

'Well, that's great,' Simon said. 'I guess I'll see you around then.' He turned to leave.

'Simon!' I called. 'Wait.'

He stopped, shoulders tensed. The breeze caught his hair, flicking it across his eyes as he turned back around.

My heart squeezed against my chest, prodding me to find the right words. I wasn't going to run away this time. I was going to say the things that needed to be said. 'I—'

'It's okay, Em, you don't have to say anything.'

'But I do. I have to tell you ... I mean ... I need to say ...' I clenched my hands into fists. Gosh, I was so bad at this! 'Simon, please.' Simon's eyes were full of regret and rejection. I needed to make this right. 'When I came back, the last thing I wanted was to be here. All I could think of was running into you and being reminded of ...' I stared at my feet. 'Of my lies. And then, we seemed to be getting along okay. I thought I could move past it all and try building a life here. Bit by bit, I began to slow down, to see that life didn't have to be big to mean something. That it was the little things that were important. Like how walking a grumpy basset hound and spending time with someone older and much wiser could brighten your day. Or how something as small as a piece of apple pie could make you smile.'

Simon's face stretched into a smile.

'Or how watching these birds, these silly little, clever curlews with their stick-long legs and funny beaks can bring you peace.' Tears had snuck their way into the corners of my eyes. 'Or ...'

'Em—' Simon took a step towards me.

'No, let me finish. And then, when I realised all of this, I ... I knew I had to tell you the truth. Which is something I should've done years ago.' I was crying now. Tears chilling on my cheeks. I blinked to clear my vision and realised Simon was also crying.

'I'm sorry. I'm so sorry. For then, for now. I'm so sorry, Simon. If I could undo everything, I would. And,' I sniffed. 'And I'm not going to run anymore.'

Simon stepped forward, and a brief moment passed when I thought he would turn away again and leave me there, but instead, he adjusted his camera over his shoulder and put his arms around me. We didn't talk. We just cried. Goosebumps pricked at my skin and I sank into his embrace, feeling his heartbeat in sync with mine.

After a few moments, I pulled away, my cheeks burning. 'Aren't you going to say anything?'

He shook his head, looked so deep into my eyes I could feel his gaze, then cupped my face in his hands and kissed me. My body fell into his; nothing else needed to be said.

CHAPTER FIFTY-SIX

Three Months Later

'HELLO? HELLO? CAN YOU HEAR ME?' Mary tapped at the phone screen.

'Yes, Grandma,' Hayley said. 'We can hear you but stop tapping the screen. Can you see us in the corner?'

Mary squinted and spotted Hayley, Emily, and David in the bottom right corner of the screen, huddled together on the familiar couch in the lounge room. 'Oh yes! There you are!'

'How are you, love?'

'Oh, it's so wonderful up here,' Mary said, her face alive with animation. 'We're at the Kakadu campground for the night. Oh, and today, we took a wildlife cruise along the Mary River!'

'The Mary River?' Hayley laughed.

'Yes! I know! Oh, Hayley, you have to come here one day. The birdlife is amazing.'

'Did you see a crocodile?' Emily asked.

'Yes.' Mary shivered at the leathery creature that the tour guide had pointed out on the bank of the river. 'Oh, they are ugly looking things but majestic at the same time.'

'Did you get some photos with the new camera I bought you, love?' David chimed in.

'I did. I can't wait to show you. And tomorrow we're taking a flight over Kakadu.'

'Sounds amazing, Mum.'

'It sure is. I can't believe I waited so long to do this.'

'You should've done it long ago, love,' David said gently.

'Well, like I always say, there's no time like the present.'

'Hey Mum, I finished the painting.' Emily reached over Hayley and pulled into shot a large canvas that dwarfed the three of them. It was a landscape of the inlet, the curlews wading in the shadows, the sky vibrant with strokes of pink and orange. A small tear pricked at the corner of Mary's eyes, making her nose twitch.

'Oh, Emily. It's wonderful. I love the colours.'

'It's not that great up close; I'm a bit rusty, but it's starting to come back to me.'

'Well, I think it's beautiful. David?' Mary continued. 'Do you think you could make a frame for it? A nice timber one?'

Emily leant over and stood the painting against the edge of the lounge, and David chuckled. 'Sure, love.'

Mary watched the screen as the image flickered on and off. 'The reception's not great here; I think I'm losing you.'

The three of them were now frozen on the screen. 'I don't know if you can hear me, but I'll call tomorrow!' she yelled before swiping at the screen. 'I love you all!'

Mary dropped her phone into the cup holder of her camp chair and leant back, admiring the canopy of towering gums overhead. She closed her eyes and let her mind block out the chatter of the neighbouring cabins and listened to the cacophony of birdlife. Many she didn't recognise. The breeze rustled the trees, and the coolness settled on her skin. She shouldn't be enjoying herself so much, she thought before quickly admonishing herself. Yes, she should. She'd waited a lifetime for this, and she'd never imagined how wonderful it would be. She thought she'd miss David awfully, and while she did miss him, he'd be there when she got home, ready to hear all about it and scroll through the photos. Emily and Hayley too. Lucy, Gordon, and the kids. She smiled to herself. Her beautiful family. They'd been through a bit in the past few months, but they'd made it through somehow. Even Lucy and Emily seemed to be getting along. Hayley was managing her time between the Bay and the city. Lucy and Gordon had sought help to get on top of their business woes, and Emily and Simon ... well, she wasn't sure what was happening, but they seemed to be close again. Things were good. And it made her heart sing. Could things be any better?

'Here you are, Mary.' Susan handed her a glass of bubbly.

'Ah, thank you, my dear friend.' Mary smiled, and they clinked glasses. Things couldn't get any better.

HAYLEY WAVED as the bus pulled away from the curb. It was always hard saying goodbye, but in a way, it made seeing each other all the better. I'd never envisaged my life like this. Being away from my daughter. But we'd grown a lot closer in that time. Sure, it wasn't the normal family arrangement, but what was normal these days? What did it matter? We were making it work, and we were happy. Anthony had secured a job in conveyancing and was actually enjoying it. He'd rented a nicer apartment closer to Hayley's school and she had own bedroom with a balcony, which she'd filled with potted plants and a fish tank. And I was settling into my own place here, too.

When I pulled up in the driveway and got out of the car, Doreen was pottering in her front garden next door.

'Emily!' Doreen, now my neighbour, called out.

'Hi, Doreen.' I headed over to the fence. Fred barked and then waddled over, his whole body shaking as he waggled his tail. I reached down and gave him a pat under the chin.

'How's your mum?' Doreen asked, brushing off her soiled hands on her apron.

'She's having a ball. Although I reckon she's missing Dad.'

'Oh, of course she is. Good on her, though. I've got some news myself, actually.'

'You do?'

'Yes, Benjamin is taking me on the Ghan from Adelaide to Alice Springs. I've always wanted to do it.'

'That's terrific, Doreen. You'll love it.'

'I will, but I was hoping you wouldn't mind having Fred for me. He's not allowed to come. And besides, he wouldn't like the train.'

'Of course I'll have him. What do you reckon, Fred? A few days at my place?'

Fred began sniffing the garden. I took it as a yes.

'How're the renovations going?'

'Slowly.' I'd spent more time than I cared to remember ripping up carpet and patching walls. 'At least the kitchen's done, so I can cook again.'

'Ah, will you be cooking up a storm for anyone special?' Doreen's eyes twinkled before she added, 'Speak of the devil.'

I turned to see Simon pull up in the driveway behind my car.

'I'll leave you to it.' Doreen smiled with a wink. 'We'll talk more about the Ghan; it's not for another five weeks.' She returned to her house and called Fred, and I went over to greet Simon.

'Hey.' He pulled me into his arms, kissing me long and hard. 'Hi Doreen!' he called when he'd finished ravishing me, waving to Doreen with a cheeky smile. She waved back before disappearing indoors with a big grin.

'I brought some leftovers from the café for afternoon tea. How's that sound? It's apple pie.'

'It sounds like you know me all too well.'

IF YOU'D HAVE TOLD me six months ago that I'd be living by myself in a fixer-upper next to a moody basset hound, running a book/art shop, teaching painting to a group of eager tweens and dating my childhood sweetheart again, I would've spat out my Gloria Jean's coffee and laughed all the way to the office. But that was Emily Mendez, not Emily Brown. I finally understand that I didn't need to reinvent myself, I needed to rediscover myself. And now, as I move towards forty, I know success and happiness isn't defined by what's listed in a Google search. It comes from inside. It's a feeling of contentment stemming from knowing and accepting who you truly are. And, from the smallest pleasures in life, like the love of your life's hot, cinnamony apple pie.

LET'S KEEP IN TOUCH

Thank you so much for reading Emily's story.

If you'd like to keep updated on all my books and publishing news, I'd love you to sign up to my newsletter which you can find at www.jfgibson.com.au

Or otherwise, feel free to connect with me on Instagram or Facebook @jfgibsonwriter

ACKNOWLEDGMENTS

Writing a book is a mammoth effort. Yet some books take much more effort than others. This was one such book.

Emily started somewhere around 2016. Back then I had no idea how to write a book and ran out of steam at the 20,000 word mark. It wasn't until around 2019 that I opened up the file and wondered if I could make something of the story. Fast forward four years, through countless rewrites, edits, and lots of tears including one very painful breakup with Emily where I'd resigned myself to the fact she would never be published, and here we are. We made it. And I have so many people to thank.

Firstly, to my editor Kelly Rigby who held my hand through multiple rewrites. Who pushed me out of my comfort zone and forced me to drill down to what Emily's story was about. Kelly gave me the support and tools I needed to 'reinvent' Emily's story into something that could not only work but be a story that meant something, and I will be forever grateful for not only her expertise, but also her friendship. Thanks, Kelly.

To fellow author, Tabitha Bird who offered her wisdom and insight into the early chapters of what would become one of the final drafts. Tabitha has a unique way of looking at a story, asking the right questions, and opening up possibilities that I didn't even realise were there. Tabitha, your assistance was invaluable, and I thank you.

To Jo Spiers of Nurturing Words for the copy edit. Jo pushes me to go deeper, fixes all my grammatical faux pas, and helps me polish the manuscript so it shines. She is brilliant and I couldn't do without you. Also, to Madeline at Creating Ink, who took care of the proofread to catch any last minute errors. Any errors that remain are mine.

To my cover designer, Stuart Bache, who once again blew me away with his concepts. I am so in love with the final cover!

Thank you to my beta readers Jodie and Pauline. Your insights into the final stages of the manuscript were spot on and I was so relieved when you loved Emily's story as much as you did!

To my dear writing friend and author Kylie Orr. A huge thank you for our messenger chats and phone calls. I know I can be perfectly honest with you about this writing hullabaloo and there's no one better to share this journey with. Thanks for making me laugh (at you and with you) and thanks for reading over my first chapters, blurbs, and synopses.

To all of my fellow Fiona McIntosh Masterclass of 2017 graduates, thanks for the support, the laughs, the venting sessions and for just being fabulous woman and brilliant writers in your own rights. We started this journey together and we will be forever joined. (Like it or not!)

To the wonderful and knowledgeable writers in the Not So Solitary Scribes Facebook group and those who join in our weekly Scribes zoom sessions. Thank you for all we share in terms of writing, publishing, and life. I'm privileged to call these women friends and colleagues.

Last year, on a bit of a whim, I began hosting live writing sessions on Facebook and Instagram, now known as Write Squad. We get together most Thursday mornings and Monday nights for a chat and writing session and we have a wonderful core group of regulars and those who pop in when they can. Write Squad is one of the absolute highlights of my week. Every one of you inspire and motivate me to keep writing. You remind me why I write and what I love about the writing community. I have also been privileged to move forward and mentor some of you and I thank you for your trust with your own writing.

Thank you to my beautiful family for putting up with me while I live in my head most of the time. I'm not really deaf or ignoring you, it's just the characters in my head are sometimes louder. I love you all and everything I do is for you.

And finally, thank you to the readers, bookstagrammers, book reviewers and all the book lovers out there. I can't put into words how much your support, feedback, and joy of reading fires me to keep writing. Thank you for choosing to devote your time to our books. It means the world and I truly hope you enjoy Emily's story.

THE FIVE YEAR PLAN

The Five Year Plan will appeal to readers who want to be whisked away from their day-to-day life and immersed in a feel-good story full of food, travel, and romance.

"I absolutely loved this book!" - Nicole, via Goodreads

At 33, DEMI Moretti's five-year plan is on track. She's moved in with her boyfriend Wil and is waiting patiently for her father to retire so she can take over the running of the family café.

But when her father blindsides her by handing the café to her older brother Nick, and she suspects Wil might be cheating on her, Demi's five-year plan crumbles like crostoli.

Determined to get things back on track, Demi travels to Italy to learn more about her Italian heritage, and to give her and Wil some much-needed space. And also in the hope that while she's away, her father will come to his senses.

But her travels don't go to plan either. Long-held family feuds, a love triangle from the past, and an unexpected new friend in Leo, all come together to make Demi question everything – especially her five-year plan.

Will Demi get her plan back on track?

Or will she realise that sometimes fate has other ideas?

AVAILABLE ONLINE THROUGH BOOKTOPIA, ALL ONLINE STORES AND PLATFORMS
OR ASK AT YOUR LOCAL BOOKSHOP

www.ingramcontent.com/pod-product-compliance
Lightning Source LLC
Chambersburg PA
CBHW010257100726
47904CB00011B/2635